MISSING

RJ COONS

ISBN: 1974692604
ISBN-13: 9781974692606

Other books by the author:
Loud Music
Three Bridges

Available on Amazon.com

DEDICATION

To my grandchildren: Will, Julia, Melissa, Zella, Matilda and Cash.

ACKNOWLEDGMENTS

I would like to thank my family and friends who were supportive and gave valuable advice. I am deeply grateful for the police, fire, and park personnel for their firsthand knowledge that they brought to the story. A special thanks to Theresa Foley, Kim Northrop and Susie Learey for their editing and computer support. Thank you, Carol Malott for your photographic magic.

Cover design by Nancy Buscher.

Chapter 1

Yellow crime scene tape stretched across the dried grass entrance to the canoe dock at Osprey State Park. The plastic warning twisted and turned in the wind, but the message was straightforward. **Police Business. Keep Back.**

Behind the barrier, law enforcement vehicles from the Sheriff's office, Florida Park Police, CSI unit, Marine Patrol and Fire/Rescue departments parked in a line along the back fence that led down to the water. A large white tent in the center of the parking field acted as the command center and was alive with a cadre of officers arranging tables and boxes of equipment. Two men in wet suits exited the tent and wheeled a hand cart with diving equipment past a red bulldozer to the canoe dock. Four other officers followed lugging tarps, portable lights, stretchers and crates of forensic materials. A sheriff's deputy stood outside his cruiser along the main road blocking all access to the crime scene.

Approaching the park's entrance off Tamiami Trail, Blaine put on her turn signal, downshifted the Mini Cooper into second, and slowly drove down the lane towards the ranger's station. Large oaks on either side shaded the roadway from the early morning sun and muffled the constant hum from the highway, a welcome introduction to the natural beauty of Osprey State Park and an open invitation to all visitors day after day, all year round.

The office door opened and Park Ranger Diana Stimson stepped out with a wave and cheery smile. Diana Stimson was a senior park ranger and a favorite of Assistant Park Manager Blaine Sterling. Knowledgeable in the park's operations, Diana, had been a member of the staff for over ten years and was dependable—a quality Blaine respected and relied upon.

"Good morning, Blaine, sorry about the early morning call, but Park Manager Forrester said he needed you here early." Diana handed Blaine the attendance clipboard and smiled.

"No problem. I have an orientation meeting today with the college. We're setting the agenda for the archeology project in the park. I'll just have more time to prepare. So what's going on that requires both park managers to be on call?"

"I'm not sure. John just instructed me to call you and I did. He wants you to meet him at the canoe dock as soon as you arrive What I do know is that we have a lot of law enforcement personnel in the park. What they're doing I haven't a clue."

"Thanks for the heads-up. See you later."

Blaine handed back the clipboard and shifted into first gear. Spanish moss hung from branches in spirals of delicate silver-grey earrings and canopied the main road in its natural beauty. Blaine glanced up and breathed it all in. *A glorious sight,* she thought. *What could possibly disrupt today's beauty?* Sadly, she was about to find out.

Chapter 2

The red and white Mini Cooper stopped in front of the yellow crime scene tape that barred entrance to the canoe and fishing dock. The shell and dirt road at the end of the tape that looped down to the canoe dock and South Creek was blocked by a sheriff's car. Flashing red and blue lights signaled urgent official business in the area. Immediately the driver's side door flew open and a large deputy stepped out. With one hand raised, he ordered, "You can't enter. This area is closed. Turn around and leave."

In two strides, the deputy hovered over the Mini Cooper and stared down at the driver behind the wheel. His hardened facial expression and body language suggested he was in no mood for an argument. Large arm muscles bulged out from his perfectly starched green uniform, and the protective vest under his shirt pushed his chest out two shirt sizes. His shaved head glistened in the sun as perspiration dripped down a young face. "I said this section of the park is closed. You need to exit the area immediately!"

Blaine opened her car door and in full park ranger

uniform stepped out. Standing in front of the deputy, Blaine at five eleven was a head shorter and at eye level to the silver name plate above his shirt pocket that read "R. Newcomb."

Blaine had dealt with big men in the past. Big men with attitudes, big men with agendas and big men that were just plain stupid. For each individual, a course of action was distinct and effective. Rapist Matt Purdy had a very sick agenda; Blaine carved rapist on his stomach to remind him of his indiscretions. Fired park ranger Remi Cole's warped attitude was stifled with persuasion that led to his own suicide. Finally, Thor Boltier, a giant of a man, was just stupid. His incarcerated father's orders to kill only led to his own demise.

Deputy Newcomb on the other hand was a different kind of big. Newcomb clearly was not deranged, nor was he psychotic. He certainly wasn't brainless. He was merely following orders mechanically. What Newcomb needed was an opportunity to adjust his rigid mindset, but without realizing he was being manipulated. A procedure Blaine Sterling had honed to perfection.

"Good morning, Deputy Newcomb, I am Blaine Sterling, Assistant Park Manager. Pleased to meet you." Blaine stuck out her hand.

Maybe it was Blaine's uniform or possibly the heat, but Newcomb stepped back and relaxed the prison guard mentality. He lowered his arm and respectfully repeated, "There is a police investigation currently under way in this area and all civilians are asked not to use this park facility."

"Do you see the gentleman talking to the deputy in front of the tent? The man with the prosthetic leg? That's John Forrester, Manager of Osprey State Park. He called this morning and instructed me to meet him at the canoe dock." Blaine waved to Forrester.

Newcomb spoke into his shoulder microphone and

immediately the deputy talking to Forrester responded. "Tell her to come on through," the voice on the other end commanded. With an agitated snarl, Newcomb mumbled something unpleasant, got back into his cruiser and in a cloud of dust peeled backwards off the shell road.

Blaine inched the Mini Cooper through the opening and when eye level to the deputy's car, rolled down her window and shouted, "Thank you for your assistance, Deputy Newcomb." She waved and drove towards the command center.

"Good morning, Blaine. This is Lieutenant Jeff Johnson of the Sarasota Sheriff's Office. He is in charge of this operation," said Forrester. "Lieutenant, this is Blaine Sterling, Assistant Park Manager." They shook hands and exchanged greetings.

So, what exactly is the operation?" Blaine asked. "There appears to be a significant amount of personnel, equipment and resources assembled here. Could someone please tell me what is the big secret?"

"I'll do better than that, Assistant Park Manager, I'll show you the operation!" said Johnson.

Leading the way, Johnson marched down the path to the canoe dock.

Chapter 3

The park's red bulldozer blocked the end of the canoe path. A thick metal chain was hooked to the bucket and wrapped around the old canoe dock, signaling the demarcation line where work abruptly stopped. A chest-high pile of waterlogged wood, broken poles and splintered planks littered the entire shoreline from the work started early that morning. The half of the old canoe dock closest to land remained intact. The other half was a heap of broken and splintered wood.

"Watch yourself walking behind the bulldozer. The mud could be a problem," Johnson called out as he disappeared behind the hulk of a machine.

Nothing could have prepared Blaine for what appeared in the dark waters of South Creek that morning. In the empty space that was once the canoe dock; a human arm broke the surface of the water and rose upward towards the sky. The chalky white skeleton arm and long boney fingers appeared to claw at its watery grave in a cry for help. The bones were thin, free of any cartilage and appeared to glisten in the sun. Not a word was spoken until two divers suddenly surfaced on either side of the arm and shouted, “The lower torso is covered in Mangrove roots. We need a saw to cut the skeleton free.”

A CSI technician wearing green hip boots marched into the water and handed them a saw. With saw in hand, they disappeared below the surface leaving only a trail of bubbles and a thin eerie glow from their lights.

Forrester was first to speak. “The volunteer work group had just ripped out the first section of dock when the arm rose out of the water. Jim Breidster was backing up the bulldozer to remove the canoe dock when George Karnedy spotted the arm. Well, all hell broke loose. The volunteers ran back to dry land and Breidster called me. I called the park police, who in turn called the sheriff's office. The medical examiner arrived thirty minutes ago along with the fire department.”

“The only department missing is the FBI,” said Blaine.

“They've been contacted and offered any assistance we may need in identifying the body,” Johnson added and walked over to the mobile work site in front of the shoreline. A small tent stood a few feet from the creek where Dr. Lenard Rosa, Medical Examiner for Sarasota County, worked arranging equipment for the investigation. Rosa, a twenty-two-year veteran of the medical examiner's office, was a master at his craft. Efficient, knowledgeable and most of all intuitive, he was a stickler for details. Rosa believed the answer to every case was in the details. Document the details thoroughly and you solve the case. “Good morning, Len, so what do you think?” Johnson called and walked under the tent.

“What do I think lieutenant? I think it's a little premature for a determination without examining the entire skeleton, but by the appearance of the arm I'm not optimistic. Now if you'll excuse me, they're bringing up the body.”

Dr. Rosa moved to the end of the table and put on his gloves and a surgical mask.

"One other point of information, Len. I have my deputies searching both sides of the creek in case this location was a dumping ground for some serial killer. I understand that you were informed that there was only one body. Will your team be prepared to process multiple homicides? That is if we find more bodies?" An awkward moment of silence filled the tent.

"Of course lieutenant. I have a carton of body pouches in the van, but let's hope I won't need them," said Dr. Rosa.

The divers floated the skeleton up to the shore where two members from the medical team placed it on a stretcher and carried it up to the tent. Without a word the team immediately went to work on the documentation protocol. Photographs were taken from every angle, head to toe. Check lists identifying body condition, dental configuration, skull disposition, physical measurements, bone shavings and bone fractures were recorded. Finally, Rosa placed a toe tag on the skeleton's big toe and wrote the number "1."

The skeleton was placed in a body pouch and was about to be carried to the ambulance for transport back to Sarasota when Johnson asked, "Well, what do you think, Doc?"

"Off the record. It's a female, length of decomposition greater than thirty years. There's a sign of head trauma, and part of her right index finger is missing."

"Missing. What do you mean missing?" asked Johnson.

"Missing, gone, not there. Could be from the watery grave, an accident or intentional? I'll have more information after the autopsy," Dr. Rosa said.

"How do you know the skeleton is female?" asked Forrester.

"The pelvic area on this skeleton is elongated. For

reproduction the female pelvic area is larger than a male. Given the size of the skeleton and bone structure development, this female could very well be a teenager," Rosa answered.

"Could the girl be Native American?" Blaine asked. "Maybe the creek was a burial site. I read that some tribes buried their dead along the banks of rivers. Part religious ceremony and a way of protecting the corpse from predators."

"Oh great, just what we don't need. I can see the headline, 'Park Disturbs Native American Sacred Burial Ground. Native Americans Protest'" Forrester interjected. "Please tell me the girl isn't Native American."

"It's too early to say," Dr. Rosa remarked. "Again, I need to do a complete forensic autopsy. More than likely I'll need to collaborate with some experts, a pathologist, an odonatologist and possibly an anthropologist before a final determination is rendered. However, I did observe a contusion on the back of the skull. More documentation is necessary before a definitive conclusion can be reached."

Dr. Rosa zipped up the body pouch and exited the tent followed by a parade of medical personnel and the body. Johnson, Forrester and Sterling waited for the entourage to leave before they started back to the police command post.

The noonday sun beat down mercilessly while the humidity climbed to an uncomfortable level, leaving everyone dripping wet as they moved across the parking field. Once under the shade of the tent, Forrester said, "Lieutenant, I would appreciate if you would forward any information to Assistant Manager Sterling. I'm leaving today for a conference in Tallahassee and would like Blaine to act as liaison between the park and the sheriff's office." Forrester extended his hand.

"Certainly. She will have full access to the case. I'm

sure the park will need to communicate with its employees and the public. By the looks of things, that chain of communication may start sooner than anticipated. Channel 6 just pulled up to the entrance to the parking lot."

Johnson turned his head and spoke into his shoulder microphone, "Newcomb, this is Lieutenant Johnson. Do not permit any news vehicles to enter the restricted area. I repeat, no one from the news media is permitted to enter."

"Yes sir," squawked over Johnson's phone.

"If you'll excuse me, we need to break down the command post and transport everything back to headquarters. Pleasure meeting you both. And Sterling, I'll be in touch as soon as we receive the coroner's report."

Johnson turned and walked over to the computer station at the rear of the tent. Orders to dismantle the operation could be heard as Blaine and Forrester left.

As they walked to their cars, Forrester said, "Why don't you go over and tell the reporter that we have no comment at this time. It is imperative that this incident doesn't get blown out of proportion. We don't want a media circus coming to the park. I'll assemble all the park rangers and volunteers in the Nature Center and update them. After my speech I'll leave for Tallahassee."

Forrester rolled down his window and shouted, "Call me if there's a problem," and drove off. Blaine drove towards the news van and reporter Bryce Faceman.

Chapter 4

The Channel 6 News van stopped against the yellow police crime scene line. Deputy Newcomb stood behind the tape with his hand raised. "This is a restricted area. No one is permitted to enter."

The van's side door opened and out stepped reporter Bryce Faceman and his cameraman.

"This is Bryce Faceman, reporting live from Osprey State Park where Channel 6 News has received news that the remains of a human body have been discovered. Deputy, can you comment on that allegation?" Faceman raised the microphone up to Newcomb's face.

Newcomb pushed the microphone away. "As I said before, this is a restricted area and you need to leave. Now!"

"I have information that a skeleton was recovered from South Creek. Was it a woman?" Faceman blurted out and pushed the microphone up to Newcomb's face again.

"I do not have any information for you. I was told to keep everyone out of the area. That's all I was told."

Newcomb grabbed the microphone and said, "Mr.

Faceman, if you jab me in the face with the microphone one more time, I'll confiscate the object and arrest you for not complying with a police department directive."

The camera filmed a close-up of the two men frozen across the screen.

At that very moment, Blaine stepped out of her car and walked towards the Channel 6 news van. To his relief, Faceman recognized her. He had met Sterling last year while working on a child kidnapping case that operated out of a house in Englewood. It turned out that Sterling called in the tip to the newspaper, which eventually, led to the freeing of the two kidnapped boys and to the dismantling of the child abduction ring. All of this while selling ice cream with her daughter.

"Hello Mr. Faceman. It's a pleasure to see you again," said Blaine and walked up to the reporter.

Faceman stepped away from Newcomb and in classic news reporting style announced, "Viewers, I'd like to introduce Assistant Park Manager Blaine Sterling. Is it true, Ms. Sterling, that a skeleton has been recovered floating in South Creek?" Faceman carefully pushed the microphone up towards Blaine's face.

"That is not completely accurate, Mr. Faceman. This morning, a work crew was dismantling the old canoe dock when a skeleton was discovered. At this time, we have no substantiated information about the body. The sheriff's office is in the charge of the investigation. When we have more information, we will report the findings to the media."

Blaine smiled for the camera, but unfortunately the lens was aimed towards Faceman.

"Is it true that the skeleton is that of a Native American and that South Creek is an ancient burial site?" Faceman asked in an authoritative tone.

"No, that is not true and to report such information

without the facts would be reckless. As I said before, it is too premature to arrive at any conclusions. We must wait for the medical examiner's report."

"And when do you believe viewers will see that report assistant manager?" Faceman asked and turned towards the medical examiner's van pulling out of the parking field.

"I don't know, Mr. Faceman. You'll have to take your viewers to the sheriff's office and find out."

Blaine smiled and walked back to her car. The camera highlighted a close-up of Faceman's surprise and then faded black.

Chapter 5

Archeologist Ryan Murphy leaned against his blue Jeep Wrangler and adjusted the angle of his Indiana Jones hat. Tipped just enough to shade the sun's rays, but not too much to hide his face and restless brown eyes. For Murphy presentation was the first step in achieving success, and Ryan P. Murphy was very successful. If you look the part and grasp the subject matter, success is guaranteed. That was his motto. The Florida Indiana Jones persona worked for him. The hat, khaki outfit, hiking boots and a length of coiled rope that hung from his leather belt all complemented the archaeological mystique.

Murphy was not surprised when he received the letter from the State Education Department congratulating him on winning the Osprey State Park Archeological Research Grant. His credentials were impeccable: four years as Sarasota County Archeologist; past curator Spanish Point Museum; Director of Florida Maritime Museum in Cortez; and a ten-year educational research project at the Blueberry Site in Highland County. Murphy's archaeological field work throughout Florida was well respected by his peers and documented in numerous archaeological field site papers housed in the Florida Master Site Publication. The two-year Osprey Research Project would highlight his illustrious reputation and hopefully catapult his career to new heights, possibly even move him to the Federal Archeology Institute in Washington, D.C.

Murphy checked his watch for the third time. "I'm positive she said eleven o'clock, meet at her office," Murphy groaned as beads of perspiration rolled down his forehead and into his eyes. He reached into his pocket and pulled out a handkerchief and wiped away the sweat as a red and white Mini Cooper drove onto the lane.

"Look, someone is driving this way," Sidney Price, one of the New College research assistants, said.

"I hope it's Ms. Sterling. I'm melting," said Dalton Marks, the other research student.

"Sorry I'm late, but we had an incident at the canoe dock and it took longer to resolve than I anticipated," Blaine said, parking next to the Jeep. Walking up to Murphy, she held out her hand. "Nice to see you again, Ryan. What's it been, nine months, since we've worked together?"

"Sadly, a little longer," answered Murphy as he shook her hand. An uncomfortable flashback of their last meeting resonated deep within his memory. The encounter was contentious and left Murphy oddly unsettled. A year earlier he, Blaine and Forrester were deep within the park's ancient cave when they disagreed on announcing the curative powers derived from the scrub jay egg. He insisted that the discovery needed to be announced to science. Unfortunately he was overruled, and the secret of the egg's healing power was to be kept secret until the scrub jay was off the endangered species list. However, with the award of the research grant, he would now have the time and opportunity to resolve the controversy and finally achieve scientific acclaim. "Good to see you too, Blaine. Let me introduce my two student researchers—Sydney Price and Dalton Marks. Both senior archaeology students from New College, exceptional researchers with two years field experience at the Bell Glade archaeological site. After graduation they both intend to pursue advanced studies in archaeology." Murphy stepped back while Blaine greeted the students.

"Look at all of you. Ryan, you're dripping wet and Sydney, you and Dalton both look like you completed a five-mile scrub jay hike. Why didn't you go into the office?" asked Blaine.

"The door was locked," Sydney said in a squeaky little voice sized to match her petite frame and short brown pixie haircut.

"Well, let's go inside and cool off." Blaine unlocked the door, and in one big push they moved down the hallway to Blaine's office at the far end of the trailer. Bathed in cooling air, their spirits immediately perked up. Decorated with maps, charts and colorful pictures of wildlife native to Florida, the room was a combination workspace for rangers and visitors alike. A computer station, couch, two antique cane chairs and a bookcase filled the back wall of the room. A large round table occupied the center of the space. Four manila folders sat on the table.

"Have a seat. I'll get some water from the kitchen. I definitely could use a cold bottle of water, and by the looks of all of you, maybe we'll need two bottles each. Take a look at your folder. I've enclosed all the necessary paperwork the Parks Department requires, Workman's Compensation data sheet, insurance release forms, educational background, license registration identification, felony conviction questionnaire and a few other forms the state requires."

Murphy scanned the paperwork and scowled. Most

of the wording didn't make sense. Highlighted in yellow were places for signatures, initials, check marks or all of the above. *Typical bureaucratic waste of time,* he thought. But he put on a professional persona and completed the forms in silence.

"Here you go. The elixir of life, cool refreshing water," Blaine said, and handed each one a bottle. "Sorry about the forms. State regulations, nothing I can do about it."

After a handful of innocuous questions, Blaine collected the forms and placed them in her out basket to be forwarded to the state. She sat back in her chair and said, "On behalf of Osprey State Park and the State of Florida, I want to congratulate you Ryan and your students for being awarded the Florida State Archaeological Research Grant. Out of the two hundred applications, your proposal was the most comprehensive approach incorporating professional and student research components for a research model and teaching tool. Your two-year design charted precisely the organizational steps for the undertaking. The strategy was masterful and outlined a course that would benefit Osprey State Park and create an archaeological research platform for colleges and research professionals around the country."

"Thank you, Blaine. I am confident that the team will achieve and hopefully exceed all your expectations pertaining to this project," Murphy said, smiling directly at Blaine.

"I expect you will, Mr. Murphy, I expect you will." Blaine blushed as Ryan's soft smile took her by surprise. "Speaking of your team, I was particularly impressed with Sydney and Dalton's essays on a momentous event in their lives." Blaine took a drink of water. "Dalton, I imagine you were overjoyed when the President of the United States entered the little luncheonette in Peoria, Illinois, where you and your Lambda Chi Alpha fraternity brothers were having breakfast."

"Overjoyed? I was frightened to death. You have to visualize a small breakfast restaurant, two blocks from Bradley University and a favorite of locals and college students. Maybe ten tables scattered about the room and counter seats for six or seven people. Eight o'clock in the morning and the place was packed, everyone eating and talking when all of a sudden the front door swings open and ten men dressed in gray suits, blue ties and sunglasses walk into the room."

"Did they say anything?" said Sydney.

"No, they just stood there. Everyone froze, and all eyes were on the men in gray as they ringed the room. Then through the front door walked the President of the United States. Everyone stood and clapped."

"What a relief that must have been." Blaine said. "What were you thinking when the gray suits entered the room?"

"I thought I was going to die. Every day there's something on the news about a gunman walking into a place of business and shooting innocent people. I thought for sure I was going to be killed," Dalton answered. "But when President Bush walked through that door and said, 'Good morning Peoria,' I screamed uncontrollably. And I'm a registered Democrat."

"What was he doing in Peoria?" asked Sydney.

"He was giving a speech at Bradley University about his presidency and then attending a major fundraiser for Republican candidates in Chicago the following night. He just decided to stop in at a local diner and talk to the people. It was amazing. He sat at our table for about four minutes, and we talked about politics, fishing and his painting. Since leaving office he found that he had time to pursue a passion he long dreamed of, painting."

"Wow that is so cool," Sydney said.

"Do you want to know what was cool about meeting George W. Bush? He listened. The former president listened to what we had to say!" Dalton leaned back in his chair with a Cheshire grin on his face.

"Sydney, I was equally impressed with your essay. You and your mother were having brunch when you saved an elderly gentleman's life. Amazing," Blaine exclaimed.

For the next five minutes, Sydney explained how she and her mother, were enjoying a delicious lunch at a quaint little country inn, a week before Thanksgiving. Between courses Sydney glanced out the window and was captivated by the vista of the long front lawn covered in snow that seemed to flow towards a small wooden dock and a handful of boats. She focused on an elderly gentleman walking on the snow-covered dock when suddenly it appeared that he lost his balance and fell into the water. Immediately Sydney told her mother to alert the hostess as she raced towards the side door leading down to the dock.

The man was sandwiched in-between two small sailboats and was unable to lift himself out of the water. Blood oozed from a gash on his forehead, and the weight of his wet clothing pulled him under. Sydney grabbed the collar of his coat and dragged him up against the dock. With both hands she managed to lift him up onto the walkway. By that time the manager and two waiters arrived, and together they carried him back to the restaurant. Thankfully he didn't lose consciousness, and the gash on his forehead was superficial. Two weeks later Sydney and her mother received a photograph and a wonderful letter from Dr. Saltin thanking us for saving his life.

"What was the picture of?" asked Dalton.

"It was a picture of Dr. Saltin on *Hewlett*, his wooden Snipe sailboat."

"Sydney and Dalton were selected for this project because of their brains and compassion, a combination destined to succeed," Murphy interjected. "Speaking of research, today I'd like to begin assembling the four solar panels that will supply power to light the cave. We have all the equipment in the Jeep, and hopefully we will put the four solar panels in today, start laying the electrical wire tomorrow and begin the research project by the end of the week."

Blaine opened her desk drawer and took out a key. "Here is the key to the cave. Make sure the gate is locked at all times. We don't want amateur spelunkers entering the area, and climbing around, especially while you're working. You certainly don't need that aggravation, not to mention the fright if a handful of strangers just drop in. Also, there's ample room for parking next to the fencing. Makes it convenient to unload equipment and adds an official presence to keep curious eyes at bay."

Murphy reached out, held Blaine's hand as he took the key and said, "Maybe I'll see you later today?" Blaine felt his grip, firm, but not overbearing; warm and comfortable.

"I don't think so. I have a pile of paperwork from this morning's episode that will occupy my day." Blaine replied and looked down at her hand. The trio said goodbye and walked outside.

Chapter 6

The outdoor craft fair at Jacaranda Plaza had ended for the day. Tony Lilly, the owner of Circus Days Ice Cream Company, and his helper Hubba Bubba drove out of the parking lot and headed back to the shop to restock supplies for the next fair. For the past three years, the white box-truck decorated with colorful balloons and circus animals was parked in the center of the midway and sold ice cream. Over the years, young and old searched out the colorful truck with an elephant roof sign that flashed every time a costumer approached. The delicious cones and cups of pure heaven were a staple at the fair and, more importantly, a money maker for Tony Lilly. One day's work put a cool, creamy, four hundred bucks in his pocket. Not bad for a New York transplant.

Past the Jacaranda Library the speed limit abruptly dropped to 30 mph. Tony eased off the accelerator and slowed down. "Got a ticket right here last year. A damn speed trap. The cops must have pulled over ten cars before I got caught in their net. It's impossible to drive 30 mph on this road. It's a four-lane highway," Tony spat out.

"How much was the ticket?" Hubba Bubba asked.

"Eighty dollars. The cop said I was five miles over the speed limit."

"Wow, that sucks," Hubba Bubba said as he blew out a big pink bubble that exploded all over his face.

"You can say that again, but the cop said I could take a driving safety class and I wouldn't receive points on my license for the moving violation," laughed Tony. "The problem was, it was an eight-hour class. What a nightmare."

"Sounds like a big waste of time. An eight-hour bullshit class." Hubba Bubba blew another bubble.

No sooner had the second wad of gum exploded over Hubba Bubba's face than the ice cream truck screeched to a halt. Hubba Bubba flew forward, smashed into the windshield and then back into his seat again. Bags of popcorn and potato chips flew in every direction while cans of soda rolled across the floor and collected at the doorway. Tony turned on his flashers just as Hubba Bubba pulled the gum from his face.

"What just happened, man?" Hubba Bubba cried out. "I think I broke my freak'n nose. Is it bleeding?"

"No, it looks fine. Sorry about the abrupt stop, but look. Two sandhill cranes are about to cross the street and I didn't want to hit them." Tony pointed to the median. "What beautiful birds. I love their red foreheads. Such regal looking birds, Grus canadensis."

"Grus whatever, I'm not really into birds, but the guy in the other lane doesn't look like he's going to stop. He's on his cell phone. Oh shit!" Hubba Bubba screamed as the driver plowed into the cranes. Hubba Bubba took out his cell phone.

"That son of a bitch. Take a picture of the car. I think he's stopping. Take it now. He's driving away. Did you get the picture?" Tony shouted.

"Got it. The car, a red BMW convertible, the guy on his cell phone and his license plate number: RIDES-1.

This guy is going down," Hubba Bubba added bitterly.

"Let's go pull the carcass off the highway. Its mate will stay by the body and grieve. The last thing I want is another Sandhill Crane run over," Tony said as he stepped from the truck.

By the time Tony and Hubba Bubba reached the dead crane, a group of drivers had gathered and were commiserating on what a tragedy they had just witnessed. Many were outraged that the driver didn't stop. One man asked if it was against the law to run over an animal and not stop. Another driver replied, "It is a hit and run offense, I think."

A woman stepped forward with her cell phone in hand and said, "I just called the police, they're on their way. Did anyone get the car's license plate number?"

"Yeah, I did." Hubba Bubba blew another bubble.

A few minutes later, a sheriff's deputy arrived. Lights flashing, he drove up on the grass and walked over to the group of people standing around the crane. "Whoever is driving the ice cream truck needs to move it, now! We have to get traffic moving again."

Tony jumped into the truck, drove across the highway and pulled in front of the deputy's cruiser. In his excitement, while exiting the truck, he forgot to duck and slammed his forehead into the overhead door jam. At six-three, skinny as a rail, his bald head absorbed the full impact of the collision and threw him backwards to the floor. Blood oozed down his head onto his wide hooked nose and across his thick lips. He grabbed an ice cream towel, wiped the blood from his forehead and face, and quickly slapped on a bandage he found in the glove box. Gazing in the mirror, he decided the colorful animal patch for children looked ridiculous, but at least it stopped the bleeding. "Okay Tony, let's remember to duck this time," he mumbled to himself and jumped down from the truck.

An overweight man with ruddy cheeks stepped

forward and said to the deputy, "The young man with the long black hair and pink bubble gum all over his face took the license plate number of the car that killed the sandhill crane." He pointed to Hubba Bubba and added, "Now, can you arrest the driver?"

The deputy looked down at the carcass, slowly shook his head and then looked up at the crowd of people standing around the lifeless crane. "I'm sorry folks, but there is nothing I can do. No laws have been broken. The sandhill crane is not on the endangered species list, so no state or federal statutes have been violated. All that I can do is call the Wildlife Center of Venice and have rescuers pick up the dead crane. Hopefully they can capture its mate and bring her back to their facility."

"Deputy, what about leaving the scene of an accident? Wouldn't that be classified as a-hit- and-run misdemeanor?" A woman in tears cried out and reached for the arm of a man beside her.

"No ma'am, a-hit and run accident only pertains to a person causing or contributing to a traffic accident. Colliding with another person or a fixture belonging to said person or persons and failing to stop and identify oneself afterwards. The law does not pertain to an accident with an animal."

"So there are no consequences. This man just drives off and that's it. That's not right," Tony snapped angrily.

The deputy raised his arm and shouted to the crowd, "There's nothing more to do here. Everyone needs to return to their automobiles and leave. I'll remain until the rescuers arrive. Thank you for your concern."

Without a word, everyone took one last glance at the lifeless crane and trudged back to their vehicles.

Once in the truck, Tony leaned over towards Hubba Bubba and said, "No consequences. We'll see about that. Call Lou Bravo and ask him to meet us at

Patches tomorrow for breakfast. Tell him I'd like to talk to him about meting out consequences."

Chapter 7

Lou Bravo backed his yellow El Camino down the driveway and onto Serpentine Lane. The clock on his dashboard read 7:55 as he neared Blaine Sterling's house. Blaine's daughter Brooke was standing out front waiting for the school bus to arrive. Brooke was a mirror image of her mother, only twenty years younger. With a long blond ponytail, bright blue eyes, a big happy smile and a contagious personality, Brooke Sterling was the neighborhood sweetheart. After the death of Blaine's husband, Lou Bravo was resolved to look after Brooke and her mother—a surrogate father so to speak. His involvement was tempered with affection, humor or concern depending on the circumstance and Blaine's approval.

The El Camino slowed down and stopped in front of 204 Serpentine Lane. Lou Bravo glanced at the newly reconstructed home and cringed. Still haunted by the night Thor Boltier threw a Molotov cocktail through the dining room window and set the home on fire, Lou Bravo remembered the fear in Brooke's eyes. The attempt to kidnap Blaine and the subsequent shooting of the arsonist at Brooke's grandfather's house put him in a pensive mood.

"Good morning Brooke," Lou Bravo shouted out the window.

"Good morning," Brooke called back and walked up to the car.

"So, Brooke any tests today?" Lou Bravo belted out with a smirk.

"We only have tests on Friday, but I have a big art project due today. Want to see?" Brooke reached into her backpack and pulled out a rolled up piece of paper. She unfurled the project and held it up to the window.

"It's beautiful, Brooke. The horse looks like it is about to jump off the page, and the buckles seem to sparkle when you move the picture. Isn't it the carousel horse your grandfather carved for you?" Lou Bravo asked. "If I'm not mistaken, isn't he restoring an entire carousel for a town on Long Island?"

"Black Beauty, isn't he gorgeous? Mrs. Wilcox, my art teacher wanted us to paint something special that we own and explain to the class why it is important. So I chose Black Beauty."

"I'm sure you'll get an A+. What if a student doesn't bring in their project today? What are the consequences?"

"Mrs. Wilcox said every day the project is late, one grade will be lowered. After the third day the student will get a failing grade."

"That is some consequence!" remarked Lou Bravo. "Has any student ever forgotten their project?"

"Yes, Willie Snook last year brought his painting in after three days. He told Mrs. Wilcox that his pet ferret chewed up all his paint brushes after his project was halfway completed. That he couldn't come to school because his father's truck broke down in a ditch after the rain storm and that his mother was unable to call the school after lightning struck the telephone pole."

"So how did Willie complete his painting?"

"With his mother's Q Tips," Brooke groaned.

"Q Tips! I don't believe it. Sounds like a fish story to me," laughed Lou Bravo.

"That's exactly what Mrs. Wilcox said. Here comes my bus Bye."

Lou Bravo watched Brooke jump on the bus, flop into a seat and pull away. Two minutes later the El Camino eased away from the curb and moved down the road towards Tamiami Trail and breakfast.

No stranger to the art of consequences, Willie Snook's outrageous tale and ultimate failing dredged up uncomfortable memories of the circumstances that brought Lou Bravo to the City on the Gulf. Uncomfortable because he had no say in the decision and that was not Lou Bravo's typical modus operandi.

Lou Bravo was a people person and loved to schmooze. At five foot five, one hundred ninety-five pounds, shaved head and barrel chest, he looked like a stocky professional wrestler. But the ring was the furthest thing from his mind. Lou Bravo was in business to make connections. For more than twenty years Lou Bravo operated Classic Touch Auto Body in Central Islip, New York. Known for quality work and reasonable prices, the business increased its profit margin year after year. Lou Bravo added another shop, hired more mechanics and took on a partner. A prominent figure in the political arena, Lou Bravo donated generously to the party machine resulting in lucrative government contracts. More business meant more money, more headaches and less control.

A two-year investigation of illegal auto repair shops on Long Island closed Classic Touch, put Lou Bravo into the Witness Protection Program and left him with only a one-way ticket to Venice, Florida. His testimony against his partner and the numerous political bribes were paramount in cleaning up the industry. So Lou Bravo knew firsthand how little Willie Snook felt about consequences. His new life centered on consequences.

Some Lou Bravo controlled, and others controlled him.

Chapter 8

The parking gods smiled down that morning. Lou Bravo put on his turn signal and eased into Patches Restaurant's parking lot. As usual, the flat slab of blacktop was packed. But at the far end of the lot, sandwiched between a white Buick Century and a brown Cadillac DST, was the last vestige of a parking spot. With the finesse of a long-haul trucker pulling into a Circle K truck stop for the night, the El Camino inched backwards and filled the spot. Lou Bravo grabbed a sweater and headed for the restaurant.

A long line of people snaked out the door and along the side of the building as Lou Bravo approached. "Excuse me, excuse me please. I needed to get a sweater for my mother. The air conditioning, you know, is too cold for her." He held up the white cardigan and squeezed through the door.

"Good morning, Lou Bravo. A bit of a chill for you today?" Jackie, the owner, called out from behind the counter, a wide grin on her face.

"It's not for me. It's for mother. She gets the chills," laughed Lou Bravo.

"Well you better get a rush on. I can see her shivering in the back corner booth. I think she's having trouble giving Victoria her order." Jackie smiled and pointed to the last booth where Tony and Hubba Bubba were seated.

Lou Bravo pushed his way around the tables to the last corner booth. "Good morning boys. And how are you this fine morning, Victoria?" Lou Bravo announced as he slid into the booth next to Tony.

With a big Russian smile, Victoria replied, "Very busy, what can I get you, Sweetie?" She reached over and poured him a steaming hot cup of coffee. Victoria Koklovia, the head waitress at Patches for the past sixteen years, was all business. She efficiently served customers for over forty years with her no-nonsense demeanor. Big, loud and often times abrupt, she was Jackie's best server.

"I'll have what the two tomato boys are having. Except make my bacon extra crispy. You know how I like it." Lou Bravo took a sip of coffee and looked over at Tony.

"Everyone in the kitchen knows how you like your bacon. Like beef jerky!" Victoria barked out and walked back to the kitchen.

"Okay, what's with the tomato red shirts? And a yellow broom logo? What genius came up with that idea? The two of you look like a newspaper ad for the Fourth of July." Lou Bravo shook his head and stared.

"They were free," Tony replied. "A guy came into the office yesterday, handed me the shirts and said if I like them, he'd give me a great price on a dozen. I think they make a statement." Tony stuck out his chest and looked as if he were going to crow when the waitress arrived with Lou Bravo's meal.

"Extra crispy, just the way you like it. Cowboy. Anyone need anything? No, enjoy your meal fellas." Victoria turned and skirted over to another table with coffee pot in hand.

"They make a statement all right. Look at us, we're trying out for the circus right after we clean your five million dollar home. No one wants a pair of clowns working in their home. My advice, lose the tomato shirts and go back to your khaki uniforms. Khaki is more professional." Lou Bravo smiled and took a bite of bacon.

"I don't know. Let's see how my clients react to the shirts today. Enough about the shirts, we have to tell you about something that happened yesterday." Tony reached over and held up Hubba Bubba's cell phone.

"RIDES-1, okay I'll bite. What does that have to do with yesterday?" Lou Bravo asked.

"That's the license plate number of the bastard that killed the sandhill crane. We were coming back from a fair at Jacaranda Plaza when I saw two sandhill cranes crossing the road. I stopped the truck, put on my flashers and waited for the birds to cross."

Before Tony could finish Hubba Bubba blurted out, "That's when some asshole on a cell phone ran right over the first bird. The cops came, but said they couldn't do a thing. It's not against the law to kill a sandhill crane. So this bastard just drives away in his red BMW convertible and there aren't any consequences?"

"Don't you have a friend in the Motor Vehicle Bureau? A Tippy something? The naked guy you picked up one night when you were driving home from the Casey Key Tiki Bar. Maybe he can find out who this guy is." Tony handed Lou Bravo the phone.

"Bobby Tiptop. Poor bastard thought he was going to get lucky that night. Instead two girls took his clothes, wallet and left him butt naked down by the water. I'll give him a call. Maybe we can visit Mr. BMW and impress upon him the virtues of appreciating the wildlife in Sarasota County."

Lou Bravo pulled out his cell phone and dialed. "Hello, Tippy how the hell are you? Still got your pants on? Hope I didn't call you at a bad time. Listen buddy, do me a favor. I need the name and address of a guy.

The license plate number is RIDES-1. Call me back at this number. Thanks."

Victoria poured another round of coffee and dropped off the checks just as Lou Bravo's phone rang. "Hello, yes, yes really. You're kidding. A carnival owner? Okay, King Amusement, 145 Auburn Road, Venice, Florida. Thanks, Tippy. I owe you one."

The three talked and decided to shadow Mr. Morty King. They would record his comings and goings, photograph the business and personal connections and finally look for any patterns in his work day. Hubba Bubba mentioned that he was at the Sarasota County Fair Friday night and that he and a group of friends plan to go back again. He would check to see if King operated an amusement ride there. They all agreed to meet back at Patches in a week, compare notes and devise an appropriate punishment for Morty King. Mr. King needed to realize there were consequences for his transgressions.

"Tony, why don't you drive by King's place of business? See what type of operation he's running. Follow him around for a day or two. Hubba Bubba, great idea to see if King Amusement operates at the County Fair. See if you can convince your friends to go tonight. Here's a hundred bucks to help you persuade your buddies to ride Moonraker." Lou Bravo picked up the check and walked over to the counter.

"How did you hear about Moonraker?" Hubba Bubba asked as they walked out the door.

"I get around. I go to the Sarasota County Fair every year. My friend, Don Maiello, from Punta Gorda, his grandson, Alex Torres, shows pet chickens at the fair. He belongs to the 4H Club of Sarasota and last year his Modern Game chicken won County Grand Champion. This year he'll be showing four of his Modern Game birds and hopes to repeat as Grand Champion. Maybe I'll see you there?"

"Speaking about getting around," Tony blurted out

as Lou Bravo got into his car. “How are you going to help with this little venture?”

“I have to see a man about a horse. No, I stand corrected I have to see a woman about a horse.” Lou Bravo laughed and drove off.

Chapter 9

Ryan Murphy is an archaeologist, not an electrician, and his bold announcement to illuminate the cave in two days was at the least unrealistic and at most unadulterated swagger. It took the team ten days to complete the task. Arrangement of the ten lithium-ion batteries each with a seven day standby reserve before recharging was cobbled together at the entrance to the cave. Next came the placement of more than a half mile of number ten electrical wire from the entrance of the cave to the back of the scrub jay alcove. After the wire was positioned, hundred twenty fifteen-watt LED lights were attached to the walls with three hundred anchor pegs. Additionally, sixteen booster transformers were wired to the electrical system at systematic intervals to equalize the amperage reduction output that routinely arose near the end of the circuit. Finally, three boxes of bandages for hammered thumbs were added to the first aid kit.

Friday afternoon with all the archaeological equipment in place and the last LED light hard wired at the back of the alcove, Murphy stood and announced, “The moment of truth is at hand, colleagues. Dalton, I bestow upon thee the honor to go topside and illuminate this prodigious endeavor."

The young man just stood there with a confused look on his face. "Go turn on the power."

"I am honored, Professor. Should I return and assist in collecting the lanterns?"

"That won't be necessary. I've decided to leave the lanterns in place in case of a power failure. Hopefully there won't be a problem, but better safe than sorry. You may leave after you turn on the power. See you back here at eight o'clock sharp Monday morning."

Murphy and Sydney finished positioning the last of the eight twenty-foot PVC poles that ringed the giant deer and would shoulder the portable micro-diffraction X-ray machine.

"That's it for today, Sydney. Monday, we'll carry the X-ray machine down into the cave, attach the unit to these support poles and X-ray the beast." Murphy looked up at the statue. "I wonder what secrets this giant has hidden all these years. This discovery is unprecedented in the annals of archaeology. Who knows what is inside? Monday, Sydney, we will find out."

"How does the X-ray unit operate?"

"It operates just like an X-ray machine in a hospital, only smaller." Pointing to the poles Murphy added, "The machine will rise at five foot increments, analyze the static formation of the object and map the interior features from top to bottom. The diffraction process will be repeated until the entire circumference of the stag is analyzed. Then an onboard computer will document the entire operation and print out a diagram of the compositional features of the structure."

"So then we get a picture of what is inside the statue?" Sydney replied.

"You could say that. However, the printout will tell us much more. From a scientific..." Murphy was about to finish when light exploded from every corner of the cave. The transformation was breathtaking. Murphy and Sydney spun round and round on the block platform in a euphoric trance absorbing the wonderment of the moment. Dark corners of the cave were suddenly illuminated, and chunks of rock that were just part of blank walls turned into works of art. Muted hues of orange, red and chalky creams flowed down the side walls and mixed together to complete nature's canvas. Flat surfaces, hidden in darkness for millenniums, sprung to life and rolled, turned and twisted magically down the walls to the floor of the cave. The ceiling shrouded in darkness lit up in shades of browns, whites and yellows. Stalactites of all sizes and shapes jutted downward like fingers reaching out to touch unwanted visitors.

"It's so beautiful, Professor. I can't believe how much more we can see now. The colors create an entirely different perspective. Details lost in the darkness now appear alive and a little scary. Look at the pictograph behind the statue."

"You're correct. The detail jumps out at you. We're looking at a story that took place thirty-five thousand years ago, maybe longer." Murphy took a deep breath. "This is an experience of a lifetime and Sydney; you will be part of an archaeological dig that will make history. No, change history. It's time to go."

"Should I photograph everything while we climb back to the surface?"

"Excellent suggestion. We'll use your photographs to document the first lighting changes."

The walk back was exhilarating. Sights before hidden in darkness revealed beauty and color, brilliant as the day they were created. Sydney began to snap pictures as they left the platform and the giant mural of the prehistoric hunt. Pictures of the pathway leading out of the cathedral gallery and of the towering ceiling revealed formations spiraling downward in nature's beauty. Sydney's camera continued to snap away. Next photographed a passageway filled with immense stalactites and stalagmites that at times blocked sections of the tunnel. Their tremendous size and girth recorded, Ryan and Sydney then moved down a long sandy riverbed pebbled with small yellow, white and gray stones. Light reflected off the cave walls like sunlight shining through tiny windows on a child's dollhouse.

"Sydney, photograph the walls. I think mica is embedded in the rocks."

"I'll get some close-ups and a few panoramic shots down the passageway." Repeated clicking sounds echoed down the riverbed and continued up the stone steps to the outside.

"Great job, Sydney. That will do it for today. Get some rest this weekend. You'll need all your strength to schlep the X-ray machine down into the cave on Monday. I'm going over to the office and ask Assistant Park Manager Sterling if she would like join us Monday morning. 'Bye."

Ryan parked in front of the ranger office. The office door was unlocked and he walked in. "Hello, anyone here? It's Ryan Murphy, Sarasota County Archaeologist, anyone here?" Somewhat full of himself and excited about Monday's experiment, he stopped and looked down the hallway towards Blaine's office.

"I'm back here. In my office," Blaine shouted.

"Hi, haven't seen you in weeks. I just happened to be in the neighborhood and thought I'd drop in and say hello." Ryan walked over to the computer station where Blaine was seated. "Hello."

"Hi, Ryan. I'm sorry I haven't stopped by the dig, but I've been swamped with work. Look at all the papers in my in-basket."

"We're going to X-ray the statue Monday morning. I thought you'd like to be the first to see what mysteries unfold. I believe it will be a historic occasion and hoped you could be part of the celebration." Ryan looked down at Blaine and waited.

"I'm sorry Ryan, but I have a meeting with John Forrester Monday morning."

"Okay, I just thought I'd ask. Maybe another time. Have a nice weekend," Ryan replied and turned towards the door.

Blaine reached for his arm and pulled him back towards the table. She stood a breath away from him and in a whisper said, "It's not just the work Ryan. It is hard for me to go down there. The memories are painful, but I'm working through them. I'll get down there, soon, but not Monday."

It just happened. Maybe it was the closeness or her touch, but Ryan leaned in and kissed her. Her lips were cool and moist and inviting. He kissed her a second time, a third and again. Then suddenly they tore off their clothes and stood naked face-to-face. Ryan reached around Blaine's waist, lifted her and carried her to the couch. She pulled him in and their bodies moved as one in rhythmic ecstasy. Their lovemaking heightened and exploded in exhausted pleasure. Together they collapsed back against the couch and hugged. They lay there silent and complete. Ryan was first to speak, "Does this mean you'll come Monday morning?"

"Very funny." Slowly Blaine turned, reached under Ryan's waist and hugged him tight, "I can't. The District Manager is meeting with Forrester and me on Monday. You must have noticed all the work on the canoe dock. A skeleton of a girl was found under the old wooden planking. We don't have any information concerning her identity, how she died or what she was doing in the park at the time of her demise. So on Monday we will develop a publicity program to inform the community about the tragedy and reassure everyone that Osprey State Park is a family-friendly park to visit."

The phone rang from under the pile of clothes

scattered on the floor. "That's mine. I have to get it. Could be the park manager." Blaine rolled off the couch and rustled through the stack of clothes until she found her green slacks. "Hello, hi Charlene. Oh I'm sorry. That's right you have an important practice. Sorry. I'm just about to leave. 'Bye."

"Who was that?" Ryan asked and watched with sadness as Blaine hurriedly pulled on her panties. If the parks department gave out trophies for good bodies, Blaine Sterling would be awarded first place, hands down. Her gym-toned body, long legs, flat stomach and firm breasts were a complete package. And she was legally blonde top to bottom. He found his pants.

"That's Brooke's babysitter, Charlene Brecht," Blaine said and smoothed out her blouse. "She has a bells final rehearsal practice tonight at the church and can't be late."

"Bells, that sounds exciting. Who's conducting, Quasimodo?" Ryan laughed and stepped into his pants.

"Be careful zipping up. Could be painful."

"It already is. I was hoping to get to second base."

"You already hit a home run champ," Blaine answered gleefully.

Ryan zipped up and said, "When can I see you again?" And touched her arm.

"I'm having a BBQ Sunday, one o'clock. Do you know where I live?"

"No, but I have a GPS," Ryan sang out in a cheery voice.

"Okay, we have to go. I'm late." Blaine turned off the light and started for the door.

Ryan reached over and pulled her close and kissed her. "I'll see you Sunday."

Chapter 10

Deputy Sheriff Jeff Johnson sat back from his computer and reviewed his report before e-mailing it off to headquarters. If he hadn't been the investigating officer, he wouldn't believe it possible that such an episode could have occurred in 2017. But it did, and Johnson was completing the paperwork.

For more than two months, on a daily basis, a motorist in a royal blue Mustang would pass Mr. Keith Freeland's house, slow down, beep the horn and aim a one-finger salute at the house. Freeland never confronted the motorist, but as time passed and the incidents increased in frequency and intensity, Mr. Freeland became fearful that the situation would escalate into something more. So one rainy Sunday morning he jumped into his car and followed the Mustang. Five minutes later the Mustang pulled into a driveway and a tall, young woman with straight brown hair and long shapely legs exited the car and walked into the house. Freeland wrote down the house address, license plate number and called the sheriff's office to ask them to investigate this individual and determine if she posed a threat to him and his family.

Lieutenant Johnson visited the woman's home, explained that the sheriff's office received a complaint that she over a period of time performed an obscene gesture and blasted her automobile horn in front of 105 Cala Court, Sarasota. The home of Mr. and Mrs. Keith Freeland. Both offenses, Johnson stated were fineable violations according to Sarasota codes # 72-456 and code# 62-409 punishable by a fine of up to a thousand dollars. The woman admitted to being the perpetrator and promised not to do it again.

Afterward, Johnson called Freeland and said, "The woman admitted to being the driver of the Mustang and the single-digit signifier. She promised to stop, but she never explained the reason for her behavior."

Freeland explained that as Neighborhood Watch Captain for his community, he may have irritated people in the course of his duties and perhaps that was why the driver drove past his home. Last year, he spearheaded a stop sign campaign to identify drivers who refused to stop at the intersection in front of his house. Freeland photographed violators and sent the pictures to the sheriff's office, which resulted in a number of ticketed drivers. Freeland surmised that she was ticketed and took out her frustration on him. Freeland's last remark to Johnson was, "I'm just relieved the entire mess is over with so I can get on with my life."

Johnson hit the send key when his phone rang. "Hello, Lieutenant Johnson, this is Len Rosa. I have the coroner's report and I'd like you to stop by the morgue this morning. There are a number of details in the report that I need to show you. Let's say ten o'clock."

"Len, please tell me the skeleton isn't Native American. I can't afford an outcry from the Native American Rights Fund Organization that we desecrated an ancient burial site. It would be a total mess. We would be required to shut down the park and protect a prolonged archaeological study of the area that could take months, maybe even years. The manpower required would be staggering and let's not forget the cost. Len, what do you say?"

"No, it's not a Native American skeleton, but I need you to see what I found."

"Thank God. I'll see you at ten."

"Hello, Assistant Manager Sterling, this is Lieutenant Jeff Johnson from the Sarasota Sheriff's Office. I just received a call from the coroner's office, and the skeleton found at the park is not Native American. That's all I have now, but I'm meeting with the coroner at ten o'clock to review the report. I'll forward you more details after our meeting. Hope this message helps." Johnson hung up and walked out to his car.

Johnson never liked visiting the morgue. Only a ten-minute drive from department headquarters on Ringling Boulevard, the trip seemed a lifetime away. A ten-year veteran of the force, Johnson made many a trip to the morgue but was always ill at ease, even though the morgue was housed in the Sarasota Memorial Hospital. Maybe it was the finality the morgue represented or maybe it was more.

Johnson pulled his black Tahoe around to the rear of the hospital and parked in the first empty spot. He pulled down the driver's side visor with his official sheriff's identification and walked over to the building.

A small, non-descript sign over an open doorway on the corner of the building read Medical Examiner Receiving. Johnson stepped into the vestibule, picked up the admittance phone on the wall and punched in the four-digit code written above the receiver. "This is Lieutenant Jeff Johnson. I have an appointment with the coroner."

A voice on the other end replied, "Dr. Rosa is expecting you. He's in Suite 4." The far door buzzed open and Johnson walked through and took the elevator to the second floor.

That's what they now call the cadaver room, Suite 4. They can call it what they want, but it's still a creepy place, Johnson thought to himself and stepped off the elevator.

The interior of the building didn't improve Johnson's well-being nor did it brighten his spirits about visiting. The drab lifeless exterior foreshadowed what was to come. The inside was even gloomier. It was cold. Not air conditioning cold, rather a walk-in freezer cold. The type of cold where everyone wears lab jackets to keep from freezing and dreams about mittens for their hands. But the worst part was the smell. The odor of embalming fluids, cleaning chemicals and death permeated every corner of the room. It seeped under the skin, melting into the bones until it choked the clean air out of you. Only a long, hot shower could bring a person back to balance after a visit to the morgue.

Suite 4 was exactly how it looked the last time he was there when it was still called the *cadaver room.* The same instructions from the Friendly Morgue Crew were still tacked to the wall: *Please write the person's name on the foot end of the bag before placing in cooler.* The whir of giant freezers, the biting chill in the air and the geometric arrangement of the stainless steel tables still occupied the antiseptic environment. The only difference was that a human body was replaced with a skeleton on the stainless steel table in the center of the room. The smell was still noxious, and Johnson could taste the familiar unpleasant burning sensation with each swallow.

"There you are, Jeff. Come over and look at this," called Rosa as he handed Johnson the coroner's report.

"Not very appetizing, all these bones," Johnson quipped and opened the report.

"I agree, but these old bones revealed a bounty of

information about this young lady. You'll notice on page two, the results of all the DNA testing. Because of decomposition we had a difficult time extracting significant DNA to develop a genetic profile. However, with the assistance of a forensic anthropologist to reconstruct the skeleton, we were able to define her ethnic origins. In addition we called upon a geochemist to examine shavings from tooth enamel and bones to analyze chemical isotopes to distinguish diet patterns and environmental chemicals in the body."

"So that's how you determined the girl wasn't Native American," said Johnson.

"Correct. DNA samples yielded key genetic markers that identified the girl as Caucasian. However, because of decomposition, mitochondrial DNA was extracted; and the results established that the girl had blue eyes and blond hair. Additionally, Carbon-14 dating on bone samples concluded that she died approximately 50 to 55 years ago. Lastly, skeletal measurements, bone maturity and dental analysis indicated that she was five foot three and was between sixteen, and nineteen years old at time of death."

"Great work, Dr. Rosa, but we are missing a most critical fact. How did this young girl die?" Johnson slapped the coroner's report against his leg and looked down at the skeleton.

"Excellent question, my dear Holmes. If you would be so kind as to step to the front of the table and take a close look at the young girl's skull. In particular, the occipital bone," Rosa answered and pointed to the back of the skull.

Johnson bent down and stared at the skull. "There appears to be a laceration down the right side of the skull. Four or five inches long. Looks as if she was hit on the head. What do you think, doctor?"

"Ten centimeters to be precise. She may have fallen and hit her head on something. She could have been hit from behind." Dr. Rosa turned the skull and traced the crack with his finger. "Probably enough force to kill a person. Hard to determine. We can only speculate because of the time factor. That's your department's job lieutenant." Dr. Rosa gently lowered the skull back down, walked over to the right side of the table and picked up the right arm.

"What's with the arm? You waving goodbye?" Johnson remarked.

"Not exactly. Take a look at her right hand."

"Shit, her index finger is cut off," said Johnson and felt his stomach starting to talk to him.

"Not exactly. The finger is cut off at the nail." Dr. Rosa wiggled the finger at Johnson and smiled. "The information is detailed on page five of the report. This girl was in some sort of accident. Hospitals, doctors and schools keep records of injuries of this magnitude."

"Perfect! How many teenage girls had a finger missing fifty years ago? Not many I suspect. We'll punch all your information into Florida's Missing Persons Data Base and see what turns up. Thanks, Doc." Johnson stepped back from the table, shook Dr. Rosa's hand and walked out to his vehicle.

Once outside Johnson took a deep breath and savored the sweet, fresh taste of paradise.

Chapter 11

Saturday morning a banana yellow El Camino pulled into the Seabourne Industrial Park turned right and drove three blocks to a single story concrete building decorated with colorful circus animals. A large red and white light bulb sign over the front door flashed "Circus Days Ice Cream Company." Lou Bravo pulled up to the door and leaned on the horn. Two minutes later a tall, skinny bald man walked outside. "Good morning Tony, let's surprise Blaine and rent an amusement park ride for her BBQ tomorrow. What do you think?" asked Lou Bravo.

"Sounds like a plan, and I know just the place, King Amusement." Tony jumped into the car and off they went.

"Did you drive past the property yet?" Lou Bravo asked and turned onto Tamiami Trail.

"No, but I Googled it and it's off Auburn Road. Maybe a ten-minute ride from here. Google Earth showed a picture of a gigantic barn back in the woods. Probably a storage facility for all the amusement rides." Tony adjusted his seatbelt and sat back.

"Here it is, Auburn," said Lou Bravo and turned.

"Ten minutes my friend. Right on the money."

"Don't thank me. Thank modern technology, you old dinosaur. The amusement company is at the end of the road on the right." Lou Bravo pushed down on the accelerator and the El Camino jumped forward and sped down the road. "A word of advice you may want to keep to the speed limit. Every now and then Venice Police lie in wait for unsuspecting drivers racing down the road. They set up a speed trap at the Saw Grass Community entrance over there to the left. No cop, lucky you."

"King Amusement Company!" Lou Bravo shouted as he jammed on the brakes and made a sharp right turn onto a dirt road. "Sorry about that, but the sign shot out of nowhere. The damn sign is so small and rusted, if you weren't looking for it, you'd never find it."

"A hell of a way to run a business." Tony groaned and pulled himself upright in the seat. "An obscured sign, a business located in the woods. What is this guy trying to hide?"

"I don't know, but we'll soon find out. Look at that!" The El Camino slowed to a crawl.

A one-lane shell road filled with bumps and holes extended more than three hundred yards into the woods. On both sides of the road, old, broken and rusted carnival rides littered the ground as far as the eye could see. Old trucks, cars and broken wagons of all colors and shapes melted into the undergrowth, painting a portrait of a bygone era. Discarded popcorn, cotton candy and soda machines stood at attention along a muddy patch of grass. Silent and unattended they waited for the next customer. A row of crushed amusement boats, cars and planes—thirty or more—abutted the road and formed a colorful metal fence of long-ago memories. Animal cages that once housed majestic beasts were now stacked two-high with open gates standing silent and empty, never to jail another wild creature again.

As the El Camino maneuvered around the many potholes, a gigantic red and white striped barn loomed at the end of the dirt path. From a distance the wooden structure resembled an assortment of colossal peppermint sticks bundled together to form a building. Two massive hangar-like doors in the center of the barn were shuttered and locked from the outside. A blue sign in large block letters above the doors read, "King Amusement Company." A single windowless door off to the right with a red BMW parked out front appeared to lead to the office.

"This is the place and I'd bet a hundred bucks that's the BMW that killed the sandhill crane," Tony said and walked over to the car. "That lazy bastard! He didn't even wash off the blood from the front bumper. Take a look."

"Unbelievable. Let's go meet Mr. Morty King," Lou Bravo barked out and opened the office door.

A small wood paneled room with a single desk, two wooden chairs and a brown leather sofa worn by time and abuse greeted Lou Bravo and Tony. Photographs, newspaper clippings, magazine articles about various amusement rides and events plastered every wall in a haphazard arrangement. Brochures on King Amusement littered the floor while half open boxes of contract forms stacked three-high filled the back wall. To say the room was claustrophobic would be a gross understatement.

Seated behind the desk and smoking a large, dark black cigar was Morty King. A short, fleshy man in his early seventies, bald, with a bulbous nose and an ugly brown mole on the side of his face. With each word he yelled into the phone his face reddened to the point one would imagine an explosion. "I don't give a damn what you think! You signed a contract! Hold on a minute."

King cupped the phone with his meaty left hand and looked up at Tony and Lou Bravo, "I'll be with you gentlemen in a minute. Please have a seat."

Morty turned his back on the visitors and in a slow controlled voice said, "Listen this is the last time I call. If I don't get my money by the end of the week, two of my associates will visit your pizza parlor and smash the place up. One week." Morty spun around and smiled. "How can I help you, gentlemen?"

"We would like to rent an amusement ride for a house party tomorrow," said Lou Bravo.

"Nothing like waiting until the last minute. Let me check my calendar. Yes, it just so happens I have one cancellation, a children's rollercoaster. How does that sound?" King smiled.

"How much?" Tony asked.

"Four hundred-fifty dollars: cash. That includes delivery of the ride, setup and removal and one operator. Half payment at signing and the remainder at the end of the party. Cash only! King smiled again.

"We'll need to see the ride," Lou Bravo answered and stood.

"No problem. The ride is already set up. Follow me." King stood, walked over to a side door and the three men walked into the barn.

The inside of the barn was cavernous. The size and shape of a factory outlet warehouse, about 50,000 square feet of interior floor space or more. Rows and rows of flood lights illuminated the entire barn highlighting every imaginable amusement park ride ever manufactured. The open space in the center of the building, the width of the two front doors was used to transport equipment in and out of the building. The rest of the barn was broken into compartments that resembled horse stalls and filled with every type of amusement park contraption King ever owned. The back section of the barn was a work space for installations, repairs and storage.

King stopped in front of the first stall and pointed to a newspaper article tacked to the wall. "That's my father Walter King. He started the business in 1955. He's shaking hands with J. P. Kiernan, the mayor of Venice. In the background you can see the first wooden rollercoaster we owned. One of the seats is preserved here in the stall. We've catalogued every event since 1955. A living museum of King Amusement Park history. For your gratification, when the new addition is completed on the Venice Archives and Museum, my entire collection of memorabilia will be displayed for the public to see." King smiled.

"That's interesting, but we need to see the new rollercoaster," interrupted Lou Bravo.

If looks could kill. King turned and marched off towards the back. "Here it is. Three red cars that hold a maximum of six children and a hundred-foot oval track. Three bumps on each side and a straight path at the end of the ride for a safe exit."

"How is it powered?" asked Tony.

"Battery powered, remote control by the operator from the center of the circle," King answered.

"How fast does it go? Does each car have its own braking system? What about seat belts?" Lou Bravo asked.

"Slow. It's a kid ride so it doesn't go fast. Maybe 3 mph we never timed it. Each car has an individual braking system, and each rider has a seat belt. Does that about answer all your questions, gentlemen?" Asked King with a curt smile.

"We'll take it," Tony said and slapped King on the back, pushing him forward into a giant stuffed polar bear propped up against the stall. "Sorry, so sorry, Mr. King, I guess I don't know my own strength."

"That's okay. No damage done. Let's go to the office and sign the papers. By the way, for an extra fifty dollars I'll throw in that cotton candy machine. That includes the cotton candy and paper cones."

"I love cotton candy. Add it to the bill," Lou Bravo replied.

“The cotton candy is for the children, not you,” Tony interjected.

“Gentlemen, you don’t have to worry. There will be plenty of cotton candy for everyone to enjoy. Here’s the contract. Fill in the address and sign on the bottom. What time do you want everything set up?” King added with a Cheshire smile.

“Everything must be ready to go at one o’clock sharp!” Lou Bravo handed the contract back to King.

“Everything looks in order. I’ll need two hundred-fifty dollars today and another two hundred-fifty cash at the end of the party.” King smiled and held out his hand.

Lou Bravo took out his money clip, peeled off two hundreds and a fifty and slapped it into his fat hand.

“A pleasure doing business with you. Enjoy the ride.” King smiled and slipped the money into his pocket.

Tony and Lou Bravo turned and left the office. Once outside Tony said, “What’s with that crooked smile?”

“I don’t know, but in a few days I’m going to wipe it off. Did you notice his left hand while he was on the phone? Looked disfigured or something.”

“I did, maybe he got it caught in the cookie jar and his mother took a rolling pin to the mischievous digits. Couldn’t have happened to a nicer guy. And that mole on his face—scary.” Tony slapped his friend on the back and the two got in the car and drove off.

.

Chapter 12

An old beat-up purple Volkswagen Bus, a vintage vehicle from the '60s and covered with painted purple flowers, pulled into Blaine's driveway. The hippie bus stuffed with boxes and bags above the windows slowly inched its way back to the garage and stopped. The driver's side door flew open to the music of *Purple Haze* by Jimmy Hendrix, and out jumped Vardi Zammiello, affectionately referred to as the Purple Lady. Miss Vardi to her friends, she was a retired art teacher from Long Island, New York, and loved everything purple.

As a young girl, Vardi hosted a monthly purple party for all the neighborhood girls. Everything was purple: purple hats, purple table cloths, purple plates, purple tea and most of all delicious cupcakes with purple icing. After the first party, Vardi was fondly referred to as the Purple Lady, a title she cherished and cultivated throughout the years.

As an art teacher, she presided over a classroom that was a magical garden of purple projects for all grades. One day each month Miss Vardi would host Purple Day, a day where everything would be purple in her art room. Paper flowers, clay models, landscape painting, portrait painting, charcoal drawing, crayon drawing, dioramas, Lego figures all fashioned in purple. At first the students thought she had gone mad; but time was the great equalizer, and soon the madness turned to anticipation.

With an armload of purple linens, Miss Vardi rushed across the lawn and began to dress the tables. Her short, curly purple hair glistened in the sun as she moved from station to station purpling each table. She reached into the pockets of her purple corn dress that flowed down to her purple high-top sneakers and took out a handful of purple clips which she affixed to the corners to hold down each tablecloth. Returning to the bus, she retrieved two boxes of supplies and continued to decorate the backyard. Centerpieces of lilacs, purple cutlery, plates and glasses, purple napkins and a single purple balloon tied to a chair completed the table settings. Next Miss Vardi hung strands of purple lights around the trunks of the palm trees and around the many low growing bushes about the yard. Finally, she unzipped a package of shiny purple butterflies and sprinkled each table with a handful of purple magic.

"It's beautiful, Miss Vardi," Blaine called from the lanai. "I'll be right over."

"Thanks, I'm glad you like it. It reminds me of the tea parties I hosted when I was a little girl." Miss Vardi gave Blaine a big hug. "Where's Brooke? I'm sure she will appreciate the shiny purple butterflies on the tables. They look like the butterflies in some of her paintings."

"You're right. They are much the same. She's getting dressed and should be down in a few minutes. By the way, Lou Bravo said he'd be over shortly. He wanted to get the barbecue started before the crowd showed up. Needed that extra time for his baked beans."

"I hear he is famous for his New York-style baked beans." Miss Vardi said. "An old family recipe. I hope the guests from Beantown won't be disappointed. You know how Bostonians are about their baked beans."

"Believe me, no one will be disappointed. Lou Bravo's beans are out of this world. Trust me; you're in for a treat, Miss Vardi. How about a hand bringing out the food?" The two walked into the house and started to arrange the platters of food on the banquet table.

Two hours later the red roller coaster cars rounded the first turn. All the guests gathered on Blaine's front lawn around the amusement park ride and cheered as the children zoomed by at a breakneck speed of 3 mph. Brooke and her friend Morgan were in the first car waving to everyone and laughing. Morgan's aunt, Marybeth Maiello, a teacher at the Pinebrook Elementary School, stood next to Blaine as their cameras snapped away. It was on the second turn that Blaine spotted a blue Jeep Wrangler pull up and park in front of her neighbor's house.

"Marybeth, he's here. Look in front of Bob and Mary Traver's house," Blaine whispered and pointed.

"Who's here?"

"Ryan. My archaeologist friend, Ryan Murphy. I told you I invited him," Blaine said softly.

"He's cute. Go get him and bring him over here. I can't wait to meet him," gushed Marybeth.

"Okay, but keep an eye on Brooke," Blaine called out as she hurried across the lawn towards Ryan.

"I will and the other eye on your boyfriend." Marybeth yelled and waved goodbye.

With unprecedented excitement of a school girl's joy, Blaine bubbled with cheerfulness. For the first time in a long time, Blaine felt her heart skip, but she understood that she had to move forward with caution. The feelings for her late husband Troy were a love at first sight, explosive, and magical. It was a love that could have lasted an eternity had he not died in a car crash. Somehow her feelings for Ryan, although sensuous and alive, were different. She had strong feelings for him and needed to explore her desires, but it would take time and he had to be patient. They both needed to be patient.

"You made it! I want you to come over and meet my friend Marybeth," Blaine said and tugged at his arm. "What do you have there?"

"A secret family recipe for the BBQ. My grandmother's tri-bean salad. Hope everyone likes it."

"It looks delicious. What's in it?" asked Blaine.

"Well if I told you it wouldn't be a secret recipe, would it?" Ryan laughed as they walked up to the rollercoaster ride.

"Ryan, I'd like you to meet Marybeth Maiello, her niece Morgan and my daughter Brooke. Ladies, I'd like you to meet Ryan Murphy. Ryan is the archaeologist working on a field study at Osprey State Park." Greetings were exchanged and Murphy was about to explain what field work he was engaged in when the clanging of a lunch bell sounded.

"BBQ is ready," Blaine called to her guests. "I hope everyone is hungry! Follow me." The roller coaster stopped and everyone paraded into the backyard.

"Come and get it folks. Plenty of BBQ for everyone, and don't forget the baked beans at the end of the table," Lou Bravo barked out from behind the grill. With plates piled high, all the guests sat down and enjoyed the backyard vittles. Two servers, dressed in purple attire, walked around refilling glasses and waiting on tables.

Lou Bravo walked over to Blaine's table with a big pot of baked beans and said, "Who's up for some more beans? How about you, young man?" Standing behind Ryan, Lou Bravo slammed down a large spoonful of beans on his plate. "That looks better. I hate to see an empty plate especially at a neighborhood BBQ. Blaine, I don't believe I've had the pleasure of meeting this gentleman?"

"Ryan Murphy, I'd like you to meet Lou Bravo, a

friend of mine and the baked bean master of Serpentine Lane. Lou Bravo this is Ryan Murphy, Sarasota County Archaeologist. He is working on an archaeological project at Osprey State Park," Blaine added with a smile.

"A pleasure to meet you, son. Any friend of Blaine's is a friend of mine. Hope you like the beans." Before Ryan could answer, Lou Bravo was gone, pushing his way around the tables and dishing out his baked beans.

"Seems like a nice man. A little overbearing, but I have to admit, his baked beans are delicious." Ryan smiled and ate another forkful of beans.

"Mr. Murphy, what do you do at my mommy's park?" Brooke asked. "Last school year, Melvin Zoomas brought in a pyramid made out of sugar cubes and showed the class how the burial chamber was sealed. Are you working on a pyramid, Mr. Ryan?"

"That's a very good question, Brooke, but no I'm not working on a pyramid. I am, however, working in a cave. And the cave holds a treasure of valuable information about how life existed thousands of years ago in Florida. As a matter of fact, tomorrow I will be conducting an experiment on a clay statue of a deer down in the cave. We are very excited that tomorrow's test will unlock a number of secrets of how early man survived," Murphy explained.

"A cave, Mr. Murphy?" Ken Brecht interjected. "How can there be a cave in Florida. The water table is so low. Wouldn't it be filled with water?"

"That's true, sometimes," Murphy answered. "We are taking soil samples to carbon date the time the cave was hollowed out by water. There was a period when Florida's sea level was approximately one hundred and thirty feet below today's level and the land extended more than a hundred miles further into the Gulf of Mexico. That could be the time frame in which the cave was inhabited. We won't know until all the data has been collected."

"People lived in the cave? How do you know? Did you find skeletons?" Morgan asked. "Isn't that so cool, Brooke?"

"There is evidence that early hunters visited the cave, performed hunting ceremonies and recorded wall drawings of the numerous hunts. That's why tomorrows experiment is so important. We'll document a giant statue in the cave and hopefully see what the object of the hunt centuries ago was," explained Ryan.

"How exciting, Ryan. I'd love to have you come to my classroom and talk about archaeology," Marybeth added. "My fourth grade class is studying Florida history and to have a visit from an archaeologist would truly pique their interest. It certainly does mine. The history aspect that is." Marybeth gave Blaine a wink.

"I'd be delighted. I'll check my calendar and email you the dates I have available," Ryan answered. Ryan took out his phone, opened his address book and said, "What's your e-mail and phone number? I'll also bring some of the artifacts from the cave. I'm certain the kids will enjoy holding a 3,000 year old Paleo-Indian spear point."

"Mommy, can Morgan and I go back and ride the roller coaster?" Brooke pushed her plate forward and stood.

"Okay, but no crazy tricks on the ride. I'll be down in a minute to take some more pictures."

"Morgan, behave yourself. No theatrics on the ride and keep the seat belt on at all times. Blaine, what a marvelous idea it was to have an amusement park ride for all the children," Marybeth added. "What an ingenious babysitter. Hours of fun that just goes round and round never leaving a parent's sight."

"Actually it was a surprise addition courtesy of Lou Bravo, the old kid at the party. He's already made two trips to the cotton candy machine and the BBQ isn't half over." Everyone at the table laughed. "If you'll excuse me, I'm going to go watch the roller coaster go round and round," laughed Blaine.

"I'll go with you," Murphy announced and jumped to his feet.

The two said goodbye and left the table.

"Does Blaine have a new boyfriend?" Ken asked. "They seem like an item and Blaine is a hot looking number."

"Oh Ken, that's not nice to say. They just work together at the park," Charlene Brecht scolded.

"I wonder if that's all they do together at the park. He couldn't keep his eyes off of her all during the meal. I think there's more to their relationship than work," Greg added sarcastically and took a forkful of baked beans.

Ryan bumped his shoulder up against hers as they reached the driveway. He smiled and rubbed her shoulder. "You have some nice friends. They all seem to care about you and Brooke very much. Especially that Lou Bravo fellow. I think I know more about your neighbors and friends than I know about you. So who are you, Blaine Sterling? I want to know everything about you. Where you're from, what you like, what you don't like, do you have any siblings, are your parents living in Florida, what about your husband and what about us?"

"Well Mr. Ryan Murphy, you ask a lot of questions. Undoubtedly it is the scientist in you. I'm not sure we have enough time to cover all the basics. We'll have to have another date to finish the inquisition." Blaine smiled.

"So today is a date, our first date? So I can count today as getting to first base?" Ryan remarked with a mischievous grin.

"Listen slugger, I think you already hit a homerun. You don't have to worry about first base any longer," Blaine said with a smiled. "About the other questions, that's a more delicate undertaking. I'm from West

Hempstead, New York. Graduated from Hofstra University, majored in Marine Biology and was offered a park ranger job on Fire Island after graduation. That job didn't work out, so eight years ago I moved to Florida and began my job as a ranger at Osprey State Park. My parents are deceased. I have a younger brother, Bobby, he's married and lives in Stanley, North Carolina ..." Blaine was in mid-sentence when Brooke ran up.

"Mommy, a man is breaking up the roller coaster and Sarah is still in one of the cars crying. Hurry, you have to stop him," Brooke cried.

"Breaking up the ride. The BBQ isn't half over why is the attendant dismantling the roller coaster, sweetie?"

"It's a different man. A bad man. He has a big hammer. He hit the man running the ride and now he's smashing the roller coaster."

"Go get Lou Bravo, sweetie. Tell him to call the police. You and Morgan run now."

Blaine and Murphy sprinted down the driveway to the front of the house and stared in horror at the scene unfolding in front of their eyes. Wielding a large sledgehammer, a short, fleshy man in his early forties, with sloping shoulders and skinny arms, pounded away at the lower tracks closest to the control box. On the ground lay the ride operator, a teenage boy no older than eighteen. Blood puddled around his head. He appeared unconscious. At the far end of the ride, in the last car, sat five-year-old Sarah Wilcox crying hysterically. Blaine and Ryan ran directly towards the car, scooped up the terrified little girl and stepped away from the ride.

"Ryan, take Sarah back to party. I'll try to reason with this guy and find out why he is destroying our ride."

Blaine walked past the coaster cars and came up behind the man furiously pounding away at the roller coaster tracks and metal support beams. By now he had completely flattened a third of the tracks and was moving over to decapitate the operation station in the center of the oval tracks when Blaine called out, "Excuse me, sir! Why are you destroying the roller coaster ride?"

Startled, the intruder spun around, sledgehammer in hand and glowered at Blaine. Eyes burning, he seethed with rage. Blaine could feel his anger, but at the same time his labored breathing and body language signaled that he was near exhaustion. The man took a deep breath and spat out a labored sentence. "That bastard King fired me because I didn't collect the final payment from a pizza store opening last week. The roller coaster broke down and the owner refused to pay me. He was twice my size, what could I do? Fifteen years I worked for that son of a bitch and he fires me. Well, this is payback. So get out of my way lady before you get hurt." He raised the sledgehammer and faced Blaine.

"I can't do that. You can't continue to destroy the roller coaster. You're frightening the children."

Before the sledgehammer reached shoulder height, Blaine side-kicked across his chest, caught the sledgehammer at its base and sent the weapon flying out of the man's hand. Surprised, he stepped back to regain his advantage, but it was too late. Blaine spun around and delivered a reverse roundhouse kick to the side of the head sending him to the ground. He rose to one knee, grabbed the sledgehammer and charged his adversary. A slashing kick to his kneecap produced a loud crack, and then the attacker collapsed screaming in pain. Lou Bravo was first to arrive and put a gun to the man's head, and together with Tony and Ryan they marched him into the house. The police and ambulance arrived a few minutes later, took the sledgehammer assailant off to jail and the amusement operator to the hospital.

"Well that's some first date if I do say so myself," Ryan whispered to Blaine as everyone began to cleanup and prepare to leave. "You really know how to grab a man's attention."

"I try my best. `Kill them with kindness,' my mother always said," laughed Blaine. "But if kindness didn't work, kick their ass my father preached."

"I sure hope I don't get on your bad side. Where did you learn to fight like that? You destroyed that poor man."

"Karate lessons, ten years at the DoJo Kan Academy of West Hempstead, New York. I'm a third degree black belt."

"Do you have any pets?" Murphy asked with a smile.

"You ask a lot of questions, Mister," Blaine said quickly and threw the last paper plate in the garbage. "I have a cat, Romeo, a brown and gray long-hair bundle of joy..." In the center of the yard a purple spectacle was about to unfold.

"Purple people lovers. May I have your attention please?" Standing on the empty buffet table, Miss Vardi dressed in all her purple glory frantically waved her arms in the air to garner everyone's undivided attention. She gyrated her hips round and round as if a Hula-Hoop was attached to her body. "Thank you. Try and say that three times fast without spitting on the person in front of you. Anyway I want to thank Blaine for the lovely BBQ, everything was delicious. I also want to thank Lou Bravo for the entertainment. There's never a dull moment when Lou Bravo is around. Nothing like a crazed maniac, the police and an ambulance to bring an end to a party."

Everyone burst out in laughter. "However, all is not lost. I have a present for everyone to take home to remember the day on a more serene note. A purple basket holding two purple cupcakes for everyone to enjoy. Thank you all for coming and enjoy the purple goodies."

After everyone said their goodbyes, Blaine handed Ryan his glass bowl with only a spoonful of salad remaining. "Your tri-bean salad was a hit. I don't suppose you could give me the recipe?" pleaded Blaine.

"As I said, it is an old family secret, but for you maybe an exception," Ryan laughed and gave Blaine a hug. "Will I see you Monday?"

"Maybe, I'll try," Blaine whispered in his ear.

"Maybe, you'll get the recipe. I'll try." Ryan laughed and walked to his car.

Chapter 13

Sunrise was an hour away when Murphy punched in the security code to open the gate to Osprey State Park. The Jeep's headlights cut through the mist as the gate slowly moved across the entrance. Crunching sounds from the gate's metal wheels echoed down the roadway until the metal frame slammed shut against the side post with a loud thud. A slow moving armadillo, frightened by the unexpected movement and caught in the beams of light, lumbered past the chain link enclosure and into the darkness.

Murphy sped past the ranger station. Empty and dark, it would be hours before a ranger officially opened the building and welcomed visitors to the park. The Jeep bounced along the road casting eerie shadows of light back and forth. Passing under the first canopy of ancient oaks, Murphy rolled down the window and breathed in the clean, fresh air. *Nature's breath of life*, he thought to himself. *How sweet it is.* He took another deep breath and pulled the Jeep to the side of the road. He switched off the headlamps, turned off the motor and leaned back in the seat to absorb the moment. In the darkness, the park erupted in a cornucopia of nighttime sounds hidden by daylight's daily confusion. Nature's concert floated through the air to nourish Murphy's heart with an all-encompassing magnificence.

Beyond the scrubby flatwoods, a high-pitched trill resonated through the darkness. A muted song, similar to a horse's whinny, repeated itself over and over again. "Amazing," Murphy whispered. "I love the screech owl songs."

The mellow calls were hypnotic and Murphy struggled to keep awake. He followed the enchanting patterns and ardently waited for the next stanza to repeat and complete the bird's song. As each song unfolded, Murphy found his thoughts drifting back to Blaine Sterling. His overwhelming desire to hold her in his arms again grew stronger and stronger. He believed in her own quiet way she had feelings for him and that their relationship would blossom and mature. He wanted to move to the next level, but understood that with the death of her husband and raising a child by herself for eight years, he would have to be patient. Unfortunately, patience was not an attribute in Murphy's portfolio. Given the choice, he would be the first to jump headlong into a risky project and damn the consequences. A style that over the years afforded him great success. Murphy smiled because he knew that was how he won the Florida State Archaeological Research Grant and the opportunity to be near Blaine. However, to win the ultimate prize, he understood that he had to make adjustments. A path he was totally committed to.

Suddenly a blinding white light exploded from behind the Jeep and illuminated the entire area surrounding Murphy's vehicle. The serenity of the darkness was transformed into chaos and confusion. Every plant and tree was radiated in brilliant greens and browns, sending unsuspecting creatures scurrying into the woods. Murphy turned around and was blinded by the intensity of the light bearing down on him. He turned to see the lights of two trucks speed past him into the night, leaving behind only two sets of red taillights disappearing into the darkness.

"Who the hell is speeding down the road at six in the morning? Certainly not campers," Murphy shouted and turned on the engine. He pulled the Jeep onto the main road and headed for the cave.

"Could they be thieves going to the cave looking for treasure?" He growled and accelerated past the campground. The entrance road was empty. Driving through the Nature Center's parking lot, Murphy spotted two vehicles parked alongside the cave. Two shadows standing at the cave entrance were silhouetted in his Jeep's headlights. Murphy reached into the glove compartment, pulled out his Colt 45 and stepped out of the vehicle.

"Hands up or I'll shoot," Murphy yelled and stepped into the gated enclosure in front of the cave. The headlights outlined two figures with their hands raised, one male and one female.

"Don't shoot! We work here. I'm Dalton Marks and this is Sydney Price. We are graduate students from New College working on an archaeological dig here at Osprey State Park. Professor Ryan Murphy is head of the project. You can call him. He will verify our involvement with the program."

"Hey, it's me, Professor Murphy. What the hell are the two of you doing here at six in the morning?" Murphy said tersely and lowered the gun.

"I couldn't sleep," Sydney mumbled and dabbed her eyes. "So I called Dalton, who said he couldn't sleep either so we decided to get an early start on the experiment."

"Why are you here, Professor Murphy?" Dalton asked.

"Great minds think alike!" Murphy exclaimed. "Let's get to work." Together they walked to the back of

Murphy's Jeep, unloaded the X-ray equipment and disappeared into the cave.

Chapter 14

Blaine put on her right turn signal, downshifted into third and turned into the park. The clock on the dash read 8:45 as she drove her red and white Mini-Cooper up to the ranger station. Through the side window, Blaine noticed Ranger Cristy Disbrow doing paperwork at the front counter as she brought the car to a stop.

"Good morning, Assistant Park Manager Sterling," Ranger Cristy said, stepping outside. Always smiling, Cristy bubbled with warmth and good cheer. No doubt she was the type who always looked at the glass as half full. A positive person, Cristy was the type of ranger Blaine wanted associated with Osprey State Park.

"Good morning Cristy. So now they have you doing morning gate duty. What happened to Ranger Diana? She was scheduled to work mornings this week."

"She called in sick. Well, a friend of hers called. You know how Diana loves sushi? Last night, she and a group of friends were at a sushi restaurant when suddenly she became deathly sick. Her throat started to close and she could barely breathe. The owners called 911 and they rushed her to Venice Memorial

Hospital." Cristy handed Blaine the attendance clipboard. "I called the hospital just a few minutes ago. The head nurse on the floor said she was resting comfortably but will remain for another day for observations." Cristy took back the clipboard.

"That's terrible! I'll call the hospital later and see how she is progressing. I'll find out if she is up to having any visitors. Maybe we can have a group stop in and cheer her up." Blaine shook her head.

"If I'd have to guess, I don't believe Diana will be eating sushi anytime soon." Cristy quipped.

"So, are you prepared for your Literacy Amongst the Trees celebration next week?"

"Yes, all ready for a big literary gathering. We have seven local authors who will talk about writing, read stories and sign books. We will have a gently used book swap table and plenty of literacy activities for all the children. It is going to be a fantastic event. Please try to attend." A big smile crossed Cristy's face. "It may be a little cold, but no rain is forecast for the entire week. That's a big plus. No one likes to visit a park in the rain."

"I noticed you were wearing your ranger jacket. Weather reports indicate that a cold front is moving down from Canada. We might even get some frost."

"I hope not. I'm going on a strawberry-picking trip in Plant City this weekend with my boyfriend and his parents. They have a cabin on a beautiful stream. I hope the weather won't cancel our trip."

"Cristy, have Professor Murphy and his students checked in yet? I forgot to look at the sign-in sheet." Blaine looked down at the clock as the dial clicked over to 8:56.

"No. The only people signed in this morning are Park Manager John Forrester and Florida Assistant State Park Director Goodie." Ranger Cristy replied.

"Assistant Director Goodie! Would that be Rosa Parks Goodie?" Blaine asked.

"Yes, it would. She signed the sheet: Assistant Florida State Park Director Rosa Parks Goodie. Is there something wrong Blaine?"

"Cristy, please describe Assistant Director Goodie."

"She's African American, short black hair, narrow shoulders and reed thin arms. She remained seated so I couldn't say how tall she was, but if I had to guess, she's short, maybe only five foot."

Exasperated, Blaine stared out the front window as her thoughts wandered to another time and place. A large, dark brown gopher tortoise lumbered along a small patch of grass in front of the canoe paddle storage shed just a few feet away. Mesmerized, Blaine watched how the huge *Polyphemus* pushed and shoved its massive hulk past the open front door and around the side. It seemed an eternity until the tortoise disappeared. A disappearance similar to Rosa Parks Goodie who disappeared from her life eight years ago. W*ell, my day is ruined,* she thought. *I might as well turn the car around and drive back home. Of all the officers from the state to attend today's meeting, why did it have to be Rosa Parks Goodie?*

"Blaine, what seems to be the problem? You look ill. Do you know Assistant Director Goodie?" Cristy looked down at Blaine and waited.

"Eight years ago Rosa and I were in the ranger academy together. It was the first week of basic training and in the self-defense class we were paired up to train together. On the third day of class we were practicing how to disarm an assailant with a knife. Rosa was first to perform the defensive moves. She was fast and mastered the technique perfectly. The instructor actually brought her up to the front of the class and made her execute the technique for the entire class to observe. Unfortunately, on my first attempt I broke her arm. My experience as a black belt was too aggressive for her tiny frame to absorb. The model pupil left the class that morning and never returned. I was informed by the instructor that she transferred to administration, and now she arrives as Assistant Director of Parks."

"It was an accident. The incident took place eight years ago. It was an accident Blaine. I'm sure she has long forgotten the incident. Don't worry."

"That's easy for you to say. You don't have to meet with her this morning."

"Speaking of meeting Assistant Park Manager, an RV has just pulled up behind you and I need to meet our new guests. Enjoy your meeting." Cristy waved as the Mini-Cooper drove off.

Chapter 15

Blaine drove down the road in a daze rethinking that unfortunate day eight years ago at the ranger academy. Over and over she tried to remind herself it was just an unfortunate accident. Accidents happen; end of story. It wasn't until she slammed down on her brakes swerving hard to the right narrowly missing a sow and three tiny piglets running across the main road that she realized what to do. Blaine took a deep breath and said to herself that she had to stop feeling guilty. It was an accident and she needed to get on with her life. She had a job to perform and the only way she could be productive was to move on and work with this woman in a positive business-like fashion. Blaine hoped that the assistant director felt the same.

Blaine pushed down on the accelerator and drove to the office.

"Good morning, John, and good morning, Assistant Director Goodie," Blaine announced as she walked into the office. "Good to see you Rosa." Blaine stuck out her hand just as Goodie stood to greet her. Blaine smiled as the two shook hands and thought to herself, *Cristy was right. She is short.*

“It’s good to see you too Blaine. What’s it been, eight years since we last met? The ranger academy if I’m not mistaken,” Goodie remarked and sat back down at the table next to Forrester.

An awkward silence hung over the room as Blaine joined them at the table. “That’s right. Eight years seems like a lifetime,” Blaine answered and turned to Forrester. “John I’m not sure if you know, but Rosa and I were cadets at the academy.”

“That’s right, Blaine and I trained together. I have Blaine to thank for the job I have today. Isn’t that so Blaine?” Rosa smiled at Blaine and continued. “In our self-defense class Blaine broke my arm, not on purpose of course, but during training. As you can see there is quite a difference in physical appearance between the both of us, but that wasn’t the reason my arm broke. Unbeknownst to me and everyone else in the class I had osteoporosis and my bones were brittle and more likely to break. The X-rays showed I had arms of a forty-year-old woman. So I transferred to administration and voila! Here I am. Assistant Director Rosa Parks Goodie. If all goes as planned, next year when Director Donald Florintine retires, I will be promoted and become the first female director for Florida State Parks,” Rosa turned and smiled at Blaine.

“It’s a small world, and here you are together again. That’s some story, but I believe we have a project to complete.” Forrester passed out the folders that were stacked in the center of the table.

“Before we begin I want to announce that the skeleton taken from the park was not Native American,” Blaine stated. “The sheriff left a message and stated that the coroner’s report confirmed that the skeleton was Caucasian. That was the only information he had at the moment, but he plans to meet with the coroner later in the day.”

“That is good news,” agreed Forrester. “I couldn’t

sleep a wink last night. All I could think about was a long, drawn-out legal battle."

"What a relief," Goodie exhaled. "I was not looking forward to conferencing with the National Congress of American Indians about protecting their tribal sovereignty. Now we can concentrate solely on the reputation of the park."

For three hours the trio talked back and forth. The conversation was oftentimes contentious, but always passionately dedicated to implementing a positive campaign for the park. The goal was to provide a platform to substantiate that the park was in no way culpable in the death of the young girl. The first position was that all park information disseminated by newspaper, magazine, radio and television interviews would be coordinated from Goodie's office and then forwarded to Manager Forrester for implementation.

Secondly, free park admission days would immediately be increased and each day would be theme driven. All of the events needed to highlight the natural beauty of the park as well as the environmental stewardship the park provided.

Next, park rangers needed to be more visible. They are the heartbeat of the park. Their presence would help reassure every visitor that the park is a safe place to commune with nature.

Additionally, during the various tours every ranger must emphasize the safety management protocol the park institutes to protect all visitors on a daily basis.

Finally, Goodie summarized the last step that needed to be implemented: The park must continue to voice its concern to protect the adored Florida scrub jays. They needed to stress the environmental steps that the park had taken over the years and will continue to take to protect their endangered habitat. At the end of her comment there was a knock on the door.

"That must be lunch," Forrester interjected. "I'm

starved. Let's take a break."

"Great idea," Blaine added and stood to stretch.

"You don't have to twist my arm," laughed Goodie. "Only kidding Blaine, it's just a joke. Please don't take offense."

"None intended Rosa. As you said, it was an accident."

That was the last of the broken arm innuendos.

Lunch was delicious, relaxing and uneventful. After finishing the last of her chicken salad sandwich, Blaine stood and announced that after sitting for more than three hours, she was going to take a walk to clear her mind and stretch her legs. She invited Rosa and John to join her, but with bemused smiles they declined. To Blaine's relief. It was a welcome reprieve not to listen to Goodie prattle on about her life.

"Blaine, if it's not too much to ask, in your travels would you please check on the canoe dock and see how far along the work has progressed? We need the job completed before the Literary Amongst the Trees event begins Friday," Forrester called out as Blaine walked towards the door.

"No problem. 'Bye."

Chapter 16

Fatigue pillages the body of its mental and physical strength without bias. Nights without sleep inflict punishment of profound proportion on a person's well-being over time. Weariness, lack of motivation and loss of mental clarity are the classic symptoms brought upon by sleep deprivation. Halfway down the main passageway, Dalton Marks began to struggle to traverse the loose sandy floor. His boots sank into the sand, and he had difficulty lifting his legs and walking forward in a straight line. "Professor what's in my backpack? Feels like five pounds of rocks," Dalton called out as he reached for the wall for support.

"No, just the X-ray equipment. If I'm not mistaken, you're carrying the laptop. It's two pounds lighter than Sydney's backpack. She's carrying the X-ray machine."

"What's the problem, Macho Man? Didn't get your eight hours of sleep last night?" Sydney quipped and patted his backpack.

"As a matter of fact, I haven't had any sleep in three days. I was working on a computer problem," Dalton answered. "Could we take a break? I need to catch my breath."

Professor Murphy walked back to Dalton and removed his backpack. "Good idea. Let's rest here before we reach the stalactites and stalagmites. I'll carry your backpack."

"So Dalton, what took three days on the computer?" Sydney quipped. "Porno for three days can really mess up a guy. No wonder you're walking funny."

"Not cool. It wasn't porno, it was a sci-fi video game called Echo. My coalition was under siege and we had to protect our space fleet."

"Wow! I heard about that game from my friend at school, Lincoln Brody you know him. He's in our chemistry class. He said over 500 thousand players from around the world play Echo. It's a huge simulation game. So what happened?"

Dalton sat down, leaned against the wall and for the next few minutes recounted the carnage that unfolded online. Dalton was fast asleep Friday night when he received the call. Star Trek Guy, a member of his online sci-fi video game, SKY Federation, warned that their system was under attack from a rival federation and was on the eve of destruction. The battle erupted after their coalition failed to make a sovereignty payment to protect a region that Dalton's coalition needed as a staging area to dock and repair their spaceships. Either the money wasn't in their account for automatic payment or one of Dalton's members made a costly calculation error. Immediately all SKY members were enlisted in regaining control of system D-S7SD.

Over a period of three days Dalton and dozens of federation members spent countless hours sending virtual starships into the conflict zone. By Saturday more than a hundred of Dalton's Goliath vessels were destroyed. These megaships were the backbone and largest ships in Dalton's federation. And at a cost of three thousand dollars virtual currency each, Saturday was a very costly battle.

However, Sunday afternoon was the turning point for SKY Federation. Titan spaceships from Minmar Star System penetrated the star gates and joined forces alongside the SKY Federation to defeat the Calori Coalition and gain control of D-S7SD system. Dalton surmised, based on data compiled from the online gaming company, that the space battle for D-S7SD was a game loss equivalent of about $500 thousand in real-world cash. It was an unprecedented battle that involved more than three thousand gamers worldwide, and one that left massive destruction throughout the galaxy. SKY Federation alone lost half its fleet of Titan vessels, twenty frigate starships, nineteen destroyers and a dozen battleships.

Although SKY gained control of D-S7SD, their losses were catastrophic. Dalton believed that the damage inflicted upon SKY Federation might take months—or even a year—to rectify. If indeed they possessed the fortitude and capital to rebuild.

"By Sunday night all I could think about was getting a decent night's sleep before work on Monday morning. Unfortunately, I received a phone call at five o'clock in the morning from guess who? Dear old Sydney."

"Me. Oh I'm so sorry, Dalton. I couldn't sleep and I thought if you were up, maybe you'd like to get started on the project early. I didn't know."

Sydney reached over and hugged Dalton. "Here drink this; it will give you a jolt of energy. I drink it all the time when I need an infusion of antioxidants. Plus if you like mango, this drink is a blast."

"Bai5, Malawi Mango, never heard of it, but it looks delicious. Thanks." Dalton cracked open the cap and downed half the drink with one gulp.

"Well, space travelers, I think it's time to return to Earth and leave all this extraterrestrial stuff behind. We have a lot of work to do. Dalton, I have your backpack. Wouldn't want these space rocks weighing you down," joked Murphy as he slung the backpack over his right shoulder.

Fifty paces later the main passageway curved and revealed a larger pathway filled with gigantic columns of stalactites and stalagmites that plunged from the ceiling or rose from the floor creating crowded columns of limestone pillars. Although wide, the tunnel was difficult to traverse what with fallen chunks of stone or pairs of collapsed totems blocking the pathway. At times Murphy and Sydney needed to remove their backpacks to squeeze through a narrow space between the pillars.

In the center of the passageway a clearing of fractured stalactites and stalagmites littered a small section of the floor. The trio needed to climb over or crawl under a half dozen combined columns to reach the end of the clearing. Looking back down the corridor, Murphy was first to notice the unusual appearance of the tunnel. The separation in the giant columns appeared out of place, juxtaposed with the entry columns and the exit columns he remembered from the initial day of the project.

"Sydney, do you have the camera?" Murphy called out and waited at the far edge of the clearing.

"Yes," Sydney replied from under a bridge formed by a fallen stalactite.

"I need to see the pictures you took of this passageway last week. Something doesn't look right. Specifically, this section of the tunnel."

Sydney pulled up the photographs from the first day, seventy in all. She fast-forwarded past the entrance stairs, main passageway to the larger tunnel and the stalagmites and stalagmites. "Oh my God, Professor, you're right. Look!" Sydney handed him the camera.

"Just as I suspected. A section of columns have fallen or broken off from the main group of stalactites and stalagmites and created a clearing of fallen pillars.

Very troubling. Sydney, retake the entire passageway. When we get back to the lab we'll sequence the initial column computer pictures and today's column images into our comparative analysis database and then determine how much of a change occurred."

"Any ideas Professor Murphy?" Dalton asked while Sydney snapped away.

"Yes, but I need to confirm something first before I make a call to Channel 6."

Five minutes later the tunnel ended, and there in front of the three scientists was the main gallery. Dozens of lights illuminated the perimeter, the center pathway and the two-tiered stone stage with the magnificent statue of the gigantic stag. The trio quickened their pace and reached the platform out of breath and eager to begin work.

"I'll set up the computer terminal and all the recording connections while the two of you set up the X-ray machine on the first rung of frame around the statue," Murphy ordered and opened Dalton's backpack and pulled out the laptop.

"It looks like these two rubber clamps on the machine are to be secured around the rung of the metal frame. Professor Murphy said we take four pictures per rung, follow the compass rose with the first setting facing north," said Sydney.

"Found it! North written on the floor at the back of the deer. Sydney, help me clamp on the machine." Together they tightened the four clamps around aluminum frame and stepped back. "We're ready. The X-ray machine is secured, Professor Murphy," Dalton yelled.

"Step back off the platform. At least five feet away. Plus you also need to wear these protective vests." Murphy held up the vests and hit enter after Sydney and Dalton slipped on their vests.

A muffled hum echoed from behind the statue while a blinking white light reflected off the back wall. Three minutes later the humming sound clicked to a stop and the white light disappeared. Murphy typed in a number of codes delineating the level, position, time and date of the images.

"Okay, the first level is documented, three more to go. All the images appear clear and distinct. Here take a look. Notice how the camera even picked up arrowheads under the outside layer of clay. Plus the inside of the statue looks hollow."

"Amazing, I can see two complete arrow points almost on top of one and other," Sydney exclaimed.

"Plus, it appears that small part of the shaft is broken off with the arrowhead. That should help to date the period of time these weapons were used." Dalton pointed to the second arrowhead. "See the section to the right? That looks like a piece of the shaft."

"Professor Murphy, will we be removing all the arrowheads from the statue?" Sydney asked. "I count four in level 1."

"We will need a representative sample from each level to take back to the lab. I'll make that decision when we complete all the imaging. Please move the machine to level 2."

The first level of images were cataloged, filed and indexed in twenty-five minutes. Next the team moved on to level 2 and repeated the procedure. When the X-ray machine completed the last frame of the west section of level 2, Murphy froze in mid compute. With the image magnified, a faint outline of a bottom section of what resembled a door or portal into the statue under the surface of the clay exterior came into view. The width of the door, positioned in the back center of the statue, appeared to be approximately twenty-four inches. The height could not be determined until levels three and four were completed.

"Oh my God, look at this! It's a door into the statue," Murphy called out.

Immediately Dalton and Sydney jumped off the platform and rushed over to the computer terminal. There under about three inches of clay, in the center of the statue, was a grainy image of a door. Flush against the body of the stag, a rectangular outline was cut into the back middle section of the statue.

"It does look like a door, Professor Murphy. But why would anybody cut a door into the statue? Unless there is something inside," Sydney added.

"The statue is hollow. There has to be something inside. Can you scan the entire cavity of the statue?" Dalton blurted out and pushed his nose up against the computer screen.

Two clicks later the computer generated a series of pictures that highlighted the entire inside up to level 2. The floor of the statue was clear of debris or any objects left behind from the early hunters. The walls didn't appear to have any drawings or discernable writings painted or cut into the clay. However, in the southeast corner of the statue, a dark mass of something appeared to be pushing up against the wall.

"There in the corner." Sydney pointed to the back section of statue. "Professor, can you enhance only that section so we can get a closer look."

"No, that's the best this computer can do. Let's finish the next two levels. Maybe the answer is there."

Murphy opened a new file, punched in Level 3 images as Sydney and Dalton clamped on the X-ray machine to Level 3 north coordinates. Ready to climb down the ladder, Sydney reached forward to steady herself when out of the dark a voice called out.

"Don't touch that arrowhead."

Chapter 17

Pieces of yellow crime scene tape stuck out of the recycling bin as Blaine walked through the main entrance to the canoe dock. All law enforcement vehicles were gone. The command tent was taken down and the boxes of medical equipment removed, but the canoe dock was alive with activity. A crew of over twenty men from the Friends of Osprey Park were hard at work removing the old dock and clearing the area for the new canoe dock. The red bulldozer was scooping up piles of broken wood while men tossed loose pieces of debris into a waiting dump truck.

All of the canoes and kayaks were moved down to the ranger station for safe launching and security. In their space was the new aluminum dock, half-assembled and ready to be installed as soon as the old dock was carted away. Blaine walked over to one of the workers leaning against his shovel watching the bulldozer dump a load of rotten pylons into the bed of the dump truck. Watching the sweeping movements of the red machine, the worker didn't notice Blaine approach. He was remembering a July night when he last drove the red bulldozer.

"Hi George, how is the new canoe dock progressing?" Blaine yelled out over the roar of the bulldozer's engine. "Hello! George can you hear me?" Blaine grabbed his jacket.

George Karnedy, a park volunteer for the past twelve years, spun around and nearly lost his balance. A large man, over six feet, broad shouldered with an athletic physique, Karnedy loved working outdoors. As a young man he spent many a day hiking and exploring the back woods of Vermont. Each season brought a new adventure and new discoveries. His favorite time to experience the magnificence of the forest was when it snowed. The silence of the forest was breathtaking. It was as if every living creature stood still and held its breath. Not a movement, a call or a hushed whisper could be detected. Only the noiseless white snowflakes falling down until the entire forest was blanketed in white.

Except for the absence of snow, George was right at home at Osprey State Park. Not only was George a good worker, he was a lot of fun to have around. He was a practical joker, testing the limits of his fellow crusty old curmudgeons with his occasional pranks. The park was the perfect forum for Karnedy's shenanigans. Everyone loved a good joke, and George was willing to deliver to his captive audience. Best of all, his stories gave all the curmudgeons a respite from their oftentimes tedious and exacting manual labor. A win-win situation for funnyman George Karnedy.

Rumor had it, because the park manager revoked his driving privileges due to a fender bender at the pole barn, George Karnedy perpetrated last year's infamous Osprey State Park Fourth of July Flamingo Caper. Not proven and fervently denied George steadfastly proclaimed his innocence.

"I didn't do it. My park driving privileges were taken away. I couldn't even drive a damn Club Car. The last time I drove that red bulldozer was when I backed it into a Club Car," George protested time and time again. "I'll tell you one thing. That was one hell of a prank. I'd like to take the credit, but it wasn't my handiwork."

It appeared that someone or some group, the night of July third, drove the red bulldozer from the pole barn over to the campground entrance where a wooden fence was stacked and ready to be assembled to hide the campground dumpster. The back section of the fence was scooped up and carted down to the lake. There a twenty-foot, plastic flamingo was inflated and tied to the center of the wooden fence. Floated out to the middle of the lake, cement blocks were dropped overboard securely anchoring the flamingo raft. The red bulldozer was left on the beach with a note taped to the steering wheel: *Happy Fourth of July from a Friend.*

On Fourth of July morning total pandemonium broke out. The park police were called. The sheriff's office cordoned off the lake. The news media showed up. Cars lined up for miles to get into the park and look at the giant flamingo raft. Campers crowded the shoreline to take pictures and selfies to post over the social media network. Divers swam out to the flamingo raft, unhooked the anchors and floated the fence back to land. The CSI team took pictures, dismantled the float, fingerprinted the exhibit and bulldozer and boxed up all the evidence. Months of interviews, leads pursued, but no arrests.

When questioned, Karnedy would smile and reply, "The Fourth of July is my favorite holiday."

"Hello Blaine. Didn't hear you sneaking up on me. Good to see you." Regaining his balance and composure, Karnedy opened his jacket and smiled. "What do you think? I had them made up for all the men." A black T-shirt with a big white skeleton in the center and underneath the drawing in bold white letters: CREW. "Get it? Skeleton crew!" Karnedy crowed like a proud rooster.

"Very funny, George, but I don't believe the dead girl's mother would appreciate the humor."

"So you know the identity of the girl? Is she an Indian? Tell me we're not tearing up an ancient burial ground. Please say that isn't happening." The big broad smile Karnedy was known for disappeared.

"No to all three questions George. No, she wasn't Native American; no, you're not desecrating an ancient burial site; and no, we don't know her identity. Not yet. We're waiting on a report from the sheriff's office."

"That's a relief. I read in the paper last year a farmer somewhere in Wyoming discovered a body on his property, a skeleton just like the one we found in South Creek. He called the police and it turned out that the skeleton was an Indian and the land where the body was found was a major burial site for the Cheyenne. The government declared his property an archaeological site of historical proportion, cordoned off half his land and for more than three years archaeologists worked to unearth an entire village. In the end, the government bought his farm and it now is part of the Wyoming Native American Heritage Museum."

"It appears we don't have to concern ourselves with the Bureau of Indian Affairs, but John wants to know when the new canoe dock will be installed. Remember, we have the Literacy Amongst the Trees program Friday and he doesn't want any reminders of the skeleton in the water episode."

"Tell John if all goes as planned we'll have the area cleaned up, the canoes back on boat racks and the new dock installed by the end of the week."

Karnedy stuck out his chest as if he was going to complete the work himself or maybe he just wanted to show off his skeleton shirt. Blaine didn't care, nor did she have the time to reply because Ranger Stephanie drove up in a Club Car.

"Excuse me, Blaine," Ranger Stephanie called out. "Manager Forrester asked me to drive you back to the office. He and Director Goodie want to finish up the meeting. Director Goodie needs to get back to Tallahassee before dark."

"Before she turns into a werewolf I imagine," Blaine laughed. "And Stephanie, it is Assistant Director Goodie, not Director!" Blaine stepped into the Club Car, turned back to George and said, "Instead of *Skeleton Crew*, you should have written *Funny Bones*. It's more befitting and less offensive. 'Bye."

Chapter 18

"Communication Protocol," written on the white board in big bold letters greeted, Blaine as she stepped inside the office. Underneath the title was a list of bullet points with explicit actions to achieve the protocol.

"Hello. Wow! You two have been busy. The entire board is filled with information. Good news, the new canoe dock will be installed on Friday. The area will be cleared of debris and the park will be brought back into pristine condition." Blaine took a seat and opened her folder.

"That's great news Blaine," Forrester replied. "I also have some good news. That is why we completed the Communication Protocol. Lieutenant Johnson called again. They identified the girl. Her name is Daisy Clearing. She was a senior at Venice High School, and her disappearance is an unsolved case from 1963."

"That is reassuring. At least now the family will have some form of closure." Blaine wrote Daisy Clearing, Venice 1963 in her folder. "Any other information?"

"No, that was it. Johnson said that they were turning over the case to the Venice Police Department since it was a cold case of theirs from 1963. He also mentioned that Venice detectives would contact us shortly."

"What was Daisy doing in the park? Was she murdered here? That is if it was a murder." Blaine asked softly.

"That's exactly why the Parks Department has a Communication Protocol. The police will be attempting to solve the case from a legal point of view. We need to defuse the publicity aspect of the crime from a communication point of view," Goodie stated. "Our concern is the public perception that Osprey State Park is a safe, family friendly destination."

"With all due respect, assistant director, a young girl is dead and I believe we have more to prove than our park is a safe place to visit!" Blaine remarked.

"I agree with both of you," Forrester interrupted. "We have a responsibility to exhibit that our park is safe, but because of the discovery of the skeleton on our property I believe we also have a moral obligation to find out what happened to the girl."

"Our role is not law enforcement. That's why we have police, judges and courts. Our position is to operate the park so everyone will enjoy their stay. That's all." Goodie folded her arms and glowered at both Blaine and Forrester.

"You are correct, assistant director, we are not agents of law enforcement. But in order to gain the confidence of the public, we need to assure them that the park was not responsible for the death of that young girl. Families will not visit our park if the spectre of doubt hangs over our head." Blaine looked Rosa in the eye and waited.

"The police have a great many cases to investigate. Just pick up the newspaper and read about the robberies, shootings, hit-and-run cases and the list goes on and on. How much time can they devote to a fifty-four-year-old case?" Forrester interjected. "Not much I surmise, but we have the time and the resources. When we receive all the facts we'll institute our own investigation and discreetly dissect the case. In short, our task has a dual purpose: finding out what happened to the teenager and absolving the park of any wrong doing."

"And how do you propose to do that, Manager Forrester?" said Goodie.

"Assistant Park Manager Sterling will command that responsibility. Blaine is organized, detail-oriented, and most of all, she is discreet. She'll interview family members, if there are any, talk to Daisy's friends and meet with the girl's neighbors—all informally. Her objective will be to ascertain information surrounding that day, determine who had contact with the girl, why she was in the park and the circumstances of Daisy Clearing's demise.

Another motive for assigning Blaine to the investigation is her rapport with one of the detectives in the local police department, a Detective Beale I believe. She is the ideal candidate to conduct all the inquiries." Forrester turned slightly in his chair and gave Blaine a wink. "Nothing like a little inside assistance to grease the beleaguered wheels of justice towards the finish line."

"Okay, you win, but I must be kept informed. I need to get back to Tallahassee. Print out the protocol and make sure the staff is on board with each bullet point." Goodie looked down at her watch, packed up her materials and walked to the door. Before leaving, she spun around and said, "It was nice seeing you Blaine. I hope we can mend fences and be friends again."

"We already have. Have a safe trip back to Tallahassee." Blaine shook her hand and smiled.

After Goodie left, Blaine and Forrester sat down and exhaled for the first time all day. They leaned back in their chairs and breathed in the tranquil silence. A muffled hum from the air conditioner floated into the room, adding to the hypnotic rhythm of the moment. Forrester was first to disturb the silence.

"We should be getting a visit from the Venice Police Department any time now," said Forrester. "As I told Goodie, I want you to handle all the details and report back to me. I will communicate with her and relieve you of the annoying minutia that float down from Mount Tallahassee."

They both laughed. Forrester blasted two bellowing wolf howls that echoed down the office halls and out into yard sending a startled scrub jay perched high in an oak tree into flight. It felt good to laugh and relieve some of the tension after a morning of disturbing circumstances.

"Blaine, are you okay with this? If not I'll understand."

"John, I'll be fine. I want to know just as much as you what happened to that young girl. Also, the reputation of the park is in question. We need to restore the public's confidence and prove that safety is our first priority. I am best qualified for the assignment, John."

"Yes, I know. I just wanted to hear it from you." Forrester stood and walked over to white board. "I'll begin informing the staff. I guess you need to wait for Detective Beale's call."

"No, I can do some research on my own. But first I want to visit the cave and see how the archaeology team is progressing. Professor Murphy mentioned that were about to X-ray the statue and that I should try to stop down." Blaine walked over to the door.

"Perfect timing. I just received Phase 1 of the Cultural Resource Assessment Survey from the State Historic Preservation Office that Professor Murphy needs to complete." Forrester pulled out the forms and handed them to Blaine. "The assessment needs to be completed and on my desk by next Friday. I'll send it off to Tallahassee after I make a copy of the findings for our files and a copy for your new best friend." Forrester smiled and turned back to the white board. "Keep me posted on Murphy's progress. 'Bye."

Chapter 19

The first step is the hardest. Thirty minutes earlier, a pair of sandhill cranes flew over Osprey Lake, trumpeting their arrival. A snowy egret foraging for frogs along the shoreline hastily flew away as the cranes swooped down and landed in their vacated stand of bulrush at the far corner of the lake. At the same time, Blaine pulled up to the cave and parked her Club Car next to Murphy's Jeep. With a backpack filled with sandwiches and drinks left over from her luncheon, she marched over to a stand of palms and disappeared behind a wall of green.

Blaine stopped and stared down at the stone steps carved into the ground that led to the cave entrance. A cold, damp push of air swept up from the cave floor and for a moment her memory was flooded with snapshots of faint lights, tunnels, large columns, a stage and a small room with birds. It was the All Trails Hike, and many of the hikers were in costume for the festive event. She recalled being carried down stone stairs by Thor Boltier dressed as a Viking. Charlie Boltier, Thor's father, was incarcerated and believed that Blaine was the moving force behind his imprisonment and had to be punished. Bits and pieces of that day flooded her memory. Long, dark tunnels, broken columns of stone, a large stage, a small room and blue birds swirled round and round in her mind.

"I escaped and you were killed at my father-in-law's farm. You and your father can never hurt me or my family again," Blaine shouted down the stairs and took the first step.

At the bottom of the stairwell, two massive slabs of stone marked the entrance to the cave. Where two stone columns met, a crack no wider than a small dog traveled up the entire rock face and disappeared into the sandy earth. Turning sideways, Blaine squeezed into the opening. As she inched forward, she felt jagged edges of stone scrape against her chest and tear at her uniform.

When she finally stepped into the main passageway, she looked down at her shirt and noticed that her pocket was torn. "I don't believe this. A new uniform and the pocket is ripped. That's what I get for trying to impress Assistant Director Goodie." Blaine turned towards the entrance and observed pieces of green cloth clinging to the rock opening. "Definitely, the entrance has narrowed since I entered with Forrester and Murphy. Or maybe I'm getting fatter. No, the entrance is smaller, but how?" Blaine marched down the main tunnel, kicking up sand and small pebbles from the dried-up river bed as she pushed forward with renewed determination.

Ten minutes later she entered a maze of stalactite and stalagmite formations. Hundreds of limestone pillars made traversing the passageway difficult, but with only a few bumps and minor scrapes, Blaine finally reached the main gallery, a cavernous space the length of a football field with a cathedral ceiling that disappeared into darkness. Watchfully, she followed the single-lighted path that snaked its way through large chunks of stone that littered the cave floor.

Finally, she reached the ancient platform and Professor Murphy's archeology team. Spotlights illuminated the giant statue Sydney and Dalton were working on and a pair of halogen lamps flooded the rest of the area where Murphy was seated.

"Hello, how about some lunch," Blaine shouted and held up her backpack.

"Great idea. I'm starving," said Dalton and stepped down from his ladder. "Professor Murphy is such a drill sergeant. Do this, don't do that! Can you believe we only had one ten-minute break and that was, let me see, three hours ago? What's in the backpack?"

"Okay, I get the message, let's break for lunch. Hi Blaine, great to see you. I guess I could use a little nourishment myself," Murphy called out. Everyone sat down at the edge of the platform while Blaine handed out sandwiches and drinks.

"My crab salad sandwich is scrumshusly delicious," Sydney playfully added with a giggle.

"What did you say? Scrumshusly delicious! What are you, three years old?" Dalton laughed out loud. "I don't even think scrumshusly is a word."

"Very funny mister know-it-all. It is a word and I used to say it all the time when I was in second grade. So there." Sydney playfully stuck her tongue out at Dalton before taking a sip of her Bai5 mango drink.

"Just because you used it in second grade doesn't mean it was grammatically correct." Dalton took another bite of his sandwich.

"Mrs. Doubtfire said it was a word and she even used it to describe the Thanksgiving feast we had in our classroom. If a teacher used the terminology, then it had to be correct." Sydney looked over and gave Dalton a stare that could freeze an ice cube.

"Mrs. Doubtfire. Like the movie, oh please, who would believe a person with that name? I rest my case. However, I have to admit these sandwiches are scrumshusly delicious," Dalton said sarcastically.

Laughter echoed throughout the cave.

After lunch, Murphy stood and took Blaine's hand and walked her over to the computer table. "I have something to show you. Something we think is amazing. Take a look at the screen." With a few strokes the monitor lit up and an image of the back of the stag appeared.

"Assistant manager, look at the middle section of the statue. The bottom six feet. What do you see?" asked Sydney.

"It appears to be a rectangle. About three inches below the surface. Very precise, all sides appear to be at right angles. It's a door," Blaine gasped.

"Correct! A stone door that appears to slide into the cavity of the statue. See the two indentations cut into the rock on either side of the door? I believe they are hand holds to pull open the door." Murphy pointed to the middle of the screen.

"Wow, that's amazing. All we have to do is pull it open and find out what's inside," said Dalton.

"Won't it be heavy?" Sydney asked.

"I don't think so," Murphy answered. "Look down at the base of the door. There is a slight spacing between the door and the floor of the statue. I believe that the hunters put sand and pebbles on the floor to assist in the sliding of the door. Ancient Egyptians used the same technique to move many of the huge blocks inside the pyramids. As a matter of fact, that's how they sealed the doors to the burial chamber. A hole at the bottom of the doorway released the sand that held up the blocks above the opening. As the sand poured out, the block fell into place sealing the opening. One of many ingenious methods using a natural resource to assist in the construction of their buildings."

"Hey, I saw a television program that said that extraterrestrials helped the Egyptians build the pyramids. Drawings on the walls of the tomb depicted beings with what appeared to be space helmets."

Dalton said. "Maybe they helped build the statue down here."

"Oh please, you can't be serious, aliens from outer space!" Sydney laughed.

"Maybe. How do you explain how they constructed massive structures with only the crudest tools? Plus did you know that the stone blocks on the Great Pyramid of Giza are so closely aligned that only the thickness of a dollar bill separates each five-ton block? I don't even think home builders today could be that precise."

"Enough you two. That's not the argument we should be investigating! We should be investigating how the method of construction of this statue mirrors the construction technique of the pyramids."

Murphy walked over to the computer station and opened up the program: Excavation Osprey Cave Archeology Initial Data Phase Operation 1.

Blaine stood and asked, "Well how old is this cave? I noticed in the main passageway a section of the wall was cordoned off and portions of soil removed. I assume you tested the different stratifications to determine the age of the cave. If I recall, in my sixth grade history class the teacher stated that the pyramids of Egypt were three thousand years old. Is this cave that old? And what about the statue? Is that three thousand years old?"

"Everyone, please take a look at this," Murphy called out.

On the screen was a diagram of what appeared to be a block of dirt. However, Professor Murphy explained that it was a vertical timeline of the stratification of the Earth's surface at Osprey State Park that he removed from the cave and examined. Horizontal rock layers of sediments of varying thicknesses composed of different shades of browns, creams and red were highlighted in the center of the screen. Alongside each layer were names, initials and numbers which reflected the density of the deposit at a specific time period.

"Simply, what the picture represents is a geologic map of a section of the Earth where we are standing right now." Murphy circled the picture with his finger. "You are looking at the rock formations that make up the structural features that delineate the relative age of the cave."

"So how old is the cave?" Dalton asked and pushed his nose up against the screen. "I can't understand any of these letters and number things."

Murphy hit another key and another geologic map appeared alongside the original drawing.

"Understandably, my dear Dalton. Voila! Now you can see we have another stratification chart to compare the physical correlation of all the column lines against each other. So, now what can you deduce from these two geologic maps?" Murphy leaned back in his chair and reveled in his presentation.

"They're identical!" Sydney said, pushing closer to the computer screen to reaffirm her discovery. Everyone took a closer look at the screen. "Where did the second chart come from and how can we now determine how old this cave is?"

"The second topographic map is part of the volume of the United States Geologic Library that is published by the U.S. Geological Survey Department. This map features the Earth's surface some twenty-two thousand years ago." Murphy tapped another key and a geological time scale of the Earth popped up next to the two maps. "Approximately the time of the last Ice Age."

"So the cave and the statue are twenty-two thousand years old?" asked Dalton.

Murphy stood and pointed to the statue. "No. The cave was carved out by rushing water when the sea level rose. The soil samples from the cave's wall along with the corresponding geological map confirm the time period, give or take a century or two. The statue on the other hand was constructed approximately five thousand years ago."

"How do we know that, Ryan?" asked Blaine.

"From the arrow points we removed from the statue. Here look at this." Murphy hit a key, the computer screen cleared, and immediately a frame of nine arrow points appeared. "These are the first arrow points we dug out of the statue. Each point is triangular in shape with a narrow base to attach the shaft of the arrow. They are approximately two inches long and both faces of the point are notched. Scientists experimented flaking pieces of chert and determined that each arrow point took one or two hours to make."

"So these Native Americans were making statues and arrow heads at the same time Egyptians were making pyramids. I rest my case Professor Murphy. There has to be a connection." Proud as a peacock, Dalton paraded around the computer table pointing at everyone and singing, "I'm the man, I'm the man."

"Dalton, there is no credible evidence in any scientific journal to support the concept that beings from outer space assisted in the construction of the Great Pyramid at Giza or any other pyramids around the world. Certainly, nothing to substantiate your claim that little green men assisted in building this cave statue," snapped Murphy as he turned to the computer screen.

"I never mentioned little green men," Dalton answered in an anguished voice and deflated posture. "I'm not some UFO fanatic checking the skies every night with my telescope looking for ET. I was merely reflecting on the point of view I saw on a television program."

"Of course not, Dalton. You're up all night playing Echo, a world famous sci-fi video game, with your Sky Federation buddies and five hundred other gamers. No wonder you're exhausted and talking nonsense," said Sydney as she turned towards Murphy with a satisfying smile. "Professor, I still don't understand how we know the age of the statue."

"Again, colleagues, let's go the video screen." There in the center of the monitor was another chart of arrow points, and at the top of the page written in bold print: **Historic Spanish Point Shell Ridge Midden 300A.D. to 1000 A.D.** Everyone froze and stared at the screen. The prints were identical. Proof that early Native Americans that settled at Spanish Point also used the cave for hunting ceremonies.

Suddenly all the lights on the stage and computer area began to dim. The computer and printer flickered on and off and then went silent. "I was afraid this would happen," Murphy said. "We installed extra spotlights around the statue, increased our computer and printer usage and as a result overloaded the battery system. We need to shut down for the day before we're thrown into total darkness."

No sooner had Murphy stopped talking than the three stage spotlights and the two lights over the computer station went dark, casting the entire area into darkness. Simultaneously, the perimeter lights along the walls and the single strand of lights that lit the pathway dimmed.

"Grab a flashlight and let's get started," Blaine shouted.

Somewhere between the entrance to the stalagmite and stalactite section of the cave and the end, Murphy sensed that the arrangement of the giant columns of limestone were altered in some way, almost as if someone or something had pushed them closer together and in certain areas may have shaken them to the floor. Climbing over or squeezing around the giant obstructions was an arduous undertaking and at times frightening.

At the final hurdle, disaster struck. A broken hulk of limestone blocked the pathway, and the only way forward was to climb over the beast. Murphy and

Dalton had completed their climb and were waiting to assist Sydney to reach the top when all the lights went out. A terrifying scream echoed down the passageway as vacillating beams of light scattered along the walls and up the limestone face. "Help me! I can't hold on," a terrified Sydney yelled and fell forward frantically grabbing at the chunks of stone to break her fall. Miraculously, Dalton caught her and cradled her in his arms before she reached the ground. Murphy rushed over and checked her vital signs. She appeared lucid, no broken bones, but he was worried about her right hand that appeared to be bleeding.

"How is she?" Blaine asked as she rappelled down from the limestone column.

"No broken bones thanks to Dalton's stupendous football catch that broke her fall." Murphy slowly moved his flashlight down to Sydney's right hand. "I'm concerned about her hand. She may need stitches. Take a look."

Blaine bent down and took Sydney's hand that was crunched up in a bloody ball. Slowly she uncurled the fingers and noticed gash marks inside the palm and down her fingers. Blood oozed from two ugly gashes in the center of her palm and seeped down her trembling hand onto her lap.

For an instant, Blaine's thoughts drifted back to the last time she was in the cave. It was in the small alcove, the scrub jay room, behind the main platform away from the statue, that she purposefully cut the palm of her hand with a knife. It was a deep, ugly cut similar to Sydney's, but last time Blaine had broken pieces of scrub jay eggs left behind by ancient hunters which possessed curative powers to stop the bleeding. Blaine's demonstration was to convince Ryan Murphy not to go public with the discovery. It worked. The secret was locked away until such time that the Florida scrub jay was off the endangered species list. But Sydney's wound would need to be attended to by traditional medical procedures. "I have a first aid kit in my backpack. We need to get her hand wrapped immediately."

Bandaged up, and physically exhausted, the beleaguered explorers trudged off in single file into the darkness. With only the light from five pocket flashlights, the trek was arduous and painstakingly slow. Finally, after numerous rest stops and one battery change, light from the stairwell signaled the end of their journey. "Hallelujah!" Dalton rejoiced loudly. "Let there be light. Freedom at last. Come; let us escape this dungeon together."

Outside, the group gathered around their cars that were parked in front of the cave and gasped a collective sigh of relief. The sun began to drop behind a line of oaks and painted the landscape a picturesque shade of red. A cold breeze blew in from the north sending a chill. "It's freezing out here," Dalton said and vigorously rubbed his arms attempting to generate heat.

"Feels twenty degrees colder than inside the cave," Sydney added and reached inside her car for her jacket.

"The weather forecast is warning of a possible frost in Sarasota County tonight and for the rest of the week," Blaine added to the cold conversation. "When I get home tonight, I'm going to cover my outdoor plants. Three years ago, I lost a Christmas palm when the temperature dropped, a very expensive loss that I don't intend make again."

"Sydney, I think I should take you to the hospital and have your hand looked at," Murphy said. "The cuts on the palm of your hand looked like they may need stitches."

"No, that won't be necessary, Professor. The bleeding has stopped and it isn't throbbing like before. Anyway, my mother is a nurse and she will definitely know what to do. I'm cold and want to go home. Like right away." Sydney reached for her car door.

"If you insist, but please call me tonight. I need to know that you are all right," sighed Murphy.

"Me too!" Dalton moaned and walked to his car. "Text me and let me know what your mother says. My money is on Professor Murphy. I say you'll need stitches. 'Bye all."

"I'll call everyone when I get home. 'Bye."

The two cars drove out of the parking lot and down the road into the night.

"Cold?" Murphy asked and wrapped his jacket around Blaine along with a tight squeeze. "Better?"

"Much better. Don't worry, Sydney will be fine. Her wound wasn't as deep as mine and I survived.

Remember. Look, no scar," Blaine opened her hand.

"I remember, but she didn't have the scrub jay eggs. Even if we had the eggs today, I wouldn't have used them. It would be impossible to explain their powers and still retain their secrets. It did run through my mind."

"Mine too," Blaine admitted.

"So are we still on for Saturday night? I started cleaning the house, even threw out all of my old Playboy magazines in the bathroom. Tonight I tackle the kitchen—that is if I get the official signal from the referee."

"Touch down for the home team," Blaine answered. "That reminds me, I have to pick up confectioners' sugar at the super market on the way home. Brooke needs to bring a treat to the sleepover Saturday night. We're making melt-in-your-mouth homemade brownies, my specialty. The kids love them."

"I could use a little treat on Saturday." Ryan groaned jokingly. "Big kids like treats too. I wonder what Martha Stewart would advise."

Blaine snuggled closer and whispered, "I can't speak for Martha, but I have your treat. It's a little red Victoria's Secret. I hope you can keep a secret."

"Oh, I can keep a secret. My lips are sealed with a kiss." Ryan leaned in and they kissed. "Trust me all I'll be doing is dreaming in red."

They hugged one last time and then Blaine said, "There's one other thing, Ryan. Forrester wants you to complete the Cultural Resource Assessment Survey and have it on his desk by Friday." Blaine reached into her backpack and handed him the survey. "Forrester will send it on to the State Historic Preservation Office Monday. Have fun." Blaine jumped into the Club Car and drove back to the office to pick up her car.

"So much for cleaning the kitchen. I guess I'll be sharpening my pencils and starting on this report. See you Saturday," Ryan shouted as Blaine drove down the road.

Chapter 20

Lou Bravo woke hungry. At five-five, one hundred ninety-five pounds and a body that resembled a short, stocky professional wrestler, Lou Bravo never missed a meal. Breakfast, lunch or dinner—he was ready to eat. However, today's hunger pangs although victual in nature had an additional degree of urgency. This morning, breakfast at Patches Restaurant with Tony Lilly and Hubba Bubba would address another dimension of hunger: the consequences of one's misdeeds and the urgency to right an injustice. Over a delicious stack of blueberry pancakes, home fries and a side of extra crispy bacon, Operation Sandhill Crane would commence. This deliciously devious caper would teach Mr. Morty King a lesson in old-time Florida justice.

After a quick shower, a head shave and a cup of espresso, Lou Bravo was out the door cruising down Tamiami Trail towards Venice. A few minutes later he passed Jokers Wild Pawn Shop, turned west on to Venice Avenue and immediately slammed on the brakes.

Narrowly missing the rear bumper of a fancy little

sports car, the El Camino jerked to a halt inches from an accident. The sudden stop shoved him up against the steering wheel where his seat belt halted further discomfort. “What the hell is going on,” Lou Bravo shouted and stuck his head out the window. Venice Avenue was a gigantic parking lot. Cars were stopped the entire length of the road up to the Venice Avenue Bridge. A police officer directed traffic in front of a patrol car parked in the center of the road across from Patches. “Give me a break. Why can’t the problem be after the restaurant?” Lou Bravo shouted at an invisible lawbreaker somewhere down the road.

Gradually, a few cars inched forward and the cause of the traffic jam came into view. Two vehicles exiting and entering Patches’ front parking lot had collided, blocking the lot and a section of the highway. “Big cars and small driveways spell disaster if you’re not paying attention,” Lou Bravo mumbled. “Especially a Cadillac and a black GMC. Somebody wasn’t watching out their back window.”

One block past the restaurant, Lou Bravo turned right and pulled into the back parking lot of Patches. Only one vehicle, a white box truck with red lettering, “Clean Sweep” painted on its side, was parked on the small patch of asphalt. Lou Bravo turned off the ignition and walked inside.

“Good morning Jackie, how’s business?” Lou Bravo asked and walked over to the owner who was standing by the door looking out at the excitement.

“I’m dying in here. Look around. Only four customers in the entire restaurant, one couple and your two buddies sitting in the corner booth. I have a business to operate and expenses that must be met: payroll, electric, water, taxes and rent. All have to be paid, but they can’t be paid when I only have four customers. I can’t have the police blocking the entrance to the restaurant all day. I’ll go broke.” Jackie pushed open the door, looked out at the empty parking lot and shook her head.

"Jackie, you worry too much. I'll bet they'll finish up before lunch and a big crowd of hungry patrons will mob the place. You'll run out of food, your cash register will ring non-stop and you'll be in the money once again. How does that sound?" Lou Bravo joked attempting to cheer her up.

"I'll believe it when I see it. A cop came in twenty minutes ago and said we now have a level 2 crime scene. The only scene more sensitive was a level 1: a murder. Now we have a whopping big crime scene." She motioned for him to look out the door.

"What are you talking about? It looks like a simple fender bender. No big deal. Two cars collided in the parking lot, the drivers will exchange licenses, insurance cards and that's it. What's the business about a level 2 crime scene? I don't buy it."

"Look for yourself!" Jackie insisted.

Outside, hidden from the roadway, a blizzard of activity transpired behind the black GMC truck. Two officers were handcuffing the driver, a tall, muscular man in his early twenties with long curly blond hair. A police K-9 handler moved his German shepherd into the back seat of the truck and then over to the front while shouting commands to the dog. Two officers were removing the side panels from both front doors while another officer in the rear was cutting open the back seat. The two front seats, along with closed boxes, cartons, open bags and backpacks, were lined up on the ground next to the black GMC.

"Maybe this isn't your run-of-the-mill parking lot accident," uttered Lou Bravo. "What the hell is going on?"

"It's the Red Bull Bandit. The cops have been looking for him for over a month," Jackie whispered. "This is the guy who's been going to Publix and walking out with a shopping cart full of Red Bull drinks. He robbed five stores in Sarasota County. It's in all the papers. Publix offered a $5 thousand reward for the capture of the robber."

"How do you know he's the Red Bull Bandit?" Lou Bravo asked.

"The cops told me when they informed me of this level 2 nonsense. Plus, look at that second backpack, the torn one. What do you see?"

"Cans of Red Bull," uttered Lou Bravo.

"Honey, that's right on the money. Something I won't get if you don't join your friends. Enjoy your breakfast." Jackie smiled and returned to her usual spot behind the cash register.

Lou Bravo snaked his way around tables to the back of the room. Before reaching his breakfast destination, Victoria, the head waitress, informed him that Tony had ordered for him: blueberry pancakes, home fries and bacon. Extra crispy, the way he liked it. He thanked her and continued to his table.

"Good morning boys, looks like breakfast has been served. Thanks for putting in my order." Lou Bravo sat down. "Looks like we have a little excitement along with our pancakes."

Tony and Hubba Bubba both had a mouthful of blueberry pancakes when Lou Bravo sidled up into the booth. After a big bite of pancake and a sip of coffee, Tony informed him that, "The Red Bull Bandit" was sitting right across from us. I could have reached out and touched him. Unfortunately, we had no idea who the guy was. Just some curly-haired bloke having breakfast."

"Yeah, what a goddamn loss," Hubba Bubba moaned. "Five thousand bucks right in front of our eyes and we didn't see it."

"Anyway, next to the window, across from the guy was an old man, maybe in his seventies, wearing a red Tampa Bay Buccaneers baseball cap. A few minutes after Red Bull sits down, Buccaneer man gets up and leaves. Doesn't finish his meal, pays his bill and walks out the front door." Tony takes a forkful of pancakes and before he can continue Hubba Bubba jumps in.

"Victoria brings our food and we're about to take our first bite when Red Bull gets up and leaves. Two minutes later we hear a crash in the parking lot and screaming. We drop our forks and run over to the door to see that Buccaneer guy smashed his brand new silver Cadillac into a black GMC truck. The old man is on his cell phone and the Red Bull Bandit is pounding on the Cadillac's window when out of nowhere two police cars pull into the parking lot. With guns drawn they rush Red Bull and handcuff him."

Lou Bravo finished a slice of bacon and asked, "So the old guy called the police? How did he know the man was the Red Bull Bandit?"

"The scorpion tattoo on the guy's neck. He saw it when the fellow sat down. That's why he left without finishing his breakfast, to call the police." Tony moaned and took a forkful of home fries.

"So that old fart gets the five grand reward for capturing the Red Bull Bandit and we get nothing!" Hubba Bubba spat out.

"That's not true boys. We didn't have to wait thirty minutes for a table. Now that all the snowbirds are gone, not waiting for a table is worth five grand in my book. What do you think?" Lou Bravo smiled and took the last bite of bacon. The trio nodded their heads in agreement and laughed.

Halfway through breakfast Lou Bravo looked over and stared at Tony and Hubba Bubba. Didn't say a word, just looked.

"What's wrong?" asked Tony. "What are you staring at? Did I spill something on my shirt? You're freaking me out with that hypnotic gaze."

"That's it! I couldn't place it at first, but now I know. What happened to the tomato shirts?" Lou Bravo bellowed. "The free shirts the two of you wore last time we met."

"For your information, they were burgundy, not tomato red. One or two clients made a comment so I made a management decision to remain with the khaki. Keep the traditional look. Some people are threatened by change, so here we are back with our traditional khaki uniforms. Happy?"

"A couple!" Hubba Bubba blurted out. "All of the clients hated the shirts. They may not have come out and said so, but I saw the looks. The final embarrassment was when we went into McDonald's for lunch and almost everyone called us, 'Tomato Boys.' It was so bad we had to eat in the truck."

"Tony, I don't want to tell you I told you so, but now that you're back in business I believe we have some unfinished business to take care of ourselves," Lou Bravo declared.

Over two more cups of coffee that Victoria cheerfully poured, the trio mapped out the course of action for Operation Sandhill Crane. Hubba Bubba mentioned that he visited the Sarasota Fair twice, had a fantastic time and even won a stuffed gorilla. The final night of the fair he spoke with Fast Eddie, the carnival operator who two years before had his game of chance, Pitch for Bottles, next to King Amusement. One night a group of men from the Florida Amusement Association showed up at King's Six Cats game of chance. They dragged Morty from behind the counter, placed his hand up against the arcade post and smashed it with a hammer. The men dismantled his arcade and carted it off the premises along with King. Rumor had it King's game was rigged and he was subsequently banned from working all Florida State and County Fairs.

"I knew the guy's hand was messed up. Wow, payback is a bitch. Couldn't have happened to a nicer man. That sounds like a business scheme King would devise. Typical King modus operandi. Cheat the customer any way you can."

Lou Bravo looked over at Hubba Bubba and smiled.

"Looks like you came up empty at the fair, but I'm glad you had a good time. What about you, Tony?"

Tony outlined the events on the days he followed King from his home to work and back home at the end of the day. King spent the majority of the day at the office. He only left some days to pick up lunch at various fast food restaurants and then returned to the office. No specific pattern. Tony thought the trips corresponded to the times he forgot to pack a lunch from home. However, the payoff happened on Friday. On Friday, King went to the Get Physical Gym at the Kmart Plaza on Tamiami Trail. Every Friday at 9:30 in the morning he worked out, or as Tony put it, *'He went to the gym.'* Like Pavlov's dogs, he parked the BMW in the handicapped parking spot in front of the gym, convertible top down, and walked in. An hour later he walked out, got in his car and drove to work. Every Friday, Tony was told by the manager.

"What a prick! He rigs his carnival games so no one can win, kills a sandhill crane and parks in handicapped parking spaces. This guy needs his ass kicked," Hubba Bubba spat out.

"My sentiments exactly," Lou Bravo replied. "And we will be the ones to deliver the ass kicking. Tony, are you positive King goes to the gym every Friday?"

"Positive! My company has the cleaning contract with Get Physical, so last Friday I went in and spoke to the manager. A cute little thing, Ryder Gale is a physical fitness fanatic and triathlon champion. She won the California Triathlon last year and is currently training for a spot on the summer Olympics in Brazil. Good chance to make the team unless the Zika Virus sidelines her and the team. She said King shows up every Friday. Doesn't do much of a workout, unless you call checking out all the females in the place a workout."

"Perfect. This Friday will be Morty King's day of retribution," Lou Bravo announced. "Operation

Sandhill Crane is now positioned in phase 2: the punishment mode."

Lou Bravo took a piece of paper from his pocket and unfolded it on the table. On the top in large letters spelled out: Purple Brush Farm. He pointed out that an old friend of his late wife, a co-ed she went to college with, Vardi Zammiello, a.k.a. the Purple Lady, owned a small farm out in the woods of northeast Venice that would play a critical part with Operation Sandhill Crane. Ms. Vardi's farm wasn't what you would call a traditional working farm that centered on animal husbandry. As a matter of fact the farm didn't grow, harvest or raise one thing. Rather Purple Brush Farm was an art camp for local plein air artists. Every spring for two weeks she would host a painting seminar and exhibition at the farm. One hundred artists, young and old, novice to professional, from all over the state would converge on Purple Brush Farm and immerse themselves in the art of Plein Air.

However, Lou Bravo was not interested in the artistic import of Purple Brush Farm. Rather he was interested in the domestic assets of the farm. Specifically, Lucy and Ethel, the two mares stabled in the Purple Lady's old barn. Left by the original owner, Ms. Vardi occasionally rode around the farm to locate a favorable spot to paint. Lou Bravo was not interested in the equestrian attributes the two horses commanded. However, he was interested in the waste matter they discharged.

"Gentlemen, once a month to supplement her income, Ms. Vardi trucks over to a small local nursery off River Road, a dump truck load of horse manure which the nursery adds to their compost and then markets as natural fertilizer." Lou Bravo stopped speaking and drew a picture of the dump truck piled high with manure hovering over a small convertible BMW. "Friday is delivery day. For three hundred bucks, the manure and dump truck is ours."

"That is a fucking amazing plan," Hubba Bubba shouted and slammed his hand on the table.

"Hey, watch your language," snapped Lou Bravo.

"Sorry, I can't wait to shovel out all that manure into his convertible."

"It's a dump truck, Hubba Bubba. The truck dumps out the manure, not you," Tony added sarcastically.

"Oh, right, dump truck. I knew that, but won't the people at the gym see the truck dumping all that crap over King's car?" Hubba Bubba took the last bite of his pancake and a gulp of coffee.

Tony took out a pen from his shirt pocket and on the Purple Brush Farm Plan drew five windows. "There are shades on all the front windows for privacy." Tony took his pen and colored in the first and fifth shade, top to bottom. "The first and fifth shades are completely down covering both windows. The second, third and fourth window remain half covered. I expect for light."

"What if we use your ice cream truck to block the three middle windows? Hubba Bubba can pull up to the front of the building at the same time we are filling up Morty's car with a dose of his own medicine." Lou Bravo raised his coffee cup and the three toasted their plan.

Chapter 21

Lego Man was standing in front of Detective Justin Beale's desk when the call came in from the sheriff's office. The eight-foot yellow, green and red fiberglass statue did not speak. However, the painted-on smile on his face spoke volumes. The one-hundred- pound celebrity had been found splashing around in the surf early that morning at the Venice Beach entertaining a crowd of beachgoers taking pictures. That commotion had drawn the police.

Beale and Hordowski were first on the scene along with a team of CSI technicians who were summarily dismissed since no crime was committed, other than creating a public nuisance. That technicality was solved when the team hauled Lego Man off the beach and back to the station.

Beale and Hordowski interviewed the two lifeguards on duty, a dozen bathers hunting for sharks' teeth, an old prospector with a metal detector and the concessionaire at the beach pavilion. No one saw a thing and didn't know how the statue got there.

Hordowski, called Legoland to see if the statue was some type of publicity stunt. Director of Public Affairs

Ms. Laura Parris got a big laugh out of the prank, but she denied any involvement. She reiterated to Hordowski that Legoland was in the business of entertaining families, not creating pranks. In addition she pointed out that the picture he emailed the company was not fashioned with Lego blocks. Rather the entire statue appeared to be a form casting. Most likely the material that was waterproof, plastic or fiberglass, Ms. Parris claimed.

"Legoland had nothing to do with the statue," Hordowski called over to Beale and hung up the phone. "Take a look at this. On the back, burnt into the statue along the waist line!"

"I see small block letters: property of Southport High School," Beale said tersely. "Those little bastards. A school prank and it's not Halloween. We'll see who gets the last laugh."

"Should we return the statue to the school?" Hordowski asked as he rubbed his finger over the lettering. "Wait a minute, there are numbers after the school name. Ten numbers, could be a phone number, should I call?"

"The last thing we're going to do is return it. Someone will have to come to the police station, explain why and who placed the statue at a public beach and then they may have their property returned. Go ahead and call the number."

"Southport High School, good morning how may I help you?"

Hordowski introduced himself, explained that they had a statue of a Lego Man, wanted to know if it was the property of the school and why it was placed at the Venice Beach. There was a moment of silence and then the secretary on the other end replied, "One moment please, I'll transfer you to the principal, Dr. Teng." Again the phone went silent.

"Hello, Detective Hordowski, this is Cecila Teng, principal of Southport High School. My secretary informed me that the police department has Ego. I have Stanley Rappaport, chairman of the Southport High Booster Club on speaker phone with me. Please tell me how you came into possession of our Lego Man?"

"We received a call from the beach that a Lego man was in the water. No one knew how it got there or who it belonged to. Back at the office we noticed your school name and number etched onto it. Now tell me why your school placed an eight-foot statue on public property." Hordowski waited.

"Detective Hordowski, the school did not place Ego at the beach," Rappaport replied. "As a school fund-raiser the Booster Club places plastic flamingos and new this year Ego, a fiberglass Lego Man on people's lawns. For a donation, club members will place thirty pink flamingos or Ego on an individual's lawn at eleven o'clock in the evening. We remove the fun prank after school the following day." The sound of shuffled papers vibrated in the background and then Rappaport came back on the line.

"Here it is: 'Dennis Miller of Englewood, Ego placed on front lawn of brother Randy Miller at 154 Heron Creek Lane, Venice. Place a hand-painted sign in large letters: CONGRATULATIONS—Big Winner'."

"So how did Ego get to the beach?" snapped Hordowski.

"You'll have to ask Mr. Miller," Dr. Teng interjected. "More importantly, when will we be able to retrieve our property? Is it possible for Mr. Rappaport to drive over to the police station this afternoon and pick up Ego? We have a client that wants the statue this evening."

"Dr. Teng, this is Detective Beale, I've been listening to the conversation, and yes, Mr. Rappaport can come to the office and pick up the statue. But first we need to speak with Randy Miller and get his version of the Ego mystery."

Mr. Rappaport gave Hordowski Randy Miller's phone

number and home address. Beale stated they would get back to them after they spoke with Mr. Miller.

Beale punched in the number and waited as the answering machine picked up the call and went through the general spiel about not home, leave your name and number and we'll get back to you bla bla bla...

Beale was half-way through his message when a voice broke in, "Hello, this is Randy Miller."

"Mr. Miller this is Detective Beale from the Venice Police Department. I just finished speaking with Southport High School and they informed me that they placed a statue of a Lego man on your lawn. Is that correct?" Beale placed the call on speakerphone.

"That's correct. I think my brother Dennis orchestrated the prank. Yes, I believe he did."

"So could you please tell me how the statue traveled from your front lawn to the Venice Beach and now is standing in my office?" Beale snapped.

"Can you keep a secret, detective?" Miller blurted out.

"Don't play games with me Mr. Miller. Right now you are only being charged with misdemeanor nuisance. Continue on this path and the charges can increase exponentially," growled Beale.

"Oh, no detective, I don't intend to be disrespectful. The truth is my wife and I are the last ticket holder in a $1.6 billion Powerball jackpot. We haven't claimed our prize because we haven't decided how to organize the money. We are still meeting with our accountant, and a financial advisor is reviewing different proposals. I told my brother that we won the Powerball, and I guess he thought it would be a nice idea to announce to the world that we had the third winning ticket."

"That still doesn't account for the statue ending up at the beach, Mr. Miller."

"I didn't want anyone to know yet. We've heard horror stories about people calling or camping out at

Lottery winners' homes and asking for money, so my son and I put the statue in my truck and drove it down to the beach around midnight."

"Congratulations on your windfall, Mr. Miller. However you will need to come down to the station and reimburse the City of Venice for creating a public nuisance, a hundred dollar fine."

The phone on Beale's desk rang. "I have an incoming call. You need to come to the station before three o'clock to pay the fine and yes, I can keep a secret. Be at the station before three or your secret goes viral! Goodbye sir."

Beale walked back to his desk and picked up the receiver, "Detective Beale."

Chapter 22

A cold case is never closed. It waits to be re-opened. The fax machine behind Beale's desk spat paper while the detective listened intently to the caller.

"Detective Beale, this is Lieutenant Jeff Johnson from the Sarasota Sheriff's Office. I am faxing over to your office all the information we have on a missing person cold case that took place in Venice in 1963."

"1963? Why are you sending it now?" Beale questioned.

"Because the missing person is no longer missing. The dead body of Daisy Clearing, a senior from Venice High School, reported missing in August 1963, has been found in Osprey State Park. Maybe I should say her skeleton has been recovered. I am faxing over to your department the medical examiner's report and the sheriff's office report. Since the original case was in your jurisdiction, we are turning the case back over to you."

"Thanks for the warning, Lieutenant."

"If I can be of further assistance give me a call. Good luck, Detective."

Beale reached over and picked up the reports from

the fax machine. With a quick scan of the first couple of pages from the Office of the Medical Examiner, Beale gleaned a smattering of particulars and a multitude of unknowns: Name: Daisy Jane Clearing; date of birth October 3, 1945; approximate age 16- 19, race Caucasian; gender female; cause of death unknown; laceration occipital bone; time of death 50-54 years ago; diagnosis death from unknown causes.

"Hordowski, after you finish the paperwork on Lego Man, go over to records and sign out a cold case file for

Daisy Clearing, August 1963."

"1963, what's that all about?" Hordowski called over from his desk as he typed the final sentence on the Lego man case and sent it to the commander's office.

"That's exactly what I told Lieutenant Johnson from the Sarasota Sheriff's Office. They found Clearing's body, or more precisely her skeleton."

"Why doesn't the sheriff's office handle the case, why us?"

"That's why you are going to records," laughed Beale. "Don't forget a flashlight. It can get a little scary along the dark rows of files."

"Very funny. I'll be back before you know it," quipped Hordowski and walked down the hall flashlight in hand.

Beale went back to the package of information and reviewed the written reports of the investigators, postmortem examination, photographs at the scene, lab photographs, skeletal DNA findings, forensic pathologist report, geochemist dental sampling and the forensic anthropologist reconstruction information. Johnson's report along with the coroner's findings were placed into the national Missing and Unidentified Persons System and a match was identified: Daisy J. Clearing a 5'3" seventeen-year-old female with blond hair, blue eyes and weighing 112 pounds. Unique feature: index finger disfigured. Reported missing on September 1, 1963. Anyone with information please contact the Venice Police Department.

"Found it! Not much inside, police report, picture of the missing girl, a poster, detective's report and a lot of dust." Hordowski called from the other side of the room.

"Here take a look at Johnson's report and the medical examiner's findings. I want to look at the cold case file." Beale opened the crusty old manila folder and thumbed through the pages; all four of them. "This is interesting, a report from the Washington, D.C. police department, a Lieutenant Gary Ley. He stated that they checked all the hospitals, jails and no one named Daisy Clearing was located. Ley contacted the March on Washington organization, but they could not provide any information on the whereabouts of Daisy Clearing."

"Yes, I read that too. It appeared she joined the March on Washington to be a part of the protest and to hear Dr. Martin Luther King Jr. speak. The march was on August 28, 1963."

"That's why her parents didn't report her missing until September 1, 1963." Beale took out his notepad and wrote, "March on Washington, August 28, 1963, and drew a picture of an obelisk." "How did she get there? Did she drive? Take a bus or train? Did another person or group take her to Washington? The lead detective, Purdy Jones, didn't say much in his report. I wonder if he's available. I'd really like to talk with him."

"On the last page, the interview with the mother, Jones indicated that Daisy took the train," Hordowski called out. "Jones is dead. There's a notation in the margin that he had a stroke in 1964. That's probably why the report is minimal. This is interesting. The coroner reported that a ten-centimeter laceration along the occipital bone was found. He left open to speculation that a blow to the back of the head could have been the cause of death."

“The real question, Hordowski, is how did Daisy Clearing end up at Osprey State Park? She was supposed to be a thousand miles away in Washington, D.C.”

Beale looked down at the 8”x10” color photograph of the teenage girl in a blue, one-piece bathing suit standing next to a palm tree. The Venice Beach Pavilion was in the background along with a parade of happy beachgoers heading for the water. However, Beale’s eyes weren’t on the beach scene. They were fixated on the young girl’s big, wide smile while his brain churned on the terrible tragedy. He could only imagine the suffering her family endured for years, and now this discovery. How will they be able to endure more sorrow, more questions?

Beale took a long slow breath and contemplated his approach. “Hordowski, check the computer for an address and phone number for Clearing. The original address on file was 145 Sunflower Lane, Venice, and the 1963 phone number listed was 284-2324. I doubt they would still have the same number, but who knows? Maybe we’ll get lucky. We need to talk to the family.”

Fifteen minutes later Hordowski returned. “Got it, same name, same address, but a new number: 941 484-2011. I spoke to Emma Clearing, the younger sister, and made an appointment for this afternoon to meet with her.”

Chapter 23

Five kerosene lanterns circled the back of the ancient statue. A yellow glow from their glass globes pushed beams of light upward in circular reflections illuminating a shadowy shine on the back section of the stag. The front of the large beast and the rest of the cave stood in darkness. Lost in a wall of black, the vastness of the main gallery loomed ominously. Only when the sound of hammers pounding against the huge statue disappeared into the faraway recesses of the cave was one reminded of its immense size.

The chalk outline of the stone door was half exposed. For three hours Professor Murphy and Dalton tirelessly chiseled away at both sides of the door, Dalton on the left and Murphy on the right. Their carbide chisels biting at the calcified clay eventually revealed the two vertical outlines where the clay ended and stone door began. Shards of broken pieces of clay lay scattered about the platform floor in a testimony of their labor and ancient safekeeping techniques.

"I need to rest, professor," Dalton shouted over the pounding of Murphy's hammer. "My hand is numb from all the pounding. I can't even grip the chisel safely. I need to stop."

Dalton put down his chisel and hammer and sat down at the back of the platform. He removed his gloves and reached into his backpack. "I'm starving. How about a lunch break?"

"Good idea, I could use a break myself," Murphy answered. "By the way, Sydney called me last night. You were right, she needed stitches, five. I feel so sorry for her."

"Yeah, she called me too and the doctor said she couldn't come back to the cave until after the stitches were removed in two weeks." Dalton laughed. "She's right-handed and it's impossible for her to write with her handed wrapped up like a baseball glove. She's freaking out."

"Since when does anyone your age write anything? She's probably texting all her friends and telling them how she happened to get five stitches. Undoubtedly, embellishing on all the minute details." Murphy took a bite of his sandwich. "I'll call her next week and ask her to come in and work at the lab. She could collate the arrow points we collected or maybe she can visit the Spanish Point Museum and systematize our arrow points with their collection."

"Great idea. I think she would love the field trip to Spanish Point," Dalton took the last bite of his peanut butter and jelly sandwich and began to rub his hands together. "Does it seem a little colder down here than it was yesterday?" Dalton pulled a sweatshirt from his backpack and put it on.

"It is. I checked the temperature and it is down two degrees. I've been watching the weather all week, and there may be a problem, but I need to do a few more calculations."

"Problem? What calculations are you talking about professor," Dalton uttered hesitantly.

"Nothing to concern yourself about. I need to call a friend of mine at Nokomis Groves."

“Are you ordering oranges? I just sent a tray of Honeybell oranges to my parents in Peoria. They’re probably squeezing an orange or two as we speak. Nothing like fresh, squeezed orange juice in the wintertime, especially if there’s a foot of snow on the ground. Can’t go wrong with Honeybells from Nokomis Groves. Plus, they’re offering a special this month, buy one get a half tray free. As a matter of fact, here we go a Honeybell orange! Easy peeling, amazing taste and no seeds. Here have a piece.”

“You sound like a commercial from Nokomis Groves. You’re right; this orange is delicious, thanks. That’s a marvelous idea, but no I’m not ordering oranges. I need some water consumption calculations. Let’s get back to work.” Murphy picked up his tools and walked over to the statue.

Dalton stood, zipped up his sweatshirt and walked over to the statue. All that remained to free the stone door was the thin white chalk line across the top of the door that marked the last remaining area of clay. “I’ll take the left side and we’ll celebrate in the middle.”

Dalton planted his chisel in the top left hand corner of the door and began to pound away at the clay. With each blow pieces of clay shattered and fell to the floor.

Thirty minutes later, Dalton struck his chisel for the last time. Exhausted, he dropped the hammer and chisel and looked down at the pile of broken clay on the platform. “Professor, do you think any of the masons that built massive monuments thousands of years ago were left-handed? Wouldn’t they keep bumping into a right-handed worker?”

“You mean like we’re doing now.” Murphy pushed up against Dalton and took his final swing. “Throughout history using your left hand was discouraged. People were demonized for being left-handed, even put to death. Oftentimes young children were forced to perform activities with their right hand to keep the evil spirits at bay. I would imagine there had to be left-handed laborers, but my guess is they worked with their right hand. Especially when the foreman was standing over them with a whip."

Murphy reached over and slowly brushed away the last remaining chips of clay that outlined the ancient door. Halfway down the side of the stone he stopped brushing and grasped the recessed handle with both hands and pulled. The stone inched forward. Only a fraction of an inch, but it moved. "Dalton, it moved. The door slid forward. Grab your side of the door and on three let's pull. Ready one, two, three pull."

Grunting and groaning the pair yanked and pulled at the door, and to their astonishment the stone moved forward crunching and grinding against the sandy floor until the opening was revealed. In what felt like an eternity, Murphy and Dalton collapsed exhausted on the floor and stared into the cavity of the beast.

"Look at the door, professor, it's a half-block stone. Five thousand years ago, those Native Americans weren't stupid. They didn't want to break their asses every time they had to open the door, so what did they do? They halved the stone edifice. Strong enough to safeguard the inside, but light enough to move with ease. Any way you look at it, it certainly worked to our advantage." Dalton knelt down to catch his breath and took a closer look at the stone block.

Murphy picked up a lantern and shined it along the floor of the doorway. "Look at this, Dalton, grains of sand covering the entire floor of the entrance. That's how they moved the stone in and out of the entryway. A five-hundred-pound block of stone moved effortlessly by maybe two or four men. Genius for such an ancient culture. I wonder what other surprises are hidden before us?" Murphy smiled.

Murphy squeezed behind the block of stone, ducked under the doorway and stepped inside the cavity of the statue. Dalton picked up a lantern and followed. The light from the lanterns danced around the room as the pair circled the cavity of the statue. The room was circular, huge, at least twenty feet in diameter, maybe more. Red-painted tree trunks, twelve in all, were affixed to the wall at equally spaced distances around the entire chamber. Murphy held up his lantern and traced their assent.

"Look the tree trunks reach the top of the room, bend over and meet in the center forming a red roof. More than likely the beams were used to support the massive weight of the clay."

"Why paint them red?" Dalton walked across the room and stood in front of one of the poles. "This pole is super smooth, and there are designs up and down the face of the wood. They're a little scary. The red color appears to jump out at you."

"Red symbolized war for a number of ancient cultures. Fighting, blood, courage all attributes of a battle. It may have been these hunters felt that they were at war with this beast. I'm guessing the twelve poles represented the twelve clans that used the cave and the poles may have recorded part of a ceremony or the hunt itself. What part I don't exactly know, but definitely something we will investigate back at the lab. Speaking of hunt, follow me."

On the west side of the room standing in a perfect semi-circle against the wall were twelve large hunting spears. Approximately eight feet in height, with a spear point the size of a human hand their smooth wooden shafts were held in place by circular holes drilled into the wooden floor constructed from tree trunks, shaved flat and joined together with clay. However, the section of floor under the spears was unique: It was painted yellow. A bright yellow, clean and void of any scuff marks or footprints. At first glance the floor looked newly painted, but Murphy's research discounted that theory. The statue was at least five thousand years old, so logic suggested the inside and its contents had to be the same age.

"Notice the floor under the spears. A painted yellow circle while the rest of the room was left unpainted. Yellow was a powerful color for ancient civilizations. It symbolized the Sun God—the creator of all living things. Most likely this cave was the location where a spiritual ritual was performed before each hunt. The spears were not only weapons of the hunt, they were symbols of the hunt. I would guess the elder of each clan brought his spear to the hunt. Take one out of its stand. Let's take a closer look at the designs spiraling down the shaft."

No sooner had Dalton pulled a spear from its stanchion than the floor started to shake. Not an earthquake-like movement, prolonged and violent, but more like a gentle vibration. Thankful for the heavy weapon to help steady him, Dalton immediately noticed how weighty the spear was. The thick shaft and stone spear point must have weighed between eight and ten pounds.

"This thing is heavy. How was it possible to throw this spear, let alone hit a moving deer?" Dalton handed Murphy the spear.

"I don't believe it was used for throwing, but for killing. The spear is much too heavy to throw with any accuracy, let alone from a distance safe enough to protect the hunter from injury. This spear was used to inflict the final *coup de grace*. After the stag was hunted and exhausted from the fight, I believe the clan leader inflicted the final blow. A mercy kill to the heart."

"Wow! That must have taken great courage to stand over a giant beast fighting for its life with only a spear. There's no way I could do it." Dalton looked down at the jagged edges on the spear point.

"You're too young to be a clan leader. Usually the most celebrated hunter in the clan would have that honor. Undoubtedly he would be the eldest." Murphy turned the shaft and examined the carvings etched into the wood.

"Professor, look at this edge!" Pointing to a notch at the shoulder of the point directly above stem of the stone projectile. "Is that blood?" Dalton asked.

"I believe it is. What a discovery. If we can extract a DNA sample who knows how much information we can glean from it: Age, sex, time of death, species, genus, family, order..." Murphy was in mid-sentence when a distant booming and crashing sound rumbled from the recesses of the cave and then came a stronger movement of the floor.

"What was that, Professor Murphy?" Dalton screamed.

"We have to leave, immediately! I thought we had time, but I was wrong. A sinkhole is forming. Orange growers have been spraying their fields with water to protect their crops from the freezing temperatures the past four nights. I was monitoring the water consumption, but my calculations may have been incorrect or the reservoirs in the artesian wells must have been depressed. With the absence of water to support the surface land, the ground above the depleted water area will collapse."

"That's what we're hearing now! The park land above us is beginning to cave in." Dalton cried out over the ever increasing booming noise.

"That's why we need to go. Grab the spear and follow me!" Murphy shouted and ran towards the door.

Suddenly the shaking stopped and an eerie quiet filtered throughout the main gallery as the pair zigzagged down the pathway leading out of the main gallery. As they entered the stalactite and stalagmite chamber, the violent shaking started up again. Caught off guard, Murphy was slammed forward against a broken limestone column that blocked the path. Still groggy, he pulled himself over the massive stone and slid down the backside of the column as another wave of movement shook the cave floor.

Murphy touched ground and was steadying himself to move forward when a huge column rolled against his legs, pinning him between the two giant columns of stone. Screaming out in pain, Murphy dropped his lantern and held on to the limestone column anticipating another violent movement.

"Oh my God, Professor, what happened?" Standing atop the first column, Dalton lifted his lantern and peered below. Silhouetted in dusty rays of light and sandwiched between two massive columns of stone was Professor Murphy. Sandwiched between two columns, arms raised over his head, Murphy didn't move.

"Professor, can you free your legs?" Dalton shouted and lay down on the column and stuck his head into the crevasse.

Murphy looked up, his face grimacing in pain. He replied in a whisper, "No." He rested his head against the stone and was silent. Another rumble echoed down the corridor. This time louder and closer.

"I'll try to pry you loose with the spear. Hold on I'll be over in a minute."

Dalton slid down the face of the column and jammed the spear butt end first into the crevice where the two columns met. He yanked down on the shaft and shouldered the wooden spear, but no movement. He tried again, but with the same result. "Oh, professor I'm sorry, but I'm not strong enough," Dalton cried out tears welling up in his eyes.

"You're talking about moving tons of limestone. No man could possibly perform such a feat. You need to leave now before the two of us are trapped down here. Take the spear and go."

"I'll be back, Professor Murphy, I promise."

"I'll be here waiting. Now go." Murphy's voice trailed off as Dalton ran down the path and out of sight.

Murphy rested his head against the cold limestone

and listened to the roar—as loud as an approaching freight train—and then silence.

Chapter 24

Beale looked guardedly at the back of his white Crown Victoria. He ran his hand across the top of the bumper and down the right side panel behind the rear wheel base. With both hands he bent down and pushed against the bumper. It didn't budge. He took two steps backwards and studied the entire vehicle.

"Not a bad job," Hordowski blurted out and opened the passenger door. "Looks like new."

"Took them long enough. Three weeks just to put on a new bumper, side rear panel, and a coat of paint," Beale snapped. "I better not complain or the boss will put me back in that beat-up Chevy Caprice. Get in. We need to interview Emma Clearing." Beale punched in the Clearing address and drove out of the parking lot with a big, contented smile.

"So how are you feeling? Still going to therapy?" Hordowski asked and put another stick of gum into his mouth.

"Finished Thursday. I'm okay. My back is still a little sore, especially if I sit too long, but a couple of aspirins in the morning and two at night; I manage." Beale turned onto Tamiami Trail and headed south. "Doctor said I should walk more. Like I'm not walking every day at work. What does he think? I sit behind a desk all day eating donuts and drinking coffee?"

"Well don't you?" Hordowski laughed. "Look. A Dunkin Donuts. Let's pull in and say hello to all your old buddies."

"Very funny. That's the last thing you need. Aren't you still on a diet? What's it called again, the McDonald's Diet or something? What's their motto: A Big Mac a day keeps the doctor away?"

"Not quite, it's called the Macrobiotic Diet and I only eat fish, chicken and fresh vegetables. I'll have you know I lost ten pounds in three weeks. If I keep it up I'll be as skinny as that young lady that smashed into your car three weeks ago at the Jacaranda roundabout."

"That'll be the day; she was beyond thin, possibly anorexic. I would guess she hasn't prepared a decent meal in years; too busy talking on her cell phone and colliding into cars," Beale uttered tersely and shook his head.

"You're not going to believe this, but your little sweetheart got into another fender bender." Hordowski laughed and reached into his shirt pocket. "I cut it out of the paper this morning. Thought you'd like to add it to your scrapbook of police memories. It's a classic. I'll read to you."

"Very funny, I don't have a scrapbook. So what did little Miss Porsche Tanner do now?" Beale turned right onto Shamrock Drive and looked for Sunflower Lane.

"SUV crashes into Venice Theatre. A Lincoln sport utility vehicle ran over a city fire hydrant and crashed into the side of the Venice Theatre missing the stage entrance door by inches. The driver, Miss Porsche Tanner, was transported by ambulance to the Venice hospital for observation. Her condition is unknown. Police recovered a cell phone from the floor of the vehicle and informed the woman on the line that her friend was in an accident and hung up. Theater goers were treated to free water display as they exited the building twenty minutes later."

"Typical! She was on her cell phone when she smashed into my car. I was three-quarters of the way around the roundabout and BOOM! A big, black Lincoln SUV smashes into me and sends my car careening up onto the center circle. Not a scratch on her behemoth of a car, but my Crown Vic needed to be towed back to the police station."

Beale turned left onto Sunflower and slowed down. "Forget about what she pays for car insurance. Two accidents in the same month. I bet her insurance premium just hit the stratosphere. Couldn't have happened to a nicer person."

"Okay, we're looking for 145 Sunflower. There's 120 on the right so 145 is on the left down towards the end of the block." Hordowski lowered the window and stared at the mailboxes as they crept down the tree-lined road. "141, 143, 147, 151 stop! We passed 145. Back up."

Beale flipped on the police flashers, put the vehicle in reverse and eased back down the road. The reverse signal beeper frightened a pair of mockingbirds from their perch high above in an oak tree and dispatched them speedily into flight. Three mailboxes back, the Crown Vic came to a stop. Across the street, a compact row of giant bamboo trees stood shoulder to shoulder like soldiers spreading across an entire drill field. Behind the stand of bamboo was a row of huge oak trees, thirty to forty-feet tall with overhanging branches that cast shadows of light over the main road. At first glance the property appeared vacant, an impression carefully orchestrated by the owner. "What's the number on the mailbox in front of all the trees?" Beale asked. "The GPS reads that we reached our destination."

"One forty-five, but I don't see a house, only bamboo

trees," Hordowski replied. "Wait a minute, at the start of the line of bamboo, looks like a narrow shell driveway."

Beale put on his turn signal and turned into the driveway. Bamboo branches clawed against both sides of the car making scratching sounds as they drove forward. Beale cringed at each scrape and dreaded the thought of what the sides of the car and new paint job would look like. Slowly the driveway widened and the bamboo forest gave way to beautifully manicured bushes, lush beds of colorful flowers and a multitude of bromeliad plants interspersed among the many large oak trees. At the end of the driveway a modern glass cottage glistened in the sunlight.

"No wonder they planted a forest of bamboo. If I had a Twitchell house, I'd plant a wall of bamboo too, but I'd add a moat," Beale blurted out and stepped from the car. "No scratches thank God."

"Okay, I'll bite, what's a Twitchell house? It looks like a tiny cottage that got lost on its way to Siesta Key Beach." Hordowski scoffed and slammed the car door shut.

"Ralph Twitchell was one of the most influential architects in the early twentieth century. He was called*:* The father figure of the Sarasota School of Architecture. He, Paul Rudolf, Jack West and two other architects formed the Sarasota School of Architecture and their buildings are renowned mid-century modern architecture marvels. And this is one of them." Beale leaned against the car and pointed up at the house. "Notice how the floor-to-ceiling glass windows and sliding glass doors merge with the environment. It's as if the inside of the house opens to the outside and the two are one with nature. That was the trademark of the Sarasota School of Architecture: the use of the natural surroundings in minimalistic clarity and integrity. Look at the slightly sloped flat roof and the yellowish Ocala concrete blocks, again a signature of Twitchell construction. If put on the market today, this little gem could easily be listed at a cool million."

"How do you know all this architecture stuff?"

"Last year I attended a World Knowledge Series lecture on the Sarasota School of Architecture at the Venice Community Center. It was an amazing slide presentation. Pictures from the 1940s in black and white and present-day slides in color of hundreds of mid-century modern architectural projects captivated the audience for over two hours. It was well worth the ten dollars."

"I didn't know architecture was your thing," Hordowski added sarcastically and walked towards the front door.

"I've always been interested in buildings, old buildings, new buildings and building things. In high school I won the physics Egg Drop Competition. It took a month to design and construct a capsule that cradled and protected an egg dropped from the school's second floor window. My design was the only capsule that successfully withstood a drop of thirty-five feet. In college my major was engineering, but during my second year a fraternity brother convinced me to go into law enforcement. So I changed my major. My parents were furious, but that's another story. Why don't you ring the bell before we get a ticket for loitering?"

A few minutes later the leaded glass door opened and Emma Clearing appeared and asked, "Detective Beale and Detective Hordowski I presume? Please come in."

The two detectives were taken by surprise, for the woman standing in front of them was the mirror image of the young girl on the missing person poster. Daisy Clearing, only years older. Same height, small body frame, crystal blue eyes, short blond hair and a big, bright, inviting smile. The only thing missing was the blue and white polka-dot dress Daisy was wearing the time of her disappearance.

"Ms. Clearing, I'm Detective Beale and this is Detective Hordowski. We'd like to talk with you about your sister Daisy."

"I've set a place out by the pool where we can talk. I trust you both enjoy iced tea?" They followed her through the small foyer that gleamed with light from an overhead skylight, into the living room and back into time. The white-walled room was decorated in vintage `50s furnishings and looked out onto the patio and backyard.

"Your home is magnificent," Beale remarked and gazed about the room in awe. "A Twitchell house, I believe?"

"Yes, Ralph Twitchell, Paul Rudolf and my father designed and built the house. My father was also an architect and worked with many of the Sarasota School of Architecture architects. The round swimming pool was my father's idea. They struggled for weeks drawing pool designs that would accent the cottage but still blend with the environment. Finally my father drew a circle, and it fit."

"Wow, the furniture looks like it's from the`50s. Are they real, I mean are they authentic?" Hordowski blurted out. "Those orange plastic chairs are unusual, but are they comfortable?"

"Yes, each piece is an original. Some pieces have been reupholstered, but everything in the room was purchased by my mother and father in the `40s when they moved in. The chairs are Lucite mid-century Tulip, and yes, they are very comfortable. If you like you can sit in one."

"The modern sofa looks brand new," Beale added. "Looks comfortable."

"Very comfortable. It's a Cherie mid-century couch. I just had it reupholstered last year in teal. If you're inclined to do so, please have a seat." Emma pointed to the couch.

"No, that won't be necessary, Ms. Clearing. However, I noticed your kitchen isn't 1950 vintage. Everything is stainless steel and contemporary." Beale smiled, pushed the sliding glass door open and stepped outside onto the patio.

"A girl has to cook, Detective. One has to make sacrifices and tweak the timetable to meet the demands of a good soufflé." Emma laughed and poured the iced tea.

"Your father was correct, the round pool blends perfectly with the patio, the bedrooms and the living room. Everything appears to flow into the backyard with the pool as the focal point."

"Thank you. Now what information do you have about my sister Daisy?"

"Ms. Clearing, I am sorry to inform you, but the body of your sister Daisy was discovered a few days ago at Osprey State Park." Beale opened the manila folder from the Clearing Cold Case file and took out the missing person poster of Daisy Clearing. The resemblance was uncanny. If Beale didn't know there was a six year difference in age, they could have passed as twins.

"Osprey State Park? That's not possible. Daisy went to Washington, D.C., to be part of Dr. Martin Luther King Jr.'s March on Washington. I saw her train tickets, $52.15 round-trip coach fare to Washington, D.C. She flashed them around for the family to see every night at the dinner table. The night before her trip she had the family sign her tickets for good luck. I drew a smiley face and signed them both. Father had to give her a two- week advance on her allowance to pay for the tickets. She only had enough money saved for a one-way ticket. Now you say you found her body at Osprey State Park?" Trembling Emma pulled a tissue from her dress pocket and slowly wiped away the tears.

"Volunteer workers were tearing out the old canoe dock and a skeleton floated to the surface of the water. The coroner's report confirmed that it was your sister. DNA samples, dental findings and an injury to her right hand all substantiated that the skeleton found at the park was Daisy Clearing." Beale pointed to the folder and added, "The death certificate is inside, and you'll need it for your records and the required funeral arrangements that need to be executed."

"We feared something may have happened to her in Washington. That maybe she fell, hit her head and had amnesia and was in a hospital as a Jane Doe. Or worse maybe she was abducted while at the rally or returning back to Venice. The police in Washington interviewed people, they retraced Daisy's movements, checked the hospitals, jails, train stations and bus terminals, but without success. Father hired a private investigator from Sarasota to go to Washington and try to find Daisy, but his results were the same; no trace of her. So we waited and prayed that one day she would walk through the door."

Emma continued that her father passed away the following year. He was inspecting a new modern home under construction in Venice that overlooked the Gulf of Mexico and fell from a third floor overhang that wasn't completely secured. He lingered for three weeks in the hospital before the doctors declared him brain dead and removed life support. Her mother never fully recovered from his death or Daisy's disappearance. Emma postponed college to care for her mother, who was suffering from Alzheimer's. Her mother's health worsened with time, and she passed away one rainy summer day while having breakfast with Emma. Emma cradled her in her arms and promised that she would be home to welcome Daisy back.

"Emma, the original investigation into your sister's disappearance didn't have many facts pertaining to the case and the lead detective, Purdy Jones, passed away ten years ago so we can't interview him. Now that Daisy's body has been identified, her missing, person cold case has been reopened and her death has been ruled a possible homicide." Beale took a sip of iced tea and waited for Emma to digest the gravity of his message.

"Purdy Jones I remember that despicable man as if it were yesterday. Big, fat, red-faced redneck detective. I was only twelve, but I recall every disgusting excuse that man spat out when he came to the house. My mother cried uncontrollably and father glowered with disbelief when he stated that Daisy must have run away from home. That the school said she was a free spirit, a hippie and probably ran off to some commune in California. I don't doubt for one second that there isn't any information in her file. Jones didn't investigate. Daisy Clearing was a runaway, case closed."

Emma picked up her glass of iced tea, and before she took a drink she added, "Homicide, you mean she was murdered? How can you say that? After fifty-four years how is it possible to prove?"

Hordowski reached into the folder and pulled out an X-ray of Daisy's skull and held it up. "If you look at the lower back section of the skull, you will see a dark shadow about four or five inches long. We believe that contusion may have been caused from a blow to the head by some person or persons, or the abrasion could be from a fall caused by some person or persons. Either way the injury was partly to blame for her death."

"So did Daisy travel to Washington, participate in the rally, come back to Florida to be murdered, or was she murdered here and never made it to Washington?" Emma looked up at Beale with tear-soaked eyes.

"We don't know yet. Most likely she never traveled to Washington and that's the reason Washington, D.C. authorities couldn't locate her. The police were looking in the wrong place. It's possible she was in Florida all this time, but why did Daisy want to participate in the March? Did she go with friends, with a school or a church group? What possessed her to want to go?" Beale took out his notepad and wrote, "March, and drew a question mark."

"Daisy marched to a different drummer. She was strong-willed and outspoken on many topics. She saw how unfairly black people were treated and confronted the discrimination head on. She wrote letters to the editor of our local newspaper, joined clubs at school, and at church she spoke about the dream of tolerance and equality for all individuals in our town. Dr. King's message of freedom for all people and the concept of nonviolence capsulized Daisy's direction and may have caused ..." Emma took a sip of iced tea and leaned back in the green and white vintage chaise lounge. A distant sadness glazed over her face.

"Did Daisy have any enemies?" Beale asked. "Anyone that you can think of that would kill your sister?"

"I was six years younger than my sister. She was going into twelfth grade, and I just graduated from sixth grade. Socially, emotionally and physically we were worlds apart. I wasn't part of her social circle, so I really didn't know what she did on a daily basis. She had lots of friends, girls as well as boys. I do remember that. They were always coming to the house asking for Daisy. We talked a little at night before we fell asleep, we shared the same room, but it was just girl stuff. Dating, dances and boys, nothing that would lead me to believe her life was in danger.

She did have a boyfriend, a cadet from the Kentucky Military Institute. The school had their winter quarters in Venice. What was his name? I recall it was an unusual name, and at twelve I thought it sounded stuck up. Let me think." Emma closed her eyes and mentally counted through the alphabet, a strategy she had relied upon to remember names since second grade. “Holden J. Winthrop III. That’s it. Handsome and rich, but skinny as a toothpick.”

“Is that the same Winthrop Realty of Venice?” Hordowski asked.

“The same. His father Holden Winthrop Jr. started the business in 1963 and now Winthrop III runs the multi-million dollar company. They have one office in Venice and one in downtown Sarasota. I read in the newspaper they just closed on a $5.6 million home on Siesta Key. A winter retreat for some unnamed buyer from Asia.”

Emma smiled for the first time all morning. “But he wasn’t in Venice when Daisy went to Washington.

All the KMI cadets went back to Kentucky in April to finish out the school year.”

“I think we’ll pay Mr. Winthrop a visit all the same. Thank you for the iced tea, and we’ll keep you informed if we uncover anything pertinent to the case. We’ll find our way out. Goodbye Ms. Clearing.”

Chapter 25

Dalton Marks collapsed on the ground a few feet from what was once the entrance to the ancient cave. Out of breath and shaking uncontrollably, he turned his head and watched the last stone step slowly slip into the hole and disappear under a river of flowing sand. On his hands and knees Dalton crawled to the chain-link fence, reached into his pants pocket, took out his phone and dialed 911. "Please help, Professor Murphy is trapped in the cave. I'm Dalton Marks. I'm at Osprey State Park. Hurry..."

The phone slipped from Dalton's hand as he fell back against the chain-link fence. Blood from a gash on his forehead dripped down across his cheek and puddled on his shirt collar.

A few hours later the park was alive with activity, all centered on the cave. "This is Bryce Faceman, investigative news reporter for Channel 6 News, reporting live from Osprey State Park. A sinkhole the size of a house has just collapsed a large section of parkland directly behind the park's Nature Center. As you can see, police and firefighters are cordoning off the area to protect campers, visitors and park personnel."

Faceman turned and pointed towards the sinkhole. Flood lights from emergency vehicles and portable generators shined down on the area revealing a large circular hole in the woods devoid of any vegetation. Palm trees, shrubs and grasses were all sucked into the sinkhole, revealing a gigantic sandy open pit. "I have with me John Forrester, Manager of Osprey State Park. Manager Forrester, can you tell the viewers what happened here?"

The camera focused on Faceman, but turned only slightly to accommodate a partial profile of Forrester in the interview picture, a subtle technique the cameraman had mastered over the years per Bryce Faceman's orders. "I just spoke with an official from the Florida Department of Environmental Protection and she stated that due to the cold weather over the past five days, growers in the area watered their crops during the night to prevent them from freezing. As a result, the water table dropped causing the ground above to collapse, creating a sinkhole."

The camera swung back to Faceman for a follow-up question and his standard up-close cameo accenting his chiseled jaw and his renowned frozen smile. "The sinkhole appears to be about ninety feet wide, and I can't even see the bottom from this vantage point. It could be a hundred feet deep for all I know. Is it going to continue to expand?"

"No! The sinkhole is not going to expand. I was informed that a geo-technical crew from the state just completed a geophysical, geochemical, drilling and hydrological survey of the area. The engineering team concluded that the fenced off area is the termination point. Now, if you'll excuse me, I have an early morning meeting in Tallahassee tomorrow."

Forrester was about to leave when Faceman pushed the microphone up to his face and asked, "One last question, Manager Forrester. What happens to the sinkhole now? You can't just leave a hole in the ground? Can you?" The camera swung back to Forrester and the sinkhole in the background.

"I believe I'll leave that question for Assistant Manager Blaine Sterling, who is standing next to the firetruck. And now, goodbye sir."

On his way to his Club Car, Forrester stopped Blaine and instructed her to say as little as possible to the reporter until he returned from Tallahassee.

Wrapped in an emergency foil thermal blanket, Dalton sat on the rear step of the firetruck and stared as the beams of light circled the ground where the cave once stood. Still dazed, feelings of guilt choked at him. The idea that he didn't do enough to save his mentor pounded away in the deep recesses of his psyche. Trembling, he closed his eyes, covered his face with both hands and wept. The sound of crashing stones and sand sliding down the sides of the cave pulsated in his ears until he heard his name off in the distance.

"Dalton, can you hear me?" Blaine whispered and sat down next to him on the step.

Dalton looked up and saw Blaine Sterling. He reached out and hugged her. They sat there until he stopped crying. "He's dead, Professor Murphy is dead. I tried to wedge the fallen rocks apart that trapped his legs, but I couldn't budge them. They were too heavy. I promised him that I would return with help. Can we go back and save him?"

Dalton looked at Blaine, but before a word was spoken he knew what her reply would be. He lowered his head.

"I'm sorry, Dalton, everything has collapsed. There wasn't anything more you could have done. Ranger Diana will take you over to the Nature Center where someone will drive you back to school."

"Assistant Manager Sterling, Bryce Faceman Channel 6 News. Manager Forrester mentioned that you could enlighten our viewers on what will become of the sinkhole." Faceman called out and waved the microphone in front of Blaine's face. The camera made a partial adjustment and half focused on Blaine Sterling.

"For now the area has been contained and the Department of Environmental Protection will develop a plan to fill in the sinkhole." Blaine took a step back assuming the interview was over.

Before Blaine could retreat, Faceman, asked, "Is the park safe? There is a gigantic hole in the ground, and hundreds of people visit the park daily. Should the public be concerned that someone may fall into the sinkhole?" The camera panned a close-up of Faceman.

"The safety of our visitors is a major priority at Osprey State Park, and I can assure the public that the park is safe and open for all to enjoy. I would love to tell you that the sinkhole will be filled tomorrow, but I don't have that information. Manager Foster will be meeting with the State Park Commissioners in Tallahassee tomorrow, and they will draft a protocol to resolve the sinkhole situation. That's all I can report at this time."

Blaine smiled and walked over to her Club Car.

The camera faded from Blaine and focused back on Faceman and the sinkhole. The police and fire personnel had left behind only the portable lights silhouetting an empty sandy pit and the yellow police tape.

"This is Bryce Faceman, Channel 6 News wishing all my viewers a very good night. And now back to the studio."

Chapter 26

Blaine parked the Club Car in front of the ranger office, a practice she never, ever did. It was an indiscretion frowned upon by the administration. All Club Cars were to be parked in the pole barn at the end of the day, locked and the key returned to the lock box in the office. That's what she always did, but not on this day. Today was no ordinary day. Quite the contrary, for today Ryan Murphy died. A man she was preparing to share the rest of her life with.

Dazed, Blaine walked mechanically over to her car, opened the door, stepped inside and drove out of the parking lot. As she pulled out onto the main road she looked down at the clock: 7:23 glowed in the center of dashboard. She took out her cell phone and called home.

"Hello Charlene, I'm leaving the office now. I'll be home in a few minutes. Have you and Brooke had dinner? What about her homework? Okay. See you shortly." She placed her phone on the passenger seat and shifted the Mini Cooper into third gear.

Sunset cast its net over the park as the landscape took on a different character and darkness welcomed a new gathering of guests. The remaining hikers finished the last loop of the Red Trail and shared a restful moment reclined on the rocking chairs outside the Nature Center exchanging their pictures of scrub jay sightings before leaving for home. Swimmers from Lake Osprey, all toweled off and dressed, gathered up their belongings and hurried back to their cars. Fishermen along South Creek collected their catches, closed their tackle boxes and abandoned their coveted fishing hole for tomorrow's fishermen. The playground stood empty, while the slides, swings and seesaws waited silently for children to return and play. The aroma of grilled hamburgers and hot dogs wafted in as campers prepared for dinner and a restful night's sleep. A hushed silence filled the darkness.

A distant hoot from a great horned owl echoed through the oaks and pulled Blaine from distant thoughts back to the park. Cool night air blew in through the car's window delivering an uncomfortable chill. Blaine began to shiver, and a bitter taste of loss overwhelmed her as tears suddenly streamed down her face. Shattered dreams of a future lost. Now only precious memories wandered through her mind.

Overcome with grief she pulled to the side of the road. The agony of her loss came cascading down and the shattered dream of a future lost ached painfully. Her body trembled as she slumped back in her seat and sobbed. "Why?" She kept repeating over and over, "Why Ryan?" as the full impact of her loss flooded her memories.

Exhausted and all cried out, Blaine wiped the tears from her eyes and looked up from her seat. Directly in front of the car and frozen in the car's headlights was a family of raccoons; two adults and a cub. Startled for a moment, the animals stood in the middle of the road and then scampered off towards the woods. The adults disappeared into the undergrowth, but a log blocked the path of the cub. A tiny squeak emanated from the furry ball and instantly a head peered over the log. In one swift move the adult jumped over the barrier, picked up the cub and disappeared back into the darkness.

"That's how I'll survive," Blaine whispered. "I'll pick myself up and move on." Blaine pulled onto the road and drove out of the park.

"Hello, I'm home," Blaine called out as she walked into the kitchen. Seated at the kitchen table Brooke and Mrs. Brecht were finishing up the last page of homework and a piece of chocolate chip cookie that remained from dinner. Hugs and kisses all around made Blaine glad to be home, but she was mindful not to let on about the tragedy that took place at the park.

"You look tired, Blaine," said Mrs. Brecht and reached for her pocketbook.

"It was an exhausting day, but nothing a hot bath and a good night's sleep won't cure," Blaine added. "Thank you for everything and say hello to Ken for me. 'Bye"

Blaine sat down in front of the plate Mrs. Brecht left for her, but food was the last thing she wanted. "So, Sweetie, you look tired too. Homework all done?"

"All except for one thing. We're going on a field trip next Monday and I need you to sign the permission slip."

Brooke reached for her backpack and pulled out the form. On the top of the paper in big bold letters were printed "The Wildlife Center of Venice Field Trip." Blaine read through the information and signed at the bottom of the page.

"Can you chaperone Mommy? It's going to be a fun trip. We're studying animals in science, and Mrs. Malott said that the Venice Wildlife Center rescues injured animals, nurses them back to health and then releases them into the woods. We will tour the center, and if there's enough time we'll help feed some of the injured animals. Mr. Barton the owner said they just rescued a baby bobcat after its mother was killed by an automobile. Maybe I can help feed it. Please come, Mommy."

"It sounds like a wonderful trip, Sweetie, but I'm not sure if I can make it. I have a lot of work next week, but I'll write a note on the bottom of the permission slip that I'll try to chaperone."

Blaine scribbled a quick note, handed the paper back to Brooke and said, "I think it's bedtime for both of us. Give me a kiss and off you go."

Brooke kissed her mother on the cheek and shuffled down the hallway to her room.

"Don't forget to brush your teeth!" Blaine called out as she turned the kitchen light off and headed for the bathroom.

The bath was relaxing, and in many ways even therapeutic, but the hot water could not wash away the hopelessness of the day. Blaine fell back on her pillow and closed her eyes, but sleep did not come easily. Over and over her thoughts drifted back to Ryan and what could have been. Their life together was in its infancy, they were taking small steps together, but in their hearts they understood they were laying the groundwork for a future together.

Gone were all the hopes and dreams. All that remained were memories, but who will celebrate his life, who will mourn his death? His parents were deceased, he had no siblings, only an aunt in San Antonio, but she resided in a nursing facility. Her memory of young Ryan had long since faded. What will memorialize his life? A mausoleum, grave site, or a headstone seemed inappropriate for the park. Something to mark hallowed ground not sad or shocking, but a destination for the living to celebrate the park. Exhausted, Blaine finally fell asleep dreaming of the time she and Ryan sat on a bench along Osprey Lake and looked out at the crystal blue water.

Chapter 27

A four-foot sandhill crane stood against the front wall of Circus Days Ice Cream Company. Its silver gray feathered body, beautiful crimson-sculpted red-topped head and long thin pointed bill blended naturally into the animal mural that decorated the entire building. Tony Lilly, the owner, was stapling a picture and the letters R.I.P to a cardboard crane when Lou Bravo pulled up in his yellow El Camino and parked up against the store front. "What's that?" Lou Bravo yelled as he stepped from the truck.

"A little something to add to Operation Sandhill Crane," Tony answered and held it up in the air. "I want the world to see what a shit Morty King really is. It's a picture of his car after he ran over the sandhill crane. I also threw in a picture of the deputy standing over the dead bird for extra effect. We ready?"

"Where's your helper, Hubba Bubba? He was told to be here Friday morning, eight o'clock sharp!" Lou Bravo looked at his watch and groaned, "Don't tell me that he broke his arm again at another mosh pit dance at the Van Wezel."

"Calm down, he's here. He's bringing the truck

around. He was working on sanding off the last of the old lettering from when we used the truck to deliver the free mattresses you won after an all-night poker game at Joey Banana's house. Remember? Can't have the name of my company Clean Sweep sticking out for the world to see, can we? Anyway I was planning on getting the truck painted. See, there he is."

Rounding the corner of the building, a big white box truck barreled forward and jerked to a stop inches from the El Camino. The driver threw open the door and jumped to the ground screaming that he was blind. Pink bubble gum covered his face and gave the impression of a circus performer as he pranced blindly around the parking lot. Tony, familiar with the malfunction, ran over to Hubba Bubba and wiped off the gum with his handkerchief. A splash of hand sanitizer removed the remaining sticky mess from his face.

"There you go, good as new," Tony announced and walked over to the truck and turned off the engine.

"Hand over all your gum, every last piece. I don't want you screwing up this operation because you had gum all over your face; understand? Give it to me now."

Lou Bravo held out his hand while a terrified Hubba Bubba handed over three packs of gum.

"Anymore?"

"No that's all. I swear."

"Now listen, I will call you five minutes before we pull into the Get Physical Fitness Center parking lot. That's enough time for you to drive over to the gym. I timed it last week. When we arrive, I will call you and then you will pull up to the gym. Make sure the truck is blocking the open windows. We don't want any of the gym rats watching the show outside. We'll pull behind King's car, drop our load and leave. Don't drive away until we are out of the parking lot and onto Tamiami Trail. Any questions?" Lou Bravo reached into his pocket and pulled out his cell phone.

"What if someone comes out and asks me why I'm parked in front of the gym?" Hubba Bubba mumbled.

"No one cares about a beat up old truck. If someone asks tell them you have engine trouble," growled Lou Bravo.

"Okay, no problem. I'll be there. You can count on me. I can't wait to see the expression on his face when he comes out and sees all the shit covering his car," laughed Hubba Bubba.

"You're not going to see him, numb nuts. You don't wait around; you drive away and go back to the office and park the truck inside the building."

"I didn't actually mean "see him," but what I meant was to picture the shock on his face," Hubba Bubba stammered.

"What's your telephone number? I want to program the number onto my phone." Lou Bravo opened up the file.

"It's 941 400-3357," Hubba Bubba reached into his back pocket and pulled out his iPhone. "Oh that's not it. That's my old number because last week I jumped into a friend's pool and forgot my phone was in my bathing suit and that was the end of the phone."

"Listen kid. I need the correct number. If I can't reach you by phone this entire operation will fall apart and we will end up in jail. So think, what is the new number?" Lou Bravo took one step closer and waited.

"Okay, I have it. You know you don't call yourself so it's hard to remember a new number, right? It's 941-400-5782. That's it."

Lou Bravo punched in the numbers. The phone in front of him rang. "Answer it."

"Hello."

"Make sure you have your phone on you at all times. Make sure it's charged and on. Is that understood?"

Lou Bravo hung up before he got a reply and walked

over to Tony's car. "Let's take your car. I want people to think I'm with you inside."

Tony pulled out of the commercial park and onto Tamiami Trail heading north. Early in the morning, traffic was light and the white Ford Focus eased into the right-hand lane and accelerated towards Venice Avenue.

Chapter 28

Tony cranked down his window and glanced up at a flock of crows passing overhead in a straight-line formation and then disappearing behind a large stand of oak trees off in the distance. "So how do we get to this Purple Manure Farm?" Tony laughed. "Pee-yew I can't breathe. Where's the air freshener?"

"Purple Brush Farm, funnyman. It's an art colony, not an agricultural farm. We'll take Jacaranda to Border and follow Border almost to the end. Her place is just before the T. Mabry Carlton Preserve. If we reach the preserve we drove too far. It's roughly twenty miles 'as the crow flies.' I drove there last week to make the arrangements."

"And how long will it take this white crow to fly to Purple Paradise Farm?"

"Again with the joke. The first time it was cute, second time it was annoying, on the third you walk to the Purple Brush Farm and I drive. Border Road is a single lane road, at most fifteen to twenty minutes. That's if we don't get clogged up behind a slow-moving tractor, then add another I don't know five..."

"Or we could just follow the crows," laughed Tony,

as another squadron of crows raced past the Focus.

Tony entered the Jacaranda roundabout and headed north. All along the east side of the highway, construction vehicles worked ripping out the landscape and preparing the land for development. A stack of trees burned in the far corner of the acreage while rows of blue sewer pipes lined the entrance to the property. A team of workers hammered in a large white and blue sign announcing the construction of Watercress Lakes, a two hundred and fifty-luxury-home development.

At the next light, Lou Bravo looked over at the construction and cringed. An orange sign with a red goose at the top read:" Future Site of a Wawa Convenience Store. Gas, food and more. Grand opening this summer."

"Do we really need another gas station? With this new addition there will be three stations all in walking distance of each other. I don't think so. I'm all for progress, but I want it to be responsible. This is irresponsible sprawl."

"Amen, brother. By the way, a bit of trivia, do you know how Wawa stores got their name?" Tony added with a sarcastic air of superiority.

"No and I don't give a shit."

"Kindly let me impart my knowledge for your self-edification. Wawa is the town in Pennsylvania where the business started. Wawa was and still is a dairy company. Its logo is the Canada goose and the Native American name for the goose sounds something like wa-wa, or maybe the call a goose makes sounds like wa-wa. It's one or the other or both."

"Thanks for the history lesson, but I still don't give a shit. The last thing we need is a two hundred and fifty-home community and another convenience store at that location. Anyway that piece of land holds a lot of memories for me."

"Memories, it was only a patch of old Florida land,

scrub oak, palms and grass where a few cows grazed. What memories could you possibly have?" Tony quipped.

"Do you know Bobby Terone? He owns Bob's Motorcycle Shop. It's in your commercial park."

"I don't know the man personally, but I pass his place of business every day on my way to work. His shop is on Warfield Avenue. Why do you ask?"

"The location for that new development is where I thought I was going to die one hot August afternoon. About eighteen years ago Bobby and I, would ride our motorcycles down to Snook Haven every Sunday. Sunday was the unwritten day for all bikers to ride down to Snookey's. Sometimes over a hundred bikers would hang out, drink beer, shoot the breeze, pick up girls and just have a good ole time."

"You're joking. I didn't know you had a motorcycle. I bet it was a big old Harley, right."

"That's right a Harley Davidson Duo-Glide. What a machine, big, bad and beautiful. I nicknamed her 'Black Beauty,' but I gave up motorcycles after I crashed one night in the pouring rain on the North Bridge in Venice. But that's another story. Anyway it was about a year after I moved down to Florida, Bobby and I were making our Sunday run down to Snook Haven. It was August, probably the hottest day of the year and humid as hell. Even cruising at 50 mph I was still sweating. Right after the Jacaranda intersection, no roundabout back then, about twenty motorcycles blocked the road. Guys were standing around shouting and cursing at each other or just cursing. Bobby and I got off our bikes, walked into the crowd and there in the center of the road was a gigantic cow or steer. All I knew was that beast was big and wasn't moving."

"Did it have horns?" asked Tony. "If it had horns it probably was a steer. They could do some serious damage if provoked."

"I don't remember. All I know is it looked pissed. So

Bobby goes back to his bike, pulls out a line of rope from his saddle bags, lassos the cow or steer, jumps on its back and the four-legged beast takes off into the bushes. With Bobby on its back."

"You're kidding. Bobby Terone rode a wild steer? So then what? He's still alive, so I guess the steer didn't trample him to death. So what happened?" Tony pleaded.

"All the motorcycle guys cheered, jumped on their bikes and took off down the road towards Snook Haven. I'm standing in the middle of the road next to my bike when a beat up red tractor roars out of the woods from the opposite side of the road and stops in front me. The old man at the wheel dressed in faded blue denim coveralls and a sweaty old, green John Deere hat that covered his stringy gray hair leaned over the wheel and shouted, 'Where's my property?' He spat out a glob of dark brown chewing tobacco juice which matched the color of his few remaining teeth. 'Are you deaf boy?' He said, 'where is my property?' In one fluid motion he reached behind the seat and pulled out a shotgun. He pointed the double barrel right at my face and yelled again, 'Where's my property?"

"Oh my God. I don't believe it. I would have had a heart attack right there on the road."

"To tell the truth, I was scared shitless all right, but I didn't believe the old man wanted to kill me; he just wanted to know what happened to his cow. So I told him my friend Bobby Terone rode off with him and pointed to the woods on the other side of the road, where they are now building that housing development."

"So what did the old man do? He didn't shoot you. Did he shoot your motorcycle?" Tony scratched his head and looked out at the new construction along the highway as they moved down the road.

"No, he drove across the road into the woods. Ten

minutes later the old man drove back with Bobby, the steer and a big smile on his toothless face."

Lou Bravo grinned and they turned onto Border Road. "Bobby was that old guy's nephew. For years Bobby spent his winter break on his farm working the cows, feeding the chickens and repairing all the farm machinery. Bobby had a gift for working on engines. That's what got him interested in Venice and motorcycles. So after the army Bobby moved to Florida and opened a motorcycle shop."

"Unbelievable. So every time you go into the new Wawa store, you can shout out for all the customers to hear, 'Where's my property?'"

"Don't bet the ranch on it, my friend."

Lou Bravo laughed and looked down at his watch. Twenty minutes had passed—a little longer than last week's trip, but they were still on schedule to reach the gym at half past nine. "See the pelican on the mailbox on the left? That's the Wildlife Center of Venice. What a fantastic organization. They rescue and treat sick, injured or abandoned animals and they don't get a penny from the government. They only subsist on donations. I know the director Kevin Barton. He's a great guy dedicated to preserving the environment and making our world a healthier place. He helped me out a few years ago with a cat problem."

"Cat problem? I didn't know you had a cat. What kind of problem did you have?" Tony stared at the mailbox as they cruised past the chain link entrance gate to the wildlife center.

"I'll tell you later. Right now you need to concentrate on the road."

"That's not a real pelican. It's a wooden figure sitting on top of the mailbox; pretty cool. I wonder if the carver used one block of wood or more. I read in the paper last winter that the Wildlife Center treated over 4 thousand injured animals. I wonder how many sandhill cranes the Wildlife Center of Venice rehabilitated. It's a shame I couldn't bring the sandhill crane King hit with his car to the center. Yeah, it's too bad."

Tony shifted in his seat and noticed another mailbox up ahead on his side of the highway. "What's the story with the mailboxes out here? Did the town have some kind of mailbox decoration contest?"

Affixed to the mailbox was an oversized figure of an artist's palette and brush painted in bright purple. Around the edge of the palette were tiny, blinking, purple lights which were connected to a solar panel at the bottom of a purple tree trunk that supported the mailbox. Tony slowed and turned onto a narrow shell road.

"Here we are," Lou Bravo shouted out, "Purple Brush Farm."

Below the wrought iron entranceway in bright purple lettering a large canvas banner read: "Purple Brush Farm Welcomes Plein Air Artists."

"Miss Vardi is having her artist workshop this week. She said today would be a perfect time to pick up her truck because the artists would be painting outside away from the barn and that we wouldn't interrupt her activities and most importantly wouldn't arouse any unwanted questions regarding our rental agreement."

"I don't believe it! What's with this purple road? What does this lady think she has a leading role in the Wizard of Oz?" Tony stuck his head out the window and looked down at the purple shells as the Ford Focus bounded down the purple shell road towards a purple barn.

The road, in dire need of repair, was pockmarked with potholes, some large and dangerously deep, able to certainly cause extensive damage to the undercarriage of any unsuspecting vehicle, a fate Tony planned to avoid at all costs. A truck driver back in New York, he skillfully, maneuvered around the impediments, past a stand of low leaning palms in the fork in the road, a handful of purple mounds that sporadically scraped against his muffler and an occasional mysterious puddle hiding unthinkable dangers below. Taking the right fork, the road led directly to a purple barn that loomed in the distance. Planted on a rise the building appeared large and impressive. Over fifty feet in height, eighty feet wide and a hundred feet long, the structure occupied a large chunk of land on one side of the property. A small corral with two horses leisurely chewing on a bale of hay completed the panorama.

On the opposite side of the property was a main house painted purple and five purple cottages that bordered a large natural pond filled with ducks and other local wildlife. Tony followed the purple road to the barn where an old, beat-up purple dump truck was parked out front. Alighting from the driver's side of the truck was a blur of purple with hand gyrations worthy of a whirling leprechaun celebrating St. Patrick's Day. Miss Vardi, a petite five foot dynamo, clad in one of her favorite purple, flowered, corn dresses, purple rubber work boots, and a purple sun hat that partially covered her curly, short purple hair, raced over to greet her company.

"Perfect timing," Miss Vardi yelled, holding out the truck keys. "Full tank of gas and a full load of shit. Have fun boys."

"We plan to," Lou Bravo laughed, "but would you go over the dump truck operation one more time? I want Tony to know the drill in case I have a problem with the other truck."

"No problem."

The trio walked over to the truck. Miss Vardi jumped up into the cab and started the engine. "First start the engine. When the beeping stops, you have enough air pressure to operate the hydraulics. Press in the clutch, move forward the transaxle lever, pull down the PTO lever which raises the box, let up off the clutch and the box goes up. Push the yellow lever to raise the tailgate. That's it. When you drive away, step on the clutch, push the transaxle back, release the clutch and the box lowers. Slide the yellow lever to right to lock the tailgate. Then drive off."

"How long should the entire process take? Let's say from the time we back up behind the BMW, dump our load and drive away," asked Lou Bravo.

"Three minutes tops," laughed Miss Vardi, "maybe less. If that's all, I have a lot of work to do in the barn today. If I'm not around when you get back, just park the truck in front of the barn. Have fun. 'Bye."

"Miss Vardi, before we leave I couldn't help wondering. I noticed two horses in the corral when we drove up. That's a gigantic barn for only two horses. Do you have other horses stabled inside? Do you operate a riding academy or something? I sell ice cream and was wondering if you'd be interested in providing ice cream snacks for your students," Tony asked.

"An equestrian school? You think I board horses? What are you mad? I only have two horses and they're for my daughters Kristen and Linnea to ride. Are you blind? Didn't you notice the banner out front? I am an artist, and for your information the large barn is for..." Miss Vardi turned and pointed a small black remote towards the barn and immediately the large purple door slid open. "Satisfied?"

The cavernous room was painted a light purple and adorned with purple strands of lights that hung across the ceiling, front to back, side to side. Along the perimeter of the barn, spotlights illuminated the entire room with a soft white hue of light. Hundreds of purple paintings adorned every wall. Clustered in groups of three or four were scenes of flowers, animals, houses, people, barns, and trees all highlighted under lights. Hanging from the rafters large paintings, some over ten feet in length, cascaded down like a purple rain of art. In the center of the room, under a canopy of paintings, twenty-five desks with laptops formed a square. In the middle of the square stood a single stool and an easel. On the second floor, the entire space was divided into numerous art stations, each containing an easel and boxes of art supplies.

"I don't see any horses," laughed Tony, "Maybe your art students would like an ice cream break before lunch? I can imagine the exhaustion from all those tiny strokes on the canvas. If you like I could arrange a little ice cream pick-me-up. What do you say?"

"I don't believe so. Happy trails, boys." Miss Vardi walked to the barn and the boys pulled away in the purple truck.

Chapter 29

Halfway down the road Tony stuck his head out the window, again stared at the shell road and said, "I forgot to ask her where she buys those purple shells. I may want to put some down on a path in my backyard that leads to the gazebo."

"What did you say? Where could you buy purple shells? I think you have been spending too much time with that bubble gum chewing moron."

Lou Bravo jammed on the brakes, brought the truck to a screeching halt and shouted, "Get out. Get out of the truck and pick up a shell. Now!"

"Okay, you don't have to get so excited. I was just curious about the purple shells. It's not a crime to ask a question is it?"

"You can answer that question after you pick up your shell."

Tony jumped out and picked up the first shell he stepped on. A splintered shell, broken many times from traffic, felt sticky and was purple on only one side. He rubbed a flat section and purple coloring stuck to his thumb. He repeated the process and more purple rubbed off the shell. He smelled the piece and detected a scent of oil or grease. "It's paint! She paints the shells; unbelievable."

"Jump in. We have to go. Before every art program she sprays the road with an oil base purple paint. Thins the paint out with kerosene and walks the length of the driveway with a hand sprayer. That's why she's called the *Purple Lady*."

"Weird! I think I'll put down pavers. Speaking of weird, we just passed the Venice Wildlife Center. I'm sure you have a weird cat story to share." Tony threw the shell out the window, sat back in his seat and waited.

Lou Bravo began with an introduction of Tubby Bling, a pain-in-the-ass customer when he owned Classic Touch Auto Body in New York. Tubby was a real character, always looking for a deal. He could never force himself to pay full price, ever! Even though he was wealthy he always tried to bargain everything down, but in the end it was his finagling that caused his undoing.

A weasel of an individual professionally and physically Tubby in many respects resembled a weasel. Short, overweight and ill-mannered, he would scrunch up his face when conducting a transaction, accenting his big bulging eyes and bushy eyebrows that moved with every word Tubby uttered.

Tubby owned Kidsland, a small amusement park and animal zoo on Long Island. Not a Disneyland type enterprise, but rides and animal attractions designed to entertain families with young children. A petting zoo where children could feed the animals, pony rides and a midway filled with cages of local and exotic animals all picture-ready for a fee. The highlight of the zoo experience was Miss Carlotta's interactive parrot show that entertained all the visitors and Tubby. The amusement park rides were geared to move the guests around the park and delight youngsters one ride at a time. A steam engine train carried children and parents around the grounds with two stops where passengers could exit or jump on. A gondola tram gave the visitors a spectacular aerial view of all the attractions and cooled them off with a light breeze as they passed over the man-made lake and the children's boat ride.

Kidsland Amusement Park was an overnight success and a financial gold mine. Tubby bought a mansion in the Hamptons, expensive cars, membership at an exclusive country club, a yacht and a hideaway cottage nestled along the Peconic Bay. It was the hideaway love nest that brought Tubby's house of cards tumbling to the ground.

"I don't get it. What does a guy in New York have to do with the Venice Wildlife Center?" Tony asked.

"Patience, my dear fellow. All will be clear before we reach the gym. I think I'll take Pinebrook to Center, and then enter the plaza's parking lot from Tamiami trail. Fewer turns and less chance to lose our cargo."

Lou Bravo returned to Tubby Bling's connection to the Wildlife Center and Lou Bravo's association with Kevin Barton.

One hot, August afternoon while relaxing by her pool and enjoying her mid-day cocktail, Mrs. Tubby Bling received a phone call from an anonymous caller detailing the love exploits of her husband and the exotic parrot lady. So began the unraveling of Tubby Bling's life and fortune. Without a prenuptial agreement, Mrs. Bling took Tubby to the proverbial cleaners. Bank accounts were frozen. Liens against Kidsland, his home, yacht, automobiles, and lastly the sale of the Peconic love nest all signaled the end of the good life for Mr. Bling. Tubby was cash poor. His assets were hijacked in litigation, and by the end of the month he barely could afford to pay his rent at a local hotel in Islandia.

One morning leaving his hotel Tubby found a note on his windshield: 'I'm sorry that I backed into the rear of your car. I'm writing this note because two people saw the accident and I don't want them calling the police, so I'm leaving you with a fake name, incorrect telephone number and a made-up license plate number. If you can afford to drive a Bentley, you can clearly afford to pay for the repairs. Have a nice day, Ralph Jockeyshorts.'

"Enraged, Tubby drove over to Lou Bravo's auto body shop. The rear bumper, trunk assembly, and back left side panel all needed to be replaced and repainted. Unfortunately, Tubby's auto insurance had a two thousand dollar deductible, and cash-strapped Tubby had only two hundred dollars until the end of the month. Even with Lou Bravo's discount the repairs totaled five thousand dollars. Tubby didn't have the money for the repair work and so begins the Kevin Barton Florida connection."

"I still don't get it. This is back in New York; Kevin Barton is in Florida. I see the gym. Do you think you can finish the story before we reach the parking lot?"

"Hold on big fella, I'm just about finished, but first I need to turn into the lot." Lou Bravo pulled the truck into the far end of the parking lot and stopped. From their vantage point they had a direct view of the gym in the middle of the shopping center, and Hubba Bubba in the white truck at the other end of the lot.

"Tubby didn't have two thousand dollars, he barely had enough money to buy gas for the Bentley, and so he offered to pay the deductible with an ocelot. He said he had papers that showed that the ocelot was worth twenty-five hundred dollars, so I bought it."

"Okay, I'll bite. What the hell is an ocelot?" Tony screamed in frustration.

"An ocelot, my dear zoological-deprived boy, is a wild cat. It looks like a small leopard, is about the size of a bobcat, and weighs about 20 lbs. Its fur is short, a yellowish color, with long, black-ringed stripes and spots over the entire coat." Lou Bravo pulled out his wallet and handed Tony a picture of himself, the ocelot, Kevin Barton, and a judge.

"I didn't know you owned an ocelot. What's with the judge?" Tony asked.

"That's where Kevin Barton comes into the story. It was a year before you moved down to Florida when the whole ocelot mishap occurred."

Lou Bravo smiled and recounted how Shadow got loose one day and killed two of his neighbor's prized Ayam cemani chickens, fondly known as the *Lamborghini of poultry.* At $25 hundred a bird Mr. Graybill sued Lou Bravo for five million dollars, compensation for loss of future revenue from the sale and reproduction contracts of his prized chickens, and an additional two million for pain and suffering he endured with the death of his prized chickens. The trial lasted three days, the jury reached a verdict in one hour, and Shadow was found not guilty due to the fact Mr. Graybill did not secure his property adequately. Graybill was fined court costs, Lou Bravo's attorney fees, and Mr. Barton's cost to retrieve Shadow from the oak tree.

"The picture you're looking at was on the front page of the Venice Journal Star. The headline read: **Ocelot Not Guilty Everything is Purrrfect.**"

"So what happened to the ocelot?" Tony asked.

"Maria said I had to get rid of it. She was worried if it got out of the house again maybe someone would be injured, and the verdict would most likely be different. The wife was generally right. So I gifted it to Kevin Barton who in turn sold it to the Big Cat Habitat in Sarasota. Give Hubba Bubba a call and tell him to move into position."

"It's time. Move your truck up to the gym. We'll start driving as soon as you raise the hood and appear to have engine trouble."

"Ten-four."

"One last thing. Don't forget when we backup to the

BMW you have to help me release the tailgate pin closest to you. Understand!" Tony reiterated with a bite of annoyance.

"I get it, I'm on the move."

Chapter 30

Planning is everything. Follow the schedule, execute the directives, maintain the timeline, and most importantly savor the outcome.

Hubba Bubba pulled the truck up to the gym blocking the three open windows facing the parking lot, he lifted the hood and looked down at the engine. At that exact moment the purple dump truck picked its way across the parking lot, backed up to King's BMW, and engaged the transaxle to raise the truck's box and all its contents. Hubba Bubba and Tony released the tailgate pins and the box rose upward to the heavens. Conversely the manure in the box cascaded down in a stream of brown noxious excrement over the open convertible.

In no time the entire cabin of the BMW was buried in a mound of steaming dark brown horse manure. Tony reached into the truck, pulled out his cardboard sandhill crane and stuck it into the center of the mound. Attached to the crane a sign read: R.I.P sandhill crane killed by this driver while talking on his cell phone. A photograph of Morty King on his cell phone, his license plate number: RIDES-1, and a policeman standing over a dead sandhill crane dangled from the crane's long black beak.

Like a seasoned college parade drill team, Tony and Hubba Bubba marched back to their trucks and prepared to drive away. Lou Bravo, as planned, was first to drive off. He jerked the truck forward, jammed on the brakes, and the last of the deposit fell onto the trunk of the BMW. He lowered the box and drove off. Hubba Bubba waited until the purple truck reached the end of the parking lot before he drove off.

"It's 10:04," Lou Bravo shouted as he eased the truck out into traffic. "Not bad for amateurs. It only took four minutes to teach that obnoxious prick a thing or two."

"Twenty-six more minutes and Mr. Morty King will be in for a big surprise. Couldn't have happened to a nicer guy," laughed Tony and rolled down his window.

"Yeah, couldn't have happened to a bigger shit. We're still not finished with King. Open up the glove compartment and take out the phone. I want you to call the cops and report a red BMW parked in a handicapped spot illegally. Then call Channel 6 and leave a message for Faceman about the horse manure dumped on the BMW. I can't wait to see Morty King on the six o'clock news."

"But won't the police trace the call and make us the ones covered in manure?" Tony asked and looked down at the phone.

"Let them trace the call. A friend of mine gave it to me. He found it yesterday on the seat of a car. People can be so careless. Make the calls." Lou Bravo turned onto Center Road and headed east.

A few minutes later police sirens wailed off in the distance. Tony looked out his window and spotted a Channel 6 News helicopter flying towards the Get Physical Fitness Center. The two high-fived and laughed.

Chapter 31

The silver Range Rover stopped at the ranger station. Ranger Diana stepped outside to greet her first guest of the day and immediately announced in her usual spirited way, "Good morning and welcome to Osprey State Park."

Behind the wheel sat a petite, blond, blue-eyed woman in her mid-sixties. Stylishly dressed in a black Armani pants suit, Diana couldn't help but think that her outfit was juxtaposed for a day of hiking.

However, visitors in many unusual forms of dress had graced the hiking trails of Osprey State Park from time to time. The most recent collection of weird costumes occurred during the All Trails Hike last January. Men painted green, pirates with parrots, Thor: Viking God of Thunder, and Wizard of Oz characters just to name a few. But most puzzling was a vintage, strawberry pink vinyl diary and a large funeral wreath of purple, yellow, and blue flowers resting on the passenger seat. "Here is a map of all the hiking trails, the entrance fee is five dollars." Leaning in Diana noticed that the woman's mascara was smudged; it was apparent she had been crying.

"I'm not here to hike," the driver answered and handed Diana the five-dollar entrance fee. "I'm Emma Clearing and I'd like to leave flowers and a diary to memorialize the death of my sister Daisy. Would you kindly direct me to the canoe dock?"

Caught completely by surprise, Diana stepped back, took a deep breath and replied, "Ms. Clearing I am so sorry for your loss. Please accept my condolences and believe me when I say that everyone at the park is heartsick over the death of your sister. We are conducting our own investigation and hope to bring some closure on this tragic discovery. Take the first right off the main road. You'll see a sign, "*South Creek Picnic Area,*" pull in and park along the fence. The canoe dock is a short walk from the parking lot."

"Thank you." Emma closed the window and drove off.

"Assistant Manager Sterling, good morning, this is ranger Diana. I know you're scheduled for a ten o'clock tour with the Disabled Veterans of Venice, but we have a situation that needs your immediate attention. Emma Clearing is in the park. She just arrived and wants to leave flowers at the canoe dock."

"Perfect, I planned to drive over to her home and speak with her this morning. Thank you Diana, I'll drive over to the canoe dock now." Blaine put down the phone and walked outside to her Club Car.

Emma was standing at the end of the aluminum dock staring down at the dark water of South Creek when Blaine drove up. The black water looked foreboding, and she shivered at the thought of her sister drowning in the evil waters below her feet. Tears flowed down her face again as they did fifty-four years ago when her sister didn't return home. Those were terrible, heart-wrenching years for the family—hoping and praying that maybe one day the front door would open and Daisy would return from Washington, D.C. But she never did.

"Daisy is home now, Mother," Emma cried out. "I kept my promise, and waited for her to return. You can now rest in peace, Mother, Daisy is home."

Emma held the funeral wreath in her hands and was about to toss the flower arrangement into the deeps when a voice called out, "Emma! Wait I need to talk with you."

Standing at the front of the dock was a tall young woman dressed in a forest green uniform. Her commanding stature and penetrating blue eyes projected an air of a no-nonsense individual. As the woman stepped forward, Emma could make out the name on the gold nameplate above her right breast pocket: Blaine Sterling Assistant Park Manager.

"It's against park regulations to dispense any form of ceremonial objects into a state park body of water as per section R-15 or is it R-51 of the Florida State Code of Statutes." Blaine called out and stepped forward.

Emma lowered her arms and waited for the park official to introduce herself.

"I'm Assistant Manager Blaine Sterling, and I am so sorry to meet you under such sad circumstances. Please except my deepest sympathies for your loss," Blaine reached out and offered her hand.

"A pleasure to meet you, Assistant Manager Sterling," Emma answered and shook her hand.

"Please call me Blaine. Let's go sit on the bench under that big oak tree next to the dock. If you wish, you may place the funeral wreath in front of the tree to commemorate Daisy's death; that's permissible. The State is extremely protective of the health and safety of its waterways. That's why the regulation is in effect. Let me help you carry the wreath."

They sat under the shade of the ancient oak and talked of memories from the past and in trepidation of things to come. Emma shared how for forty-four years her mother kept Daisy's room exactly the way it was on August 26, 1963. Every morning her mother would tidy up the room hoping that it would be the day her daughter would return. Ten years ago her mother passed away, but before she died her mother made her promise to remain at the house and wait for her older sister to return. It was then that Emma got up the courage to pack up Daisy's belongings and redecorate her bedroom. And not until yesterday, after Detective Beale informed her that they found Daisy's skeleton at Osprey State Park, did she haul out of the closet a packing carton with some of her sister's keepsakes.

Emma took out of her pocket an old faded pink diary and nestled it in her lap as she spoke. "I broke the lock on the diary with a bobby pin more than fifty years ago. Not intentionally, it was an accident. I sneaked into Daisy's bedroom and found the diary tucked under her mattress. I knew she wrote in the book every day and I wanted to see for myself what was so secretive. Before I could read the first page Daisy came in with a friend and went crazy. She ripped the diary from my hand and chased me out. That's how the lock broke." Emma flipped the vinyl strap back and forth.

"Is there an entry on Daisy's last day?" Blaine asked.

"No, but the night before there's one. A very troubling one based upon what Detective Beale said." Emma flipped to the last page dated Sunday, August 25, 1963, but before she read the entry she whispered in a soft voice. "He said maybe Daisy never left Venice."

"That could be a possibility. Please read the passage."

"Tomorrow I leave for Washington, D.C. I can't wait to be part of history. From what I've read the march will have thousands of people arriving from all over the country. I'm packed, have my ticket and can't wait to leave. I'm worried that Win will not take me to the train station tomorrow. We argued about me going to

Washington and he left in a huff. Anyway, I'm ready. My new red suitcase is packed. My blue and white polka-dot dress is pressed and hanging over my dressing chair waiting for morning. Good night, diary. I can't wait for tomorrow."

"Who's Win?" asked Blaine.

"Win was her boyfriend, Holden J. Winthrop III. They called him Win for short. Because he bragged about being such a winner" Emma barked out. "He was nothing but a stuck-up rich kid who went to the Kentucky Military Institute. I was only twelve, but I realized he was only using my sister. I despised him."

"Why does the name Winthrop sound familiar? I know I've heard that name before, but where?" Blaine looked back towards the water and thought.

"On the television! He's the real estate salesman shouting at everyone to buy one of his homes. 'My deals are *HUGE,* Venice and Sarasota, *HUGE.'* The guy is a real jerk, but he's loaded. He sells million-dollar homes all the time. He has an office in Venice and one in Sarasota on Main Street in that new high-rise, the Vista." Emma looked down at the diary and smoothed out the page with the palm of her hand.

"Oh yes, how could I forget? The commercials are comical, jumping around and screaming about the deal he is going to make everyone. It is beyond belief how he can make any sales. I do have to say for a man in his seventies he appears fit and reasonably handsome. Perfectly groomed gray hair, tall, strong jaw, small nose, and a boyish face that made him appear younger than he is. Add a military uniform; no wonder Daisy fell for him. Wait a minute, I read somewhere that all the KMI cadets went back to Kentucky in April to finish out the school year. What was Winthrop doing in Venice in August?" Blaine looked down at the diary.

"That's right. What was that creep doing here in August? I didn't know it at the time, Detective Beale wasn't aware of it, and that redneck detective Purdy Jones sure as hell didn't question Winthrop. Did he take Daisy to the train station. And if not, who did?"

A tear fell from Emma's eye and landed on the last page of the diary and circled the word hope. She looked down and stopped crying.

"That's the question. If not, what happened to Daisy that caused her to end up at Osprey State Park?" Blaine uttered in a low-pitched tone from the deep recess of her pained heart. "Emma, my boss has asked me to investigate the death of your sister and attempt to understand the role Osprey State Park contributed to her demise. Could I please have Daisy's diary? Maybe I'll uncover some clues that will help solve the mystery. I'll return the diary after I read every page."

"Of course, but after you finish reading it you should give it to Detective Beale." Emma handed Blaine the diary and smiled.

"I'll walk you to your car." Together in silence they walked up the path to the parking lot. Blaine waved goodbye and brokenheartedly watched Emma drive out of sight. She looked back at the flowers resting against the old tree and said softly to the park, "I promise to find the answers, and the first step will take place tomorrow morning." Blaine took out her cell and called Lou Bravo.

Chapter 32

Everyone from the Get Physical Gym spilled out the front door, circled the red BMW and looked down at the steaming brown mess percolating in front of them. The crowd pushed and shoved to get a closer look, but all the patrons were careful not to push too close. Morty King, front and center, still dressed in his lime green sweat suit, turned bright red and exploded with a barrage of expletives that would embarrass a seasoned X-rated porn star.

“Who the fuck did this to my car? I’ll kill the son of a bitch.” Morty looked around at the crowd for any indication of culpability. “Did anyone see anything, hear anything, anything at all? Horse shit doesn’t just fall from the sky. Some bastard dumped this crap onto my BMW. So did anyone see who did this?” King shouted.

“I saw a white truck parked out front,” Rider the gym manager called out. “A tall, skinny guy got out and was checking his engine. That’s all I saw.”

“I was on the treadmill alongside the windows, but like Rider said, the truck blocked the view of the parking lot. Couldn’t see the BMW or any other vehicle in the lot." A voice from the back called out.

"Mommy, why is there a sandhill crane standing on the top of the pile of stinky dirt?" a young girl holding her mother's hand asked.

"It's a sign, Dear. It says "rest in peace," and there is a photograph of this car and a policeman looking down at a sandhill crane," the mother explained.

"Mr. King, isn't that your automobile in the photograph? If I'm not mistaken, doesn't your license plate read: RIDES-1?" a muscular man shouted out from the crowd.

"Well yes, but..." Morty was stopped mid-sentence with the arrival of a deputy sheriff.

With blue and red lights flashing, the patrol car picked its way through the crowd up to the handicapped parking spot and the BMW. The deputy opened the car door and walked over to the red BMW covered in manure. Standing head and shoulder over everyone in the crowd, the young deputy surveyed the situation and made a mental note of the specifics. "May I have your attention! The sheriff's office received a complaint of an unauthorized automobile parking in a handicapped zone. Who owns this BMW?"

"I do," Morty King raised his hand and stepped forward.

"Sir, what is your name and would you please explain what happened here?" The deputy took out a small pad.

"My name is Morty King and I'm not exactly sure what happened here. I was in the gym and someone yelled out that a car was covered in horse manure. Everyone ran out to see, and this is what we found." Morty pointed down at his car.

"May I see your license and registration Mr. King?" The deputy held out his hand and waited while King fumbled with his wallet.

"I can't hand over the registration. It's in the glove compartment which as you can see is covered in horse manure."

Turning the license over twice the deputy remarked, "I don't see a notation on your license where it denotes that you are handicapped. I don't even see a handicapped placard attached to the mirror and your license reads: RIDES-1. Are you handicapped Mr. King?"

"Well not exactly. I do have a problem with my right leg, but I don't have a handicapped classification. Not now, but I intend to apply for one as soon as I have my car cleaned."

"He has a handicap deputy. He doesn't know how to read. Every Friday he parks in the handicapped spot and goes into the gym. It's disgraceful," a woman behind the BMW called out.

"It's also against the law and subject to a two hundred-fifty dollar fine," said the deputy tersely and ripped off the ticket and handed it to Morty. The crowd burst out in cheers and clapped fervently.

"What about my car? I can't drive it like that. What can I do?" pleaded Morty.

"Call for a tow truck, Mr. King. And Mr. King, you need to concentrate on your driving, not your cell phone. If you weren't on your phone maybe that sandhill crane would be alive today and your car wouldn't be filled with you-know-what. Have a good day sir."

Morty stood in the parking lot all alone looking up at the sandhill crane perched on top of his car. He reached into his fanny pack and took out his phone. "Hello Martha, I'm still at the gym. Would you call a tow truck for me? I can't start my car. No, I didn't lose my keys. Also call the insurance company and have them give the tow company the address of the nearest claims office. I'll be waiting in the parking lot."

"Smile, Mr. King! Hello viewers this is Bryce Faceman reporting live for Channel 6 News where Amusement Park owner Morty King has just found this BMW covered in well...See for yourself viewers."

As customary for every opening segment of Bryce Faceman's news report, Faceman insisted that the camera focus solely on the newscaster, hence the nickname "*The Face*." So from a close-up of the narcissistic reporter the camera slowly moved to King and the BMW.

"Mr. King, why would someone dump a load of what appears to be horse manure over your car?" The camera moved back to Faceman.

"I have no idea. I was exercising at the gym and I came out to this! Just look at my car. It's ruined. It will be impossible to clean up that shit."

The camera panned a quick shot of the car and then back to Faceman.

"How do you explain the sandhill crane statue standing on top of the manure? Are the perpetrators leaving a message?" The camera remained focused on Faceman. "I believe there is a photograph of this car and what appears to be a dead sandhill crane. Care to comment on that information Mr. King?"

"I have no comment. I have no idea who took the picture or when it was taken." The camera slowly moved away from Faceman to King with a puzzled look on his face.

"The R.I.P notation represents rest-in-peace. Is that referring to the sandhill crane or to you, Mr. King? What's your opinion?"

"I have no opinion. All I know is if I find out who did this, I'll kill the son of the bitch. Anyway, my tow truck is pulling up, I have nothing more to say. Move out of my way. I need to talk to the driver." King pushed past Faceman and walked over to the truck.

Immediately the camera focused back on Faceman with his perfectly combed black hair, big bright smile and intense brown eyes. Looking straight at the camera, the reporter ended the news report: "This is Bryce Faceman, Channel 6 News saying goodbye."

Chapter 33

Winthroprealestate.com read like a used car advertisement on a Friday night. The one-page web site glorified the exceptional experience Winthrop Realty extended to its clients and all of Southwest Florida. Winthrop touted the marketing, accounting, mortgage, and contract services it provided in all the steps of home ownership. Highlighted over and over were the *huge* selection of homes, *huge* sales incentives to its customers and *huge* savings for the clients. Color-picture listings of homes in the Sarasota, Manatee, and Venice areas packed the entire page in a dizzying array of listings. Under each photograph in bold letters was Winthrop's slogan: *It's huge Florida.*

"I found it. Winthrop Real Estate. Do you want the Venice or Sarasota office?" Hordowski asked. "Wow, no wonder this guy is loaded, all the homes listed are one million plus. What's the commission on a $1,549,000 home on Bird Key?"

"I think it's six percent. Sometimes the home owner can make a deal and drop it down to five, maybe. Get the Venice address, I'll meet you outside."

"That's $92,940 commission on one house. I'm in

the wrong business," exhaled Hordowski as he threw the calculator down on the desk and printed out the web site.

"So what was the commission? Let me guess eighty-five, no ninety thousand," Beale barked out and headed west on Venice Avenue.

"$92,940. Can you believe that? One house ninety thousand bucks. What if the broker sells two or three places? He'll be millionaire before the age of forty. No wonder Winthrop is rich," Hordowski looked down at the webpage. "The address is 207 Tamiami Trail. I think it's near Miami on the left side of the highway."

"You know the broker only keeps half the commission. The other half goes to the owner of the realty company: Winthrop," Beale pointed out and looked down at the GPS.

"Take a look at that line of crap. The entire window is painted red white and blue; IT'S HUGE VENICE-HUGE HOMES-HUGE SELECTIONS-HUGE SAVINGS" Hordowski laughed. "There's a parking spot right under HUGE," Hordowski drooled until he was out of breath.

"Very funny. Behave yourself in there. This guy could be our killer." Beale pulled open the door and the detectives stepped in.

"Good morning, gentlemen and welcome to Winthrop Realty. How may I help you?" asked the receptionist seated next to the door.

"I'm Detective Beale and this is Detective Hordowski. We would like to see Mr. Winthrop."

"Do you have an appointment with Mr. Winthrop?"

"No," Beale replied and clipped his badge back on to his belt. "We don't require appointments."

"Come in detectives, please come in," Winthrop called out from his office. Rising from behind his desk, Winthrop stuck out his hand and said, "Welcome to Winthrop Realty, I've been expecting you. Please have a seat."

"Expecting the police is an unusual pastime," Beale responded and wrote in his notepad, "Waiting for police with a big question mark."

"Well detectives, after the headline story in the Venice Journal Star about Daisy Clearing's skeleton being discovered, what better individual to interrogate than the boyfriend?" Winthrop leaned back in his chair grinning from ear to ear and oozing an air of superiority.

"Yes, the original report stated that you and Daisy were friends." Beale opened the Daisy Clearing folder and looked down at his notes. Highlighted was Holden Winthrop III, KMI boyfriend.

"We were more than friends, we were in love. Come take a look around the room and you'll see pictures of my time at the Kentucky Military Institute and pictures of Daisy and me together. We were happy and talking about a life together after I finished college."

Together they walked around the office looking at pictures, banners, posters, even Winthrop's KMI uniform standing in the corner at attention. The room was a virtual repository of KMI artifacts chronicling Winthrop's four years at the military school.

"So what happened Mr. Winthrop?" Hordowski began. "Why didn't you and Daisy get married and settle down in Venice?"

"She went to Washington, D.C. and never returned. That's what everyone believed, until now." Winthrop walked over to a gold, ornately framed picture in the center of the back wall, "This picture is a favorite of mine. It was after a Sunday dress parade. Hundreds of people turned out to watch the cadets in full uniform march, and of course local girls were there looking to meet a cadet. This was the first time Daisy and I met. I remember it was hot as hell in that dress uniform, but Daisy asked my friend Larry to take our picture. Being a gentleman as all cadets were, we obliged and here it is today. The rest is history."

"History, what do you mean by history, Mr. Winthrop?" Beale asked and wrote in his notepad, "Cadet Parade, met Daisy Clearing, and drew a camera."

"We were an item, started dating and fell in love. Take a look at the date—January 10, 1963. That was KMI's first dress parade, and from that day on we were inseparable. Here we are waterskiing off Snake Island across from the Crow's Nest Restaurant. Back then the island was about twice the size and boaters from all over would raft up and party all day long. Check out Daisy in that bathing suit. What a body.

Over here is a picture of the Valentine's dance. That night was magical. Formal attire required, dress uniforms for the cadets and ball gowns for all the girls. Daisy was radiant. The only problem, all those damn buttons, a real pain to, well you get the idea ..."

Winthrop grinned and walked over to a basketball sitting on a stand under a green and white banner that read: *1963 Game of the Year.* A little worn-out and cracked by time and handling, Winthrop picked it up and spun it with one finger. "1963 game ball, KMI vs. Venice. It was a home game, our gym is now the Venice Theatre. The gymnasium went wild when I made the final basket. We won 60-31 and I scored a record twenty points. We won both games that year and KMI owned bragging rights for the rest of the year thanks to my performance. I was a hero and was handed the game ball."

"Is this your graduation picture, Mr. Winthrop?" Hordowski asked pointing to a large photograph of a cadet shaking hands with an officer and receiving a diploma.

"It certainly is, Detective, Ormsley Hall, May 26, 1963, Lyndon, Kentucky. That's the Commandant of KMI with me. I look stunning in uniform if I don't say so myself. No wonder the girls took a shine to me." Winthrop pointed to the picture and said, "Not only was I handsome, but I was intelligent, hardworking and resourceful. I was an honor student, an officer, an athlete, and received an academic scholarship to the University of Kentucky. But I imagine your file has all that information. I trust it also states that I started college that August." Winthrop started to count the fingers on his left hand. One, two, three, four, his thumb moved back and forth.

"It does Mr. Winthrop," Beale answered. "I assume that's the reason Detective Jones didn't have your testimony. You were in Kentucky at college when Daisy's parents filed the missing person's report. But what we can't understand was how did Daisy's body end up at Osprey State Park? She was supposed to be in Washington D.C."

"That's what everyone believed. She wrote me in July saying she had her ticket and was going, and that was the last I heard from her. I called her parents, but they were too upset for words. They mentioned that they hired a private detective who went to Washington, but he found out nothing. The local police believed she ran away from home and would return when she needed money." Winthrop walked back to his desk and sat.

"One last question, Mr. Winthrop. What do you think happened to Daisy Clearing?"

Beale turned to a new page in his notepad, and wrote, "College alibi and drew a big UK."

"I told you I don't know why her skeleton was found in Osprey State Park. Why don't you interrogate some her friends from high school? She belonged to some political club, and a few of the students were weird. Question them," Winthrop snapped and took out a cigarette.

"Weird? What exactly do you mean by weird? Mr. Winthrop?"

Beale wrote, "Weird club and drew a picture of a school."

"Daisy said they were always talking about freedom and civil rights. One of the girls and Daisy organized a protest in Plant City over workers' rights in the strawberry industry. I believe it was in the newspaper. They were arrested. Yes, I would advise asking some of the members why Daisy didn't go to Washington, D.C." Winthrop continued to count fingers.

"When was this strawberry protest and who participated in the demonstration with Daisy?" Beale asked and wrote, "Lying in his notepad, and drew a strawberry."

"I don't know who or how many people were involved, but it was during strawberry season in February. The reason I recall February was she missed a dance at KMI and I was left standing at the door with a wilted corsage in my hand. She made up for it the following night when I sneaked out of the dorm and we drove down to the beach." Winthrop took a long drag on the cigarette and blew out a perfect circle into the air.

"Thank you for your time, Mr. Winthrop. We'll be in touch if we need anything more. Have a good day." They shook hands and the detectives left the office.

"He's hiding something," were the first words Beale uttered when they reached the car. "His story seemed rehearsed. Sounded like one of his real estate commercials for television. Something just doesn't sound right, and if doesn't sound right, it is wrong. Did you see him counting his fingers? A nervous tic when he lies. Here take the keys I need to check something while you drive back to the station."

"I also think the pompous ass is lying, but how did the girl get to the park? Did she drive there before going to Washington? If so, why? What was at the park that would make her alter her trip arrangements? Someone had to drive her there. But Winthrop said he was in Kentucky. Perhaps she went to the park after her trip to Washington and was murdered."

Hordowski eased over into the right hand lane, turned onto Venice Avenue and accelerated over the bridge. A powerboat passed under the bridge north towards Sarasota leaving a white foamy wake behind, and Hordowski dreamed again of boat ownership.

"Nothing in the original police report suggested that Daisy's car was missing, so someone drove her to the train station or to the park. The entire report concludes that Daisy Clearing went to Washington, D.C. and disappeared, end of investigation." Beale remarked and flipped through his notepad. "There has to be a connection between Washington, the park and, if I had to guess, Winthrop."

Beale wrote, "Dump site with a big question mark."

"Or was her body just dumped at the park? If so the killer must have been familiar with the operation of the park." Beale closed his notepad.

"You're not suggesting the park may be a dumping ground for murdered girls. And we might have a serial killer on the loose in Venice, Florida." Hordowski drove through the police gates and parked in the rear lot.

"It's just a theory, but I'll tell you, if I was a park official, I'd be extremely concerned about the park's connection to this death. Negative publicity can be a bitch."

Beale checked his notes and suggested that Hordowski locate some of Daisy's high school political club friends, especially that strawberry festival girl, and check out the dates Winthrop attended the University of Kentucky. Beale planned to drive over to Osprey State Park and talk with Blaine Sterling to find out if she had any idea why Daisy Clearing ended up on her doorstep. He was confident that the park was already gathering information on Clearing and that Sterling was leading the investigation. Her skills and determination made her the perfect candidate for the job, and if not mistaken Beale was confident that she had already started compiling a dossier on Daisy

Clearing. Beale also recognized that the park was anxious to put the girl's death to rest with as little negative publicity as possible, so solving the case would be beneficial to both agencies.

Chapter 34

PokeStops and animated monsters turn an ordinary morning into a battleground for teenage players and deranged creatures. Four teenagers with their faces buried in their cell phones crowded up against the front door of Patches Restaurant when Tony Lilly and Hubba Bubba pulled into the parking lot. The kids didn't appear to be waiting in line, only standing in one spot and looking down at their phones.

"See those kids by the door," said Hubba Bubba. "They're probably playing Pokémon Go, a new mobile-phone game where Pokémon creatures appear at different locations in real time, and kids try to capture them."

"Pokémon what?" Tony asked and slammed the truck door shut.

"Pokémon Go, it's the latest craze in videoland. Players walk all over town looking for creatures to capture on their cell phones. I bet there's a Pokémon character near the restaurant. See the girl pointing at the roof, the one with the yellow hat that looks like a mouse? She just shouted, 'Geodude.' It's a creature that looks like a rock with arms. She must have just captured one."

In unison the foursome frantically waved their phones at the roof, moved away from the door, and shuffled back towards the rear of the restaurant.

"Well I can say one good thing about Pokeawhat's Go; the game made them go, leaving the entrance free and clear," laughed Tony and pulled open the door.

They got a friendly smile and warm greeting from the owner Jackie as she escorted them to the last empty table in the back. As usual the room was packed with locals, but that morning with the addition of Pokémon gamers eating and staring at their phones searching for animated monsters, every available table was occupied.

"Good morning boys, what are you having today?" The waitress asked, holding a tablet in her left hand and looking unusually bewildered.

"Victoria, don't tell me you're playing Pokémon Go?" Tony asked shaking his head in disbelief. "What is this world coming to?"

"Way to go, girl," Hubba Bubba shouted and slammed the table, startling the elderly couple across from them. Victoria Koklovia, a large, buxom waitress with a no-nonsense personality, looked completely befuddled.

"Oh no, it's this new digital dining system all the waitresses have to use. Everything is now computerized, Jackie wants all transactions punched in on this iPad, and she informed everyone that Patches needed to move into the twenty-first century, but I'm having a terrible time decoding the different orders. I mix up some of the picture items and when I go to pick up a customer's plate, it's the wrong order. So much for moving into this century."

"Don't give up. It takes time for an old dog to learn new tricks. We're waiting for some more people. I think we'll just have coffee," Tony smiled and opened his newspaper.

"Thanks for the compliment. Do you want your coffee in a cup or poured over your brainless head?" Victoria turned and walked over to the coffee station in the rear of the room.

Ten minutes later Lou Bravo turned into the Patches' parking lot nearly running over a skateboarder gliding down the sidewalk and staring down at his cell phone, oblivious to the world around him. He jammed on his brakes, slammed down on his horn, and shouted out a few choice words to the misguided youth. Unfortunately, or fortunately depending on one's perspective, his greetings fell on deaf ears as the skateboarder headed for the Venice Train Station. Lou Bravo parked and walked into the restaurant. Jackie smiled, handed him a menu and pointed to the table in the back where Tony and Hubba Bubba were seated.

"Good morning boys," Lou Bravo called out and sat down. No sooner had he sat when the waitress walked up to the table, slapped down a cup of coffee and left. "Good morning, Victoria nice to see you. What's wrong with her?"

"Tony called her an old dog," laughed Hubba Bubba and pushed against Tony's arm.

"What's that all about Tony? Now we're going to have problems every time we come into the restaurant?" Lou Bravo took a sip of coffee and waited.

"That's not exactly what I said. She's having trouble with the new computer system Jackie installed last week. I was trying to reassure her that it takes time but she would eventually master the system. You know how long it takes an old dog to learn a new trick? I was just attempting to use a little psychology to relieve some of her stress. I guess it didn't work."

"Great job, Sigmund Freud. You better apologize to her before we leave. Speaking of characters from the past, who the hell is that with Blaine? The guy looks like Mr. Spock from Star Trek."

All three turned and studied the man approaching with Blaine: tall, lanky, straight black hair combed onto his forehead, black pants, boots, blue crew shirt with an upside down triangle insignia, and pointy ears all made for a perplexing individual. Blaine stopped at the table.

"Good morning. I'd like you to meet Myron Weeder, aka Star Trek Guy, president of my computer club. He's on his way to Tampa for the Comic-Con event, but I persuaded him to come to our meeting first. That's the reason for the costume." Blaine smiled and performed all the necessary introductions just as Victoria arrived to take everyone's order.

"Man that is so cool, all the comic book publishers, pop culture programs, movie industry people, toys, games, and celebrities all in one spot for four fantastic days. I'd kill to be there," Hubba Bubba blurted out just as the waitress arrived with the food. "If I gave you some money, do you think you could pick up a Comic-con event program for me?"

"I'll try," answered Star Trek Guy.

"I hear they're having a special screening for the new Star Trek movie. Do you think you could get an autographed copy of the Star Trek program?" Hubba Bubba pleaded and poured maple syrup over his pancakes. "I guess that's why you're dressed as Spock?"

Star Trek Guy smiled, raised his hand, parted his fingers between the middle and ring finger, and gave the Vulcan salute.

"So Blaine, why have you called for this delicious breakfast meeting?" Lou Bravo asked, took a bite of bacon, and smiled. "Extra crispy, just the way I like it, and the reason is..."

"I need your help." For the better part of the meal Blaine explained how she was given the responsibility to discover what happened to Daisy Clearing and what role if any Osprey State Park contributed to her demise. Blaine mentioned that she met with Emma Clearing, Daisy's younger sister, and that she gave her Daisy's diary and suggested she meet with Holden Winthrop III, Daisy's old boyfriend. Before Blaine could continue Lou Bravo interrupted her.

"Winthrop, isn't he that real estate salesman from Venice? The guy yelling on television, 'It's Huge Florida!' That guy tried to sell me a house when I first moved to Venice. What a self-absorbed jerk. He wanted to push me into a million dollar place right on the Gulf. I told him to get lost and used another realtor. Anything I can do to make that pompous ass suffer, count me in."

Lou Bravo looked over at Tony and Hubba Bubba and gave them the Lou Bravo do-or-die stare.

"Count us in also. What's the plan?" asked Tony.

"I need to talk with Winthrop and find out what he knows about Daisy's disappearance. In her diary Daisy writes about how they argued about her going to Washington, D.C. He didn't want her to go, but the unusual thing was ..."

Before Blaine could finish her sentence, Hubba Bubba interrupted, "Why was she going to Washington?"

"Daisy was going to join the March on Washington on August 28, 1963, one of largest civil rights rallies in American history. The train trip from Venice to Washington took two days. Daisy was scheduled to leave Venice on August 26 and arrive early morning on the 28. Her last diary entry on August 25 said she was packed and ready to leave but was upset with the fight she and Winn had that day pertaining to her trip."

"So what's the problem? Winthrop didn't want her to go. I remember watching the march on television, there were thousands of people standing in front of the Lincoln Memorial and listening to Dr. Martin Luther King Jr. give his `I Have a Dream` speech. I would be worried if my girlfriend wanted to travel to a strange city and march around with 200 thousand people," Tony blurted out and looked around the table for moral support only to notice blank stares, and confused looks.

"The problem," Blaine answered, "is that Holden Winthrop III should not have been in Venice on August 25, 1963. All the cadets and teachers from the Kentucky Military Institute left Venice in April to return to their school in Lyndon, Kentucky. I need to find out if he is connected in any way to Daisy's death or at the very least what he knows about the discovery of her skeleton in Osprey State Park."

"So what's the plan and how can we help?" Lou Bravo sat back and took a last bite of bacon and waited.

Blaine unfolded the real estate section of the paper and placed it in the middle of the table. A big red circle highlighted the Winthrop Realty Open House advertisement. In large bold print the words: "Huge house, Huge savings, Huge deal," a picture of the home, the price, address and the date for the open house filled the page.

"Wow what a house! It's made of glass," Hubba Bubba groaned. "Four bedrooms, five baths, theatre, pool, three car garage, on the Gulf, many upgrades, and nestled in a quiet cul-de-sac. Asking price: $3,299,000." He pushed his face up against the picture and sighed, "I could never afford a house like that."

"If you won the Florida Lottery you could," Tony laughed and playfully slapped Hubba Bubba on the back. "On second thought I don't think you're the nestled in a quiet cul-de-sac kinda guy. I see you hanging out with your buddies, drinking beer on the beach in a small cottage in Key West or maybe Englewood."

"My idea is for Lou Bravo and me to question Winthrop at his open house while you and Hubba

Bubba block off the road leading down to the house. This way no prospective buyers can walk in and interrupt our meeting," Blaine offered and pointed to the map on the advertisement.

Tony leaned in and said, "How do you propose Hubba Bubba and I stop prospective buyers from driving to the Open House?"

"That's where Myron comes in," Blaine answered with a big smile and looked over at Star Trek Guy.

From his pants pocket Star Trek Guy pulled out a small, black plastic box the size of garage door remote and placed it in the center of the table. Innocuous in size, shape, and color, the object was designed to serve just one a purpose. A violation of federal law if found on a person and subject to a $10 thousand fine, Star Trek Guy carefully passed over the red button on the top of the appliance and pressed the green one. Immediately pandemonium spread throughout the restaurant. A silent catastrophe was unfolding at all the tables where gamers sat enjoying breakfast. Furiously, individual players punched away at their devices exasperated with every stroke that touched their keypads. Blank screens appeared in the spaces that once were filled with magical monsters and unimaginable challenges to be conquered. A half dozen players ran from the room with panicked expressions leaving behind plates of uneaten food and dollar bills for the waitresses to clear off and collect.

Victoria looked down at her iPad and smiled. Nothing worked! No items, no prices, no icons, no iPad this morning. She pulled out her notepad and pencil and cheerfully announced to one of the regulars, "Good morning Ed, what can I get you?" Up at the main counter a blank screen and a locked cash register greeted Jackie with alarm. In a panic she checked all the plugs running from the cash register to an outlet bundle behind the counter. All secure. She powered down the computer and waited.

Star Trek Guy pressed the red button and quickly put the box back into his pocket. Suddenly a joyous roar from the tables echoed throughout the room. Gamers yelled, clapped, and held their phones high in the air as cell phones lit up, the cash register opened and all the iPads operated flawlessly. Everyone was overjoyed with the return of service; all except Victoria, who was dispirited when her iPad went on line. "So much for the good ol' days," she said and ripped out the order from her notepad. "So Ed, what are you having again?"

"Star Trek Guy is a computer genius. Not only is he president of our computer club, but the interior of his 1971 classic Volkswagen Bus is a replica of the bridge of the Starship Enterprise and outfitted with computer technology that NASA would envy," Blaine said softly. "As you observed, the cell phone-blocking device he designed can disable cell phone communication at a press of a button, plus a whole lot more, but I'll let him explain."

"The blocking device will disable all cell phone frequencies at a range of up to a hundred square meters plus reroute all calls to my computers in my bus and deliver a prepared message explaining that the open house Winthrop is hosting has been cancelled due to unforeseen circumstances and is rescheduled for the following Saturday. For further information please call Winthrop Realty at (941) 484-2000."

"Unforeseen circumstances, what the hell does that mean?" Lou Bravo blurted out and gulped down the last of his coffee.

"That's where Tony and Hubba Bubba come in," Blaine interjected. "They will be parked at the entrance to the open house driveway. All cell phone communications in the area will be cut off via Star Trek's bus that will be parked at the top of the lane. So whatever excuse they mention, no one will be able to substantiate it."

"And what is the unforeseen reason that the open house has been cancelled?" Said Tony sarcastically, looking directly at Blaine with a blank expression across his face.

"I got it! A friend of mine, Spike Chandler has a pet boa constrictor. The thing is about ten feet long, weighs about twenty pounds, and is always getting out of its cage and slithering around the house. We can tell all the drivers that Mr. Winthrop reported seeing a large snake on the property, and for safety concerns, the open house has been canceled." Hubba Bubba, feeling full of himself, folded his arms across his chest, which was twice the size it was two minutes ago, and sat back in his chair.

"That's a great idea, but let's say two snakes have been reported in the area, and we'll have your friends in a cage for all the drivers to see. Do you think your friend would let us borrow his snake for a few hours?" Blaine asked.

"Tell your friend we'll give him a hundred bucks to rent the snake. I'll have some rescue company lettering on the side of my El Camino and on your truck, Tony," Lou Bravo barked out. "That should convince every prospective home buyer that the open house has been canceled."

"I don't want snake lettering painted on my truck. Besides, Clean Sweep lettering is already painted on both sides advertising my janitorial business."

"I'll buy magnetic lettering," added Lou Bravo. "All we need to do is slap the sign on the vehicles and off we go. We're snake hunters, but we need a name, something that people will believe. Nothing stupid like Snake Boys. Anyone have a suggestion?"

"Venice Reptile Rescue," Blaine replied. "The sign needs to have a picture of a large boa constrictor, an alligator, map of Florida, and a fake telephone number linked to Star Trek Guy's computer. That should help legitimize the operation."

Lou Bravo looked down at the advertisement. "The paper says the open house is this Saturday, ten in the morning until four in the afternoon. That gives us two days to prepare for Mr. Holden Winthrop III's intervention party. Let's meet at Tony's warehouse at nine o'clock and then drive to the Open House together." Everyone nodded in agreement and finished their meals.

"Before we leave I'd like to present to Tony a security computer hat that I have been testing and hope to market by the end of the year. On the visor is a miniature camera and audio device that records real-time events a person is experiencing and sends the information back to a central computer for storage at my lab." Star Trek Guy handed a hat to Tony and Hubba Bubba.

"Wow, these hats are cool, I dig the teal green color, and it goes great with our khaki uniforms. Plus the fancy scroll lettering, Clean Sweep on the front, really stands out. People will definitely get the idea that we are a cleaning company. I'll start wearing mine today," Hubba Bubba squealed and quickly pulled on his hat.

"Blaine mentioned that you operated a janitorial service and most of your work is performed at night. The cameras are equipped with infra-red technology, the pictures are developed with daylight clarity precision, and the audio transmission can pick up crystal-clear reception up to thirty meters. If you don't mind I'd like to test the accuracy of the product while you and your employees perform your duties for a one-month trial period."

Star Trek Guy pressed a key on his cell phone and activated the hats.

"That would be fine, but how do you turn the hat off? There will be times I don't want it recording my business; you know what I mean." Tony took off the hat and felt around the brim for a switch.

“You just did. The program is heat sensitive to body temperature so when the hat is removed it positions into a sleep mode program and is not activated again until you put it back on your head.”

“Don’t wear the hat Saturday!” Lou Bravo barked, and pointed at Hubba Bubba. “We don’t want to do any advertising that day. Understand?”

Hubba Bubba nodded. He got the message loud and clear.

Outside everyone watched in awe as Star Trek Guy waved the trio a Vulcan salute and pulled out of the parking lot. “I hope this guy knows what he’s doing,” Lou Bravo groaned and shot Blaine a skeptical glance. “If not, all of us may be spending some real time in jail watching reruns of Star Trek instead of depending on the expertise of a make believe Star Trek impersonator.”

“You worry too much. See you Saturday,” smiled Blaine and gave him a Vulcan wave.

Chapter 35

Locals call it the Big Squeeze. Drivers who ply the road daily call it something less endearing and scream it out their windows at the workers at each backup. The two mile construction zone on Tamiami Trail at the Venice loop pinched the southbound, four-lane highway into a compressed, angled single lane, and added at least twenty minutes to the commute.

Detective Beale cursed as he joined the line of cars stopped behind a flagman standing in the middle of the road. A dusty, beat-up, black dump truck piled high with dirt, rocks, and concrete inched forward onto the road and jerked to a stop. A workman, dressed in a clean uniform, presumably the foreman, ambled over to truck and shouted, "What's the problem?"

The driver frantically moved and turned in his seat, as he attempted to restart the engine. Banging his head on the steering wheel, the driver sat motionless for a time. Then in a panic he threw open the door and with hammer in hand ran over to the front of the truck, opened the hood, and smashed away on the engine. With each blow a metallic sound echoed down the road increasing in volume with each strike.

Beale couldn't understand what would possess a person to go berserk and pound away at his vehicle with such violence just because it stalled out in the middle of the road. In Beale's mind this could possibly be an extreme case of road rage that could escalate into something more tragic. Beale was about to exit his car when the truck driver slammed down the hood, jumped into the truck, and started the engine. A cloud of black smoke rose from the chrome exhaust stacks behind the truck's cab as the diesel roared to a start. "Battery cables, loose connections, happens all the time. All I need to do is hammer it a few times, and the problem is solved," the driver yelled and inched up onto the highway.

As the truck crossed the lane, Beale laughed out loud when he spotted the name of the trucking company painted on the side of the cab's door: Hammer Trucking. "Now there's a man who takes his work literally," Beale thought to himself. "I wonder if all drivers are issued a company hammer for emergency road repairs."

Beale eased off the brake as the flagman waved the cars forward. Traffic was still bumper to bumper until the Winn-Dixie Shopping Plaza, and then with the four-lane highway open, cars accelerated and raced north on Tamiami Trail.

Twenty minutes later, Beale was in bumper to bumper traffic again. But this time it was at the entrance to Osprey State Park. Coming to a complete stop, Beale counted ten cars lined up in front of him and the taillights of two vans driving down the road past the ranger station. After what seemed an eternity, Beale finally pulled up to the ranger station and rolled down his window. Standing in the doorway was Ranger Rob Collins, a recent transplant from Colorado's snow country, enjoying the sunny warmth of Florida. "Welcome to Osprey State Park. Are you here for the Literacy Amongst the Trees Program?"

"No, I'm Detective Beale and I'm here to see Assistant Manager Sterling." Beale held up his credentials.

"She is up at the Nature Center where the literacy program is taking place. If you have a book to donate, today's admission fee is waived," Ranger Rob announced.

"That's why the backup, free admission. See my badge? That's my admission. Have a nice day." Beale pushed down on the accelerator and drove away.

Ranger Rob waved goodbye, turned to the next visitor, and said, "Welcome to Osprey State Park..."

Beale followed the line of cars down the main road that passed under a lush, green canopy of leaves from ancient oaks that bordered both sides of the road. Spanish moss cascaded from thin, green branches like dusty lace curtains filtering out the bright summer sunshine. A cool breeze blew in through the window and Beale breathed in its sweet country nectar.

At the top of the hill the landscape took on a drastic transformation that minutes before was totally green, and beautiful. Off to the left and right of the road, a burnt-out forest of trees and grasslands greeted visitors. Unsightly at first glance, both sides of the road were the site of a controlled burn the previous month that cleared more than fifty acres of the scrubby flatwoods. Overgrown and smothering the food source of the Florida scrub jay, and a possible site of future uncontrolled wild fires, park officials cleared the land with fire to ensure a safe and fruitful habitat for wildlife to thrive in.

The parking lot was packed, but Beale managed to squeeze into a spot against the split rail fence that ringed the picnic area adjacent to the Nature Center. He followed a group of women carrying armloads of books up to the Nature Center. "Here let me get the door for you," Beale called out and pulled open the door to the porch where people were gathered looking at books.

"Thank you," the ladies called out, and disappeared into the crowd of book lovers reading, laughing, and perusing the novels that lined a large table in the center of the room.

Beale didn't see Blaine, so he turned and walked over to the Nature Center. Inside Blaine and a group of women were listening to Brenda Spalding, a local author and co-founder of ABC Books 4 Children and Adults, finish talking about her new novel *Honey Tree Farm,* an exciting story about a young couple who after their car runs off the road finds refuge at a farmhouse. There an old woman recounts the story of how she came to live at Honey Tree Farm.

Amongst rousing applause and cheers, Beale called over to Blaine, "Assistant Manager Sterling, may I have a word?"

Blaine looked up and waved just as her phone rang, "Hello. Yes, I'll be there in a minute. I'm at the Nature Center. No, don't do a thing; keep your distance."

Blaine walked across the room and said, "Hi detective, we have a problem at the campground. Care to join me?"

"Sure. What's the problem? Don't tell me it's another ATV digging up the park again. I remember the night when we arrested that big guy and his family. What was his name, Charlie something? He's still in jail for driving the boat when that ranger shot you. What was that guy's name?" Beale opened the back door and they walked down towards the lake.

"Charlie Boltier, and no it's not another ATV bulldozing the old section of the park," said Blaine. "The camp host spotted a man walking down the road with a fishing pole, a Bible, and mumbling something about fishing for Jesus."

"So what's the problem, maybe he's a very religious fisherman? Last time I heard it's not a crime to fish with a Bible," laughed Beale.

"No, but it's against the law to fish naked. And by the screams coming from the lake, I would say that the naked fisherman had arrived."

"That's him," the camp host shouted as a cluster of adults and children exited the water and hurriedly left the beach. "Wally Longfelder. You can't see because he's waist deep, but he's not wearing a bathing suit. I can tell you that!"

Standing in the center of the swimming area, waist deep, Bible raised to the sky, and singing "Onward Christian soldiers," was a short man, with weightlifter's arms, broad shoulders, bald head and a back covered in tufts of brown hair, fishing.

"Mr. Longfelder, fishing is not permitted in the swimming area. Please move over to the side embankment or to the closest fishing dock." Blaine shouted. The fisherman didn't budge.

"Mr. Longfelder, you need to leave the swimming area now. It's a safety concern. We don't want any bathers injured by stepping on a discarded hook or getting hooked from an unsound cast. The fishing is far superior over by the reeds. Just last week a ten-year-old girl caught a monster sunny. Right over there." Blaine pointed to the stand of cattails off to her right. The fisherman didn't budge.

No sooner had Blaine pointed to the reeds she marched across the beach and into the water. She wrapped her arms around the fisherman and hugged him tight. His large arms fell to his sides and he began to cry uncontrollably. "She left me. My wife left me for someone else," he mumbled between the tears.

Still holding him tight, Blaine turned the fisherman around and they both walked towards the shore where an EMT operator waited with a blanket. Still sobbing, Mr. Longfelder was placed in an ambulance and taken to the hospital for observations.

"That ended well. Except for one thing; I hope your

cell phone isn't in your pocket," said Beale.

Blaine reached down into the sand and picked up a phone.

"Pretty tricky. I never saw you drop it. Great planning. However I hope you have a change of clothes back at the office, or you're going to be very uncomfortable for the rest of the day." Beale smiled.

"I do. Follow me back to the office. I'll put on dry clothes, and we can have our meeting. I have something to give you." They walked off the beach to their vehicles and drove back to Blaine's office.

Ugly black clouds piled together over the lake. A light drizzle fell and tiny round circles dotted the lake's surface like freckles on a young child's face. A jagged flash of light broke behind a line of pine trees, crossed the sky, and reflected off the water a mirrored glow upwards into the dark clouds. Seconds later a clap of thunder shook the sky and hailstones the size of marbles rained down from above. Blaine and Beale raced up the stairs to the office, slipping and sliding over a layer of white hailstones that covered the wooden structure.

"We just made it," Blaine said. "I'm going to change out of these wet clothes. Have a seat. There's water in the fridge."

Rubbing his head, Beale flopped down on the couch and said, "I got hit in the head getting out of my car and I think I have a small bump right in the center. Ouch. I can just imagine what my new paint job is going to look like after the storm; ouch again."

He looked out the window and watched the hailstones bounce off the Crown Victoria. "That doesn't look good," he thought and collapsed back down on the couch.

"Dry again. I feel like a new person. So Detective Beale, what information about the murdered girl can you share with me?" Blaine sat down at the conference table and waited for Beale to join her.

"Before I begin I would like to convey my deepest sympathies for the death of Ryan Murphy. It was such a tragedy. I'm so sorry for your loss. I was wondering what is going to happen to the cave and his body?" asked Beale.

"Thank you. It was such a shock. The project was progressing well, everything seemed safe and they made significant discoveries. I was inside the cave the day before the accident and nothing appeared unsound, especially to indicate the presence of a sinkhole." Blaine reached over to her desk, grabbed a file folder and a pink diary. She removed a letter from the folder and handed it to Beale. It was from the State declaring that the cave area was safe, and that the park could re-open the grounds to the public.

"That's good news," said Beale.

"Next month we're having a memorial service at the site. A plaque to commemorate Ryan Murphy's life and the work he performed at the dig will be permanently displayed. Local and State officials will be present as well as a contingent of Native American representatives who will accept the artifacts Ryan's team unearthed. So now, detective, what news do you have pertaining to the death of Daisy Clearing?" Blaine opened her notepad and waited.

Over the next hour, as heavy rain pelted the office, Beale outlined the report from the coroner's office, the meeting with Emma Clearing, the cold case file report, the notes from Detective Purdy Jones, and finally the meeting with Winthrop. The volumes of information led Beale and Hordowski no closer to solving the crime than it did Jones in 1963. "Right now Hordowski is checking on Daisy's high school friends, and the train station. Maybe someone can tell us why she was in the park and not Washington, D.C." Beale closed his notepad.

"I also spoke to Emma Clearing. She stopped by the park to lay a wreath at the foot of the canoe dock in honor of her sister. She mentioned that she spoke with you, and after your visit she found Daisy's diary. I think you need to look at her last entry." Blaine pushed the pink diary across the table.

Beale flipped to the last page and turned red. "That lying bastard. He said he was in Kentucky attending the University of Kentucky. I knew his answers were too pat."

Trying to regain his composure, Beale closed the book, reached into his coat pocket, and took out his notepad. He wrote, "Talk to Winthrop, and drew a picture of the diary with an exclamation mark."

"I photocopied the diary yesterday so I could give it to you. So the questions remain, who took Daisy to the park? Did Winthrop drive her to the train station? Did she travel to Washington, and then come back to park? Why was she murdered, if indeed she was?"

"We are checking on the train ticket angle attempting to find out if she boarded the Venice train or not. One thing I do know is that we will be interviewing Mr. Winthrop again."

Beale stood, thanked Blaine for the diary and left. The rain had stopped. Beale ran his hand across the cruiser's hood and smiled. No damage.

Once outside his cell phone rang, Hordowski was on the other end, and reported that he had a few names of Daisy's friends, but wasn't too successful with finding anything substantive at the train depot.

"I have some news. Sterling gave me Daisy's diary, and Winthrop was in Venice at the time of her death. That bastard lied. We need to interview him again on Monday."

"How did Sterling get the diary?"

"Emma Clearing visited the park and gave it to her. Anyway, I'll be in Tampa on Saturday for that Neighborhood Policing seminar. We'll visit Holden Winthrop III Monday morning."

Beale clicked off and drove out of the parking lot.

Halfway down the road a gopher tortoise lumbered across the blacktop, its thick brown legs laboriously pushing against the macadam moving its hulk painfully forward. Beale jerked the car to a stop and stared at the beast pull and slide in front of his vehicle. “That’s how this case is progressing,” Beale said to himself. “Painfully slow.”

Chapter 36

Three orange construction cones blocked the entrance to 3047 Gulf View Lane. On either side of the long cobblestone driveway two vehicles stood with lights flashing. The name Venice Reptile Rescue Coalition in bold red, white, and blue lettering was pasted to their doors. Tony and Hubba Bubba, dressed in matching khaki uniforms, stood alongside the El Camino that housed the pet boa constrictor and waited for the first potential buyer to arrive. They didn't have to wait very long.

At eleven o'clock a red, Porsche Boxster convertible roared up the lane and screeched to a stop inches in front of the cones. The agitated driver, a middle-aged man, bald, overweight, and wearing too much gold, and his female companion half his age were irritated to see a barricade impeding their journey. "What's the meaning of this? I have an eleven o'clock meeting with Mr. Winthrop to look at a house."

"I'm sorry sir, but Mr. Winthrop canceled the open house today," said Hubba Bubba as he stepped forward to get a better look at the car, and the young lady.

"He didn't tell me the showing was cancelled. I drove all the way from St. Petersburg to see this house, and now my meeting is cancelled. We'll see about that."

The driver pulled out his phone, dialed, and listened. A pre-scripted recording apologized for the inconvenience and stated that today's open house has been re-scheduled for next Saturday. It emphasized that Mr. Winthrop would compensate in a huge way all prospective home buyers that were turned away. The driver slammed his phone down on the console and glowered up at Hubba Bubba.

"I'll give you a hundred bucks if you let me see the house," said the driver.

"No one is permitted to drive past the barricade," Tony answered and stepped up to the car.

"What is the problem? Why are employees of the Venice Reptile Rescue Coalition blocking off a public road? Do I have to call the cops?"

"Snakes sir!" said Tony. "When Mr. Winthrop arrived this morning he saw a large snake slithering through the bushes alongside the pool. He contacted our organization and we captured a ten foot boa constrictor about an hour ago. Our people are still on site and believe they have cornered another snake under the porch, but they are having trouble extricating the reptile. Would you like to see the boa we captured?"

"Of course not. This whole experience has been a big waste of time. I don't plan on staying one minute more, and you can tell Winthrop to go shove his *Huge House Deal.* I won't be back."

"Oh honey buns, I'd love to see that big old snake. I'll take a selfie with that bad ole snake. Please..."

Without a reply she was out of the car and walking over to the yellow El Camino. Hubba Bubba pulled off the canvas tarp. There in a glass-enclosed aquarium the size of a small desk was the snake. Curled up in a ball, the yellow and brown snake sprang from its corner position and smashed into the glass trying to attack the visitors. Immediately, the young lady took out her phone and clicked away.

"Here take a picture of me next to the snake." She handed her phone over to Hubba Bubba. He took three pictures in different stages of crazy facial expressions, and then she was back in the car speeding back out of the neighborhood without even a thank you.

Two minutes later a red and white Mini Copper drove up. "How's business?" A voice asked, "We saw a shiny red convertible speed away. The driver looked annoyed. Any problems?" asked Blaine with a smile.

"No problems at all. The young lady wanted her picture taken with the snake. That sealed the deal. They were out of here like a bat out of hell."

Tony picked up a cone, and the Mini Cooper drove down the driveway. The cobblestone pavers circled the front of the house ending at a three-car garage where they parked next to a bronze Jaguar EJ with vanity plates HUGE 1.

The full page advertisement did not do the house justice. The two-story glass and white concrete front was breathtaking. Two thirty-foot glass-enclosed entrance doors surrounded on both sides by massive clay pots filled with fan palms added a welcome touch of nature. A sign standing next to the door instructed visitors to enter. A Chihuly chandelier hanging from the foyer ceiling intensified the grandeur of the home with its multicolored glass appendages gleaming in the sun. Beyond the foyer marble stairs led to the second floor where Winthrop stood with arms open wide. "Welcome, I'm Holden Winthrop. Please come up, and enjoy the view."

The upstairs living room was beyond belief, Blaine thought. The entire room was glass, with a panoramic view of the Gulf from every corner. Elegant contemporary furnishings, a stone fireplace, a grand piano, and a collection of Florida landscapes adorned the walls. "The view alone is worth three million, don't you think?" said Winthrop as he held out his hand.

"At least," Blaine replied and shook his hand. "I'm Blaine Sterling, and this is my friend Lou Bravo."

Lou Bravo returned an acknowledged nod and unbuttoned his sports coat. Winthrop glanced down and then quickly looked back at Blaine.

"As you can see this custom-built home is equipped with every modern convenience a discerning homeowner could demand. Expansive rooms, a spacious master suite, separate guest rooms, a professional kitchen with state-of-the-art appliances, an oversized dining area that seats ten comfortably. Outside a vanishing pool set in a lush garden of palm trees and flowers offers a hidden oasis looking out at the Gulf of Mexico and your own private beach." Winthrop stepped away from the windows and said, "I am told that the owner has been transferred back to Dubai and is anxious to sell. Let me show you the master suite."

"I'm not interested in purchasing the home, Mr. Winthrop; I'm only interested in speaking with you about Daisy Clearing." Blaine pulled out the pink diary from her purse.

Winthrop's face flushed, and in an irritated tone, he asked, "What's this all about? I spoke to the police a couple of days ago and told them everything I knew about the case." Winthrop stared at the diary, glanced at Lou Bravo and then quickly back at Blaine. He began to count the fingers on his left hand. One, two, three, four, his thumb moved back and forth in an agitated cadence. "Who are you?" The finger counting continued.

"I am the assistant manager at Osprey State Park and I am investigating the death of Daisy Clearing and what if any implications the park may have contributed in her death. Emma Clearing gave me Daisy's diary and it appears that you were in Venice at the time of her death. A point of fact Daisy wrote in her diary. She was worried that you were not going to drive her to the train station, which you conveniently neglected to tell Detective Beale. Would you like me to read the entry, Mr. Winthrop?"

"No that won't be necessary. Yes, I was in Venice. My father opened his real estate company in August and we were living in Venice. In 1963 that buffoon of a detective Purdy Jones didn't bother to question me because he assumed all the KMI cadets were back in Kentucky, plus he was convinced Daisy was in Washington, D. C. When he phoned my parents they informed him that I was attending the University of Kentucky."

"But you weren't at the university yet, so did you take Daisy to the train station?" Blaine took a step closer and waited. Winthrop began to count fingers.

"No, I drove her to the park. I thought I could convince her not to go, but we argued. She wouldn't listen to a word I said. She said she had to go, that the country was on a collision course regarding civil rights and that she wanted to be part of the march. She believed that the March on Washington would change the lives of Americans, and she had to be a participant. So I left her at the park."

"That's it. You just drove away," Blaine stared straight into his eyes.

"Yes, I drove away. We broke up that day. I told her she had to decide between that damn march or me. She said she was going to Washington. So I left her there all dressed up, red suitcase in hand, and defiant expression on her face." Winthrop cleared his throat, and added, "I wanted to spend the rest of my life with her, but she chose to go the Washington, or so everyone thought." The finger counting continued.

"Why did you drive her to the park?"

"We loved the park. It was our special place, plus we could make out without anyone hassling us. We were teenagers." Winthrop laughed, and stopped counting his fingers.

"Where in the park did you leave Daisy?" asked Blaine.

"Back in the `60s there wasn't much to the park. A single dirt road wound through brush and trees and stopped at a picnic areas near the lake and the creek. I parked near the lake. There were people picnicking, and I think some kids fishing in the lake. It was a long time ago. That's all I can remember."

Winthrop's finger counting started up again.

"Why don't you talk to some of her friends from school? She belonged to some political club. They were a bunch of nut cases—always complaining, or protesting about something wrong with this or that. Go see her friend Strawberry Girl, a Gilda something. I forget her last name, but that fruitcake is on the front page of the newspaper. Talk to her," Winthrop coughed out.

"The Venice Journal Star?" asked Blaine, and looked over at Lou Bravo.

"I have one in the car," said Lou Bravo.

"Yes, the Star. She chained herself to a banyan tree last night to protest the bank's decision to cut the tree down to expand their parking lot." Winthrop started finger counting. "They were thick as thieves, always planning another protest. Talk to her. She may know something. Now if you'll excuse me, if you're not interested, I have a house to sell. Good day."

Blaine smiled. Lou Bravo flipped his jacket open enough for Winthrop to view the butt of his Glock 29. They walked down the stairs, and back to the car.

"We're done here, Tony. Please call Star Trek Guy and tell him to put Winthrop back on line. Thanks for everything."

"I need my paper. It's on the floor," Lou Bravo called out. "Nice bubble Hubba Bubba. Try not to get it all over your face...Too late."

"Speaking of newspapers, I read last week about a purple truck dumping horse manure all over a BMW convertible and leaving a sandhill crane sign accusing the driver of killing the bird."

Blaine removed the article from her pocket and waved it in the air. "I was wondering if you and your friends were responsible for this bit of mischief?"

"Mr. King needed to be taught a lesson. Talking on your cell phone while driving puts people and animals at risk. Tony saw him on the phone when he killed the sandhill crane. He kept on driving, didn't even turn around to see what he had done."

Lou Bravo folded his paper over to the front page. There covering the entire page was a picture of a woman perched high on a banyan tree, and chained to a large branch. The headline read: Venice Resident Protests Banyan Tree Death.

"Gilda Gooseberry. That's the name of the Strawberry Girl. If I had a name like that I'd change it to Strawberry Girl in a heartbeat." Lou Bravo held up the paper.

"She looks a little old to be climbing trees," Blaine said. "From the looks of her, maybe a letter to the editor would have been a safer strategy." Blaine turned onto Tamiami Trail and drove south back to Tony's building.

"She's seventy, owns a tree farm in East Venice, and is a pro-environment activist. She was arrested last year for demonstrating in front of the Whole Food Market in Sarasota for their proposed expansion over wetland property. She refused to plead guilty or post bond and spent three days in county jail."

The front page picture showed a woman dressed in brown and green camouflage fatigues and a red beret nestled within a clump of thick branches high in a banyan tree. Her thin weathered face lined by sun and age was eclipsed by her wide, cat-like green eyes that stared defiantly at the camera. A rope was attached to a small bucket that she used to send down messages or haul up supplies. Over her head, an American flag flapped in the wind, and below the flag a large sign read: “Save Our Banyan Tree.” Hundreds of cards and letters adorned the sign supporting the protest. On the ground groups of people were photographed circling the tree or marching back and forth on the sidewalk in front of the bank. More than a hundred demonstrators were recorded on the first day, and organizers predicted the same number of protesters the following days.

“So should we join the circus?” said Lou Bravo.

“No, I don’t think so. You’ve helped enough. I think I’ll go by myself in a couple of days when the melodrama has calmed down. Anyway, Brooke and I are going to spend Sunday with her grandfather. He finished restoring all the carousel horses, and on Monday the last nineteen horses will be trucked to Greenport, Long Island, and placed with the twenty other horses to complete the center attraction along their harbor walk carousel.”

“No problem. Call me if you need a hand, or a gun.”

“I don’t think that will be necessary. Thank you for everything.” Blaine pulled up to the Clean Sweep building, dropped Lou Bravo off, and drove away.

Chapter 37

Mountains of confectioners sugar covered the plate of homemade brownies that sat on the back seat of Blaine's Mini Cooper as she and Brooke drove down the driveway. Brooke turned around and stared at the brownies dreaming of the soft chocolate delights melting in her mouth. "Do I have to put the brownies in the trunk?" said Blaine. "It's the third time you turned around and looked at them."

"They smell delicious. Do you think I can have just one?" Brooke moaned.

"No, they're for Grandpa Connelly. How would it look if you walked into his house with sugar spots all over your pink dress?" Blaine down shifted and merged onto I-75. "Please turn around we'll be there in about one hour, and then you can have a brownie."

Twenty minutes later Blaine exited onto Route 64, a two-lane highway with nothing but empty expanses of farmland and palm trees. An occasional cow pushed up against the fence that bordered the road, but other than that there were miles of unspoiled land. A semi-trailer carrying a load of building supplies sped by from the opposite direction, creating a wind that practically forced their car off the road. With a white-knuckled grip on the steering wheel, Blaine, steadied the vehicle and kept driving towards County Road 674. "Wow, that was a big gust of wind. Good driving Mommy," said Brooke.

"Thanks Sweetie, we're getting closer. The sign we just passed said six more miles until our turnoff."

"Mommy, do you think Grandpa Connelly is sad when he sees us?"

"Sad, why would he be sad?" Blaine said in a surprised tone. "He seemed happy to me. Why would you ask such a question?"

"Maybe because we remind him of his dead son. The baby he and Grandma gave up for adoption when they were first married. And then to be told that he died in a car crash trying to find his birth parents—the memories are so sad." Brooke looked over at her mother. A tear rolled down the face of the nine-year-old.

"Oh Sweetie, no! Grandpa Connelly is so happy to have us as part of his family. Don't ever think he is sad to be with us. Yes, he misses your father deeply, so do we, but he is so happy to have a granddaughter and daughter-in-law." Blaine reached over and squeezed her daughter's hand.

"I guess you're right. Every time we see him he's smiling, and telling jokes. He must be happy." Brooke smiled and wiped away the tear. "Oh Mommy, is this turn where Daddy crashed into the woods?"

"Yes it is. Rutland Road and 675. And it took eight years before a news helicopter covering an accident spotted your father's car in the woods. Hold on Sweetie, I'm about to turn and then drive over to the Fish Camp. Weee..."

"Fantastic, maybe we can rent a rowboat and go fishing," Brooke shouted as her body was pushed against door.

The Mini Cooper made a left and continued a few

yards onto a cracked shell parking lot, that rolled up to an old, weathered cedar shake building with a screened in wraparound porch. Laughing hysterically, the pair clambered out of the car and up the steps to the fish camp. The screen door slammed behind them as they stepped inside. The store hadn't changed since their visit last year. Fishing equipment of all varieties, brands, and styles filled the room from floor to ceiling. Ancillary items for the fishing family were for sale: hats, waders, buckets, nets, hooks, fillet knives, and numerous cleaning supplies.

"Hello ladies. Welcome to the Myakka Fish Camp. How can I help you?" A voice from behind the counter asked. There standing next to a vintage brass Michigan cash register was Boaty Johnson, a lifelong fisherman and owner of the establishment. Weathered from seventy-three years of fishing, boating, and working on the waters of Florida, his leathery body scarred by time and the sun, he still retained a handsome roughness attributed to living outdoors. Boaty's big smile, bright blue eyes, and cheerful sense of humor were his trademark introduction to the fish camp.

"Hello, I'm Blaine Sterling and this is my daughter Brooke. We were in your store last year and inquired about renting a boat to go fishing; but due to unforeseen circumstances, we never did get a chance to do any fishing."

"I remember. You're Dillon Connelly's daughter-in-law and granddaughter, and I believe you wanted to rent a canoe. How can I help you?" Boaty smiled and moved from behind the counter.

"I stopped in to thank you for notifying the police that Thor Boltier was going to burn down Dillon's barn, and more than likely shoot us attempting to put the fire out. We are very grateful that you had the courage and moral fortitude to call the authorities." Blaine stuck out her hand.

"Well thank you, Missy. That Thor was always a mean son of a bitch. I'm sure it was his old man who put him up to it; you know on the account he is in prison for driving the boat when that fired ranger shot you. Dillon is a good man and a hell of a woodcarver." Boaty took Blaine's hand, and immediately pulled her in, and gave her a mighty bear hug. "I guess the two of you are going up to Dillon's to see the horses. What a show. I'd swear those horses were alive and kicking, especially that big black one. I looked straight into that horse's eyes and I felt the cold shivers. I'll tell you that horse was looking right back at me. Yes sir, right back at me."

"Grandpa had a horse show," said Brooke. "How come we weren't invited?"

"It was last Saturday. Everyone from town was invited. I would say over a hundred people showed up, maybe more. He probably wants to give you both a private tour. In a way it was better you weren't at the community show because of the incident." Boaty immediately covered his mouth as if to retrieve the last word he uttered, but it was too late. The proverbial cat was out of the bag.

"Incident, what incident?" asked Blaine with a tone of agitation.

"Oh it was nothing," said Boaty, attempting to undo the damage he created moments before. "Just two teenage girls fooling around and getting hurt. That's all. I'm sure Dillon will tell you the rest." Just then the phone rang. Relieved, Boaty walked behind the counter and picked up the phone. "I need to take this, it's a supplier, please give my best to Dillon for me. Hello, fish camp."

Blaine and Brooke waved goodbye and walked back to the car. Blaine pulled out of the parking lot and headed towards Dillon Connelly's house. "Mommy, what is an incident?" asked Brooke.

"It's when something happens that could be a

problem."

"What kind of problem?" Brooke asked.

"I don't know Sweetie. Probably nothing at all, but I plan to find out when we get to Grandpa's house."

Five minutes later, a large green sign, "Connelly's Woodcarvings and Furniture," directed them to a narrow driveway that emptied onto a large, gravel parking fronting Connelly's farmhouse and studio. They parked up against the white, split rail fence that bordered the entire parking lot, picked up the brownies, and followed the brick path to the house. Dillon Connelly waved from the wrap-around porch and yelled, "Just in time for lunch."

Seated, Blaine and Brooke relaxed in the imposing beauty of their surroundings. Lush floor and hanging plants dotted the porch with color and a hint of jasmine. White wicker chairs, tables and a love seat arranged along the back corner of the porch looked out onto a small pond covered with water lilies, pickerelweed and arrowhead plants. Just beyond the pond, acres of forest land untouched by construction, or human demands completed the vista. "I hope everyone likes tuna salad sandwiches, potato salad, lemonade, and let us not forget—homemade brownies for dessert," crowed Connelly as he passed the plate of sandwiches.

Everyone helped themselves. Even finicky eater Brooke took a large spoonful of homemade potato salad, which was out of character, but a welcome change for her mother.

"Well, Brooke, all the carousel horses are glued, sanded and painted; and tomorrow they will be trucked to their new home in New York. Would you like to take one last look before they ride off into the sunset?" Connelly asked.

"Oh yes, Grandpa, but first I have to have one more brownie."

"Isn't that your third brownie, Sweetie," teased

Blaine. "By the looks of all the confectioners sugar on your dress, someone would think you finished the entire plate."

"Who's counting anyway? We're having a party, a going-away party for Grandpa's beautiful horses, cheers." Brooke smiled, and popped a brownie into her mouth. Powdery sugar sprinkled down on her new pink dress, already covered in white creating a winter wonderland effect from top to bottom. Everyone laughed.

Blaine took a sip of lemonade and waited for the cool liquid to slowly refresh her taste buds with a sweet tang of lemon before she spoke. Choosing her words carefully, she leaned in and said, "Dillon, we stopped in at the fish camp to thank Boaty for calling you and the police to warn everyone that Thor was planning to burn down your barn. During the conversation, he mentioned that two girls fell off a horse and were injured. He appeared uncomfortable, and I got the impression that he regretted mentioning the incident in the first place. Is there more?"

"A little more, but nothing to be concerned about." Dillon took a long, slow drink of lemonade, and for the next few minutes detailed the incident. The two teenage girls, Cindy and Mindy, the daughters of Coach Corky Corchran, the high school football coach, started fooling around the moment they stepped into the barn. They thought it would be cool to send a selfie of themselves on top of a horse to all their friends. They jumped up on the back of the horse, the rear leg collapsed, and both girls fell to the ground. Cindy was shaken, but fine. However, Mindy complained that her hand and wrist was sore.

The father, a big imposing man, muscular physique, known to have a bad temper and prone to get physical at times, complained in very colorful terms. It appeared that Mindy was the high school's only tuba player and was scheduled to have a tryout for USF

Marching band after Friday night's football game. A full scholarship and a permanent position in the band would be awarded if she had a favorable review. Mindy's wrist was fractured, two of her fingers were broken, and a cast up to her elbow made it impossible to play the tuba. Corchran threatened to sue for the lost scholarship monies, pain and suffering, and intimated that he would cut up the horse into little toothpicks. "It's been a week and nothing has happened, so maybe Mindy will get another tryout and Coach Corchran has calmed down."

"I hope so, but to be on the safe side you need to report the incident to the police. He sounds like he could be violent." Blaine took a last drink, inhaled deeply, and shot Dillon a skeptical glance.

"I did. So now, let's go see those horses, ladies," Connelly announced, and off they went.

Chapter 38

The red barn sparkled in the late afternoon sun. The old hulk of a barn stood proudly with a new coat of paint in what was truly a tribute to farming's past and tomorrow's future. All the old splintered wooden planks were repaired, a new front window was installed, and commercial rollers made opening the large, wooden barn door effortless. "What do you think of the old barn?" Connelly asked.

"It looks like new," chirped Brooke. "I love the new red color, it's shinier. Grandpa, what happened to your arm?"

"You're not going to believe me, but I slipped on a banana peel." Connelly laughed.

"Is that really true, Grandpa?" asked Brooke.

"It sure is. I finished eating the banana but didn't realize that the peel fell on the ground. When I left the table, boom, down I went," laughed Dillon. "Only a sprain."

"Well, that's a relief," Blaine said. "I, too, think the barn looks new. It must have cost a fortune."

"No, my neighbor is a painter. It's his slow season, so he gave me a great price and finished the entire barn in time for the open house. I still have money left over from the carousel project so I contracted him to complete some needed repairs inside the house. Definitely need a new bathroom. That's priority number one."

Halfway up the path Connelly noticed that the barn door was partially open. "That's strange the barn door is open. I distinctly remember closing the door and hooking the hasp last night. I'm sure I did. It's the same routine every time: Turn the lights out, pull the door closed, and hook the padlock on the hasp."

"Maybe the padlock wasn't secure, it slipped off, and the door moved a little," said Blaine. "There Look. The lock is on the ground."

Connelly picked up the lock, hooked it through the open hasp, and watched it hang in place like a brick. He pulled down on the metal padlock, yanked at the hasp, grabbed the door and shook. Still the lock remained in place. "No way could this padlock have fallen. Someone removed it."

"Grandpa, I hope no one stole the horses," said Brooke, as she grabbed her mother's hand.

"I do too, Brooke," Dillon said and stuck his head inside the barn. Without light only faint outlines of the carousel horses were visible. Two rows of horses lined the center gallery and disappeared back into the darkness. At first glance Connelly was relieved that the horses were not disturbed, but a nagging sensation that something was not right filled the air. He took a deep breath and knew. "Blaine do you smell that?" Connelly stepped back from the opening while Blaine pushed in.

"Gasoline. It smells like gasoline. Do you store gas for your tractor in the barn?" Blaine inched her way into the barn, and listened.

"No, that's the problem," said Connelly and pushed inside next to Blaine. "Someone broke in and poured gasoline...Listen, do you hear that?"

"Yes, sounds like splashing water."

"Splashing gasoline. Someone is in the barn now pouring gasoline all over the place. Next he will set the place on fire. We have to act fast. There's only one way out, and that's past us. Do you have your cell phone?"

"No, it's in my pocketbook on the porch." Blaine inched back outside and took Brooke's hand. "Brooke you need to go back to the house and call 911, and tell the police that someone is about to burn down Grandpa's barn. Give them the address, and then stay in the house and wait until Mommy and Grandpa return. Do not come back to the barn, understand?"

"Yes, I understand." Blaine gave Brooke a hug and sent her on her way.

Blaine walked back to the door and listened with Connelly as the splashing became fainter and fainter. Suddenly the sound of a metal can rolling along the cement floor echoed in the darkness. They immediately realized the gravity of the situation; the intruder finished pouring out all the gasoline. The next act would be to light the match.

"He has to come to us. The guy can't set the fire and then run to the front door. So let's just lock the door. Tell him to give up and we won't call the police. How does that sound?" whispered Blaine.

"No, he won't buy it. If he believes he's trapped he'll go crazy and destroy everything in sight. The guy has to be disturbed to attempt to get away with a stunt like this. Maybe we should wait for the police."

"There's no more time left. He's finished dousing the barn with gasoline, and the next step will be to torch it and watch it burn to the ground. I'm going inside. You stay here in case he gets by me."

"No, wait. I'll go in. It's my barn. I can do it," said Connelly.

"Dillon look at you. Your arm is in a sling. You can't confront some maniac intent on burning down your barn. Our last resort is you locking the barn, and holding him for the police. When you hear me say horses, turn the lights on." Blaine slipped through the opening and into the darkness.

Following the line of horses Blaine's eyes slowly became accustomed to the dark. The faint shadows at the front of the gallery changed into more distinct forms as she walked towards the rear of the barn. A small, blueish light waved from side to side a few feet to her left, and then a large form approached from behind a red stallion. "Beautiful horses don't you think?"

The ceiling lights exploded with the illumination of an airport runway guiding a 747 towards the terminal. Standing in front of Blaine was a big man, dressed in black with a ski mask covering his face. He clicked off the small flashlight, and Blaine noticed the size of his hands—big meaty hunks like that of a weight lifter. But that wasn't the only thing that was big. His arms, chest, and shoulders all complemented a weightlifter physique. "The private tour is over. It's time to leave," said Blaine and took a step closer.

"Who says?" said the arsonist and reached into his pocket. "This lighter says when the tour is over, not you lady." In his left hand he held a silver flip lighter. He flicked the wheel with his thumb over and over again. "What are you doing here? At the open house Connelly said he was going to visit his granddaughter, had a present to give her before the horses were shipped back to New York. The barn was supposed to be empty."

"That was last week. Yesterday he fell, and sprained his wrist, so there was a change of plans. We decided to drive up to the farm."

"That's too bad for you," Corchran spat out.

"You realize there's only one way out of this barn, and that's through the front door. If you set the place on fire it will be impossible to escape. You'll be trapped and burn to death. Give yourself up and we can both walk out of here alive." Blaine took a half step closer.

"Lady, you seem to forget that I'm twice your size. If I have to I'll snap your neck with one hand and leave you here to burn along with all the pretty horses." Corchran put the lighter back in his shirt pocket, reached down to his belt and pulled out a knife. "I guess we'll have to go to plan B."

"What, you're going to kill me?"

"Get into that locker or I will kill you," Corchran waved the knife in front of Blaine's face.

Her side kick to his head sent Corchran reeling backwards into a horse. Dazed and completely surprised at the ferocity of the impact, he instinctively lurched forward and jabbed at her face. Blaine sidestepped the attack and delivered another kick that sent shock waves up through his right arm. The strike broke two fingers and sent the knife flying across the floor disappearing, under a cabinet against the far wall. Screaming out in pain, Corchran grabbed his broken hand and charged Blaine with the force of an attack dog. A crushing blow to his right kneecap dropped the big man to his knees, and then to the floor. The attack was over, and all the fight in Mr. Corchran was gone. He knew it, and so did Blaine as she reached down and removed the lighter from his pocket. "It's over. Now get up."

Halfway down the gallery, the barn door flew open and four deputies rushed in and surrounded Corchran and Blaine. They removed Corchran's mask, put him in handcuffs and marched him out of the barn. Dillon almost fainted when he saw Corchran appear in handcuffs sandwiched between the two deputies.

"Corky, is that you? Why would you want to burn down my barn? I thought the girls were fine after the accident." Connelly stood there staring into the man's eyes waiting for an answer.

"Mindy lost the scholarship all because of your damn horses. Her hand was so swollen she could hardly move her fingers and her tryout was terrible. That's why!"

A deputy placed Corchran in the back seat of a patrol car and drove off. Fire personnel scoured the barn for accelerants that may have been left behind. Finding none, they placed fire retardants throughout the gallery to absorb the gasoline covering the floor and left.

Back at the house Blaine and Dillon reassured Brooke that all the horses were safe and the arsonist was taken to jail. Blaine mentioned that Brooke was going on a field trip to the Wildlife Center of Venice on Monday and that they needed to leave shortly to get her organized for the class trip. "We're studying animals in science, and Mrs. Malott organized a trip to the wildlife center where they rescue and heal injured animals," said Brooke with an excited smile on her face.

"Well, before you leave I have a little present to give you," said Connelly, and walked into the house.

"A present for me, Mommy. What could it be ..." Before Brooke could finish her sentence, Connelly stepped onto the porch carrying a hand-carved table lamp.

"Oh Grandpa, it's beautiful. A black beauty lamp with white horseshoes around the lampshade. Can you plug it in?" Brooke pleaded.

Connelly placed the lamp on the wicker table, plugged it in, and turned it on. The horse's shiny black coat glimmered in the light, and a golden saddle with silver buckles reflected light out into the room and onto a wooden base. Its tail and mane were made from natural brown horse hair, and leather straps that hung from a brass bit in the horse's mouth added to the unique quality of the lamp.

"It's a work of art Dillon. Thank you." Blaine leaned over and kissed him on the cheek.

"Grandpa, look at his eyes. I think they're looking at

me. I love it, thank you so much," said Brooke and gave him a big hug.

Goodbyes were said, Blaine put the lamp in the back seat, and drove off.

It was an early night with Brooke's class trip, and with Blaine's visit to Strawberry Girl scheduled for Monday morning, a good night's sleep was just what the doctor ordered.

Chapter 39

Five thousand was paid upfront, and another five thousand promised when the job was completed. The dark green Honda Civic pulled off onto the shoulder of the road fifty feet from the blinking purple mailbox. Hidden in the darkness were two men dressed in black and wearing dark ski masks.

They stepped from the car, walked to the back of the vehicle, and opened the trunk. Inside sat two red, plastic gas cans purchased earlier in the day from a local 7-Eleven, each filled with three gallons of gasoline. Alongside of the cans was a four-foot sandhill crane sign. The tall man picked up the sign, leaving the two gas cans for the other.

Waiting for their eyes to adjust to the darkness, they slowly walked along the road to the front gate that led down to the Purple Brush Farm. The tallest of the pair easily squeezed between the metal bars on the gate. The second man, short and stout, had a more difficult time pushing through the gate. Holding his breath and sucking in his stomach while his compatriot pulled his arms, he eventually fell to the ground inside the fence.

Retrieving the gas cans they sidestepped the shell

driveway and walked along the grass bordered by palm trees that lined the road leading down to the barn. Unfortunately, the intruders were unaware of the infra-red cameras hidden amongst the palm trees that recorded every move the two late-night interlopers made. A beeping on the Purple Lady's phone alerted her of the unwelcome visitors, and on the handheld screen she could watch as they neared the barn. The two red gasoline cans one man was carrying were cause for alarm. Clearly their intent was to do damage to her property, and possibly to herself. She dialed 911, and alerted the authorities that two men dressed in black were on her property and carrying what appeared to be two containers of gasoline. Miss Vardi hung up, grabbed her shotgun from the gun cabinet, and marched over to the barn.

Suddenly lights along the roofline of the barn went on, illuminating the front of the structure, the parking lot, and the purple truck parked at the end of the lot. "Shit," the tall arsonist whispered. "Quick! Run towards the bushes. We need to get out of the light!"

Out of breath, the second arsonist collapsed on the ground and said, "Now what? The place is lit up like a Christmas tree, and there is no way we can get to the barn in that light."

"Just wait. It's a motion detector. The light will go out. Calm down." Three minutes later everything went dark. "Okay, maybe the old lady will think it's an animal setting off the sensor and just go back to sleep. You need to walk beyond the palm trees to the back of the barn. Start pouring the gasoline and walk around to the front, and then light the place up."

"What are you going to do?" said the other man.

"The boss said he wanted the sign on the purple truck. Preferably sticking out of a broken windshield. Now get moving. I want to be home before daylight." The two moved out from behind the bushes, and crept back into the darkness.

Time seemed to stand still and weigh heavily on the Purple Lady. With each step closer to the barn she feared that her efforts would be too little or too late. But she pushed forward and was only a few feet from the barn door when spotlights from behind the barn burst on casting a muted glow that partially outlined the front section of the barn. At the corner of the barn, closest to her, she spotted the shadow of a person splashing a liquid up against the purple walls. Up and down lines of liquid zigzagged across the barn walls like some crazed artist's painting. As he rounded the corner, the front spotlights erupted with light, and she could clearly see the horror unfolding in front of her eyes. She knew she had to act immediately. The man's back was to her when she pointed the shotgun and shouted, "Drop the gas can, Mister, or I'll blow your brains out!"

The arsonist spun around, threw the can to the ground, and raised his hands. "Please don't shoot me lady, please," he begged.

"Where's your friend? The tall one. Where is he? I want..."

"Right here," a voice from behind called out.

Miss Vardi didn't finish her sentence. A crushing blow to the back of the head jerked her forward, causing her right hand to flex and pull the trigger. She collapsed and fell to the ground in an unconscious heap.

The shotgun blast lifted the arsonist off his feet and threw him backwards, spread eagled on the ground.

"Roadie, oh shit Roadie, this is so fucked up," a voice moaned. A rock dropped from the man's hand as he stared down at the large hole in the chest of his friend. Blood oozed from the wound and down over what was left of his shattered upper torso. His dark brown eyes were open with a frightened surprised glazed expression looking back.

"This is for you old friend," said the man as he

reached into his pocket and took out a book of matches. With one strike the book of matches ignited, and in one fluid motion he threw the fire torch against the barn. Instantly the wooden planks exploded in flames as yellow and red flames raced up the walls towards the roof.

In the distance sirens blasted their horns to herald their approach. The tall man raced up the shell driveway to his car.

Chapter 40

Daybreak brought long swaths of red sky across the eastern horizon. The crimson glow that welcomed the morning also foreshadowed the approach of a change in the weather. Blaine looked out her bedroom window and marveled at nature's beauty, but she recalled the old seafaring adage: "Red sun in the morning, sailors take warning. Red sun at night, sailors' delight."

"We need the rain," she said, and looked over at the clock on her night stand that read 6:45 a.m.

Blaine rolled out of bed, dressed, and plodded into the kitchen where she poured herself a glass of juice. Her thoughts were on Brooke's class trip and getting things organized before she left for work when a soft knock on the back door pulled her thoughts back to the present. "Good morning Blaine, I hope I didn't startle you," said Mrs. Brecht, the babysitter. "You did say seven o'clock."

"You're right on time, Charlene. Brooke's backpack is on the table. The only thing left to pack is her lunch and a snack. Both are in the refrigerator. I'll try to be home early. I can't wait to hear all about the animals at the wildlife center, and of course tonight is mac and cheese Monday. Can't be late for that family tradition."

"Can I make you some breakfast? It won't take long. All I need to do is add another egg to Brooke's omelet." Mrs. Brecht reached into the refrigerator, and pulled out a carton of eggs. "You have a full dozen. What do you say? You can't go to work on an empty stomach and perform your best. Isn't that what you tell your daughter every morning?" Mrs. Brecht held up two eggs and smiled.

"Thank you very much, but I'm picking up breakfast at the Upper Crust Café and Bakery this morning—a peace offering so to speak. Have a great field trip, Sweetie." Blaine gave Brooke a kiss on the cheek, and headed out the door.

The Upper Crust Café had an early morning line for breakfast that extended out the door and on to the sidewalk as Blaine pulled up and parked in front of the restaurant. Blaine waved to Nancy Gutierrez, her favorite server at the café, who was standing at the front window talking to another server while arranging the scone display. Blaine always requested Nancy as her server because she was a pleasure to be around. She was cheery, polite, efficient, and over the past five years the two had become friends. Blaine wiggled her way through the line to the front counter and called out, "Hi Nancy. Busy this morning, and it's only eight o'clock."

"It sure is. Blaine, I'd like you to meet my sister Gail Pudenz. She finally moved down to Florida," said Nancy, and gave Gail a friendly shove.

"Pleased to meet you, Gail, and welcome to Venice. Nancy told me that for the past five years in her Christmas cards she would beg you to leave the cold Illinois weather for sunny Florida. I guess her persistence finally paid off," laughed Blaine.

"That and last year's winter," Gail smiled.

"Nancy, I'd like four blueberry scones and two large cups of coffee with cream, please," said Blaine.

"I'll get the scones," Gail called out. "Blaine, I was wondering, can you tell the difference between the blueberry and the raspberry scones?" Gail pointed to the trays of scones in the window.

"I can't, but I'm not a server."

"That's what I said to Nancy, so I suggested that we arrange the trays in alphabetical order: apricot, blueberry, chocolate chip, cinnamon raisin, cranberry/orange, plain, and raspberry. That way the two berries would never be side by side. What do you think?"

"That sounds reasonable, but that is a decision left up to the owner, not me—especially this morning. I need to get going," Blaine remarked and handed Nancy a twenty dollar bill.

"I'm sure Linda will welcome my idea, especially after the nasty email she received last week from an irate customer who was given two blueberry scones and two raspberry scones instead of the four blueberry scones he ordered. Yes, I believe I will tell her. I'll talk to her this afternoon after my shift is over. Thank you Blaine."

"I think Blaine has heard enough, Gail. She needs to be on her way, and we need to serve the other customers," Nancy smiled, handed Blaine her order, and change.

"It was nice meeting you, Gail, and good luck with your scone dilemma." Three minutes later Blaine was out the door, breakfast in hand, and driving down the road to Strawberry Girl.

The banyan tree stood alone in the morning mist. The demonstrators, the police, and the curious had all gone home. Only the banyan tree remained, a bastion of time standing tall and proud. Long curving roots fell downward from its canopy to the ground. Their thick woody limbs spread like jail cell bars, one after another forming a network of long wooden trunks anchored to the earth supporting the old, massive tree.

So large was the stately structure that it occupied the entire lawn on the south side of the bank and a section of the rear parking lot. High above the ground a complex branching of roots and large glossy green leaves crisscrossed to form a nest-like structure where Strawberry Girl made her home. An old blue tarp covered nature's capsule providing shelter from the rain and a warm, safe home for the intrepid protester.

"Hello, Gilda Gooseberry, are you awake? I'm Ranger Blaine Sterling, and I'd like to talk to you about your friend Daisy Clearing." Blaine walked closer to the tree and looked up for any movement. "I have breakfast, Strawberry Girl. Hot coffee and blueberry scones." Instantly, a head popped out from behind the blue tarp.

"Why didn't you say that in the first place?" resonated down through the branches as a blue bucket, and rope ladder were lowered. "Place the food in the bucket and climb up the ladder." The red beret covering a head was a dead giveaway. The Strawberry Girl was alive and feisty as ever.

Hand-over-hand Blaine followed the bucket up through tree limbs and clumps of leaves into a nest-like capsule of branches lined with blankets and pillows likely used for comfort and support. Cheap, plastic solar-operated lanterns hung from overhead branches supporting the blue tarp that protected them from a heavy downpour that had just started. Strawberry Girl didn't wait for Blaine before she started to eat. She was already devouring a second scone by the time her guest sat down. "I hope you don't mind, but I was starving." Strawberry Girl stuck out her hand. "Nice to meet you Ranger Blaine. How can I help you?"

Blaine reached out and returned the greeting. Gilda Gooseberry looked older in person than her photograph portrayed. Time had been hard on her. Scars from unyielding childhood acne pockmarked her weathered, narrow face, and years of working outdoors compounded the aging process with long deep wrinkles along her forehead and down both sides of her face. Her green eyes never seemed still, but continually darted from side to side seemingly searching for something or someone. It was difficult to see her hair with the red beret pulled down close to her forehead. However, thin wisps of gray hung off to the side of her hat revealing its natural color. But Strawberry Girl had a warm smile and a firm grip, two important attributes Blaine admired in an individual.

"I have been instructed to investigate the death of Daisy Clearing and determine if the park was in any way complicit in her death. However, before we begin I must ask you how you got the nickname 'Strawberry Girl.' The rumors bantered about didn't seem to follow the same line of thought expressed in Daisy's diary. Do you think you could enlighten me with the true story?" Blaine reached into the bag of scones and handed one to Strawberry Girl.

Strawberry Girl laughed and almost chocked on a piece of scone. A big gulp of coffee and a napkin righted the situation, placing her in a pensive mood and ready to talk. "You are the perceptive young lady; no one ever asked me that question before. Everyone assumed I was the one who organized the free strawberry giveaway. I'm beginning to like you more and more, Ranger Blaine, and of course thank you for the coffee and delicious scones."

"The paper said that the Plant City demonstration was organized to protest the terrible working conditions of the migrant workers harvesting strawberries on Plant City farms. That the protest was peaceful until a mob rushed the strawberry fields and started picking all the strawberries. Police were called and groups of demonstrators were arrested. Daisy wrote that the two of you were arrested. What I can't understand is why a peaceful protest turned into a mob of strawberry pickers." Blaine took a bite from the last scone and leaned back against a pink sequined elephant pillow.

"Because Daisy and I and the strawberry mob weren't part of the demonstration," said Strawberry Girl and laughed uncontrollably, almost spilling the last of her coffee all over her brown and green camouflage pants.

Over the next half-hour, Strawberry girl explained how Daisy, a track star in high school, loved to jog every morning, rain or shine. The morning of the demonstration, she was out early running on a dirt road that bordered the main highway and a large strawberry field. In the center of the field was a farmer shooting at hundreds of birds on the ground eating strawberries or flying overhead. She yelled at him to stop but he reloaded his shotgun, and continued shooting. She raced back to camp and explained that they couldn't participate in the protest but had to teach the farmer a lesson.

The two drove into town, bought two large pieces of plywood, a can of red paint, two brushes, a half dozen stakes to anchor the plywood signs, and fifty pint baskets for the strawberries. Back at camp they painted: "Free Strawberries" and a big arrow pointing right on one board, and "U- Pick Here" on the second plywood board. That night they set up the signs and waited for daybreak. Dozens of cars drove down to the field. Families piled out of their vehicles and started picking strawberries.

The farmer was outraged and called the police. The mistake Daisy and Strawberry Girl made was to hand out the pint containers to all the people. They should have just left the containers below the U-Pick sign, and let the people take one.

They were arrested along with a handful of other demonstrators, but to their advantage their cellmates were two women from the American Civil Liberties

Union who subsequently represented them in court.

"The charges were dismissed, and to this day I still communicate with them on a regular basis. As a matter of fact they will join the protest on Thursday. So the real story behind the name is thanks to my dear friend Daisy. She was the real rebel behind the protest which we didn't participate in."

"That's some story," said Blaine, "but now I need some information about her Washington trip. Daisy wrote in the diary that she was worried that Winthrop wouldn't drive her to the train station, which he didn't. He told me they argued about her going to Washington, they broke up, and he left her in the park."

"That was the explanation everyone believed for over fifty years—that she went to Washington, D.C. and disappeared; until last week." Strawberry Girl took her last sip of coffee and placed the cup in a recycling bag next to the opening in the tarp. "My money is on Winthrop. I believe he became enraged when Daisy told him she was going to Washington, and he killed her. I heard all his friends at school were making fun of him for dating a girl who was going to the March on Washington, and as you know in the South it wasn't very popular to be a civil rights activist. He had a bad temper. You must have read the diary entry about the Snake Island quarrel. She told me all about it after I got out of the hospital. My money is on Holden J. Winthrop III, he killed her," Strawberry Girl spat out.

"Hospital. Why were you in the hospital?" said Blaine.

"I'll tell you later," Strawberry Girl answered. "Now, tell me what Daisy wrote about the Snake Island trip."

"Okay, I remember reading about it. She mentioned that Snake Island was across from where the Crow's Nest Restaurant is today, and on weekends Winthrop and a group of friends would spend Saturday's water skiing and partying on the island. A friend's uncle who lived in Venice let the boys use his boat on the weekends. He worked on Saturdays so the speed boat was available. It was the weekend before the KMI cadets left to go back to Kentucky for the spring semester, and Winthrop was in one of his obnoxious moods all day. Nothing seemed to please him. He kept falling off his skis, sand was on his sandwich and the beer wasn't cold enough. It was one complaint after another. It was close to sunset when all of a sudden Winthrop decided it was time to go. Everyone was looking forward to seeing the sunset, but he would have none of it. He jumped into the boat and sped away leaving Daisy and the two other couples stranded on the island."

"Daisy told me at first everyone thought it was just one of Win's practical jokes and that he'd come back shortly with another six pack of beer and an incredible story about his sudden departure. But that bastard didn't return!" Strawberry Girl said angrily.

"No, he didn't," replied Blaine. "Daisy wrote that the sunset was magnificent. She actually painted an unbelievable water color of the island and the sunset that covered two pages of the diary. It was dark, Winthrop hadn't returned, and the idea of spending the night on the island was beginning to seem like a reality. They built a fire in hopes that someone would see the light and rescue them. Not a single boat passed the island, and by eleven o'clock the odds of spending the night on the island were almost guaranteed. Then out of nowhere Skip Hargus ran into the water and started to swim across the channel towards the mainland. He shouted that he was going to get help and disappeared into the darkness."

"I was friends with Skippy Hargus. He was in the Political Club with Daisy and me, and no matter how difficult the club's discussions became, Skippy found a way of defusing the argument and bringing the group back on task. How he got mixed up with Winthrop in the first place is beyond me," Strawberry Girl said tersely, and looked outside. "It stopped raining. Looks like a good day for a demonstration. Oh I almost forgot, it was Skippy's uncle who owned the boat. That's probably why Winthrop befriended him."

"Then Daisy wrote that around midnight a Venice Police boat pulled up to the island and rescued everyone. They were brought back to the dock where all the parents waited frantically for their return. The police stated that they received an anonymous call that five teenagers were stranded on Snake Island." Blaine knew what the next entry said, but she waited for Strawberry Girl to complete the line.

"Skippy's body was never found. The police and Coast Guard searched for over two weeks before they called off the search. Authorities believed that the current in the channel was so strong that it dragged him out into the Gulf, and he drowned. I'll never forget that day," Strawberry Girl spat out.

"Okay, now tell me what Snake Island, and the hospital have in common," asked Blaine.

"The date. I remember that day very well. It was Saturday, April 4, 1963, and I was in Sarasota at the Big B Barbershop on Main Street," said Strawberry Girl as she removed her red beret, and pushed back a handful of thin gray hair. "See this! A cop clobbered me on the head that morning because Curtis Price and I were sitting on the sidewalk in front of the Big B Barbershop, protesting that the shop wouldn't cut a Negro's hair." An ugly dark purple scar zigzagged from her right temple up to the crown of her head. "Forty-three stitches, a concussion, two days in the hospital, and one night in jail for resisting arrest," laughed Strawberry Girl. "Resisting arrest; I couldn't even open my eyes with all that blood flooding down my face, let alone resist anything. Yes, I remember that day very well. How could I possibly forget?" Strawberry Girl put the red beret back on.

Blaine could hardly speak. The horror of that day was so overwhelming it took all of her energy not to throw up. She closed her eyes and tried to erase the image of such brutality, but to no avail. The picture of a police officer beating a seventeen–year-old girl so brutally that she needed medical attention was unconscionable. Finally, Blaine took a deep breath, gathered all her strength, and in a whisper said, “Gilda, I’m so sorry.”

“Thank you. I’m fine, but Curtis was another story. I didn’t see Curtis until a week later when he walked into the Political Club meeting at school. He didn’t say much. The bruises were still visible, and he walked with a limp. But his eyes told the story. He was never the same, and at the end of the school year he moved to New York.”

“Let’s get back to Daisy. I know you believe Winthrop is the killer. But just for argument’s sake, let us assume Winthrop is telling the truth. Who would Daisy ask for a ride to the train station?” Blaine looked straight at Strawberry Girl and waited. All of the scones were devoured and Blaine could sense she was beginning to lose interest in the inquiry. “She wouldn’t ask a complete stranger, so who is left in the park that could provide her with transportation to the station? A ranger?”

“Ranger Milt? Don’t make me laugh. That would be the last person anyone would ask for help. We nicknamed him, behind his back that is, ‘Uncle Milty,’ after Milton Berle the famous comedian. You probably weren’t born yet. It was back in the `50s. He even looked like Berle—big nose, glasses, and a cigar in his hand all the time. But Ranger Milt wasn’t funny.” Strawberry Girl shook her head, and frowned

“There was only one ranger for the entire park?” asked Blaine. “How was it possible for one man to run the park?”

“It was impossible. Ranger Milt spent the entire day

cleaning, repairing, building, or chasing away troublemakers. He didn't have a minute for himself, let alone to take Daisy to the train station, and Daisy knew it."

"Didn't he have to collect entrance fees at the ranger station, and assign campground sites? How could he do any work if he was working the ranger station?" asked Blaine.

"The park was much smaller back in 1963. There wasn't a campground, it was free to enter the park, and so there wasn't a ranger station. No Nature Center, no developed nature trails, and the lake wasn't like it is today. It didn't have a sandy beach, just weeds and grass, and an occasional alligator. There were only two picnic areas and a wooden boat ramp. That was it, but it was a beautiful park back then, and still is today."

Strawberry Girl abruptly stopped talking and rolled up her sleeve. There in the middle of her right forearm was a tattoo of a strawberry. "Daisy and I got them right after we were released from jail. A testament to our commitment to help our fellow man."

"There has to be something else. There has to be someone else. She just wouldn't let Winthrop leave without knowing someone at the park could take her to the train station. She prepared for months. There was no way she would have let him go if she needed him for the ride. Think! Who would she turn to?"

"Oh shit. How could I've been so blind? It had to be Fix-It Freddy. What a fool I've been. She went to see Fix-It Freddy," screamed Strawberry Girl.

"Okay, I'll bite who is Fix-It Freddy?" laughed Blaine.

"Fix-It Freddy was a homeless person. A Vietnam veteran who lived in the park with four other men back where the campground is located today. One day after taking pictures of the park for an art project, Daisy couldn't start her car. Out of nowhere this humongous black man steps out of the woods and asks if we need any assistance. I'll never forget because he used the word *'assistance.'* Who uses the word assistance? Someone with an education. He looked under the hood, and voilà! The engine started. Daisy asked him his name and he said, 'Fix-It Freddy' because he fixed all the bicycles in the camp.

After that day Daisy and I and some of the Political Club members would bring food and other basic necessities to the camp once a month." Strawberry Girl's eyes seemed the glow with excitement, and the broad grin across her face reminded Blaine of the Cheshire cat in *Alice in Wonderland.*

"I knew it, I knew it!" Blaine shouted. "But the problem is where he is now? There are no homeless camps in the park at the present time, so what happened to the camp, and what happened to Fix-It Freddy? What is his surname?"

"He never said. He told everyone he was in the army, and that he serviced all types of military vehicles while stationed in Vietnam. A year after Daisy disappeared, the park hired two more rangers, started charging a fee to enter, and removed the camp and all its residents."

"Okay, but where is Freddy now?" asked Blaine in a frustrated tone.

"I'm sorry Blaine, but I don't know. I wasn't there when they bulldozed the homeless camp, and when I walked over to the camp nothing remained but a bent-up bicycle." Strawberry Girl sat back against the pillows and closed her eyes.

"I don't believe this. We have the next piece to the puzzle, and now it doesn't fit. How can a giant of a man disappear? Someone had to see him. Can you call any of the club members and see if they know Fix-It Freddy's whereabouts?"

Blaine's excitement was noticeably reduced by the latest revelation that Strawberry Girl didn't have

Freddy's address, but after fifty-four years who would? It was a disappointment but not a total loss. She gave Strawberry Girl her card, thanked her for her time, and climbed down the ladder just as the police were arranging orange safety cones beside the road. Blaine smiled and walked to her car.

Chapter 41

The pink vinyl diary looked very much out of place on Beale's desk when Hordowski walked into the police station. The frayed edges of the book along with a broken lock indicated that the item had some age to it, or at least was written in. Curiosity got the better of him and he picked it up and flipped through the pages. The handwriting was amateurish, swirling letters and doodles littered many of the pages along with dried flowers, newspaper clippings, and of course, hearts. The diary obviously belonged to a teenage girl. On the front page in flowing bold pink cursive lettering was the title: "Property of Daisy Clearing."

"I don't believe it. I'm gone for just a weekend, and you're writing about me in your diary. How thoughtful," laughed Beale, as he sat down.

"Very funny. Where did you get it?"

"Blaine Sterling gave it to me. Emma Clearing found it after we interviewed her, and she left it with Sterling when the two met at the park. Take a look at the last entry." Beale opened the Clearing file.

"That lying S.O.B. He was in Venice all the time. We should go to his office and arrest him for withholding information in a murder investigation. I had my suspicions about that guy from the get-go. He just seemed too slick. So the question remains: Did Winthrop drive Daisy to the train station?" Hordowski handed the diary back to Beale.

"We'll drive over to his office, but first what did you find out at the Venice Train Depot? Was she on the train or not?"

"That's impossible to prove. In the early sixties people bought their tickets with cash or check, so the only record of a transaction was the number on the sold ticket that was later matched to the corresponding ticket number at the destination. No names, just numbers to verify travel." Hordowski took out a folder from his desk, and opened to a page with timetables and schedules stapled together. "However, all is not lost. A docent at the depot showed me a white notebook of letters passengers wrote Donald Decoster, the station agent from 1963 to when the depot closed in 1975. Wouldn't you believe it there was a letter from Daisy Clearing thanking him for all his help organizing her trip to Washington? It was dated August 26, 1963, two days before the March on Washington, the day she was scheduled to leave."

"So we still don't have proof she boarded the train," said Beale. "What about her friends? What did you find out about them?"

"I went over to the Venice Museum and Archives where Michelle Hamm, the curator, dug out a 1963 Venice High School yearbook. There on page 35 was a picture of Daisy Clearing, a junior, and a headline that she was a member of the Political Club." Hordowski removed two pages from his folder. "I wrote down the names of the club members, and one of them still lives in Venice, a Gilda Gooseberry. She owns a nursery out near River Road. I googled a half dozen of the other members, and what a collections of misfits. One guy raises rare Arawapa goats in the hills of West Virginia;

two members, a man and wife, are part of a Michigan militia that profess the overthrow of the government; the president of the club was killed twenty years ago when the Greenpeace boat he was in collided with a Russian whale ship and the list goes on in the same vein."

"Okay, let's drive over to Winthrop's office and find out the reason he lied. We can see Gooseberry after that," said Beale as he picked up the diary.

Beale turned onto Venice Avenue and headed west. Early-morning traffic was light, but when they reached Tamiami Trail, traffic came to a standstill. The bridge was up, and a line of cars extended beyond the light to Montgomery's Carpet shop. Beale turned the engine off, looked out the window and sighed, "We're going to be here for a while."

"So how was the conference?" Hordowski asked.

"It was an eye-opener," said Beale. "I was debriefing the chief while you were writing in your diary." Beale held up the shiny pink diary.

"Not funny. So what did the chief say?" Hordowski reached over to grab the little pink annoyance, but Beale was too quick, and he switched it to the other hand.

"He is going to contact Tampa and arrange for our department to participate in the de-escalation training program. We don't have the same problems as Tampa, but the live scenarios and actual situations to help officers assess and reduce tense encounters will be a tremendous benefit to the department."

"I agree. Every day we read about situations where police are confronted by a gunman. There are too many shootings. One life lost is one too many. Any step taken to assist in better policing I believe is welcomed. I'm sure every officer is on the same page. The bridge is going down."

Two traffic lights, and three minutes later they pulled into Winthrop's parking lot and squeezed into a space in front of the *Huge* sign painted on the picture window. They walked inside and asked the secretary if they could see Mr. Winthrop.

"Good morning, detectives. And to what do I owe the pleasure of your visit so early in the day?" Winthrop called out from the inner sanctum of his office. "Please come in."

Winthrop stood, and with his renowned TV smile in place he readied himself for battle. But disaster immediately struck team Winthrop, and the infamous smile quickly evaporated as the vanquished warrior collapsed into his chair after noticing the pink diary in Beale's hand. "I can explain," a pitiful voice uttered.

Beale and Hordowski took a seat. "We're waiting," said Beale.

For the next twenty minutes, Winthrop explained how the original detective believed Daisy had run away from home and disappeared somewhere in Washington, D.C. In his mind the case was closed, and for over fifty years it was. Winthrop's parents also mentioned to Purdy Jones that their son was attending the University of Kentucky. And since all the KMI cadets returned to Kentucky in April, that information eliminated Holden as a suspect in her disappearance. As a result Winthrop decided not to contradict the original investigation and refrained from adding any new facts until a park ranger interrogated him last Saturday.

"Was that ranger Assistant Park Manager Blaine Sterling?" Beale asked.

"Yes, and some thug with a gun that looked like a short professional wrestler. I told her I drove Daisy to the park to try and convince her not to go to Washington, but she had her mind made up. She was going. We broke up, and I left." Winthrop started to count his fingers.

"So you're saying you didn't drive her to the train station," Hordowski said tersely.

"That's correct, I left her at the picnic area with her red suitcase."

"Were there other people in the area?" Beale asked and wrote in his notepad, "red suitcase, and drew a picture of a suitcase."

"There were kids fishing in the lake, people barbecuing, and some type of big family party." Winthrop's finger counting sped up.

"Did you recognize any of the people?" Hordowski interjected.

"I don't remember. It was more than fifty years ago. I have no idea, but I did tell the ranger to go see Daisy's friend Strawberry Girl, a Gilda something. They were in a high school club together. She may know what happened to Daisy."

"Gilda Gooseberry. I wrote that name down from the Venice yearbook. She's Strawberry Girl and a member of the Political Club. She still lives in Venice and owns a nursery out near River Road," said Hordowski.

"That's her name. Gilda Gooseberry what a nut case. To protest the poor working conditions of the migrant workers she and Daisy put up a sign that read: "Free Strawberries" alongside a strawberry field in Plant City. Hundreds of people trampled up and down the rows of strawberries and destroyed the field. Daisy and Gilda were arrested, and so began the saga of Strawberry Girl," Winthrop added sarcastically.

"Daisy mentioned the Plant City protest in her diary. That she and Strawberry Girl were in the same jail cell with two ACLU protesters, and that the American Civil Liberties attorneys represented them pro bono, and that they won the case." Beale held up the diary, and waved around the page that had a big red strawberry and the phrase We Won in red.

"So you have no idea what happened to Daisy?" said Hordowski. He stood, and waited for a reply.

"No idea. You need to talk to Gooseberry, and today is your lucky day detectives because you can find her up a tree in Venice," laughed Winthrop and handed Hordowski his newspaper. "That whack job is still protesting. What is she seventy years old, or older, and still she continues to demonstrate. As you can see, she climbed an old banyan tree the bank wants to cut down to build a parking lot. If anyone knows what happened to Daisy, she does. Good luck getting her down." Winthrop's fingers moved back and forth.

Beale and Hordowski looked at the paper and shook their heads. "I think we need to pay Gilda Gooseberry a visit. We'll be in touch, Mr. Winthrop," said Beale.

Winthrop looked out the window and watched the white Crown Victoria drive down the road towards the bank.

Chapter 42

A police officer walked up to the white Crown Vic stopped alongside the orange barricade cones that lined the street in front of the banyan tree. “You can’t park here. This is a restricted area. People will be demonstrating all along the street, and we can’t have any vehicles blocking access to road.” Beale and Hordowski stepped out of the car and immediately the officer recognized them. “Oh, sorry detectives I didn’t recognize the vehicle. How can I help you?”

“That’s okay, Officer, we want to talk with the lady in the tree. Shouldn’t take long.” Beale and Hordowski walked over to the tree, and looked up. “That is some big tree. How tall would you guess it would be?” asked Beale.

“Has to be over forty, fifty feet, maybe more. It is big, and I would also guess maybe a hundred years old. What a beautiful tree. Maybe that old lady has a point.” Hordowski reached over and grabbed one of the hanging roots. “This branch is anchored to the ground, it’s solid as a rock. I bet all of the other trunks are the same,” Hordowski remarked and grabbed another trunk. “Solid as a rock!”

"Hello Strawberry Girl, I'm Detective Beale. I'd like to ask you some questions about your friend Daisy Clearing," shouted Beale. He waited, but no reply.

"Ms. Gooseberry, please we just need a minute of your time." Again no reply, only the rush of leaves singing in the wind.

"Gilda Gooseberry, don't make me remove you from this tree and escort you to the police station. We need some answers in Daisy Clearing's disappearance."

"If you attempt to extricate me from this tree, all I need to do, is make one phone call, and over five hundred protesters will show up; and news reporters will televise you dragging off a helpless seventy-one-year-old lady. How would that play out on the six o'clock news, detective?" shouted a voice from above. "Not very well I predict."

Beale took a deep breath and readied his answer, "I don't want our meeting to end in confrontation. All I need are a few questions answered."

"I already told a park ranger everything I know about Daisy's disappearance. If you want any information about Daisy, question her. I have other pressing issues to contend with, so goodbye Detective."

"Was that Ranger Blaine Sterling?" shouted Beale.

"Yes, and she brought coffee, and scones."

"Okay, we're leaving, but if I find that we need further details from you, we'll be back. Do you understand, Ms. Gooseberry?" Beale wrote in his notepad, "Bring donuts next time, and drew a strawberry."

"Don't forget the coffee and scones," a voice called out from behind the blue tarp.

"That went well, Detective. Looks like someone will be driving to Osprey State Park," laughed Hordowski.

"Very funny, but first we need to go back to the station. We need to look at the diary more closely and find out what Daisy wrote about that Plant City protest.

Chapter 43

Blaine slid a Patti Hyland CD into the console, and immediately her favorite country and western song, *"Crazy,"* filled the cabin of the Mini Cooper with its soft tones and lilting melody. Patti Hyland was her go-to music when she needed a moment to think and collect her thoughts or just for fun music to listen to. For Blaine, country and western music reached down into the soul of a person and put to rest all the problems of the world with a song. Blaine pulled out of the parking lot and drove north on Tamiami Trail to the park. Halfway through "Walkin' After Midnight" Blaine's phone rang. Already stopped in bumper-to-bumper traffic at the construction site on 41, Blaine pulled off and took the call.

"Hello Blaine, this is John Forrester. Good morning."

"Good morning, John, I just had a curious meeting with Gilda Gooseberry, aka Strawberry Girl, an old friend of Daisy Clearing, and quite a bizarre character. I'll give you all the details in a few minutes. I'm on my way to the park and should arrive on time for our meeting."

"That's the purpose for the call," said Forrester. "I need to go the Tallahassee this afternoon and meet with Director Goodie and finalize the arrangements for Ryan Murphy's memorial. So I need to postpone our meeting until I get back."

"Did you say Director Goodie? Director Dr. Rosa Parks Goodie? I thought Director Florentine wasn't retiring until next year?" A surprised Blaine coughed into the phone.

"I was just as surprised as you, but at his yearly checkup he was diagnosed with stage two prostate cancer and decided to retire early. So now we need to work with Director Goodie on both the memorial and the Daisy Clearing mystery. But before I hang up, who is this Strawberry Girl?"

"There isn't enough time. I would need at least thirty minutes to explain, but take a look at yesterday's paper, and you'll get a tiny glimpse of the people Daisy Clearing associated with. Don't be surprised. We'll talk when you get back."

"One last thing before I hang up. Are we any closer to finding out what happened to Daisy Clearing? I'm certain Director Goodie will ask me if we're making progress on the case. Are we?" Forrester waited on the other end.

Blaine hesitated before answering, took a deep breath, and said, "No."

"That's disappointing, but I'll inform Director Goodie that we're picking up on a delicious lead that may move us closer to solving the case."

"John, please congratulate Director Goodie on her promotion and convey to her my heartfelt joy that I am certain her new position as director will bring. You may want to bring her a small basket of strawberries to make your news more palatable." They both laughed before hanging up.

Blaine pulled back onto the highway, turned on the CD, and eased forward at a breathtaking 10 mph.

Traffic opened up just as Patti Hyland belted out “Back in Baby’s Arms,” another of Blaine’s favorite songs. Blaine’s mind drifted off thinking of Goodie’s good fortune and how she turned adversity into success. Who would imagine that a broken arm that derailed a career as a park ranger, would morph into an administrative position that commanded the entire State of Florida Department of Parks? Blaine smiled and savored the good fortune that her old friend now enjoyed. She realized it was probably her karate kick that channeled Goodie’s energies to the position that she was destined to hold. Blaine was happy for her, and deep down inside she welcomed working with her and looked forward to rekindling an old friendship.

Blaine downshifted into second gear, and pulled into the park as Patti Hyland started to sing “I Fall to Pieces.” She stopped at the ranger station, rolled down her window, and smiled as Ranger Diana stepped outside. “Welcome back. How are you feeling?” Blaine asked, and signed the logbook Diana handed her.

“Fine, thank you,” said Diana. “I think I’ll take a pass on sushi for a while. I don’t believe my body could take another food poisoning episode. Cooked food from now on. Dalton Marks and Sydney Price just pulled into the park. They’re waiting for you at your office.”

“Thanks, Diana. Have a nice day, ‘Bye.” “Back in Baby’s Arms” echoed through the trees as Blaine drove to her office.

It had been weeks since Blaine last saw the two archeology students, and she was excited with a touch of apprehension to see them and find out how they were coping after the death of Professor Murphy. It could have been the shock at Sydney’s short pixie-style haircut or Dalton dressed in black, but something didn’t feel right. The most disturbing aspect of the snapshot was that their body language seemed to express a distance or detachment from one another.

A condition Blaine recalled covered in a psychology class she took at Hofstra University. A state of mind common when a tragedy occurs.

"Hello you two. Good to see you both. Let's go into the office and get out of the sun," Blaine said and opened the office door.

"Good to see you, Ranger Blaine," Dalton and Sydney replied.

"So Sydney, I see you have a new hair style," said Blaine.

"Yes, I thought I needed a change—a major change after what happened. I'm in therapy and working through the whole experience. The short hair was one way to move forward with my life," Sydney laughed and messed up her hair.

"Well that's some statement," said Blaine. "As my old psychology teacher professed, 'Bold statements help one move on from adversity,' and I believe you're headed in the right direction."

"As for you Dalton, why are you dressed in black?"

"I'm also in mourning. After Professor Murphy's death I went back to my apartment and thought I'd console myself with some computer game escape. I logged onto Echo and inadvertently opened a default portal to D-S7SD, the docking station we battled for and captured last month. Well I unleashed a disastrous attack on Sky Coalition which culminated in the total destruction of our Titan and Goliath starships, and ultimately the elimination of the Sky Coalition. So you could say I'm mourning the death of Professor Murphy and, in a small way, the death of Sky Coalition."

"Professor Murphy's death is a major loss in all our lives, and it will take time for us to heal. I realize we all mend in different ways, but our goal is the same: to remember a kind and gentle man who was a part of our lives, and I'm certain he'll remain in our hearts forever. Ryan would want us to go on with our lives and be productive caring individuals in a world that has many challenges to address."

Blaine walked over to her desk, picked up two boxes and carried them over to the conference table. She handed Sydney the smaller of the packages and instructed them to open them. "To help bring some amount of closure, and to commemorate Professor Murphy's work in archeology, the Park's Department wants you both to present to the Seminole Tribe delegation from the Tribal Historic Preservation Office all of the artifacts from the cave which will be housed at the Ah Tah Thi Ki Museum on the Big Cypress Reservation. Sydney, you are responsible for the arrangement of all the arrow points, and Dalton you need to place the ceremonial spear in your case."

"What a beautiful walnut box," Sydney remarked as she opened the glass top. "The blue velvet lining will definitely accent the different-sized arrow and spear points. It looks like the box can hold all the artifacts we catalogued from the dig." On the walnut border framing the glass top, a small gold plaque read: *Native American Artifacts, 2017 Osprey State Park, Professor Ryan Murphy Sarasota County Archeologist.*

"Mine looks like a gun case, but with a glass top and no lock," said Dalton. "The ceremonial spear will glow inside this red velvet box." Dalton opened the box, and rubbed the silky red fabric. "Thirty-five thousand years ago this spear was held in a hunting ceremony by one of the clan leaders right here at Osprey State Park. Now this important treasure will be returned to their descendants thanks to the work of Professor Ryan Murphy, and the volunteers from college."

"Manager Forrester is attending a meeting in Tallahassee to finalize the memorial service for Professor Murphy. I'll call you both after he returns and notify you both on the exact date and time of the ceremony."

“Sounds like a plan,” said Dalton, and picked up his box with a groan. “Heavy bugger.”

“We’ll head back to the archives building to start preparing the artifacts for the ceremony,” Sydney added, as they walked towards the door.

“Nice seeing you both. Stay well.” Blaine hugged them both, and returned to her computer. Five minutes later there was a knock on her office door.

Chapter 44

Beale quickly thumbed through Daisy's diary until he came upon a large red exclamation mark at the top of a page dated February 10, 1963. Period 6 lunch! In large print the entry began: *Gilda didn't eat lunch today, instead she left the food line, walked over to where we were seated, stepped on a chair, and jumped up on the cafeteria table holding her lunch tray. Slowly she lifted the tray over her head and screamed, "I can't eat this food!"*

The words jumped off the page as Beale scanned each line attempting to better understand Gilda Gooseberry. So this is where the birth of her activism began, he thought.

There was complete silence. Everyone froze, stopped talking, stopped walking, stopped everything, and looked up at the girl standing on the table holding a food tray. "Meatloaf with gravy, mashed potatoes with gravy, and mixed vegetables boiled into extinction. Kids don't eat this crap for lunch! We want pizza, hamburgers, salads, soups, hotdogs," she shouted.

Mr. Winkel, the wood shop teacher who had the misfortune of being on cafeteria duty rushed up to our table waving his arms in excited, exaggerated gyrations in hopes of convincing Gilda to come down. Unfortunately, his plea did not persuade her to sit nor refrain from screaming out vehement comments about the cafeteria food. "If you don't come down this instant, young lady, I'll be forced to get the assistant principal," Mr. Winkel called up to her and moved closer to the table, a misstep he would soon regret. "Gilda, this is my last warning; please come..."

Mr. Winkel could not finish his warning for an explosion of food rained down over the cafeteria. First Gilda's tray, and then the entire cafeteria erupted in a shower of food from all directions. Gilda was suspended for three day and had to perform twenty hours of community service in the cafeteria for her part in the food fight.

"This Strawberry Girl was some piece of work. She starts a food fight in the cafeteria, gets suspended, and has to perform community service cleaning the cafeteria. Sounds like the type of girl you would have dated Hordowski."

"Very funny. I'll have you know I was a clean-cut all-American boy in high school. Varsity football team, student council president, homecoming king, and more. I don't think Gilda Gooseberry would be in my circle of friends." Hordowski gave Beale a wink and went back to organizing the papers on the Political Club members he just received from Daytona Beach, and North Dakota.

"So you think Gooseberry is a strange bird? Well I was just handed information on the last two members of the high school Political Club. Talk about weird. Listen to this. Johnny *'Pork chop'* Brown makes and sells online *ghost guns,* military-style semi- automatic assault rifle kits with no serial numbers making them untraceable. No background check necessary, and it is legal. This upstanding citizen sells them right out of his garage in a Daytona Beach neighborhood."

"Unbelievable! No wonder this woman is the way she is today. But the question that needs to be asked is were all of Strawberry Girl's actions born from indoctrination while a member of the Political Club, or were her actions a manifestation of her own personal beliefs?" Beale waited for a reply.

"I don't know. What difference does it make? She's still a nut case who hung out with nut cases. Anyway, it gets worse. The last member of the club was just arrested in North Dakota for criminal trespass and engaging in a riot at the Dakota Access Pipeline. Bobbie Jo Morabetto, reality television actress, was taken into custody after she locked herself to a construction crane at the site. Her trial will be held next month in Mandan, North Dakota."

"I guess Ms. Morabetto will be getting some actual reality soon enough," laughed Beale, and continued flipping through the diary until a page full of strawberries caught his attention. It was dated March 2, 1963, Strawberry Festival, Plant City, Florida. Beale skimmed over the entry, paying particular attention to the protest, the arrest, and Gilda's involvement. Beale noted that both girls were committed to the protest, but Daisy appeared to be the catalyst behind the free strawberry giveaway. They spent one night in jail, all charges were dropped, and Daisy was grounded for two weeks.

In April Daisy and Strawberry Girl were involved in another protest. This time the event took place in Venice and netted the pair a two-day suspension from school. It appeared that the chemistry lab door opened into the hallway causing what Strawberry Girl believed to be a hazard to people walking in the hallway. Daisy wrote an editorial in the school newspaper, "Doorway to Danger," explaining the hazardous condition the lab door presented.

Strawberry Girl went to the principal with a student petition asking that the door be reversed before a serious accident occurred. Both requests were denied stating that a reversed door would pose a fire violation. As a result on April 1, 1963, April Fools' Day, at seven o'clock in the morning, Daisy and Strawberry Girl chained themselves to the chemistry lab door. Three hours later the police, firefighters and administration finally extricated the two protesters from their chains, and a trip down to the Venice Police Station ended the standoff.

The final act of protest Strawberry Girl perpetrated occurred during graduation, a fitting venue for Strawberry Girl to say goodbye to the establishment. Daisy, a junior, had a front row seat to the shenanigans that erupted during the principal's address to the students. Out from behind the seated graduates, five strawberry beach balls flew into the air and began their bounce all across the stage and into the bleachers. Back and forth, up and down, and across all the rows for ten minutes or more, strawberries flew in the air until Mr. Jehelca, the assistant principal, corralled all of them except for the very last one that bounced off Principal O'Brian's head and into a waste paper basket behind the podium, a form of poetic justice to end the school year. There was no doubt who instigated the parade of strawberries, but there would be no suspension that day. All that Principal O'Brien could do was glower at Gilda Gooseberry when he presented her diploma. Strawberry Girl smiled, and waved to the crowd.

"That Gooseberry was quite a handful back in the '60s. I'd hate to be her teacher, let alone her principal. I don't like her behavior today, and she's in her seventies and still causing problems. I can't imagine all the trouble she perpetrated back then." Beale closed the diary. "I think we need to drive out to Osprey State Park and see what information Sterling has on this Strawberry Girl."

Beale and Hordowski were about to leave when

Beale's desk phone rang. Beale picked up the receiver: "Hello, Detective Beale speaking, how can I help you?"

"Detective Beale, this is Sheriff Jeff Johnson. We worked together at Osprey State Park on the skeleton case. By the way, how is that case progressing? The reason for the call is that I may have some information on another case you are working on that took place in Venice."

"Hello sheriff, good to hear from you. Unfortunately the Osprey case has reached an impasse, but we're about to head out to the park and meet with the assistant manager and speak with her about the case. So what information do you have for me?"

"Last night two men attempted to burn down Vardi Zammiello's barn. The arsonists were caught on the farm's surveillance cameras, and Zammiello called the police. The fire department and police arrived within minutes and put out the fire before any real damage occurred. Zammiello shot one of the men and killed him. The other arsonist escaped before we arrived, but before leaving he broke the windshield of Zammiello's purple truck and left behind a sign of a sandhill crane sticking out of the broken window."

"Did you say purple truck?" Beale asked. "Is this Zammiello called the Purple Lady?"

"The same, Detective. Everything on the property is painted purple, including the driveway leading straight to the purple barn. I was surprised she didn't paint the two horses in the paddock purple," said Johnson. "Anyway, the sandhill crane sign is the same sign from your horse manure dumping case over at the Get Physical Gym in Venice."

"The same sign. That can't be a coincidence. What about the dead arsonist? Have you identified the dead man?" Beale asked.

"No. We ran his prints through CODAS, but nothing. No identification on the body either. Wore jeans, tee shirt, and sneakers. But something very strange; he had five thousand dollars in his pocket."

"Five thousand dollars. Who walks around with five grand in his pocket? Not me that's for sure," said Beale, as he sat down.

"Had to be a payoff. I think this guy was paid five thousand to start the fire, and probably five more when the job was completed. That's our theory, but it's the sandhill crane sign that may be your connection. One other piece of evidence, he had grease under his fingernails. Open Face Gear Lube, a type of lubricant used to grease the wheels on carnival rides. A heavy-duty type of grease to withstand extreme heat and hours of wear, and almost impossible to wash off."

"Morty King owns an amusement company, and a sandhill crane sign was planted in his car. Can you send me all the information you have on this arson case?" Beale jotted down a note, "Get Physical file, and drew a picture of a sandhill crane."

"It's on its way. Good luck, and let me know if I can be of further assistance," said Johnson.

"Thanks," said Beale. "I believe we'll drive out and impound that purple truck and question Vardi Zammiello. Nice talking to you." Beale hung up, and said, "Hordowski, change of plans. Get your jacket we're driving out to talk to the Purple Lady."

"What happened to the drive out to the park?" Hordowski asked.

"That can wait. We just got a tip on the Get Physical Gym horse manure dumping. We need to see the Purple Lady and her purple dump truck. Bring the King file. I want to look at the pictures of the sandhill crane poster."

Chapter 45

The yellow school bus came to a complete stop in front of 204 Serpentine Lane with both caution signs flashing. The side door opened, and out jumped Brooke Sterling clutching a picture of a sandhill crane in her left hand and frantically waving to Mrs. Bretch, her baby sitter, with the other. Brooke skipped up the driveway and into the house.

"I have a snack ready for you, Brooke, but first wash your hands, and then you can tell me all about your class trip to the Wildlife Center of Venice." Mrs. Bretch poured a glass of milk for Brooke and a cup of tea for herself.

Brooke raced from the bathroom to the kitchen table and sat down in front of a plate of homemade cookies and the glass of milk. After one quick gulp of milk and a bite of a sugar cookie, she began her story. "It was the best field trip ever. The bus ride was great. Mrs. Malott let everyone listen to their electronic devices the entire bus ride. I sat next to my BFF Nancy Buscher, and we listened to music the whole bus ride."

"What's a BFF Brooke?" Mrs. Brecht asked, and refilled Brooke's milk glass.

"Best friend forever. We do everything together. She is definitely my best friend." Brooke took a bite of cookie and another big gulp of milk.

"Slow down, Brooke, you don't have to finish your milk with one swallow. Now please tell me about the wildlife center. What did you enjoy the most?"

"Everything. The place was awesome, and Mr. Barton, the Director, he knows everything about wild animals plus he has a ponytail." Brooke giggled and took a bite of the last sugar cookie.

"I believe Kevin Barton is the director of the Wildlife Center of Venice," said Mrs. Brecht.

"Whatever. The bus stopped in front of a big metal fence with the name Wildlife Center of Venice. The bus driver had a difficult time opening the gate, but while he worked on the gate handle I noticed a beautifully carved pelican mailbox next to the fence. I knew at that moment I was going to love the field trip. Finally we drove in and parked. A volunteer met us and took the class around the back to their animal hospital where Mr. Barton was working."

"What was he doing?"

"He was putting a sandhill crane in a hammock-like swing. One of the bird's legs was broken when a car hit it, and so Mr. Barton made something to take weight off the broken leg. How cool was that?" Brooke smiled, and slowly finished her milk.

"That is cool, but what does the center look like?"

"It's big. There's an animal hospital where they care for the sick and injured animals. Also part of the building is the nursery where they feed the baby birds and baby animals by hand. Julie, a college volunteer, was using an eyedropper to feed a baby rabbit. She said it takes almost half an hour to feed one rabbit. She started volunteering at the center when she was in middle school. When I get to middle school, I'm definitely going to volunteer at the wildlife center."

"That is an admirable goal, Brooke, and I'm certain the center needs plenty of volunteers, considering it takes a half hour to feed one bunny. So tell me more."

"There are lots of cages for animals, a large screened building for injured flying birds, and other screened buildings for pelicans, owls, deer, sandhill cranes and other injured animals. They also had a building for tools and supplies and a big pond in the middle of the property for ducks, geese, and even a pelican to swim in and get strong. I was excited to see how Mr. Barton and all the volunteers worked so hard to help the animals, but I'm sad that there are so many injured animals and birds hurt every year. Mr. Barton said that the center cares for about four hundred injured animals a day. That is so many, Mrs. Brecht." Brooke looked up at Mrs. Brecht with a sad expression.

"It is a great many injured animals, but with more people moving to Florida and new housing developments being built each year, the habitat these animals enjoyed is being destroyed more and more. As a result, accidents with automobiles are commonplace. We are very fortunate that people like Kevin Barton and the Wildlife Center of Venice are helping to care for the many injured animals." Mrs. Brecht picked up the dishes, and walked over to the sink. "Oh, your mother called earlier and said to remind you that tonight is mac and cheese night and she would try to be home early."

"Mac and cheese, fantastic! I better get working on my homework right away. Mrs. Malott wants the class to write a story about the field trip and then read it to the class tomorrow. I have an idea that may help stop so many sandhill cranes from being hit by cars." Brooke picked up her backpack and walked back to her room.

An hour later the front door flew open, and in marched Blaine. "I'm home," Blaine called out as she walked through the front door and headed towards the kitchen. "Hello, where is everybody?"

Simultaneously Brooke and Mrs. Brecht burst through the living room and together said, "Hello."

All three went into the kitchen where Mrs. Brecht had already set the table for dinner. "Can you stay for some mac and cheese, Mrs. Brecht? It shouldn't take long to prepare, and it will be scrumsedelicous," said Brooke.

"I'd love to, Honey, but Mr. Brecht and I are going over to some friends for dinner. Maybe next time. Enjoy your mac and cheese. 'Bye."

"So Brooke, tell me all about your trip while I prepare dinner," Blaine said.

Over a heaping plateful of scrumsedelicous mac and cheese and salad, for the next half hour Brooke recounted in detail from start to finish her trip to the wildlife center. She explained how a volunteer fed a baby rabbit, how Mr. Barton made a sling hammock to support an injured sandhill crane, and described the many cages that held recuperating animals. Finally Brooke mentioned that when she entered middle school she would like be a volunteer at the Wildlife Center of Venice.

"What a wonderful experience, and I think your desire to be a volunteer is admirable," said Blaine. She reached out and squeezed Brooke's hand.

"That's what Mrs. Brecht said, 'admirable,'" laughed Brooke.

"Well it is admirable. You mentioned that the center responded to over three thousand rescue calls last year. I'm sure they could use a volunteer like you to help. As a matter of fact they probably could use a hundred more volunteers, especially with the closing of the Pelican Man's Bird Sanctuary in Sarasota. Now the Wildlife Center of Venice is the only rescue center in the area."

"Mommy, I also have an idea that may help stop so many animals from getting injured or killed every year. Mrs. Malott wants the class to write a story about the field trip and then read it to the class tomorrow. Mr. Barton told the class that sandhill cranes were injured the most from accidents with cars. My idea is to start a fundraiser to have signs made to warn drivers that sandhill cranes cross the road. If drivers are aware that sandhill cranes live in the area, maybe they will be more careful driving down the road. What do you think of my idea?"

"Brooke, I think that is an amazing idea, and I'm positive Mrs. Malott will too. I'm not a hundred percent sure, but you may need permission from the City of Venice before you put up the signs. Mrs. Malott can investigate the legal aspects before any digging takes place. I would be happy to help with the project, and I'm positive Lou Bravo would volunteer to dig the first hole." Blaine smiled and took a bite of mac and cheese.

"Lou Bravo would help?" Brooke asked with a skeptical glance.

"Oh yes. Lou Bravo is very fond of sandhill cranes, and he is an expert in digging holes. I'm sure he'll join in the fun," laughed Blaine.

"If you say so. May I be excused? I want to finish my story, and then take a bath."

"Of course. I'll clean up here, and then come up and kiss you good night," said Blaine.

A short time later with the dishes cleaned, Brooke's lunch in the refrigerator, homework checked, and a quick bath, Blaine sat down on Brooke's bed, pulled the covers up around her chin, and gave her a kiss good night. "You look tired Sweetie, get a good night's sleep, and good luck with your report tomorrow. I believe your idea to save the sandhill cranes is admirable." Blaine tickled her around her cheeks and the two of them laughed together.

"Oh Mommy, there was one other thing about our trip. There was a fire at the Purple Lady's barn. Julie said two men tried to burn down her barn Sunday night. She also said that the Purple Lady shot one of the men."

"Was Miss Vardi hurt?" Blaine asked

"Julie didn't know."

Blaine walked into the kitchen and called Vardi Zammiello.

Chapter 46

Purple Brush Farm doesn't grow vegetables, nor does it raise livestock, but it does cultivate one's imagination. "The color of the day, Hordowski, is purple, and you are about to have a Purple Lady experience. I hope you like purple." Beale smiled, turned onto Border Road and accelerated.

"Okay I'll bite. Who or what is a Purple Lady? Is it a drink?" asked Hordowski.

"It's not a drink. It's a person, and that's all I am going to say. However I will promise that you are in for a real surprise, Detective."

"More surprised than when we went to Arthur Dunn's glass house? A house made from Coca-Cola bottles that his father stole when he was fired from the company. What was it, five trailers of Coke he buried on his property? What a whacko."

"Ten trailers. That's twenty thousand bottles of soda. That man must have hated Coca-Cola, but to answer your question you will be more surprised. Take a look."

Beale made a sharp right onto a small driveway and slowly bumped down the palm-lined road into Purple

Brush Farm. “I don’t believe it, a purple road! Stop the car I have to get out and walk it myself,” shouted Hordowski.

A few steps down the broken shell road he bent down and picked up a purple shell, turned it over, and scratched the bottom with his fingernail. He picked up another, repeated the same process and yelled, “They’re painted. All the shells are painted purple. That is so bizarre! I can’t wait to see the rest of the nuthouse,” he said sarcastically.

“Get in. We need to get a look at that purple truck and talk to the lady of the farm,” said Beale.

The road curved to the right. There on a hill at the end of the crushed shell road loomed a large purple barn with an attached corral and two horses shading themselves under a giant oak. A purple dump truck was parked alongside the barn. On the opposite side of the property was the main house, a long flat one-story ranch, painted purple, and five purple cottages in a semi-circle facing a pond. Beale parked next to the truck.

“What is that walking towards us? From the barn! That purple thing with short curly, purple hair in a long, purple flowered dress that resembles a tent. Is that the Purple Lady?” Hordowski coughed out. “You were right, Beale, I am more surprised. I’m actually flabbergasted. I wonder if she’s wearing a purple thong.”

“Funny you should mention that because I asked her the same question when we first met at Osprey State Park. Maybe you would like to broach the underwear question, or maybe ask her about her tattoos. If you think you’re flabbergasted now, wait until she shows off her body tats. That’ll be a real eye-opener.” Beale pointed to his chest, and stepped out of the car.

“What was she doing at the park?” said Hordowski.

“Painting. She was painting an old, abandoned

railroad bridge along the Legacy Trail not far from the park's untouched section of land. It started to rain so she bicycled over to the Nature Center on her purple bike blasting "*Purple Rain*" by Prince from a purple radio hanging from the handlebars. It was quite a sight. Here she comes now."

Purple Lady never walked. She sashayed with bold, exaggerated movements, flashing her purple until she reached her destination, a technique she perfected over the years to compensate for her five-foot frame. "Good morning gentleman, how can I help you?" asked Miss Vardi, and extended her hand.

"Good morning, I'm Detective Beale, and this is Detective Hordowski." Both detectives returned a greeting. "We're here to talk to you about the events of last night and your purple dump truck." Beale took out his notepad.

"My dump truck? What do the fire and shooting have to do with my dump truck?" Miss Vardi asked dully.

"We received a call from the sheriff's office regarding your fire and the shooting of an unidentified white male. In addition Lieutenant Johnson implied that your purple truck may have been involved in an active investigation in Venice involving a red BMW."

"My truck hit a red BMW? That's impossible." Miss Vardi walked to the front of the truck and scanned the entire front section. "I don't see any damage. You said my truck hit a BMW? What proof do you have to substantiate that allegation?"

"I didn't say your purple truck hit a BMW. It was reported to our office that a purple dump truck was seen in the parking lot after a load of horse manure was deposited onto the red BMW." Beale wrote, "Purple Lady didn't know someone saw truck, and drew a truck."

"Who said they saw a purple truck?" Miss Vardi blurted out.

"A concerned citizen leaving the Dollar Store saw a notice of a reward for information about the incident and called Mr. King, the owner of the BMW," Hordowski answered.

"Well, you don't know it was my purple truck in the parking lot. I'm sure there are hundreds of purple trucks in Florida. How could your eyewitness prove it was my vehicle? Did he or she take down the license plate number?" Miss Vardi moved to the back of the truck and pointed at the license plate. "Can't miss this plate, Detectives, that is if you really did see my purple dump truck." Three heads looked down at the vanity plate which read: PURPLE.

Hordowski opened the manila folder he was carrying, pulled out a picture and handed it to Beale, who in turn handed it to Miss Vardi. "We don't have the plate number, but we received this picture of your truck with a sandhill crane sign sticking out of a broken window," said Beale. Hordowski handed Miss Vardi another picture. "Our CSI team took the second picture: the red BMW in question with a sandhill crane sign sticking out of the pile of manure. The two signs look very much alike, and we are here today to bring the sign back to our office. A repo truck will arrive shortly to transport your truck back to the station. Here is the warrant for the transfer of property."

Miss Vardi handed the pictures back, and for the first time she appeared to be less animated and somewhat befuddled. "When did this dump truck event occur, Detective?"

"Last Friday," said Hordowski, "at around ten o'clock in the morning."

"Well detectives, last Friday I was teaching a plein air art class to twenty-five women. I will give you the enrollment forms, and you can call each one to verify my alibi," Miss Vardi stated with renewed spirit.

Beale wrote in his notepad, "Twenty-five artists, drew a picture of a truck and a question mark." "Miss

Vardi, we were informed that you have security cameras on the property. That's how you were alerted that arsonists were in the process of setting your barn on fire."

"One arsonist. I saw one man splashing gasoline against the barn. The other guy wasn't on camera, he must have been vandalizing my truck, and then came up behind me and clobbered me on the head." Miss Vardi reached up and ever-so-slowly rubbed the back of her head. Her eyes closed with the initial touch followed by a pained expression that enveloped her face while she moved her fingers up and down the short purple hairs. "Would you like to touch it, Detective? It's still sore, and I can feel a goose-egg bump back there."

"I don't think that will be necessary," said Beale. "We also need the security disc for last Friday, the day you were teaching the art class."

"The sheriff took the disc, but last Friday's recordings won't be on the disc; it's been erased," said Miss Vardi. "Every seventy-two hours the security camera records over the previous recordings and starts a new security session unless the owner manually transfers the episodes onto another disc, which I didn't."

"How convenient," Hordowski muttered under his breath.

"I resent the insinuation, Detective. There were absolutely no wrongdoings on my part. And for your information, since the security installation every recording was erased. The reason for the erasure was strictly monetary. The security system is an inexpensive package and does not feature a save picture rescue option." Miss Vardi put her hands on her hips and stared at the Detective.

Beale intervened, calmed the situation down, and thanked Miss Vardi for her cooperation. "Before we leave, can we have that list of artists?"

Miss Vardi scurried up the path to the barn and in no time returned with the list, which she handed to Beale. If looks could kill ... She shot Hordowski a look of indignation, said goodbye, and walked back to the barn.

On the way back to the car Beale took out his notepad and wrote, "Who borrowed the truck, and drew a question mark."

"She's lying," Hordowski said as they pulled out of the parking lot. "She knows something. It has to be her truck, and as soon as we confirm that the sandhill crane sign we have is the identical sign from Morty King's BMW, she's toast."

"So when we get back to the station, why don't you go over to the sheriff's office drop off the sign, and ask Johnson if you can look at the Purple Lady's disc. Maybe we'll get lucky and find that something from last Friday is retrievable. Then on your way back visit King Amusement and ask Morty what happened to the sandhill crane sign that was sticking out of his BMW. I'm going to take another look at Daisy Clearing's file and see if there is anything we may have missed." Beale turned onto Border Road, pushed down on the accelerator, and felt the power of the Crown Vic's 215 hp V8 motor thrust the car forward along the highway.

Hordowski rolled down the window and let the cool breeze fill the car's cabin with a gust of fresh air while he watched the Purple Lady's property disappear in the distance. "That reminds me, on a number of cold case files there's written in big, black ink Chilled-4, Chilled-6, Chilled-10, and so on. Do you have any idea what that means?"

I was asked to open a cold case from 1951. On Halloween night, a Black man was shot behind the Standard Oil gas station where the Lucky Dog restaurant is today. No witnesses, no murder weapon, no motive for the killing. The case lay unsolved for almost fifty years when the department received a call from the Venice Hospital on Halloween night." Beale stopped at the light at Pinebrook and put on his turn signal.

"You're joking! Fifty years to the day you get the tip that solved the case? I don't believe it; sounds like a prank call to me," Hordowski blurted out and shook his head in disbelief.

"Believe it, Detective. I took the call." Beale turned left onto Capri Isles Blvd. "It was a little after eleven o'clock. A doctor from the hospital, Dr. Joseph Solinas, said a patient wanted to confess to a crime he committed fifty years ago. I drove over to the hospital, met the doctor who informed me that Mr. Doyle was in an automobile crash, and during surgery had a heart attack, and due to his age and poor physical condition would not survive the night."

Beale turned left onto Deerfield and slowed to a crawl past the Fifth Third bank. "Doyle looked like crap, bandages all over his head, left arm in a cast, and one leg hanging from a sling over the bed. It was a miracle that he could speak at all, but he did. He described how he was fooling around with the gun where he worked part-time pumping gas behind the gas station when a Black man walked up behind him and startled him. He turned around and the gun went off. He was sixteen, panicked, ran home, and hid the gun under the floor boards in his bedroom. The murder was front page news, but after a few weeks, and with no arrests Doyle moved on with his life. But recently in poor health and with the auto accident, Doyle decided to clear his conscience and confess."

"And this has to do with Chilled-4 written on the cold case files, how?" Hordowski asked.

"Patience, Detective, patience. You're never going to make lead detective if you don't have patience." Beale pulled into the police parking lot, and backed into his spot next to the side-entrance door.

"Okay, okay I get it, but let's finish the story before

our shift is over," Hordowski barked, and unbuckled his seat belt.

"You know Detective Weber? He's commander of the school resource officers, the old guy with bad acne. He told me back in the '50s that the old police station didn't have air conditioning, and there were weeks when the temperature lived in '90s, so when the fans couldn't cool down the place, detectives took a chilled bottle of beer from the ice box to cool off. The number next to "Chilled" signified how many beers were consumed before the case was closed. Weber heard that a number of detectives requested the tough cases just to cool down and drink beer, but that was never verified to his knowledge. Venice chill ended when the new police station was opened and central air conditioning cooled the entire department."

Hordowski walked over to his cruiser, opened the trunk and placed the sandhill crane sign inside. "Thanks for the history lesson, Detective. See you tomorrow."

"Don't forget we have a meeting with the Chief at eight o'clock. Hopefully you'll have some definitive information on that sign, and I can dig up something from Purdy Jones' report." Beale walked inside the station as Hordowski pulled out of the parking lot.

Chapter 47

Meetings never go as planned, especially early morning ones scheduled under duress by someone from outside the department. Beale was first to arrive. Hordowski rushed in five minutes later out of breath and a bit disheveled. The chief's office was empty, but the conference room across the hall was full of people. Beale had a feeling that the room was selected not for convenience but to send a message of authority.

Seated at the head of the table was the chief, to his right the mayor, the city attorney, and director of tourism. Across from them was the chief of detectives and two empty chairs presumably, for the two guests of honor who were unceremoniously late.

"Detectives, welcome. Please sit down so we may get started," said the chief. "I'm certain everyone knows each other, so I'll forego formal introductions and proceed with the meeting." Seven heads automatically turned in acknowledgement; and with a cursory smile, each member at the table readied themselves for battle. "Detective Beale, what have you uncovered pertaining to the Daisy Clearing case?" asked the chief.

Beale began his testimony with a review of the cold case file on Daisy Clearing which, concluded that most likely Daisy Clearing succumbed to some wrongdoing in Washington, D. C. He quoted the testimony of the parents that she bought a train ticket, packed her red suitcase, and had a train schedule that the station master organized for her. This was acknowledged by a letter Daisy wrote found in the train depot display case. Beale also summarized the report written by a private detective the Clearings hired to search for their daughter, but in the end nothing conclusive was noted. Finally Beale shared a Washington, D. C. police report stating that Daisy Clearing was not identified as missing, injured or hospitalized, which led the Venice Police Department to label the case unsolved.

"However, Detective, with the discovery of the body of Daisy Clearing, you must have additional information," the mayor interjected.

"That is correct, Mr. Mayor. We have a subsequent statement from her boyfriend, Holden J. Winthrop III. Because of an argument over her participating in the March on Washington, he didn't drive her to the station but left her at Osprey State Park." Beale waited for a reply.

"Is that the real estate mogul from Venice? The guy who screams his deals are huge?" The city attorney asked.

"The same," answered Hordowski. "And not only do we have his testimony, we also have Daisy Clearing's diary." Hordowski held up the pink diary. "However, information from the diary ended on August 25, 1963, the night before she was scheduled to take the train to Washington, D.C., so we can't confirm or deny that she got on the train."

"What were Winthrop and Clearing arguing about, and why were they in the park?" The city attorney asked.

"Winthrop was embarrassed to have his girlfriend

participating in a civil rights demonstration. His friends chided him constantly about his 'nigger-loving girlfriend' until on the day of her departure, he told her she had to choose between Washington or him. She chose Washington, and he drove off."

"Detective Hordowski, I still don't understand why Winthrop drove to the park. Why not drive to the train station, and if she chose Washington, just leave her there to board the train? Why leave the poor girl stranded in the park?" repeated the attorney.

Hordowski looked around the room and realized that the rest of the people in the room were also questioning the rationale behind the location and that they were waiting for an explanation. Hordowski took a deep breath, collected his thoughts, and said, "Sex. The park was their special place, so Winthrop believed he could sweet talk Daisy into staying and then have sex in the back seat of his car." No one commented, but the disquieting expression on their faces spoke volumes.

Beale sat quietly for a moment, and then with a mischievous grin on his face blurted out, "Now that sex is out of the way, I am sorry to say that to date nothing substantive was found to establish that Clearing took the train to Washington, D.C. However, the diary provides information about her high school friends who may shed some light on her disappearance." Beale opened his folder. "In particular, a Gilda Gooseberry, aka Strawberry Girl, a close friend of Daisy, whom as you all must have read is now protesting the destruction of a banyan tree in downtown Venice." Beale held up a photo of Strawberry Girl perched on a limb high above the ground.

"We are well aware of Ms. Gooseberry's protest, Detective, and hope to resolve the conflict sometime today, but how can she help?" asked the mayor.

"Unlike the diary entries pertaining to Winthrop that

were solely about dances, parties and sex, Gooseberry's entries talked about specific protests, places, feelings and other people they encountered along the way."

"So why haven't you interviewed this Strawberry Girl, Detective?" asked the attorney.

"We attempted an interview, but as you can see conducting an interview with a person of interest forty feet in the air was ... well, fruitless. However, she did inform us that she gave an interview to an Osprey State Park ranger and that we should interview her." Beale folded up the picture of Strawberry Girl, and placed it back into his folder. "We intend to interview Assistant Park Manager Blaine Sterling after this morning's meeting."

"I'm curious, Detective Beale. How did Gilda Gooseberry come to be called 'Strawberry Girl'?" the mayor asked.

"It's a long story, Mr. Mayor. Maybe another time, sir." Beale looked over at the mayor, and to his relief the mayor nodded in agreement.

"Before the detectives march off to interview Assistant Park Manager Sterling, I would like to present information on the Daisy Clearing case that directly impacts the financial well-being of our city each day that the case remains unsolved." The director of tourism stood and walked over to a bulletin board in the front of the room and turned it around. "If I may have your attention, I would submit that the City of Venice is losing tourist dollars every day."

Plastered over the board were front-page pictures from the Venice Journal Star of reporter Bryce Faceman and color photographs chronicling the Daisy Clearing case. The first picture titled "Venice Girl Murdered in Park," showed Faceman standing on the broken canoe dock. In the next picture, Faceman was shown standing in front of City Hall interviewing a passerby with a headline, "When Will Public Get

Answers to the Daisy Clearing Murder?" Another headline, "Did Daisy Clearing Board the Train," pictured Faceman standing at the Venice Train Depot.

Finally, the last illustration depicted Faceman standing outside the Sarasota Hospital with his arm around a human skeleton and the headline, "Where is Venice Girl's Autopsy Report? Head Injury Proves Murder!"

"Gentlemen, every day the media covers Daisy Clearing's case is a day that the City of Venice loses tourist dollars. People are not visiting our beautiful city, which translates into people are not checking into our hotels, people are not eating in our restaurants. They are fearful that the murderer is still free, and as a result they are not purchasing gifts from our local merchants. We are moving into the height of the tourist season, and to date the finance department has calculated that the City of Venice has lost more than one million dollars in lost revenue." The director turned the board around and walked back to her seat. "So, detectives, I say to you. When will you solve the Daisy Clearing case? The city is hemorrhaging, and it's only a matter of time until the patient loses all of her assets."

The chief rose, cleared his throat, and said, "This case has gone unsolved for over fifty years. Information from the initial investigation was minimal, and it is only now that we have a new direction as to what happened to Daisy Clearing. I am confident that our team of detectives will now be able to resolve this case. Does anyone have any further questions for Detectives Beale or Hordowski?"

The director of tourism raised her hand. "It's not exactly a question, Chief, but an observation compounding our public relations trustworthiness. To make matters worse, we have a seventy-one year old environmental fanatic living in a banyan tree in downtown Venice. Every day she tweets to thousands of viewers about her daily confrontation with the establishment and her difficult living conditions. And that news hound Bryce Faceman is spewing out daily reports about her fervent commitment to save the banyan tree. His negative assertions only add to damage the reputation of our good city, and I fear for our bottom line."

"The city is aware of the banyan tree incident and all its implications. Presently the city attorney is in contact with the bank and has presented a proposal we feel will bring this matter to a peaceful resolution," said the mayor. "I am not at liberty to put forth the details of the plan; however I am confident that the bank and Ms. Gooseberry will be satisfied. I want to thank you all for attending the meeting. Have a good day."

On the way out, the chief handed Beale an envelope from forensics and said, "This may be of some use when you interview the assistant park manager. Keep me informed."

"Will do, Sir," answered Beale as he and Hordowski walked outside. "Why don't you drive while I look at this report from forensics, but first tell me about the disc, and what King had to say about the sandhill crane sign?"

Hordowski pulled out of the parking lot and turned north on Capri Isles Blvd. towards Edmondson Road. "Nothing on the discs. Gooseberry was right about the erasers. Nothing from Friday's art class. Just the fire." Hordowski turned off Edmondson onto Pinebrook, and headed north towards Laurel Rd. "King is another story. I know he is lying through his teeth. He said he had no idea what happened to the sign and that the insurance company informed him that the car was totaled and was towed to Nicely's Recycling and Renewable Parts Company in Sarasota."

"I know that place," said Beale. "It's a gigantic junkyard back in the woods off Tamiami Trail. For five bucks you can hunt around for hours until you find your part, remove it from the vehicle, and then pay for the part back at the office. They have acres of cars, trucks, and busses. You name it, they have it."

"And if they don't have what you want, they can get it for you. Everything is on the computer. These guys aren't some Florida crackers collecting junk off the street. They have everything catalogued on their computers. They knew exactly where King's BMW was, and guess what?" Hordowski laughed.

"The sign wasn't there!" answered Beale.

"Bingo. The car was there, and the load of horse shit still covered the seats, but no sign."

"Why am I not surprised, Detective Hordowski?" said Beale, as he held up the forensics report. "Because there is only one sandhill crane sign. That's what forensics concluded, plus they found fingerprints from King and two other unidentified individuals. No prints from the Purple Lady."

"So the fire and BMW are linked together by the sign. How?" Hordowski asked, and turned right onto Tamiami Trail. "I don't believe the Purple Lady dumped the manure over the BMW. Do you?"

"No, I don't, but she is hiding something. What I do know is when we get the forensic report on the truck, and if the two unidentified prints from the sign and truck match, then you will have an answer." Beale slid the report back into the manila folder and looked out the window as a squadron of pelicans skimmed inches from the water in perfect formation. "Slow down, the entrance to the park is coming up. Try not to fly by it like those pelicans."

Chapter 48

Bryce Faceman stood in front of the old banyan tree as police attempted to control a large crowd that formed along the street and sidewalk across from the huge tree. The cameraman focused on a close-up of the newscaster with his perfectly combed hair, big white smile, and a $1600 custom-tailored suit. “Hurry up, she’s coming down,” Faceman yelled at the cameraman.

“All set; ready when you are. Three, two, and one: You’re live.”

“Good morning viewers, this is Bryce Faceman reporting live from downtown Venice where Gilda Gooseberry is right now coming down from the banyan tree and ending; her successful protest to save this old, beloved tree.” Faceman pointed to the tree, and the camera panned up through the tree limbs to highlight Gooseberry’s descent.

The crowd that swelled to over three hundred erupted in screams and shouts of joy and began to push closer towards the tree. The police line gave way in the center, and a handful of protesters ran towards the tree shouting “Save the tree.” Like a house of cards, the police line collapsed, and all the protesters ringed the banyan tree just as Gooseberry touched terra firma.

A bit wobbly on her feet, Gooseberry smiled and waved to the crowd. She held up the peace sign, and the crowd went crazy. Faceman grabbed her arm and said, “Ms. Gooseberry, how does it feel to be standing on the ground after weeks of protest up in the tree?”

“It feels solid. There were nights that the wind blew with such force I thought I’d be thrown to the ground, but I persevered, weathered the storm, and here I am now.”

“I am told that the mayor intervened and brokered an agreement between you and the bank. Is that correct?”

“Yes it is. I was not going to leave the tree until another site was selected for the bank’s parking lot. That was my position from the start, and I was prepared to remain up in the tree for as long as it took to save her.” Gooseberry waved to the crowd. “I want to thank the many supporters who helped me throughout this ordeal and say that today is a victory not for me but for the environment. Thank you all.”

The camera focused on a close-up of Faceman, and in a sarcastic tone, the reporter said, “There is a rumor that the city gave the bank the rights to lease the public parking space across from the bank because your protest was costing the city money. Do you think that’s why the mayor agreed to your demands?”

“I don’t know, you’ll have to ask him yourself. Personally I don’t give a damn what his motive was. All I cared about was saving the banyan tree. Anyway, I’m leaving Venice and taking a long overdue vacation in Cannon Ball, North Dakota.” Gilda smiled and walked over to a friend leaning against the banyan tree.

“Isn’t that the area where the Indians are protesting the oil pipeline?” Faceman shouted.

Gooseberry turned and shouted back, “They’re

Native Americans. And for your edification, there are many other protesters from around the country in North Dakota rallying with the Native Americans to support their struggle against the oil giants of the world. An old friend from Venice High School just invited me to join the protest and I'm going. Her name is Bobbie Jo Morabetto. She's Italian."

The camera panned back to Faceman, who was silent and without his classic bright smile, until reality kicked in and he uttered, "This is Bryce Faceman saying goodbye from Venice."

Chapter 49

The phone on Blaine Sterling's desk rang four times before she picked up the receiver. With the receiver in one hand, Blaine hit the send key with a free finger and off went her reply to Director Goodie's request for an update on the Daisy Clearing matter. "Hello, Blaine Sterling, Assistant Park Manager, how may I help you?"

"Good morning, Blaine, this is Strawberry Girl. I won! The bank caved in. The banyan tree is saved and will see another day to spread its long roots down to earth."

"That's wonderful news, but what convinced them to stop the parking lot project?" asked Blaine.

"Not what, but who convinced the bank," laughed Strawberry Girl. "The mayor intervened and offered the bank parking space across the street. They agreed, end of protest, and now I'm off to Cannon Ball, North Dakota."

"That's where the pipeline protest is unfolding. I heard that more than a thousand protesters were camped near the oil construction site, and organizers believe another thousand people will arrive within a month. Why there? Isn't there another environmental cause closer to Florida, a state a little warmer than North Dakota? I read it snowed there last night, and another six inches was predicted by tomorrow."

"I'll bring a coat. Anyway, I told you the other day I choose my battles based upon need, not meteorological forecasts," chuckled Strawberry Girl. "But that's not why I called...well not exactly."

"Okay, Gilda Gooseberry, I'm all ears."

Over the next twenty minutes, Strawberry Girl explained how Bobbie Jo Morabetto, an old friend from high school who was protesting in North Dakota, called her last night asking her to join the demonstration for old time's sake. That invitation ignited a conversation about the Daisy Clearing disappearance, and to her surprise, Bobbie Jo said she saw Fix-it Freddy last year. He was a Salvation Army Bell Ringer at the Publix Supermarket in Venice.

Bobby Jo recalled that it was the day of Publix's Holiday Fest party, where free food and drinks were offered to all the customers. A commotion at the hot dog station caught the eye of Bobbie Jo, a handful of customers, and the store manager Melody Pruitt, who, was questioning Freddy about eating a handful of hot dogs and why he was not outside by his kettle. Melody, who is a most welcoming manager, mild mannered, and always accommodating to customers, was deeply concerned that day over Freddy's presence in the food court. She explained that his responsibility was outside at the Salvation Army kettle, not eating inside. Ms. Pruitt had two employees usher Freddy out the door and threatened to write a letter of reprimand to the Salvation Army if she saw him inside again.

"That is fantastic news, Gilda. I'm sure the Salvation Army will have some documentation on Freddy. More than likely he is living in the Venice area. Well thank you, Strawberry Girl. Please promise me you will stay warm in North Dakota, but if you can't stay warm, promise me you will stay safe."

"You're welcome, but don't bank on the Salvation Army being family-friendly to your request for confidential records on a volunteer bell ringer. I would bet you they'll be just as hard-nosed as the bank."

"I have that bureaucratic red tape already unraveled, and he just walked into my office," Blaine laughed.

"Catch the bastard that murdered my friend, Blaine Sterling." They both hung up.

"Hello, Detective Beale and Detective Hordowski. I imagine your ears were ringing. Strawberry Girl and I were just talking about you," Blaine said, and offered them a seat at the conference table.

"I'm impressed how Gilda Gooseberry gives you an interview, then phones you at your office, and I can't even get a statement from her. Why is that?" scoffed Beale.

"Maybe it was because you didn't bring blueberry scones," said Blaine.

"I told you we should have brought donuts, but you said no," Hordowski said jokingly.

"Very funny: The two of you make a great comedy team, but this case is no laughing matter. The chief wants answers, and right now we don't have any leads. Blaine, I'm hoping that you might have some information that will kick start our investigation." Beale opened the pink diary to the last entry and said, "Daisy wrote that she was worried that Winthrop wouldn't take her to the train station. She mentioned it on the last page. Winthrop admitted he left Clearing at the park alive with her ticket, her suitcase, and her headstrong attitude. So what did Clearing do? Her mind was made up to go to Washington, so she had to ask someone for a ride to the station, but who?"

Blaine opened her agenda book where she was jotting down notes from Strawberry Girl's phone call. "Fix-it Freddy. Daisy had to ask Fix-it Freddy."

"And who is Fix-it Freddy?" Beale asked, and wrote in his notepad, "Fix-it Freddy, and drew a big question mark."

Blaine looked down at her notes and with a smile said, "He was a homeless man who lived in the park, and his job was to fix the bicycles at the homeless camp. Daisy, Strawberry Girl and Bobbie Jo Morabetto would bring food and a variety of sundry items to the camp once a month. Daisy knew he had a bicycle and would most likely take her to the station."

"Bobbie Jo Morabetto, she's that protester in North Dakota who was arrested for chaining herself to some tractor. They were all in that Political Club in high school, I have the report on my desk," Hordowski blurted out.

"That's correct, Detective. The very same." Blaine mentioned that Bobbie Joe called Strawberry Girl last night to invite her to join the protest in North Dakota. Strawberry Girl agreed because the bank decided not to cut down the banyan tree, but rather accept the City of Venice's offer to rent the parking lot across the street. During the conversation Strawberry Girl asked Bobbie Jo if she knew what happened to Fix-it Freddy, and she replied that she saw him at the Publix last Christmas, ringing a bell for the Salvation Army. "Fortunately for us, he was being reprimanded by the manager, Melody Pruitt, for eating food from the Holiday Feast rather than ringing his bell."

"Now we're getting somewhere," said Hordowski. "This guy sounds like trouble. Maybe this is our murderer. I'll call the Salvation Army and get Freddy's last name and then check CODIS to see if he has any priors." Hordowski puffed out his chest as if he solved the case. Beale wrote in his notepad, "Salvation Army, and drew a kettle."

"I wouldn't jump to any conclusions, Detective. From Bobby Jo's portrayal of Fix-it Freddy, he did not sound like a criminal. On the contrary, all this guy wanted to do was to help people, not murder them," said Blaine. "However, he may have additional information pertaining to Daisy Clearing's disappearance."

"My money is still on this Fix-it Freddy guy," Hordowski said tersely, leaning back in his chair, and stretching out his arms in victory.

"Either way, Fix-it Freddy is our best lead. Let's see where it takes us before we make any rash judgments about the man. On another note, Blaine, why would your friend Vardi Zammiello take her purple truck and empty a load of horse manure onto Morty King's BMW?" Beale said in his most avuncular voice.

"That's absurd. I saw the six o'clock news report with Bryce Faceman about Morty King, a sandhill crane, and a BMW covered in horse manure. There was no mention of the Purple Lady. How can you make such an accusation?" snapped Blaine. "What proof do you have?"

"An eye witness saw a purple truck leaving the parking lot at the time of the incident," Hordowski scoffed.

"Did your eye witness see the Purple Lady driving the truck?"

"No," Hordowski answered.

"Did the witness take down the license plate number?" said Blaine

"No, he didn't."

"And I suppose Miss Vardi has the only purple truck in Florida! I spoke with her the day after you and your officers storm trooped onto her property, interrogated her, confiscated her truck and threatened to arrest her if she didn't cooperate."

"Blaine, we didn't storm troop onto Vardi Zammiello's property. We were investigating an arson fire and the probable connection to a vandalism case in Venice," Beale interjected.

"Miss Vardi told you she was teaching an art class

at the time of this vandalism incident in Venice, which I'm sure you verified, so I suggest you concentrate on identifying the individuals who attempted to burn down her barn." Blaine picked up her planner, pushed back her chair, stood and extended her hand. "I hope the information on Fix-it Freddy will assist you in finding the person or persons responsible for Daisy Clearing's murder. If there is nothing more to discuss, I need to hurry to a ranger meeting at the Nature Center in five minutes."

"I think we have everything we need. Thank you for the information, and we will keep you updated." The detectives said their goodbyes, and left.

Blaine sat down and dialed Lou Bravo's number: "Hi, I need you to find someone."

Chapter 50

Back at the office, Hordowski phoned the local Salvation Army on Albee Farm Road, but he was rebuffed by the Volunteer/Resource Development Coordinator, Patricia Horwell, who informed him that all personnel files were housed at their headquarters in Lutz, Florida. Horwell provided Hordowski with the Lutz number, but she added that more than likely he would require a court order to obtain any personnel records.

Hordowski had greater success with Captain Warren, Human Resource Director of Southwest Florida who, after listening to a detailed commentary regarding the murder of Daisy Clearing, provided him with Freddy Coop's address without hesitation. Warren also acknowledged that Coop was no longer on their bell ringer volunteer list and apologized for any inconvenience the Salvation Army may have created with the centralization of their documents.

"I have Freddy's address. He lives in Venice, 102 Alligator Drive," Hordowski called out with a smug grin that enveloped his face. "Let's go pick him up."

"Not so fast, cowboy. I'm not convinced that Freddy

is our man. I don't believe we should go charging over to his house and arrest him for murder. I just finished a section in the diary, and this guy seems to be a peaceful, easygoing giant that was tagged Fix-it Freddy because he helped everyone in the camp fix their bicycles." Beale held up the diary with a picture of a big man working on a bicycle.

"Just because this guy fixes bicycles doesn't mean he's a saint. Maybe he wanted a little action with Daisy, she said no, and he killed her. The guy's a giant. That's how it describes him in the diary: over six foot, muscular body, thick arms, a weight lifters chest, and big fleshy hands that could squeeze the life from a little girl. He is a monster of a man. With all that strength, what chance would a teenage girl have if he lost his temper? None."

"Again, just because he's big doesn't mean he's a murderer. Daisy described how Freddy spent more than a half-hour taking a bike apart after a man from the camp, Buffalo Bill, caught his pants leg in the chain of his bicycle and couldn't get free. He managed to drag himself and the bike into camp and collapsed in front of Freddy's tent. Buffalo Bill's jeans were wound so tightly around the chain that his right foot became wedged between the spokes, and the bicycle frame exacerbated the pain." Beale closed the diary and stood. "We need to take it slow, Detective. Remember, all we need is information. When all our ducks are in order and an arrest is warranted, then he'll be arrested. Let's go question Fix-it Freddy."

Alligator Drive was a short drive from the station, maybe five minutes down Tamiami Trail if traffic wasn't backed up along the construction zone. Unfortunately, traffic was backed up. A dump truck carrying a load of blacktop material blew a tire and tipped over, dumping its entire load of steaming-hot blacktop onto both lanes of the highway. Two yellow front-end loader trucks and a dozen workers feverishly worked to clear a single lane of highway so traffic could move forward. So a five-minute drive turned into a fifteen-minute wait. Finally traffic limped along until they passed the construction site where the highway opened up into four lanes. Three minutes later, Beale turned right on to Alligator Drive and immediately spotted Fix-it Freddy's residence five houses down on the right-hand side.

"Look at all those bicycles! There has to be at least fifty bikes, maybe more," Hordowski said, pointing to the collection of bicycles that lined the entire driveway.

"Do you think it's Fix-it Freddy's place?" laughed Beale, and pulled up to the curb.

"What gave you that idea, detective? Could it be all the used bicycles on the driveway, or the wooden sign hanging from the lamppost that reads: Fix-it Freddy's Place?"

"Not exactly. It's the giant of a man working on a bicycle in the carport," Hordowski laughed.

"Brilliant detective work, Sherlock, now let's go interview Mr. Coop."

Fix-it Freddy's home was a small concrete block house, single-story, painted a pale yellow faded by time and weather. A cracked concrete driveway led to a carport filled with bicycles, bicycle parts and a small work area where a large black man stood hunched over a bicycle repairing a tire.

"Mr. Freddy Coop?" Beale called out, as he stepped forward with his shield held out in front for Mr. Coop to see. "I'm Detective Beale, and this is Detective Hordowski. We would like to talk to you about the disappearance of Daisy Clearing."

Freddy stood up straight and walked over to the two detectives. When standing, he was a good head taller than both men, who were six foot tall themselves. He reached out his hand, and the detectives couldn't help but notice the strength and massive size of his hand.

"Pleased to meet you, Detectives. I saw the news

about Daisy's body being discovered at Osprey State Park last week. How can I help you, gentlemen?"

"We were told that Daisy and other students brought food to the homeless camp where you lived back in the '60s. We also have information that you and Daisy were friendly," said Beale. He took out his notepad.

"That's right. She was a very nice girl. She truly cared about people like me and the other homeless people in the camp. I was shocked to hear that her body was found in the park." A blank look covered his face. His eyes darted back and forth from one detective to the other looking for an answer.

"When was the last time you saw Daisy, Mr. Coop?" Beale asked, and wrote in his notepad, "Last time Freddy saw Daisy, and drew a question mark."

"I saw her the day she was taking the train to Washington. She walked into camp dressed in a blue and white polka dot dress and carrying a red suitcase. Her boyfriend left her at the park, so she needed a ride to the train station."

Beale wrote, "Daisy went to homeless camp, and drew a suitcase." "Did you take her to the station?" Hordowski asked.

"No, someone stole my bike so I couldn't take her. Maybe if I had my bike she would be alive today. I feel responsible. I let her down. If I'd only had my bike," Freddy moaned and covered his face.

"So what did Daisy do?" Beale asked.

"She walked out of the camp and back to the picnic area. That was the last I saw of her. I should have walked back with her. Why didn't I walk back with her?" Freddy wiped a tear from his eye and turned away.

Beale wrote in his notepad in large letters, "Innocent, and drew an exclamation mark." "Freddy, you are not responsible for Daisy's murder. There was no way you could have known she would be killed at the park. Like everyone else you believed she went to Washington, D. C. Thank you for your time, and if there is anything else you can recall about that day, please call. Here is my card." They shook hands and walked down the driveway.

Halfway down the driveway Hordowski called out, "Where do you get all these bikes?"

"Garbage pickup is Wednesday, so every Tuesday night I drive around the neighborhoods and pick up bicycles left in the trash. I take them apart, clean them up, repair the frames, put new tires on, and sell them. Gives me spending money. I'll give you a good deal on that ten-speed next to you. What do you say?" Freddy yelled back.

"How much?"

"For you, Detective, ten bucks!" Freddy replied.

"You got yourself a deal, Mister," Hordowski called out, and took out his wallet.

"You got yourself a fine bicycle, Detective," smiled Freddy, and slipped the money into his pocket.

Hordowski placed the bicycle in the trunk, hopped into the car, and sat back against the seat. As the car pulled away from the curb he said with a smile, "He's not our guy."

"I agree. Unfortunately, we're back to square one. Who killed Daisy Clearing? The chief isn't going to be happy." Beale turned onto Tamiami Trail, eased into the right-hand lane, and accelerated. "So what are you going to do with the bike?" Beale asked with a skeptical glance.

"Wouldn't you like to know, Mr. Nosey Parker? I'll give you one hint, Venice Half Triathlon."

"Good luck, Mr. Glutton for Punishment," sang Beale, and moved into the left hand lane, and back to the station.

Chapter 51

Pizza on Friday night had been a family tradition since Blaine was a small child. Her parents would either order a large pie with extra cheese and half pepperoni, a salad, and a side order of meat balls and spaghetti delivered to the house, or they would go to their favorite pizzeria, Momma Leonia's in Hauppauge. It was the family's way to end the work week and welcome the start of the weekend. Pizza on a Tuesday night was unusual, very unusual. It either meant something very good or something very bad.

"Hello, Pizza Lady, I'm home, and the pie is right out of the oven," Blaine called as she walked through the front door, and headed towards the kitchen. "Hello, where is everybody?"

At the same moment Brooke and Mrs. Brecht burst into the living room and greeted the pizza lady with a joyous, "Hello. The pizza smells delicious Mommy, but today is Tuesday. We have pizza on Friday. Why are we having pizza today?" asked Brooke.

"To celebrate your idea to save the sandhill cranes. Let's go into the kitchen and have dinner, I'm starved." Blaine pushed open the kitchen door, and set the food down on the table that was already set for dinner.

"Can you stay for a slice of pizza, Mrs. Brecht? It looks scrumsedelicious," Brooke giggled, and pulled a slice apart, and placed it on her plate.

"I'd love to Honey, but I need to go home and make dinner for Mr. Brecht. Thank you for the invitation, and enjoy your pizza. 'Bye."

"So Sweetie, tell me about your day. Did Mrs. Malott like your report? What did the class think about your idea about the sandhill crane signs? Tell me everything," Blaine implored, and spooned out a helping of spaghetti and meatballs, and a small portion of salad onto Brooke's plate.

Over two slices of pizza, a half plate of spaghetti, and two forkfuls of salad Brooke, explained how Mrs. Malott loved her report, thought the idea of sandhill crane signs placed around town was an excellent suggestion, and as a class project she asked each student to design a sign to present to the city council. The principal came into the class after lunch, said that he spoke to a council member, and that the class would present their Save the Sandhill Crane project to the city council on Tuesday. Lastly, Brooke said that Mrs. Malott ordered the bus, handed out a permission slip, and asked the kids to invite their parents to attend the city council meeting.

"That is wonderful news, Brooke. I will definitely be there. I'll call Lou Bravo and ask him to invite Kevin Barton from the Wildlife Center of Venice to the meeting, and I'm sure Mr. Barton will inform other wildlife groups in the area to attend. I'm so proud of you Brooke." A little embarrassed from all the attention, and accolades bestowed upon her, but at the same time honored that her idea may help save a sandhill crane from a torturous death, Brooke asked to be dismissed to finish her homework while Blaine cleaned up from dinner.

"I'll be in shortly to say good night Sweetie," Blaine

called out, "but first I need to make a call." Blaine made a quick check of thc room and, satisfied everything was clean and put away, she turned on the dishwasher, switched off the kitchen light, and walked into the living room to make her phone call. Exhausted from the day's harried schedule, she plopped down on the couch, leaned back against the pillows, and dialed Lou Bravo's number.

After three rings the voice on the other end said, "Hello, Blaine, how are you?"

"Fine I hope I haven't interrupted your dinner, but I need a favor."

"No, I finished a long time ago. How can I help you?" Lou Bravo answered in a curious tone.

"I told you that I was asked to investigate the Daisy Clearing murder. Well, I reached a dead end until today when I was given the name of a person of interest that may help solve the crime." Blaine reached into her purse and took out a piece of paper.

"The Clearing thing is all over the news. A person would have to be living in a cave not to know about the case. So what is your new information, and how can I help?" Lou Bravo asked and turned off his television.

"Today I went over to Publix and spoke with Melody Pruitt, the store manager whom I was told had the name of the man who was a Salvation Army Bell ringer last year, the same individual who fifty-four years ago lived in a homeless camp at Osprey State Park when Daisy and two other girls brought food to the camp. I have his name, but no address."

"Why did the manager have this guy's name? Usually volunteers just show up, and volunteer. There wasn't any sign-up sheet when I volunteered two years ago. What's his name?"

"Fix-it Freddy, Freddy Coop. You're correct, there wasn't a sign-in sheet, but Freddy spent more time eating the free food Publix offered than ringing the bell. Pruitt confronted him and sent a blistering letter to the

Salvation Army. She kept a copy of the letter on file and gave it to me with a big smile. Can you get his address?" Blaine asked.

"No problem. I have a friend at the DMV. I'll call him tomorrow. Anything else?" Lou Bravo turned on the television. "By the way your friend Bryce Faceman from Channel 6 news is on. He's interviewing some old gal, Strawberry Girl, who just climbed down from a banyan tree in Venice. You should listen to this lady take Faceman to task. What a firecracker."

"She's the one who gave me Fix-it Freddy's name. Also, can you come with me to meet Mr. Coop in case he's the murderer?" Blaine turned on the TV, and waited for an answer.

"I'll see you tomorrow. I'll also bring a friend along as an extra added attraction." They both hung up, and at the same time turned off the television.

Chapter 52

The yellow El Camino stopped behind the school bus in front of Blaine's house. As if on command, Brooke Sterling bounded out the front door and raced across the yard for the waiting bus. With an overloaded backpack swaying from side to side and one arm clutching long rolls of colored papers, the spirited student appeared to teeter on disaster as she attempted to balance her belongings and manage the steps into the bus. However, with the agility of a nimble gazelle, she successfully entered the bus, took her seat, and waved goodbye to her mother on the stoop and Lou Bravo sitting in the El Camino.

"Good morning, Blaine," Lou Bravo shouted. "Are you ready to go? I have Coop's address."

"I'll be down in a minute," Blaine replied and walked inside to retrieve Daisy's diary notes.

Lou Bravo thought it strange that Blaine was in uniform, especially when she had mentioned the other day that she had the day off. He did have to admit she looked impressive in her forest green shirt with dark green shoulder epaulets, Florida Park Service patches on both sleeves, dark green pants and polished black boots. Standing close to six feet tall, with straight blonde hair tied in a ponytail, and an athletic physique, Blaine Sterling projected an air of official business. The car door opened, and she slid in. "I thought you had the day off."

"Change of plans. Anyway, I thought the uniform would add a little drama to our meeting with Fix-it Freddy."

"His address is 102 Alligator Drive. I drove over there earlier this morning to check the place out. It's only about five minutes away, but the weird part is Freddy sells bicycles from his house. He must have a hundred recycled bicycles lined up and down his driveway. Most likely, he collected old bicycles from the neighbors' garbage, fixes them, and puts them out for sale. Some of them, I have to admit, looked like new."

"That's why he was called Fix-it Freddy," said Blaine.

"That's the good news. The bad news is that Freddy's a giant. I watched him put out the bikes this morning. That man has to be almost seven feet tall, and has a body like Goliath. He's huge." Lou Bravo uttered, and pulled away from the curb.

"I know, Daisy described him in her diary. But unlike the Biblical Goliath, she depicted Freddy as a 'Gentle Giant.' He's now probably seventy-five-years old, and I'm sure he has mellowed with time."

"I hope you're right. Here we are. Need a bike?" Laughed Lou Bravo as he pulled to the curb.

An elderly couple stood in the middle of Freddy's driveway surrounded by bicycles of all sizes, colors and makes. Lou Bravo and Blaine overheard the woman say to Freddy that they just arrived from the colds of Michigan and wanted to purchase two bicycles to ride around town. Nothing expensive, but bicycles that would be safe and easy to handle.

The big man pointed to two tricycles, one red, the

other blue, both sporting an orange flag sticking up from a rear metal basket. Freddy grabbed the red bicycle in his massive hands, picked it up, and dropped it to the cement. “Sturdy as a tank, and easy to turn,” he said and jerked the handle bars back and forth. “I’ll sell you the pair for fifty dollars,” Freddy gave the blue bike a shake, and smiled.

The old man looked at his wife, then back at the bicycles, and made a counter-offer of thirty dollars for both bicycles.

“Forty dollars, and that’s the lowest I will go,” declared Freddy. “Do we have a deal?”

The woman reached into her pocketbook and handed Freddy two crisp twenty dollar bills which he stuffed into his shirt pocket. The big man picked up both tricycles and walked to the back of the couple’s car and placed them in their trunk.

“Welcome to Florida, enjoy the warm weather, and I hope you have fun riding around Venice. Tell your friends if they need a dependable bicycle, Fix-it Freddy’s is the place to shop. ’Bye now.”

Freddy walked back up the driveway to where Lou Bravo and Blaine were looking at a refurbished royal blue Royce Cruiser. “That’s a beauty, a vintage ’70s bike. Runs like a charm. I can let you have it for sixty dollars, and that’s a great bargain.”

“We’re not in market for a bicycle today. However they all look in excellent running condition, and when it’s time for a new bike, I’ll definitely stop by,” said Blaine. “My name is Blaine Sterling, and this is Lou Bravo. I am the Assistant Park Manager at Osprey State Park, and I have been placed in charge of investigating the murder of Daisy Clearing whose skeleton was discovered in the park a few days ago.” Blaine offered her hand.

“Yes, I saw the news report on the television. It was awful,” Freddy uttered and let go of Blaine’s hand. He reached over and shook Lou Bravo’s hand.

"Wow that's some grip, big fella," Lou Bravo barked out, rubbing his fingers in hopes to bring back the circulation.

"Oh sorry. I didn't mean to squeeze so hard."

"Freddy, I read Daisy's diary, I also spoke with Strawberry Girl, and know you were friends with the both of them. On the day Daisy was scheduled to take the train to Washington, D.C., did you see her?" Blaine looked up at the big man and noticed a tear his eye.

"Yes, her boyfriend left her, and she needed a ride to the train station, but someone stole my bike the night before so I couldn't take her. I told the two police detectives the same thing yesterday. I told them I didn't know how she got to the station. Now I find out she never got there." Freddy looked down and rubbed the handle bars of the Royce bicycle with a rag he pulled from his back pocket.

"Did she say anything to you about how she planned to get to the station?" asked Blaine. "Was she going to walk to the station?"

"No, it was too far. Plus she had on a pretty new blue and white polka dot dress, new patent leather shoes, and a big red suitcase that I carried back to the picnic area for her. The suitcase was fairly heavy. It would have been impossible for her to carry it to the train station." Freddy stepped over to the empty space in the driveway where the two tricycles once stood and began to rearrange the remaining bicycles when he said, "Especially with a broken handle. I had to wire it together for her."

Lou Bravo moved next to Blaine and said, "So then what did you do?"

Freddy didn't answer right away. Instead a faraway stare appeared to transport him back to that hot August afternoon. Under the shade of the ancient oak trees, Freddy remembered a large family gathering celebrating a child's birthday. He recalled tables gaily decorated with pictures of circus animals, jumping clowns, and balloons, but most memorable were the large platters of food that filled the entire table. He could not remember a time when so much food was displayed in one place. The main attraction Freddy pictured was a small children's rollercoaster that bumped along the rails in the center of the grass, entertaining groups of children who screamed with joy at every turn. A rainbow-colored donkey piñata hung from a large scrub pine tree behind the picnic tables and spun in circles while the birthday boy swung blindly at the candy-filled treat in hopes of unlocking its treasures for all the children circled around. Finally, a fleeting flash of a pink carnival cotton candy machine and a carnival employee spinning its sugary pink magic to the delight of all the hungry children streamed before his eyes.

"There was a big party taking place. It was a child's birthday party. There was a kiddie rollercoaster carnival ride, a cotton candy machine, a donkey piñata, and tables full of food. Daisy recognized someone at the party. She was going to get a ride from him," Freddy gasped.

"Did she say his name? Remember Freddy, please remember," Blaine implored.

"No, she didn't, but she did say it was someone from school."

"Are you sure she said it was a boy from school?" asked Lou Bravo.

"Yes, she said, him. I'm positive," Freddy repeated.

"Did you see Daisy talking to the guy?" Lou Bravo asked again, but this time garishly loud.

"No, I dropped her off near the party and left to look for my bike. That was the last time I saw her. I'm sorry I didn't do more, but I had no idea someone would kill her. I feel so ashamed." Freddy looked away, hung his head, and sobbed.

"Freddy, you have nothing to feel ashamed about. There was nothing you could have done differently.

You took her to someone she recognized, whom she thought would help her. That was an admirable thing to do. Daisy had no idea that the outcome would be her murder. How could you have possibly known? You're a good man, Freddy Coop." Blaine reached out and hugged the big man.

"Thank you," Freddy whispered. "Will there be a funeral?"

"The skeleton is still in the county morgue, but I'm sure Daisy's sister, Emma, will have a ceremony as soon as the authorities finish their investigation. She lives in Venice. You should give her a call. I'm sure she would want you to attend the service." Blaine smiled and said goodbye.

Freddy smiled back, said goodbye, and turned to Lou Bravo, "So mister, can I interest you in that Royce bicycle? I'll give it away for fifty dollars, and that's a steal. What do you say?" Freddy picked up the bike, and held it over his head and said, "She'll fit fine in that pretty yellow El Camino."

"I'm not a bicycle kinda guy, but I can appreciate the hard work and craftsmanship you put into fixing all these fine bicycles. I once owned a car repair shop back in New York, and I remember the hours of hard work it involved to repair a broken vehicle. So throw that bad boy in the back of my truck, and here is your original price." Lou Bravo took out his gold money clip and peeled off three twenties. "Keep the change, and keep fixing things, Fix-it Freddy."

No sooner had the El Camino pulled away from the curb than Blaine's phone chirped. "Hello, John. Yes, I should be at the park shortly. I just finished interviewing Fix-it Freddy, a man who knew Daisy Clearing. I'll explain the connection at the meeting. Meet you at the workshop building? Okay. See you in a few minutes, 'Bye." Blaine turned off her phone and shook her head. "I'm dreading my meeting with the park manager. I'm no closer today to finding the murderer than I was at the start of this investigation. I'm not convinced that we will ever find out who killed Daisy Clearing, and that is a crime."

"Don't give up. You never can tell when the tiniest detail will help solve the big mystery. Anyway, are you prepared for tomorrow's city council meeting?" Lou Bravo asked and turned onto Serpentine Lane.

"I think so. Brooke has her speech almost memorized. The class painted beautiful sandhill crane crossing signs for the members of the city council to see, and Kevin Barton informed Brooke's teacher that his organization and the Audubon Society would have representatives at the meeting. It all sounds very exciting," Blaine crowed. "Too bad my meeting with Park Manager Forrester won't be as exciting. Thanks for the ride," said Blaine and stepped out of the car. "See you tomorrow."

"Speaking about speaking, Tony and Hubba Bubba want to speak to the council members tomorrow. That's what I call interesting," Lou Bravo added sarcastically and drove away.

Chapter 53

Thirty minutes later, Blaine pulled up to the park's workshop building, a cobbled gray-white clapboard structure that for years had operated as the official hub for the park's volunteers and the mainstay for all the park's building projects. She drove around to the back past the pole barn and carefully squeezed her Mini Cooper between Forrester's black pickup truck and a straggly old slash pine, terribly scarred over time by vehicles pushing in. Blaine took a deep breath and walked inside.

"Blaine, come over here, and look at this," Forrester shouted and waved her over. "What do you think?" Standing in the center of the room, Forrester and four volunteers, aka *old curmudgeons*, moved aside to allow Blaine to see what all the fuss was about. There on the cement floor were two gray granite memorial stones. Polished, both were the size and shape of a loose-leaf binder. They reflected the morning's sunlight with brilliant rays of white that filtered upward in all directions. The beams appeared almost spiritual in the dusty air of the workshop creating an air of reverent beauty.

"They're beautiful, John! I love the rough-edged stone cutting, combined with the highly polished face; they will truly commemorate the life of Ryan Murphy and the historic importance of the Native American cave. I'm having trouble reading the epitaphs etched into the stones. Can you read them please?"

"The first one reads," said John,

"RYAN L. MURPHY

June 3, 1977- April 16, 2017

Sarasota County Archeologist

Unearthed the past so all could see the future"

"The second," he continued:

"Ancient Native American Ceremonial Hunting Site

3000 A.D. - 1000 A.D.

Sacred Land To Be Preserved Forever"

"The volunteers are about to drill a small hole in the back of the stones and cement a two-foot bar in place which will anchor the stone at the memorial site that is being prepared as we speak. So let us get out of their way so they can work. We'll go over to the office where we can review the details of the memorial service, and you can give me your report on Daisy Clearing." Forrester and Blaine said goodbye and drove back to the office.

Once there, Forrester opened a folder on the conference table titled Memorial Service Osprey State Park. He handed Blaine a single sheet of notes and began to talk on each bullet point outlined in the report. Blaine would welcome all the speakers and visitors, then introduce Forrester. Forrester would say a few words about the park and officially dedicate the memorial site. Next, Blaine would introduce Dr. Wilbur Franklin, President of the Sarasota Archeology Department of New College, who will speak on the important contributions of Ryan Murphy to the field of archeology. Blaine would then introduce the Director of Florida State Parks Dr. Rosa Parks Goodie, who along with Sydney Price and Dalton Marks would present to Willie Henry, Director of Ah-Tah-Thi-Ki Museum, in Big Cypress, Florida, the artifacts collected from the cave. Mr. Henry would speak about the At-Tah-Thi-Ki Museum and the importance of the artifacts to the Native American experience. Lastly, Blaine would invite everyone to lunch behind the Nature Center.

"The memorial will be held at eleven o'clock on May 23rd and let's hope for good weather," Forrester said.

"Sounds like a straightforward program, and I'm assuming there will be free admission to the park that day." Blaine asked and underlined the date.

"Yes, I asked Ranger Diana Stimson to organize the publicity for the memorial service, and I instructed her to contact the media. God knows we need all the positive coverage we can get, and this ceremony will indeed garner favorable sentiment. Now what about your report on the Clearing case?" Forrester closed his folder, and took out a notepad.

"Unfortunately, John, I don't have good news. I've concluded Daisy didn't travel to Washington but was murdered in the park." Blaine reached into her attaché case and handed Forrester her report.

"That's a bit disheartening, but continue. There may be something we can build upon."

"Winthrop confessed to driving Daisy to the park. And after an argument over her going to Washington, he drove away leaving her at the park in a new blue and white polka dot dress, new shoes, and carrying a red suitcase."

"How do you know that really took place?" asked Forrester.

"Because there was an eye witness, Fix-it Freddy. He lived in the homeless camp at the park. Once a month Daisy and some of her friends would bring food to the camp, so after Winthrop drove off, she went to find Freddy, and ask him for a ride on his bicycle to the train station."

"So Fix-it Freddy murdered Daisy!" Forrester blurted out.

"No, Freddy was a gentle giant. A huge man close to seven feet tall, probably tipping the scale at three hundred pounds, and strong as an ox, but no killer. All he did was repair everyone's bicycles at the camp."

"So, you believe this Fix-it guy? How do you know he's not lying?" Forrester looked down at the report and added, "I'm just not sold on this man's alibi."

"John, I'm certain he didn't murder Daisy. The entries in Daisy's diary painted a very specific picture of Fix-it Freddy. Time, and time again, she described him as a kind, caring man. All he wanted was to repair things that were broken. Never once did she mention that he was prone to violence." Blaine, paused for a moment and in a controlled voice said, "He's not our murderer. Someone else murdered Daisy Clearing."

Forrester leaned back in his chair and smiled. "That's why he's called Fix-it Freddy. I get it. So why didn't he ride her to the train station?"

"Someone stole his bike, so he walked her back to the picnic area where a big party was going on. Daisy told Freddy she knew a boy at the party and that she would ask him for a ride. Freddy left to look for his bicycle, and that was the last he saw of her." Blaine turned her report over and folded her hands.

"Okay, so who's the boy at this big party? Is he the one who murdered Daisy, or not?" asked Forrester

"I don't know to both your questions," Blaine uttered almost in a whisper.

"Blaine, the answer to your two questions may be in this room. You mentioned a party, a big party, how big?" Forrester bellowed.

"There were tables of food, a large piñata, balloons, a cotton candy machine, and a children's roller coaster ride. What does that have to do with finding the boy?"

"It may have everything to do with his identity. I hope," Forrester answered. He pushed back his chair and walked over to the bookcase at the far end of the office. Forrester called out, "You said 1963 is the year Daisy disappeared, right?" He pulled off the shelf a thick, white loose-leaf binder titled: Osprey State Park Yearbook 1963 and sat back down.

"A yearbook for the park! I had no idea the park kept a photo album of the park," Blaine answered in amazement.

"It's more than a photo album. This album and all the others since the inception of the park in 1955 chronicle all the major activities that took place that year. Scrub jay 5-10K run, building the Lake Osprey Trail, prescribed burns, All Trails Hike, installing water lines, building a new canoe dock and even this year's Literacy Amongst the Trees event. Maybe extravagant parties were archived. Let's hope." Forrester opened the binder.

The first three pages contained letters from the Florida Park Service about budget cuts and regulations, a list of park awards, and lastly a newspaper clipping of a controlled burn. Bored with the content of the three previous pages, Forrester flipped to page four and walked over to his desk to answer the phone. As soon as he picked up the receiver, there was an ear-piercing scream from the back of the room.

"Oh my God, it's her, Daisy Clearing! There's a picture of her in her blue and white polka-dot dress," Blaine called out. "John, come look!"

"I'll have to get back to you later," Forrester barked into the phone and hung up. "How do you know it's Clearing?"

"Her sister showed me the 1963 missing person's poster. It's Daisy. I'm positive. Look, she's holding a red suitcase and talking to a boy next to a cotton candy machine wearing a funny white hat. He's operating the cotton candy machine." Forrester sat down and stared at the photograph.

"I see the piñata in the background and the tables of food just like Freddy described, but who is that boy?" Forrester squinted, and took a closer look.

"There's the children's roller coaster ride. And there's a mole on the side of the boy's face. John, I know who the boy is. It's Morty King, the owner of King Amusement Company." Blaine gasped in horror.

"How do you know it's Morty King?"

"King was on television being interviewed by Bryce Faceman after someone dumped horse manure on his car. It was impossible not to notice the mole on his face. That boy has the same mole. Take a look." Blaine pushed the yearbook in front of Forrester.

"I see the mole, but lots of people have moles. That doesn't mean it was a teenage Morty King!" Forester insisted.

Blaine pulled the photo album in front of her, leaned down almost putting her nose up against the picture, and stared. She looked up, smiled, and said, "Look on his shirt. There's a blue name tag pinned to his pocket. What does it say?" Blaine pushed the album over to Forrester who in turn scrunched down and scrutinized the photograph.

"Morty," said Forrester. "It says Morty, and I only know one Morty, which is Morty King, owner of the King Amusement Company. Not one of the top ten boy names of 1963 I would think," laughed Forrester pointing at the photograph.

"Now we have a lead, John. Morty may be the murderer, or he may not be, but right now we have solid evidence that he was the last person to see Daisy alive. This photograph may be the proof we need." Blaine turned the album around, pushed it over to Forrester, and said: "Notice the little blue roller coaster in the foreground. Look down at the second car; what do you see?"

"King Amusement. That's the proof we need. Are you going to inform Detective Beale about our new discovery?" Forrester asked.

"I'll call and update him. However, tomorrow I'm going to city hall with my daughter's class to petition the city council to put up signs warning of sandhill crane crossings. It was a project Brooke dreamed up after her class visited the Wildlife Center of Venice. So I need to help her prepare her presentation. I'll need the picture," said Blaine.

"No problem," said Forrester and handed her the photograph. "Just keep me posted so I can stay one step ahead of Director Goodie."

Chapter 54

A sense of urgency filled the air as the seven members of the city council took their seats while men, women, and children spilled into the chambers and took their seats. Mrs. Malott's class was first to march single-file into the room, and sat in the first two rows. Behind them, Blaine, Lou Bravo, Tony Lilly, and Hubba Bubba squeezed in. Next sat Kevin Barton and ten volunteers, all dressed in their blue Wildlife Center of Venice shirts, followed by members from the Audubon Society. Lastly, a handful of local activists rounded out the contingency to support the sandhill cranes. The remainder of the room held spectators and concerned citizens requesting to address the city council or just listen. One citizen in particular caught the attention of Tony Lilly, who gave Lou Bravo a nudge as he walked up to the city clerk's counter to fill out the request to speak form.

The mayor called the meeting to order with one tap of his gavel. City council attendance was taken, and then the mayor asked everyone to rise for the invocation and the Pledge of Allegiance. Next he officiated a promotional ceremony for a Venice firefighter followed by the city manager presenting the Employee of the Year Award to a city worker for his devoted service on the job.

The first two speakers talked about the importance of a park alongside their community and implored the council members not to approve the construction of a new police station on park land. The third speaker asked the Council to install more trolley signs alerting the public where pick-up and drop-off locations were stationed.

Brooke Sterling was next. She sat down at the presenter's table in front of the council and spoke into the microphone. Her words were soft, and at times the mayor asked her to speak louder into the microphone so that she could be heard. Brooke spoke about the class trip to the Wildlife Center of Venice and how moved she was with Mr. Barton's talk about the injured animals his organization helped every day. As a homework assignment she wrote about a way to help reduce sandhill crane accidents caused by cars. Brooke held up her sign and asked that the council to consider putting up sandhill crane crossing area signs on Venice city roads to help reduce sandhill crane fatalities.

Next Tony Lilly spoke about witnessing a sandhill crane killed by a careless driver talking on his cell phone. "The driver never stopped, just kept on driving, and talking on his cell phone. I showed the deputy a picture of the red BMW and the license plate number, but there aren't any laws against killing a sandhill crane he informed me. That's why I believe sandhill crane signs are necessary to help stop the killing."

If looks could kill...Morty King spoke next about canceling the city's implementation of an automated trash program. He stated that the large trash cans the city is issuing would be an eyesore and too large for homeowners to maneuver from the home to the curb and back. Storage of the large cans would put some homeowners in jeopardy of violating an association's bylaws if the large cans were left outside.

On his way back to his seat he gave Tony a look that could only mean trouble. But trouble was just beginning as two wildlife center volunteers maneuvered the metal cage that housed an injured sandhill crane down the aisle to where Kevin Barton was about to speak. Halfway down the aisle the cage tipped sideways, and the hook that latched the enclosure caught on the armrest of an aisle seat opening the door and releasing the crane. The crane with a heavily wrapped right wing jumped out and began to flap around. With only one good wing, flight was unbalanced and jerky, allowing the crane only short bursts of flight.

"Don't be frightened," Barton yelled, and ran towards the crane heading straight for the seven council members seated at the dais. In mid-stride, Barton wrapped his arms around the frightened crane. Cradling it against his body, he walked back to the righted cage and placed the crane safely inside. With the crane securely locked up, Barton and the two volunteers pushed the cage up to the speaker's table.

"Members of the City Council, the Wildlife Center of Venice treats over three thousand injured animals a year. On average the center receives nine pages of calls a day requesting assistance with injured animals. Most of the injuries are human-related. If the implementation of sandhill crane signs save one crane from injury, the Wildlife Center of Venice supports that initiative because that means that the center will have that much more time to devote to helping other injured animals."

The mayor thanked Mr. Barton for a compelling presentation as well his courage in corralling the injured crane, thus protecting all of the visitors and council members from a frightful experience. He then announced that all the requests for audience participation in the meeting were concluded, but then asked Brooke to return to the speaker's table. "Young lady, I was impressed with the sincerity of your presentation, and I'm going to instruct the city manager to investigate the cost of placing sandhill crane signs on designated city roads and to report back to the council next month." He then asked Brooke to give the city manager her poster so he would have a design to work from. Brooke smiled, handed the sign to the city manager, and walked back to her seat.

Mrs. Malott gathered up the children and walked out of the building to the awaiting bus. Blaine followed and walked alongside Brooke, congratulating her on a job well done before she stepped into the bus. Blaine stood on the sidewalk and waved goodbye as the school bus drove out of the parking lot. No sooner had the bus disappeared from view than an angry scream from behind shattered the morning quiet.

"So you're the bastard that saw me hit that crane! I bet you also dumped that horse shit on my car," Morty King screamed as two of his goons pushed Tony Lilly against a car.

"Get your hands off me you, filthy murderer," Tony shouted.

"I'll do more than put my hands on you. Maybe I'll burn down your ice cream building, Mr. Lilly. Yeah, maybe a fire will popup just like the fire at that Purple Lady's barn. That was the color of the truck that dumped all that crap on my car, purple. She has a purple truck. But I expect you already know that, Mr. Lilly, don't you?" King raised his fist and was in mid-swing when Lou Bravo, who had just walked outside, grabbed his arm and spun him around.

"The party's over, boys," Lou Bravo shouted and jabbed his gun into Morty's side. "Tell your henchmen to let Tony go or I'll shoot you. Florida has a *Stand Your Ground Law*, and this could be a perfect time for a test. What do you think, Morty? Ready for a test case?"

"Let him go," Morty squealed. "This isn't over. Believe me I'm not through with the two of you." King's two henchmen released Tony.

"You need to leave or I'm calling the police," Blaine said as she pushed in next to Lou Bravo with her cell phone in her hand. "Do you understand, you need to leave now!"

"That won't be necessary lady, we're going," King barked out. "You two better watch your backs because I know you were responsible for wrecking my car. Payback time is right around the corner." The three stepped back and walked to King's new red SUV.

Blaine, Hubba Bubba and Lou Bravo held Tony, and the four stood alone in the parking lot having a group hug. Tony looked shaken, but he smiled and said he'd be fine. "I'm glad I spoke. I wanted that man to understand that there are consequences for one's actions and that his behavior will not be tolerated."

"Speaking of consequences, I need you to look at this photograph," said Blaine, as she pulled out a yellowed 4x6 color photograph from her breast pocket and handed it to Lou Bravo.

"Okay, I see a picnic scene at a park. Children riding in a roller coaster, adults seated at a table full of food, a kid trying to bash a piñata hanging from a tree, and a pink cotton candy machine. So what?"

"Look at the cotton candy machine, what do you see?" Blaine said tersely, pointing to a girl in the picture. "That's Daisy Clearing."

"It is. There she is wearing the blue and white polka-dot dress and holding a red suitcase. Where did you find this picture?" asked Lou Bravo.

"The park records a yearly album of events. Forrester has the entire collection in his office dating back from 1955 to the present. That picture was from 1963, the year Daisy disappeared. On the back is written August 26, 1963, Osprey State Park, the day

Daisy was scheduled to leave for Washington, D. C. What else do you see?" Blaine handed the picture to Tony.

"That kid operating the cotton candy machine ..." Tony put his nose to the picture, and shouted, "It is Morty King! The kid with the funny hat is King."

"Let me see," barked Lou Bravo, and grabbed the picture. "You're right. I see that ugly mole on his face, and the blue name badge says Morty; it's him. So that bastard killed Daisy Clearing, and he has the nerve to threaten us with payback. Let's see who has to pay back now."

"So we have the mole, the blue name tag, and the date of the picture as evidence Morty King was with Daisy in the park, but all that proves is that he may have been the last person to see Daisy alive; not necessarily that he's the killer. It's all circumstantial evidence. We need more than a picture, we need concrete evidence," Blaine added with a sigh.

Tony reached over and took a closer look at the picture. Turned it sideways, to the right, to the left, upside- down, and back right-side up. A big smile covered his face, and he slammed the photo back down on the yellow hood of the El Camino. "You need concrete evidence. It's right there in the picture. The red suitcase. The red suitcase will convict Morty King of murder, and I know where it is."

No one moved. No one spoke a word. The three journeymen just stood frozen in time and let the statement hang in the air full of immeasurable consequences for Morty King. It was a moment to cherish, and try to absorb that after all this time the answer to the death of Daisy Clearing was right in front of them. Unfathomable, that after more than fifty years, how was it possible for a suitcase to still be intact? But more unbelievable how could Tony Lilly know its location? The trio waited for the answer.

Blaine was the first to speak. Tentative at the start,

but then focused and steadfast in her delivery. "Tony, you do understand how important it is for me and the park to find out what happened to Daisy Clearing. I hope this is not a joke, but rather you do have concrete evidence for the whereabouts of the suitcase."

"Oh yes, Blaine, I do. No one wants to put Morty King in jail more than me. The suitcase is in King's barn," Tony stated smugly, and pointed to the picture. "When Lou Bravo and I rented the roller coaster for your party, King gave us a tour of his company barn where all the amusement rides were stored. King's father who started the business in 1955 every year put together a display that highlighted the events the company performed. I saw a red suitcase in the 1963 exhibit."

"That's right! I remember seeing a red suitcase just like the one in the picture. I remember and thinking at the time how it seemed out of place, squeezed between a broken blue roller coaster car and a yellow plastic duck. It has to be Daisy's suitcase." Lou Bravo handed Blaine back the photograph.

"This is the evidence the police need. Why on earth would King have Daisy's suitcase? Because Daisy Clearing didn't need it any longer. She was dead," Hubba Bubba blurted out. "He killed her and had to get rid of the evidence. Simple as that."

"It's not that simple," Blaine answered. "We don't know that the red suitcase in the picture is in fact the same suitcase in King's barn. Secondly, I doubt if the police could obtain a search warrant based upon a fifty-four-year-old picture. We need to see if it is positively Daisy Clearing's red suitcase in that barn, then the police will have a case." Blaine looked over at Lou Bravo and without saying a word they both understood what the next chapter in Daisy Clearing's diary had to include.

Across town Star Trek Guy's computer collated the voice and video data accessed from Tony's and Hubba

Bubba's hats. That information, upon Blaine's instructions, was forwarded to Detective Beale's computer terminal.

Chapter 55

A line of cars with their turn signals flashing slowly inched forward into Patches' front parking lot hoping for a coveted spot close to the door on a rainy morning. Third in the procession of vehicles was Lou Bravo's yellow El Camino that he managed to successfully squeeze into the last parcel of blacktop at the far end of the lot. An anxious line of customers stood patiently waiting to move forward into the restaurant as Lou Bravo excused himself and walked inside. Jackie, the owner, smiled, and pointed to the back where Tony and Hubba Bubba were seated drinking coffee. Lou Bravo smiled back and snaked his way through the room, apologizing as he jostled one table after another until he finally reached the last booth and sat down.

"What? Is Jackie giving away free bacon with every breakfast special?" Lou Bravo joked.

"That will be the day when she gives away anything for free," laughed the waitress who walked up to the table right behind Lou Bravo with a pot of coffee in her hand. "Speaking of bacon, I believe you like yours extra crispy," she replied and filled Lou Bravo's cup.

"Good morning, Victoria. Yes extra crispy is the way

I like it, and I'll have the egg special today, scrambled, and home fries. Thank you."

Victoria took Tony's and Hubba Bubba's orders and marched back to the kitchen. "So, gentlemen we have some unfinished business to complete tonight. Tony, I'm sure you will be pleased with this endeavor, and Hubba Bubba, you'll just enjoy the thrill of the mission."

Before Lou Bravo could finish the details of the undertaking, Tony held up a newspaper, placed it in the middle of the table and pointed to the headline. "Have you seen this? The Greatest Show on Earth Closes after 146 years. The Ringling Bros. and Barnum & Bailey Circus folds its tent after 146 years."

"The circus is closing for good," Hubba Bubba mumbled. "How is that possible?"

"The article says that the circus was losing money for the past ten years, and that Field Entertainment decided that this would be their last year of operation." Tony turned the page, and pointed to the last paragraph at the bottom of the article and read. "Field entertainment is under contract with King Amusement Company to purchase the big cat production for $4 million. The contract will be finalized at their Ellenton, Florida, office tonight."

"That is great news. Not the circus closing, but King traveling to Ellenton to sign the contract." Lou Bravo took a drink of coffee, and over breakfast he outlined the operation. The plan was for Tony and Lou Bravo to break into King's barn, check to see if the red suitcase belonged to Daisy, take a picture of the suitcase in the 1963 display stall, and forward all the facts to Detective Beale. Hubba Bubba was to stand guard at the entrance to the property and alert Tony if anyone approached. Now with King in Ellington, the night break-in would be a breeze.

"I can't make it tonight. My band has a gig in Bradenton," Hubba Bubba insisted. "How about tomorrow night?"

"No, it has to be tonight," Lou Bravo snapped angrily, and downed the last bit of coffee in his cup. "Since when have you been in a band?"

"Since high school. We're called the Stinky Puppy. I play guitar, Mo plays drums, and Aqua plays the keyboard and sings. It's a punk rock group."

"Don't invite me to your next performance, but good luck tonight," Lou Bravo added sarcastically and finished the last of his eggs.

"I only have one question. How are we going to tell if the suitcase belongs to Daisy Clearing?" asked Tony.

"Good question, my dear Watson, and the answer is: Her initials, D.J.C., are stamped in silver on the suitcase under the handle." Lou Bravo stated smugly, and continued. "Blaine called me last night after she found in the notes from Daisy's diary that her father had her initials embossed on the suitcase to help his daughter identify it if it was lost or stolen. Daisy wrote how delighted she was to see her initials every time she picked up the suitcase. Blaine also said that Daisy put her ticket, signed by her family, in the side pocket of the suitcase."

"That sounds like a plan to me. What time will you pick me up?" asked Tony.

"Eight o'clock, Dr. Watson," said Lou Bravo jokingly.

"See you then, Mr. Holmes," laughed Tony and looked up at the dark clouds racing along the skies. "I think we'll get some rain. We definitely need it."

"If it's raining tonight wear boots and a rain coat. We'll be doing some walking."

Lou Bravo picked up the bill and the trio walked to their cars

Chapter 56

A steady rain beat down on the yellow El Camino as Lou Bravo switched on the windshield wipers, drove down his driveway to pick up Tony, and then on to King Amusement Company. It was usually a five-minute drive to Tony Lilly's house, but with the rain and the traffic Lou Bravo arrived twenty minutes late. Tony, a natural born worrier, was pacing back and forth in his open garage dressed and ready to go in a yellow rain slicker and white boots. Lou Bravo couldn't believe his eyes. Here they were going to conduct a clandestine operation on a private business, and his compatriot was dressed as the Gordon's Seafood fisherman.

"What's with your outfit? A yellow rain coat and white boots? The only thing missing is a neon sign announcing we are burglarizing King's barn. We want to be inconspicuous, not stand out like a fish stick commercial for television," Lou Bravo shouted. "You need to change."

"I have another rain coat, but I don't have any other boots," Tony called back.

"Okay, get another coat. I guess the boots will have to do. Hurry up, we need to get going. I don't want King returning early from his meeting with the Ringling circus people and finding us in his barn."

Three minutes later Tony was seated in the car, suited up in a navy blue rain coat and white boots while he and Lou Bravo barreled down Tamiami Trail towards King Amusement Company. Once on the amusement company road, Lou Bravo slowed down and poked his way forward, searching for secluded place to park near the entrance to the property. A few yards from the entrance, Lou Bravo turned off the black top and pulled alongside a thick stand of palm trees. From the bed of the truck he unfolded a camouflage car cover, and he and Tony stretched the fabric over the vehicle. Once on the cracked shell driveway, Lou Bravo stopped and asked Tony, "Can you see the El Camino?"

Tony pointed his flashlight back towards the palm trees and made a quick sweep of the area. "Can't see a thing. Anyone driving up to the entrance won't realize that a yellow El Camino is parked a few yards away."

The two plodded along the shell road moving their flashlights side to side searching for firm ground to step on as they moved deeper onto the property. Old, broken amusement equipment lined both sides of the roadway forming a mountain of junk towering above them. "What if one of the wagons comes loose and falls?" Tony whispered and pointed his light up to the wooden wagon fifteen feet above his head.

"You get squashed like a bug," laughed Lou Bravo. "Look at the barn. I don't see any vehicles in the parking lot. I guess King is still in Ellington. Let's step it up."

Stopped in front of the two barn doors, Lou Bravo noticed that the old brass padlock hanging from the two rings was not clamped shut, but hanging open. "It's unlocked," he said quickly, and pulled the lock away from the rings, pushing the door open slightly.

"What luck! Now we don't have to walk around the barn looking for a way in," Tony said softly and squeezed through the opening.

"I don't like it. Why would King leave the doors unlocked?" Lou Bravo stepped inside and walked over to where Tony had stopped and waved his flashlight into the first stall. "It's too easy."

"Maybe an employee forgot. King is away, and you know what they say when the owner is away," laughed Tony.

"Yeah, I know the workers don't work, but I still have an uncomfortable feeling about it. This is 1955. Let's get to 1963."

Four rows down, two flashlights lit up a red suitcase sandwiched between a yellow duck and a blue roller coaster car along with a menagerie of puppets, clown suits, hoops, juggling pins, and a broken wagon. "There it is," Tony said and climbed over a wagon, and pulled at the suitcase. "It's Daisy's suitcase alright. The initials D.J.C. are stamped into the leather."

"Open it up and find the ticket," Lou Bravo ordered. "Hurry. I want to get out of here as soon as possible."

Tony pushed the two lock buttons sideways, allowing the silver lock bar to snap open and free the top of the suitcase. He lifted the top and like a madman rifled through the clothes and side compartments until he found the prize. With a big smile, he waved the ticket in the air.

But his moment of joy was abruptly cut short when suddenly the entire barn exploded in blinding light. Hundreds of circular globes hanging from the ceiling lit up and shot down beams of incandescent light over every inch of the barn. Every stall from the front of the barn to the back was bathed in light, and standing in the center of the barn was Morty King along with his two henchmen from city hall.

"The party's over boys. It's payback time," shouted

Morty, and pointed his shot gun at the two intruders. "I knew you'd be coming, I just didn't know the day. After I told you that I arranged to firebomb Zammiello's barn and threatened to do the same to Lilly's ice cream warehouse, I knew the two of you would show up. And here you are."

"It's over, King. We didn't come here in retaliation for the firebombing. We're here to obtain proof that you murdered Daisy Clearing and dumped her body under the canoe dock. The red suitcase is the evidence that will throw you in jail for the rest of your life," Lou Bravo shouted.

"Bullshit! Tie these fools up to the two support beams facing the new construction area," King bellowed, and waved the shot gun at their heads. "That was over fifty years ago. How are the authorities going to prove I killed that stuck-up bitch?" howled King.

"Because you have the suitcase. You couldn't leave it at the canoe dock, someone would find it, and implicate you. So you took it. I bet your DNA is all over the handle, sides, and maybe on Daisy's ticket. Care to make a wager, killer?" shouted Lou Bravo.

"I told her I'd take her to the train station, but first I wanted to make out. She laughed, told me to forget it, and that she only kisses her Kentucky Military Institute boyfriend. She was screaming like a banshee. I had to shut her up. I was afraid someone would hear her and arrest me. I smacked her in the face. One hit, that's all. She fell and hit her head on a metal dock cleat. It was an accident. I didn't mean to kill her. It just happened."

"Accident? Why didn't you report the accident to the authorities instead of stuffing her body under the canoe dock? To a jury that sounds like the actions of a guilty man," Tony screamed.

"How the fuck can the cops arrest me if the suitcase is destroyed and you two bozos are nowhere to be found?" King walked up to Tony and shoved the shotgun up against his face. "Below, right where you are standing, Mr. Sandhill Crane Guy, is a twenty-foot pit that will be filled tomorrow with cement. Actually the entire back section of the barn will be cemented to accommodate the new circus equipment I purchased from the Ringling Bros. and Barnum & Bailey Circus. The plan is for you two boys to be part of the cement party, but twenty feet down."

"I hate to ruin your little scheme, but in two minutes Detective Beale and a Venice SWAT team will burst through your barn door and arrest you for the murder of Daisy Clearing, the firebombing of Vardi Zammiello's barn, and the attempted murder of Lou Bravo and myself. How's that for a plan Mr. Amusement guy?" laughed Tony.

"Sounds like a fairy tale to me," King shouted, lowered the shotgun to Tony's groin area and smiled.

"You think so? Take a close look at the baseball cap I'm wearing? This cap is outfitted with fiber optics, audio and video capabilities that record and transmit every action, and every word that takes place within a twenty-foot radius. All your accusations, confessions, and threats have been recorded and sent to a central terminal and then relayed to the Venice Police Department. Every time we had contact with you, Mr. King, a file was developed and transmitted to the authorities."

King snatched the cap from Tony's head, pulled, and tugged at the brim and sides until a hair-thin, transparent fiber was exposed. His eyes bulged out in surprise while his face turned beet red as he realized that he had unknowingly hung himself. At the same moment, the barn doors burst open and in stormed the SWAT team and Detective Beale.

"Put the rifle down, sir," echoed down the walkway. "Sir, put the weapon down. Now!" King took a step towards the officers, raised the shotgun to his shoulder, and pointed. A single shot echoed through the barn.

"Good evening. This is Bryce Faceman reporting live from outside the King Amusement Company barn in Venice where the owner, Morty King, is holding two men captive." The camera moved from a classic close-up of Faceman to the barn fifty feet behind the yellow police security line. "Wait one minute. There appears to be some action taking place as I speak."

Faceman turned and faced the camera waiting for another cameo close-up. "Directly behind me the SWAT team, guns drawn, just charged through the huge front doors and into the barn." The camera panned the red and white barn, police vehicles, a SWAT van, one fire truck, an ambulance and the police command truck. "I heard a shot," Faceman screamed. "I definitely heard one gunshot from inside the barn!"

Faceman turned back to the barn as the SWAT team exited the building surrounding two civilians. "It looks like the stand-off with King has ended, and the two hostages are now safe. Yes, it appears the police are shepherding the two men into the command vehicle—a short, rotund man and a tall skinny man."

The camera focused on the command truck after Faceman yelled, "This operation is not over. SWAT team officers are escorting two other men from the barn. Both are in handcuffs. It's difficult to see, but I believe they are being placed in a squad car, and now two medics just entered the barn pushing a gurney."

The camera moved from the barn back to Faceman for a final close-up. "There are many unanswered questions revolving around this police operation, but you can be sure that this reporter will find the answers. This is Bryce Faceman reporting from Venice, and now back to the station."

Chapter 57

After two days the preparations for the memorial service were completed. The two marble headstones were laid at the base of the cave steps away from the lake trail, facing Lake Osprey. A wooden podium stood in the center of the grassy area, and off to the left, chairs reserved for the speakers and invited guests were arranged in a semi-circle awaiting an eleven o'clock introduction.

Blaine arrived early and went directly to the memorial site. She wanted to spend time alone with Ryan. To feel his presence, and tell him how much she would miss him. She knelt down and touch kissed his headstone. She ran her finger across the rough letters and spelled out his name in her mind. Tears rolled down her face by the time she reached the letter Y, and for the first time grief overwhelmed her. For months the work on the memorial, the investigation of Daisy Clearing, the firebombing of the Purple Lady's barn, not to mention the raising of a child, occupied all her hours. Now with the finality of the marble grave marker in its resting place, Blaine relived the pain and sorrow of death once more. The same overwhelming feeling of grief as when she was informed that her husband Troy died in a car crash attempting to connect with his birth parents nine years ago. However, this time she was stronger and promised that his memory would live on in her heart as she faced each day without his love.

At eleven o'clock Blaine stepped up to the podium. "Good morning, I'm Blaine Sterling, Assistant Manager of Osprey State Park, and welcome to the memorial service for archeologist Ryan Murphy and the dedication of a sacred Native American ceremonial hunting cave. At this time I'd like to welcome our speakers, special guests and all the visitors here today. It is my pleasure to introduce John Forrester, Park Manager."

Forrester spoke about the history of the park, how it had grown over the years, and thanked all the volunteers for their many hours of service. Next, Blaine introduced Dr. Wilbur Franklin, Director of Archeology at New College of Florida, who at great length extolled the dramatic work in the field of archeology performed by Professor Murphy and his field site team. Then Blaine gave a warmhearted introduction to the Director of Florida State Parks, Dr. Rosa Parks Goodie, who along with Sydney Parks and Dalton Marks presented to Willie Henry, Supervisor of Ah-Tah-Thi- Ki Museum, the depository for Native American artifacts in Florida, all the artifacts from the cave. Mr. Henry graciously accepted the case of arrow points and the ceremonial hunting spear on behalf of all Native Americans and promised that the Osprey artifacts would be prominently displayed at the museum. Lastly, Blaine thanked the speakers and visitors and invited everyone to enjoy a luncheon provided by the Friends of Osprey State Park now being served behind the Nature Center.

On the way to the luncheon, Blaine and Brooke were stopped by Henry. "I'd like you to keep one of the arrow points here at the park as a physical reminder that Native Americans walked on this piece of ground and left behind an everlasting legacy for all to see." Henry opened the velvet case, and handed it to Brooke. "Would you like to select one, young, lady?"

"Oh yes!" Brooke replied, and reached in, and pulled out the biggest one.

"Excellent choice, little one. Now all the visitors will have the honor to view and enjoy the beauty and craftsmanship our ancient brothers created thousands of years ago." Henry smiled, and took back the box.

"Can you sit with me and explain how the Native Americans made arrowheads?" Brooke asked holding the grayish brown projectile in her hand.

"I'd love to, but I'm leaving for Cannon Ball, North Dakota, and have to catch a flight out of Tampa in three hours." Henry smiled and touched Brooke on the head. "Maybe one day you and your mother can visit me at the museum, and I will teach you how to make your own arrow point."

"Can we, Mommy, can we?" Pleaded Brooke, and tugged on her mother's hand.

"That would be a wonderful idea for a summer trip. We would be honored to visit you at the Ah-Tah- Thi-Ki Museum. You mentioned that you're joining the protest against the Dakota Access Pipeline. A woman I just met from Venice, Strawberry Girl, left to join the demonstration. I know there are thousands of protesters, but if you see her please say hello for me."

"Strawberry Girl? What kind of a name is that?" asked Henry.

"That's a long story, but one I'm sure she will recount if the two of you meet. Gilda Gooseberry is her birth name," Blaine said jokingly, and waved goodbye.

On the food line, Blaine bumped into Detective Beale who informed her that Morty King was dead, shot last night by the police while holding Lou Bravo and Tony Lilly hostage. That King confessed to killing

Daisy Clearing, burning Vardi Zammiello's barn, and what connected all the events was the killing of the sandhill crane. Beale stated that a final report would be sent to the parks department absolving Osprey State Park of any involvement in Daisy Clearing's death.

"That is wonderful news. Not Mr. King being killed," said Blaine. "Now, finally the cloud of suspicion has been lifted, and we can concentrate on the business of park management, not crime investigations."

"Also I sent an email to your friend Star Trek Guy thanking him for all the computer technical stuff he performed throughout the investigation. Thanks to his compuvideo hat, Lou Bravo and Tony Lilly are alive today. But you probably already know that."

"Yes, he emailed me last night. I am so grateful for his help and your work to bring closure to a fifty-four-year-old murder," Blaine smiled and picked up her food.

"One thing you don't know is that we dropped the horse manure investigation against Lou Bravo and Tony Lilly. Morty King didn't officially press charges, and as a result the department will send out a notice of cancellation tomorrow. Case closed." Beale smiled at Blaine.

"Fantastic! Do you want to sit with Brooke and me at lunch? She has a table over by that big oak tree."

"Thank you, but I have to get back to the office and prepare for a case meeting with the chief. Enjoy your lunch." Beale said goodbye, and walked back to his car.

Blaine carried hot dogs, chips, and water to the picnic table where Brooke, John Forrester and Ranger Diana Stimson sat waiting to enjoy a delicious lunch. Halfway through the meal, Blaine gazed across the lake and her thoughts focused on the memorial site and the beautiful tribute that unfolded for her beloved Ryan and an ancient culture he worked so hard to preserve. She smiled and understood the magnitude of placing the two headstones side by side for eternity.

After her last bite of hot dog, Brooke said in a very effervescent tone, “I know where we can put the arrow head. In the display case at the ranger station. It will be on view for every visitor when they walk into the room.” A big smile enveloped Brooke’s face. “What do you think?”

“What a perfect suggestion,” Forrester and Diana remarked in unison. “Blaine, you have the key to the display case,” Forrester added. “Why don’t you and Brooke put the arrow point in the case today?”

“Are you ready, Brooke? Let’s go and deposit a part of history for all our visitors to enjoy.” Blaine took her daughter’s hand and they left to complete the circle.

83730955R00191

Made in the USA
Columbia, SC
12 December 2017